'A fresh and highly disturbing take on t
winner … no question' Eva Dolan

'A moving and compelling account of a form of violence that remains cloaked in shame and ribald imagery in society. Malone perfectly balances storytelling with a brutal commentary on a dysfunctional relationship' Sarah Ward

'A dark and unnerving psychological thriller that draws you deep into the lives of the characters and refuses to let go. This is a brilliantly written book; I could not put it down' Caroline Mitchell

'A chilling tale of the unexpected that journeys right into the dark heart of domesticity' Marnie Riches

'Michael J. Malone is one of my favourite writers and his new novel does not disappoint. While on the surface this is a departure in genre for Malone, his incredible skill with language and prose remains, and his talent for characterisation really comes to the fore, creating a story that will I won't forget in a hurry. Malone is a massive talent … get on board now so you can brag you were reading his books long before the rest of the world' Luca Veste

'A tightly wound page-turner with real emotional punch' Rod Reynolds

'An unsettling and upsetting story that kept me enthralled, horrified and quite often in tears. Dark, disturbing and peppered with his trademark humour, *A Suitable Lie* is a fantastic read, and, as a writer, Malone just gets better and better' S. J. I. Holliday

'A disturbing and realistic portrayal of domestic noir with a twist. The humour and emotion laced within the darkness was just the right mix for a shocking yet compelling read' Mel Sherratt

'The plot was fast paced and flowed seamlessly. There were times when I wondered if I just might die from excitement' – Noelle Holton, Crime Book Junkie

'He's got the knowhow, the knowledge of police work and the machinations of detective work and its trials and tribulations' *Scots Magazine*

'Big, bold themes and terrific humour amidst the darkness' Tony Black

'Tough, funny, dark and so in your face it hurts' Ken Bruen, novelist

'*Beyond the Rage* is a deeply personal thriller that will keep the reader turning those pages with twists and turns designed to keep the heart pumping. The best yet from a writer who has always delivered' Russel D McLean

'*Beyond the Rage* is a thoroughly enjoyable novel. It is also quite a rare beast, a crime novel that has a criminal as its central character. The characters are nicely drawn and very credible' Undiscovered Scotland

'Vivid and powerful … a harrowing depiction of what it is – and isn't – to be a man' *Scots Magazine*

'Remarkable story told with rare skill, *The Guillotine Choice* is at once fascinating, moving and thrilling. Malone writes beautifully. A wonderful achievement' Chris Ewan

'*The Guillotine Choice* is a beautiful homage to courage, resilience, and compassion; it is a vibrant proof that human nature can remain good, even in the heart of the darkest, most evil of places' Jacques Filippi, The House of Crime and Mystery Blog

'Powerful and emotional ... If you want to read a book that grabs your emotions and takes you on a roller coaster ride, this is it' Linda McHenry

'Malone's writing is effortless, expressive and taut' *Crime Review*

A SUITABLE LIE

ABOUT THE AUTHOR

Michael Malone is a prize-winning poet and author who was born and brought up in the heart of Burns' country, just a stone's throw from the great man's cottage in Ayr. Well, a stone thrown by a catapult. He has published over 200 poems in literary magazines throughout the UK, including *New Writing Scotland*, *Poetry Scotland* and *Markings*. His career as a poet has also included a (very) brief stint as the Poet-in-Residence for an adult gift shop. *Blood Tears*, his bestselling debut novel won the Pitlochry Prize (judge: Alex Gray) from the Scottish Association of Writers. Other published work includes: *Carnegie's Call* (a non-fiction work about successful modern-day Scots); *A Taste for Malice*; *The Guillotine Choice*; *Beyond the Rage*; and *Bad Samaritan*. His poetry includes: *In The Raw*, *Running Threads* and *Lip Synch*. Michael is a regular reviewer for the hugely popular crime fiction website www.crimesquad.com. This novel marks a major departure for Michael Malone.

You can follow him on Twitter *@michaelJmalone1* and on Facebook at *www.facebook.com/themichaeljmalonepage/*, or visit his website: *mjmink.wordpress.com*

A Suitable Lie

MICHAEL J. MALONE

**ORENDA
BOOKS**

Orenda Books
16 Carson Road
West Dulwich
London SE21 8HU
www.orendabooks.co.uk

First published in the UK in 2016 by Orenda Books

ISBN 978-1-910633-49-6

Typeset in Garamond by MacGuru Ltd
Printed and bound by CPI Group (UK) Ltd, Croydon CR0 4YY

SALES & DISTRIBUTION

In the UK and elsewhere in Europe:
Turnaround Publisher Services
Unit 3, Olympia Trading Estate
Coburg Road
Wood Green
London
N22 6TZ
www.turnaround-uk.com

In the USA and Canada:
Trafalgar Square Publishing
Independent Publishers Group
814 North Franklin Street
Chicago, IL 60610
USA
www.ipgbook.com

In Australia and New Zealand:
Affirm Press
28 Thistlethwaite Street
South Melbourne VIC 3205
Australia
www.affirmpress.com.au

For details of other territories, please contact *info@orendabooks.co.uk*

To all the lost souls. May each and every one of you find your way back to life and love.

'It's not the size of the dog in the fight that counts
– it's the size of the fight in the dog'

Ike Eisenhower

Prologue

I don't know how long I walked for. My heels slammed on to concrete until they almost went numb. Fists tight in my pockets, I walked and walked.

And walked.

Light from a shop window spilled on to the pavement just in front of me. What was a shop doing open at this hour? For the first time I noticed my calves were so cold they had no feeling in them. My watch read 6.30. What the hell was I doing? I had been walking for hours wearing only boxer shorts and a t-shirt under my coat; on my feet, a pair of mule slippers.

What the hell was I thinking?

The shop door opened, a small, bald man came out and propped an advertising board for a newspaper against the wall. He stared at me as if I was an idiot searching for his village.

'Looking for my dog,' I muttered, feeling as if I had to offer this total stranger an excuse for the way I was dressed. He shrugged and walked back into his shop. The newspaper headline on the board read, 'DIVORCE DAD KILLS KIDS'.

As I turned and walked away from the shop, I realised just how weary I was. Each step was an effort and each time my heel jarred on to the ground, shockwaves reached my spine. The banner had sapped what strength I had left. What kind of a world did we live in where someone would think such a crime was their only way out? What kind of a god would countenance such an act? I stumbled to a halt. What on earth would drive a man to do such a thing? Only an extreme emotion would result in such a dreadful action. Was it desperation, anger, jealousy? A disturbed mind's version of an act of love?

I willed myself to continue walking and my own situation pushed its way to the front of my thoughts, like a small child in a crowd shouting, 'What about me?' What about me?' Would I ever feel that desperate?

The banner blazed like a warning.

I would have to find a solution. I would have to find a way out of this trap.

At last, my circuit brought me home. The door was unlocked, I pushed it open and walked inside. Pausing by the living room door, I saw her curled up in a chair. Fast asleep. Even in the weak light I could make out the silted lines of mascara that ran from her eyes and down the pale expanse of her cheeks, almost past her nose.

She had obviously fallen asleep waiting for me.

And that was the first time I thought about murder.

BOOK ONE

1

It was a Sunday, the day we met; Sunday 7th July 1996. I've no idea why I remember that. It just stuck. And it would be nice to say our eyes lit on each other across a crowded dance floor, cos that's romance, eh? But, no, it was a smoke-filled bar at the local rugby club.

I've no clue why she was interested in me, I was one of a type. The room was filled with broad-shouldered, thick-limbed, flat-bellied young men, so why would she pick me? My first thought was that it was ghoulish curiosity. After all, it wasn't like I hadn't encountered it before. Being a widower with a toddler before you reach the age of thirty does have a certain appeal, as my young brother Jim told me when he dragged me out that night.

'You need to get out of the house,' he said. 'All work and Disney movies makes for a dull life, brother.'

'Suits me just fine, Jim.'

'You'll thank me for it,' he countered. 'The ladies love a tragedy. They'll be throwing their knickers at you soon as you walk in the door.'

It was an image that filled me with horror. Having lost the only woman I'd ever loved, the thought of a group of women looking at me with wide-eyed, open-mouthed sympathy was more than I could bear.

'C'mon, Andy,' he pleaded. 'I told Mum I'd drag you out tonight. You know what she's like if I let her down.'

'You'd think she'd get used to that,' I grinned.

'It's been arranged anyhow.' He shrugged. 'Mum's coming over in…' he stretched his right arm out in such a way that his silver Tag wristwatch edged out past the cuff of his Thomas Pink shirt – my brother is a slave to the high-end brands – '… in forty-five minutes to put the wee fella to bed.'

I groaned. Once Mum was here it would all be over. Mrs Boyd doesn't take no for an answer.

Jim wore a sly grin like it was a badge of honour. 'Game's a bogie, big man. Go get your good jeans on. And wear that light-blue shirt I got you at Christmas. Makes you look less like a morgue assistant.'

'Do I have to?' I made one last effort at resistance.

He winked. 'Your nutsack must weigh a ton, brother. What is it, over four years since Patricia died? Time to get them emptied.'

I shook my head. Looked him up and down and made a face. 'You look so refined. But you've really just stepped out of a cave, haven't you?'

When we walked in the door of the club an hour later, the smell of my son, Pat's Thomas the Tank Engine pyjamas still lingered in my nostrils and that tuft of hair on his crown stuck in my mind. I'd have given anything to be back there, tucking him in, reading *The Gruffalo* to him one more time. Instead I fought the churn in my stomach and allowed Jim to push me inside.

A few of the guys came over, slapped me on the back, told me it was good to see me. Like it had been a long time, even though I had played a game with them just the previous weekend. But I knew what they meant. Since Patricia died it had been nothing but work and Pat. And the occasional game of rugby when injuries meant they were struggling for players.

As Jim led me through the crowd to the bar, a Spice Girls song came on and I was for turning and leaving. Jim sensed my movement and with a hand on my back he pushed me forward. What the hell was I doing here? A lot of nods were sent my way. Ayr was a fair-sized town with a village mentality. Everybody knew everybody. I'd gone to school with most of these guys. Their parents knew my parents.

My parent.

Another tick in the Andy Boyd tragedy box. Father died of

a massive heart attack just when the boys were approaching the troublesome teenage years.

'You know Louise, don't you?' Jim said over the babble.

I hid my reaction. Two minutes in the door and he was already trying to set me up. To be fair, he'd made a good choice, I thought as I looked at Louise. I recognised her. She'd been a couple of years below us at school and had grown into herself rather nicely in the intervening time. I remembered a shy girl: look at her and she'd try to hide her blush under her long fringe.

I gave Louise a nod and a tight smile. No point in misleading her. There was as much chance of me hooking up with anyone that night as there was of Ayr winning a European championship.

Next up on the DJ's version of a fun night was somebody singing what sounded like *Ohh, ahh, just a little bit*. Yeah, I'm all over that, I thought as I turned away from Louise, faced Jim and asked for a pint of lager. He gave an almost imperceptible shake of the head and waved at the barmaid.

Pint in hand, heart feeling as solid as if someone had poured fast-setting concrete into my chest cavity, I took the chance when Jim was distracted by Louise's blonde pal to walk across to the far corner of the room.

I took a seat, crossed my arms and legs and surveyed the crowd. I was in a room full of people – most of whom I knew – but I'd never felt so alone.

That was when I saw her. Shoulder-length blue-black hair; black turtle-neck, short-sleeved sweater. Very little jewellery. Minimal make-up. Yet she was easily the most attractive woman in the place. She was surrounded by guys, but she was looking at them as if they held as much attraction for her as a pile of dung.

She took a sip of her red wine. Looked away as one of her would-be suiters cracked a joke. Judging by the way he threw his head back in laughter, he thought it was hilarious. Her cheeks barely budged in response.

She saw me looking.

I looked away.

Moments later, as Celine Dion was chuntering away, she sat beside me.

'Fancy helping out a bird in bother?'

I sat with that for a moment.

'Cos a damsel in distress doesn't sound Ayrshire enough?' I asked at last.

She made a 'well done' face. 'You're about the only guy in here who would have got that.'

'And what's bothering you?' I asked. 'Or who?' I added, thinking about the guys who had been surrounding her earlier.

'New girl in town. I know nobody,' she said as she looked around the bar. 'I was asked here by some guy. Ken something. And now he's creeping me out.' Keeping her arms straight, she tucked her hands between her knees and gave a dramatic shudder. 'Wouldn't be surprised if his mum's called Norma and he stabs shower curtains in his spare time.'

I followed her line of sight. Saw a guy who grew up on another estate. We used to play football with him. The jumpers-for-goalposts kind. He would have been better taking the place of one of the jumpers.

Never took to him. His gaze would meet yours for less than a second before it slid off, as if he was afraid you would read his mind. We found him one day down the River Ayr throwing stones at the swans and avoided him from then on.

'Ken Hunter,' I answered. 'His wife, Sheila, works in my office.'

'What a prick,' she said, leaning back and to the side, as if this would make her less visible to him. 'Didn't say he was married.' She looked at me. Her eyes were large, clear and an intoxicating blue. 'You'd rather be somewhere else, eh?'

I gave a non-committal shrug.

She stood. 'Let's go. We can rescue each other.'

Thinking, *why the hell not?* I followed her outside. 'Where are we going?' I asked when I caught her at the door.

'I don't know. You're the local.' She scanned the playing fields and the tall, full-leafed trees beyond. 'Is the beach far from here?'

Half an hour later we were walking alongside the low grey wall that holds the sands of Ayr beach from being blown into the town. The tide was in, the waves had their lazy on and we could see the sweep and curve of the bay ahead of us. And out to sea, holding up the skyline, were the hills of Arran. A cool breeze was coming in off the water and, despite the early summer evening sunshine, I could see her arms stipple with the cold when she crossed them.

'Nice,' she said. 'No wonder you've never left town.'

'How did you…?'

'It's written all over you,' she smiled. 'Born, bred and buttered Ayrshireman, eh?'

On the way down here our chatter had been light and unaffected, and, to my surprise, without any awkward silences. She was an easy girl to talk to.

'It's Anna, by the way,' she said as she took a seat on the wall. I sat beside her, being careful not to get too close.

An elderly couple walked past with a yellow Labrador. Judging by the colour of its coat it was just out of the sea and it chose that moment to give itself a shake, spraying us both with droplets of sea water. Anna's laughter was loud and unrestrained.

The couple were profuse in their apologies. The dog approached us and nudged Anna's hand with its nose. The woman tutted. 'This is Dave, by the way.' Her pride in the dog evident. 'Greedy bugger's looking for a treat.'

'Not the only one,' the man said and gave me a wink. 'Jeez, hen, you're all wet. You'll catch your death. Here have my fleece.'

'No,' Anna stretched out the syllable. 'I'll be fine. Honestly.'

The man offered her it again. It was clear he was momentarily caught up in the glamour of her. I glanced behind me at the sea and thought of mermaids and their siren call.

'C'mon you,' the woman said and gave him a nudge. 'Offering

young women your fleece. They'll be calling the cops on you.' She set off, and with a regretful air, man and dog obediently trotted after her.

Anna waited until the couple were out of earshot. 'At least the natives are friendly.' As she said *friendly*, she looked into my eyes.

Discomfited and flattered, I looked away. She was way out of my league. What the hell was she doing with me?

'We were getting round to the introductions, before Dave showered us…' The pause at the end of her sentence a request for my name.

I told her. 'And what brings you to my home town?

'I've just been sent here. Work.'

'What do you do?'

'Nothing special,' she smiled at me. There was a light in her eyes and a blush to her lips and I felt my thawing into the human race continue. 'I work for the Royal Bank,' she explained. 'But don't be asking for a loan. I'm just a teller.'

'Wait,' I sat up. 'The Royal? Which branch?'

'The one at the top of the High Street.' She cocked an eyebrow at my sudden interest.

I mentally reviewed the staff there. We were expecting a new team member, but that wasn't until next week.

'I don't start until next Monday. I've got a few days holiday to take first.' She held her hands out. 'Thought I'd take in the sights first.'

A file had arrived on my desk the day before. The name came to me.

'Anna Reid?'

'How the hell do you know that?' She straightened her back.

'Andy Boyd,' I reached out, shook her hand. 'I'm based at the branch at the other end of the town. I'm your new boss.'

She threw her head back and laughed. 'You're at it.'

I shook my head slowly. 'Nope. Not long promoted.'

'Wow. What are the chances?'

'It's a small town.'

'Hope I made a good first impression?' She tilted her head to the side.

'I think your new boss is already thinking that HR have been very kind to him.'

'Bet you say that to all the girls.'

'Only the ones that laugh at my jokes.'

'You tell jokes?'

'On high days and holidays. Maybe the odd funeral.'

She lifted her legs up and swung round on her backside so that she was facing out to sea. I followed suit and in a silence usually only possible between long-time friends we stared into the distance and watched the sun as it painted the distant Isle of Arran and its crown of clouds in shades of red, amber and gold.

I sneaked a look at her. She caught me, nudged me in the side and gave a little giggle. I couldn't help but join in.

My sensible voice warned that our employers might not take kindly to any fraternisation between us. My usually unheard devil voice was louder. It said: fuck it.

Our shoulders were all but touching. My hand was on the wall, within centimetres of hers. I felt the heat of her skin on me as she slowly moved her pinkie and linked it with mine. I looked down at how our little fingers were joined and looked up and beyond the horizon.

A smile warmed my face. My heart gave a little twist and I couldn't help but feel, maybe, I was about to get a second chance at happiness.

'So, when do I get to meet this new girlfriend of yours then?' my mother asked in the middle of the reception area of the bank.

She'd popped in to apologise and say that Nana Morrison was going to pick Pat up from the nursery as she had a game on that afternoon. My mother the would-be champion bowler. I had my suspicions that she'd taken up this new hobby only to allow the Morrisons time with my son. I was almost tempted to visit the bowling club to see if anyone had ever heard of her.

'Mum,' I chided. 'You know how I feel about the Morrisons.' In the months after their daughter – my wife – died, they tried to get custody of Pat. I was still working through my resentment towards them.

She tutted and waved away my complaint.

I looked around me to check who might have overheard. 'And another thing – don't be giving the gossips ammunition.'

'Why the secrecy, Andy?' She gave me that look, reached out and prodded me in the stomach. 'People will be happy for you, son.' She smiled at me and moved the hand that had just poked me up towards my tie as if she was about to straighten it against my collar, but stopped herself before she could finish the action. I looked to the ceiling and felt like a teenager.

The top of her head barely made my chin, even with her jolt of thick white hair, which went well with her purple, sleeveless summer dress. And all the beads. When she had reached pensionable age, my mum had read the Jenny Joseph poem and run with it.

'Mum.' I made a face and fought down a cringe. Here I was, the manager of a large part of a massive organisation and with nothing more than a look my mother could have me behaving like a shy, thirteen-year-old.

'Can't a mother be pleased with her son?' she asked, squaring her shoulders and looking around herself, taking in the counter and the team of staff working behind it. Her expression said, my son's your boss and he's done me very proud indeed.

I often wondered what my mother would have made of her life if she'd had the same ambition for herself as she'd had for her sons. She had a bullet-eyed view of the world and an ability to assess what was going on around her that often left me feeling inadequate. Not that I agreed with her on every occasion; she was my parent after all, and a young man has to find his own way in the world.

'I hear she's a bit of a looker,' she said.

'You've been talking to Jim.'

She hoisted her bag – a garish orange – into a more comfortable position on her shoulder. 'At least *he* tells me stuff.'

'Aye, well, Jim's got a big mouth.'

I understood Mum's perspective. She was understandably curious. Anna was the first woman I'd shown more than a passing interest in since Patricia's death four years before. But I wanted to be sure we had something before I introduced her to my family. And, more importantly, before she met Pat.

He often asked about his mum. He understood – as much as a child could – that his mother was 'in heaven' and he had recently begun to ask if he was going to get another one.

Perhaps the answer to his question was in the fact that every moment away from Anna had my stomach twist with longing. It would have been easy to have her over at mine every night, ask her to stay till morning. But my sensible side kept reminding me that it had only been four weeks since we met. Who knew where this was going?

Except I did know.

From that moment on the wall down by the shore.

Could I afford to fall in love again? My grief for Patricia had almost broken me and I was self-aware enough to know that part of me was holding back because I wasn't sure I could go through that again. What if I let this love take over and I lost her as well? There wasn't just me to think about this time.

'This is more than a wee fling, isn't it, son?' My mother was studying my expression.

'Haven't you got a bowling match to prepare for?'

She snorted, pleased she could still read me.

'I knew that your father was the man for me on our second date.'

'Yeah, I know all the stories, Mum.'

'So, tomorrow night.' Thursday was late opening at the branch. 'When you come to collect Pat, bring whatsername…'

'Anna.'

'… with you. We'll make it casual. A friend dropping by. It'll be easier for Pat that way.'

I nodded, seeing the sense of what she was saying. Plus – I was allowing myself to relax into the idea now – it meant I would get to see more of Anna. Trying to juggle her, the job and Pat was becoming increasingly difficult.

The next evening, I picked Anna up from our other branch. Well, around the corner from our other branch. I wasn't quite yet at the stage where I could allow my colleagues in on the secret.

Anna sat in the passenger seat with a long, slow exhalation, followed by a deep breath and then a tight smile.

'Hey, gorgeous,' I said and leaned across to kiss her cheek. As my lips pressed against the cool of her skin I felt her face rise in a smile and caught the delicate heat and spice of her perfume. I read the sigh and the tight smile that welcomed me. 'You're not nervous are you?'

She shifted in her seat and clicked her seatbelt into place. 'Feel like I'm sixteen…' she paused. Reflected. 'No. Don't think I was this nervous when I was sixteen.'

'You'll be fine,' I said. 'Mum's great.'

She raised an eyebrow, then reached across and patted my hand. 'Just what you should say.'

'She is. Honest.' I took her hand and gave it a little squeeze. 'She never comments on our girlfriends. Never judges.' I studied the traffic, saw a space and moved into the stream of cars that flowed down Miller Road.

Anna laughed. 'She's a mum. She'll be judging.'

'If she does, she'll keep it to herself.'

'Yeah. Well.' Anna looked away from me, out of her window. 'You're a man. You guys miss all that stuff.'

'What stuff?'

'Reading between the lines.' She turned back to me. 'That's where women communicate.' She took another deep breath. Exhaled. 'Anyway. How do I look?'

'Fantastic.' I took my hand from the gear stick and gave hers another squeeze. She had changed out of her bank uniform and was wearing black jeans and a bright-pink top. 'And Mum loves colour, so you'll fit right in there.'

Anna pulled at the neck of her top. 'Jesus,' she laughed. 'I can't believe how nervous I feel. This is ridiculous.'

'It's also very cute. Makes me love you even more.'

She pinked. 'And that right there is the best thing you could have said, Andy Boyd.' She picked my hand up to her lips and kissed the back of my fingers.

Mum made lasagne for the adults and mince and potatoes for Pat. He was openly curious about Anna, hardly taking his eyes off her for the first ten minutes. Then he handed her one of his dinosaur toys, which was a clear sign of his approval.

'What's his name?' Anna asked as she eyed the lump of plastic in her hand.

'Let Anna eat her dinner in peace, Pat,' said Mum.

'Diplodocus,' answered Pat, demonstrating that, no matter how much trouble kids had interpreting the world of adults, the Latinate name of a long-dead species was, quite literally, kids' play.

'Is he your favourite?' asked Anna.

Pat snorted. Looked over his shoulder at a box in the corner. His toys had all been tidied up before we came to the table and he was clearly itching to get back to play with them. 'Velociraptor. He's my favourite cos he's small and fast.'

'Just like you,' I said and rubbed the top of his head, mussing his hair. He stuck his tongue out in response.

Once we'd finished eating, Anna insisted on helping mum with the dishes.

'Another woman in my kitchen?' asked Mum with mock seriousness. 'Cherish the thought.' She smiled to show that was exactly what she meant. 'Next time, for sure, Anna. This time, why don't you take the easy way out and make the coffee?'

'Deal,' said Anna with a grin.

Pat and I launched into the box of toys while the women went into the kitchen, no doubt to begin the dance in earnest. A few minutes later Anna emerged with a tray of cups and a cafetiere. She was wearing an expression that was half pleased, half harassed.

I sent her a smile of enquiry. She smiled in reply. My male brain read that everything was fine. And this was confirmed a short time later when Mum pulled Pat onto her lap.

'Why don't you let this wee guy stay with me tonight?' Mum asked. 'Let you guys do some adult stuff.'

I raised an eyebrow. Anna blushed.

'Adult stuff?' I asked.

'Go to the pub. Go for a walk. A drive? Do something without this…' she reached under Pat's arms and give him a tickle '… wee monster.'

'Great idea.' I stood up. Although Anna and I stole every moment we could with each other, we had rarely managed to spend a full night together. Waking up with her in bed beside me had so far been a rare treat during our short romance. 'You okay with that?' I asked Anna.

She gave a coy nod to my mother and a smile to me that promised much.

'Right.' I rubbed my hands together. 'Let's get this Verocirictor into his bath.'

'Velociraptor, silly,' replied Pat.

Between us, Mum and I wrestled Pat into the bathroom and out of his clothes. Once the bath was run, I plunked Pat into the water and placed an enormous tower of bubbles on to the top of his head.

I turned to leave the bathroom.

'Thanks, Mum,' I said. 'I'll pick him up on the way to work in the morning and take him to nursery.'

She nodded and almost gave herself a wee hug, she looked that pleased to have him all to herself.

'And don't be spoiling him.' I warned.

She tutted. 'Silly Daddy. That's my job.'

I gave her a look, wanting to know what she thought of Anna, but didn't ask, knowing she tended to keep her own counsel.

'Have fun, son,' she said and got down on to her knees at the side of the bath. She studied me as if she wanted to say something. Then settled for, 'But just take this for what it is, eh?'

3

Certainty that Anna was the woman for me arrived in a setting that would have had a film director purring. After a wedding meal for friends of mine at the Marine Highland Hotel in Troon, Anna and I went for a walk. With the fairways of the famous Troon golf course before us and the hills of Arran melting into the horizon, I steeled myself to ask the question.

It was too soon.

Was it too soon?

What if she said no?

The late-August sun painted the scant clouds above Goatfell a deep crimson. We stood in silence, Anna's head resting on my shoulder as we enjoyed the calm after the happy tumult of the wedding. Anna looked up at me, her button nose begging for a kiss. I obliged. She giggled and rubbed the spot with the palm of her hand. A feeling settled over me, a cloth of silk floating to land on a cragged rock. Carefully I examined it.

I had known plenty of moments of pure joy with Pat, but since Patricia's death there was always something missing. The rough and blemished surface of my soul needed to be clothed in silk and colour. I needed a woman in my life.

'You never talk about, Patricia,' she said quietly, as if unsure of herself, and studied my expression for a reaction.

'You've just thrown me from my…' I looked into her eyes, trying to judge what was behind the question, and feeling somewhat deflated. 'I was just about to…'

'And now you're deflecting me from my question,' she said with a small smile. She stepped in front of me and held both of my hands.

'I want to get to know you, Andy. And that means I need to know everything…'

'But … I was just about to…'

'I can handle the fact you were married before. We all have a past. You didn't just appear in my life, fully formed as Prince Charming.' The breeze lifted a lock of hair and gently left it in front of her right eye. She tucked it back in place, her gaze never leaving mine.

'Prince?' I snorted and resisted the urge to pretend to fart.

'She must have been pretty special for you to fall in love with her.'

'Well out of my league, actually.' I leaned forward and kissed her lips. 'Just like you.'

'You don't need to do that, Andy.' Her eyes were full of understanding. 'I'm not threatened by the thought of your dead wife. In fact I'm impressed at how you've dealt with it all and provided a lovely home for your wee boy.'

'Yeah. Andy Boyd: model father.' I stepped to the side and, holding her right hand pulled her along with me as I walked towards the golf course that nudged on to the grounds of the hotel. Truth was I read the clear-eyed honesty in her remark and couldn't handle the compliment.

We came to a deep sand bunker and, seeing that there were no golfers about, Anna removed her shoes and sat on the edge, trailing her toes in the cool of the sand.

'Mind your dress,' I said. 'You'll get dirty.'

'It's just a dress,' she grinned and patted the turf. 'Have a seat.'

If she didn't mind getting grass stains on her dress, I didn't mind getting them on my suit, so I sat beside her. She sighed and rested her head on my shoulder.

'This is lovely. Thanks for bringing me, Andy. Couldn't have been easy to introduce me like that to all your friends.'

'Strikes me that they'd better get used to you being around.'

'Yeah?' She poked at my thigh.

'Yeah,' I said and kissed the top of her head.

We sat in silence for a time, enjoying the breeze, the stretch of grass and beach, and the moment with each other.

'I can't imagine how tough that would have been. You get the wonderful gift of a beautiful boy and your wife dies at the same time. That would have pushed lots of guys into permanent residence in the local boozer.'

'Aye. Hidden shallows me.'

'Stop it,' she said, admonishment light in her smile. 'You're fooling no one, Andy.' She looked into my eyes, hers warmed through with empathy. 'Died in childbirth.' She shook her head. 'Poor woman. That's the kind of thing you don't expect to hear nowadays.'

'Patricia had a heart condition. She'd had it since childhood actually, but was determined she wouldn't be defined by it, you know? Went skiing, horse-riding. All kinds of physical things that pushed at her limits.' I smiled at the memory of her determination. Saw her in her parent's kitchen arguing with her father that she would do whatever the hell she wanted. 'Her parents tried to wrap her up in cotton-wool. God she hated all of that.'

'I think I would have liked her,' Anna said.

'I don't know anyone who had a bad word to say about her.'

We sat silent for a moment.

'Her heart?' asked Anna. 'Was that the…'

I nodded. 'The doctors advised that she shouldn't get pregnant, that it would be too much for her.'

'But she was determined to have a child?'

'No, it was an accident. We'd kind of resigned ourselves, you know? We'd have each other and that would have to be enough.' I shrugged. 'And I was fine with that. Patricia was on the pill. I was lined up for a vasectomy…'

'And she fell pregnant…'

'Yeah. She had a tummy bug. Couldn't keep anything down for about a week. And that was enough to let my wee swimmers in.' My laugh was tinged with sadness as I remembered that was how she described it to my mum. 'Patricia point blank refused any medical intervention. Her parents wanted her to have an abortion. They blamed me…' I had a memory of her father at our front door, pleading with me to talk her out of having the baby, saying I was holding a gun to his daughter's chest. 'They were beside themselves with worry throughout the pregnancy.'

'You can understand that, surely?' Anna asked.

I turned to her and saw the sparkle of a tear in the corner of her eye. I gave her hand a squeeze.

'Course I do. I was scared too, but Patricia convinced me she could handle it. She sat staring at the photo of the first scan for hours. Pat was nothing but a dot, but you'd have thought she could see his wee face there.'

Anna sniffed. Wiped a tear from her cheek. 'Jesus, it's heartbreaking.'

'I think she knew…' I turned to face Anna. I'd never articulated this thought to anyone before. Couldn't trust myself to say the words out loud. 'In fact, I'm sure she knew her heart couldn't deal with the trauma of childbirth; it was as if she felt she was leaving something better behind, you know? She nearly died when she was a teenager and she felt that every moment after that was a bonus. And this baby was the biggest bonus of them all.'

As I said the words, I felt the last piece of an easing. As if I had finally and fully put Patricia to rest.

Anna sniffed again. 'I don't know if I could be that brave.' She got to her feet. Wiped down the seat of her dress. 'C'mon, let's head back to the wedding.' I stood and helped her get the grass off her dress.

'Cheeky,' she laughed as I touched her backside.

Then, hand in hand we walked back to the hotel. I chose a rather sedate pace because I didn't quite want the moment to be over and I still had an unanswered question to ask.

'Anna.' I turned to face her and held her slender fingers in mine. She looked up at me with a small question in her eyes and a smile that caused a catch in my throat and a tightening in my chest.

Given what we'd just been talking about I wasn't sure of my timing, but it was there, burning in my mind and heart, and I had to spit it out.

I couldn't believe we had only met eight weeks before and yet in that instant I was never more sure of anything in my life.

'Anna,' I said, my voice quivering and barely audible.

'Andy?'

'We're getting on really well, aren't we?'

She nodded; a question in her eyes.

'You love Pat, don't you?'

'He's a wee dreamboat.'

'Would it be ok if I asked you something?'

Her answering nod was slow. She too seemed caught up in the moment, her eyes wide with expectation.

'Do you want to go inside? I'm freezing,' I said.

'Oh, Andy.' She thumped my arm, turned and walked back towards the hotel.

'Anna,' I reached her in three easy steps. 'I'm sorry, honey. I just got nervous there. But there really is something I want to ask you.'

'Yes?' she looked up at me, suspicion shrinking her eyes.

'I want to ask you…' I licked my lips. 'I mean, what I want to say is…'

Anna said nothing, she merely looked up at me with an unreadable expression.

'Well, what I want to ask you is…' Shit, I really was nervous. 'You and me are getting on really well. Really well. And I was wondering…' For Christ's sake just say it, man. 'How do you fancy getting hitched?'

Anna turned and walked away.

I was stunned.

'Anna?' I caught up with her again.

She turned and smiled and thumped my arm again. 'Gotcha.'

The stag was held two weeks before the wedding. The two-week hiatus was supposed to give me time to recover from whatever tricks the lads would play on me. Having participated in the humiliations of a few of my friends over the years I thought two weeks would be just about enough.

While I waited for Jim to pick me up in the taxi, Anna paced the living room. She had come over to my house to make sure I was going to be drinking on a full stomach.

'So where's that brother of yours taking you?'

'Just to the club for a few drinks and then into town for a wee pub crawl,' I answered, choosing my words carefully.

'Who's all going?'

'A few of the guys from the club and one or two of the guys from the bank.'

'Guys from the bank are going as well?'

'That's not a problem, is it?'

'You're not long promoted to Branch Manager, Andy. You need to be careful what your colleagues think of you.'

'It's a stag night, Anna. There's nothing I can do about what they think of me.'

'What do you mean? Why? What's going to happen?'

Big mistake, I'd said far too much. 'Little pranks get played, Anna. It's just the way it is.'

'And what about that brother of yours? I'll bet he's organised strippers and everything.'

'He'd better have strippers, or there'll be bother.' I grinned to show I was joking.

'You big bugger,' Anna said, taking a swipe at my arm. 'You better behave yourself.' She stepped towards me and pushed me over on to the chair I had been standing in front of.

I grabbed her as I fell and we landed in a tussle of arms and legs. Reaching for her ankle I pulled off her shoe and started to tickle. She clenched her teeth against the need to laugh and struggled to free her foot.

'Stop it. Stop it.' Then a laugh escaped through her teeth. With little effort I pinned her down and, panting like a St Bernard, licked her all over her face.

'Yuck. Stop that, you big lump,' she laughed. I stopped licking and started kissing, swallowing her laughter. Her tongue sought mine.

We both groaned, then giggled when we realised we had moaned in perfect time with each other.

Mouth to mouth, both of us laughing, made us laugh even more. I fell back on to the floor away from her. She saw her chance and jumped on top of me. Pinned me down.

'Got you,' she said and leaned forward, her long hair falling either side of my head, tickling my ears. 'So much for the big, strong rugby player.'

'I'm putty in your hands.' I said as she took both my hands and stretched them out above my head.

She kissed me. 'Love you, Andy Boyd.'

I pushed her over as easily as if she weighed no more than one of the cushions on my sofa, and once I'd reversed our positions I returned her kiss.

'Can't believe we're actually going to be married in two weeks' time.'

'Anna Boyd,' Anna said as if trying the name out for the first time. 'Works for me,' she smiled.

Anna pushed me off and returned to the chair. She smoothed her hair. 'By the way, I meant to say that my transfer came in today.'

The organisation we worked for wasn't too keen on couples working in the same branch. As Branch Manager I had been copied in on the transfer, but worries about what Jim had planned for my stag night had thrown it out of my head.

'Right,' I said. 'How do you feel about going to Kilmarnock?'

'You knew already? Course you did.' She gave a smile. 'S'fine,' she said with a shrug. 'There's worse places to work.'

I had been thinking about Anna's job recently. Where she might be transferred to. How she might feel about it. She didn't share my ambition, seeing work as a means to an end. Once in the office she'd put in a shift, but that was it. When she walked out the door of an evening all thoughts of the bank receded.

So watching her with Pat just the previous day had given me an idea. I had no clue how she would react when I put it to her, though. I chewed on my bottom lip for a moment.

'I remember when I was young and Mum was working, I had to come in from school, make up the coal fire, peel the potatoes and make the tea for us all. I knew we needed the money but I would have loved to have my mum waiting in a warm house with food on the table. Sounds terrible, I know, in this day and age, but there you go.'

'It doesn't sound terrible.' Anna held my hand and her eyes moistened, as if she was ahead of me. 'It sounds lovely. It sounds just like what every child should have.'

She paused. Looked deep into my eyes, hers full of love. 'Pat's had such a traumatic start to his young life. Wouldn't it be great if together we could give him that stability?'

The tone she used for that last sentence held an inflection of yearning, as if this was something she'd missed out on herself.

'Fancy me writing a letter of resignation? Telling the bank to piss off?' she asked.

My chest tightened as the implications of this hit me. I was about to get a new wife and she was willing to set aside her own needs for me and my son.

'I think that would be a fantastic idea.' I clapped my hands.

She brushed away a tear with her fingertips. 'You are a lovely, lovely man, Andy Boyd?'

'And I just love you to bits.' I leaned forward and kissed her on the lips. 'So that's it decided, you're going to be a stay-at-home mum.'

'What about your mum?' Anna gripped my hand. Her expression had moved into neutral and I couldn't read anymore if she was pleased or disappointed with the suggestion.

'She could still help out. Let you go shopping or for coffee with your pals.'

With a squeal she jumped into my arms. 'Andy Boyd, you are a saint. I hate that bloody job and it would be fab to look after Pat and the house.' She got to her feet and did a daft wee dance. Squealed again. 'I've always dreamed of having my own house and family.' She stopped dancing, grew still and gave herself a hug, looking into the distance as if a bad memory crouched there.

But then she brightened and fell into my arms again. 'Andy, thank you. You have just made me the happiest woman in the world.' She kissed my nose, my forehead, my right ear, my lips. 'Thank you, honey. I'll be the best wife you could ever wish for.'

Just then a voice sounded from the door.

'Do I need a shoe horn to separate you two'? Jim's voice filled the room. '… Or will a bucket of cold water do the trick?'

'Hey, Jim.' Anna pushed off me, sat up in the sofa, smiled at my brother and smoothed the creases in her trousers.

'Do you not believe in knocking?' I said. Even to my ears my tone sounded too stern, but I didn't want Jim to think that nothing was going to change. I was getting married and he would have to learn to respect our privacy. But at the same time I felt bad at being so abrupt with him, he'd been coming and going as he pleased for years.

'Right, big guy.' Jim clapped his hands. 'Taxi's waiting.' He then looked around the room as if waiting to be ambushed by a miniature cowboy. 'Where's the wee man?'

'He's with Nan and Papa Morrison,' I answered.

'Yes,' added Anna. 'I've got the night off. I have my box of chocolates, my nail varnish and a nice romantic movie.' She pulled her feet under her.

I leaned down to give her another kiss. 'Love you,' I whispered.

'Love you too,' she replied.

Jim made a gagging sound.

'Let's go,' I said. 'Wish me luck, sweetheart.'

'Anything happens to him, Jim Boyd, you'll have me to contend with.' Then she looked at me, smiling. 'Bye honey.' She folded her arms, stuck her tongue out and then fixed her vision on the TV set. 'Don't have too good a time.'

In the backseat of the cab Jim turned to me, eyebrows raised in question.

'Nan and Papa Morrison?' he asked. 'You aiming for a sainthood or something?'

'Leave it, Jim. I have my reasons.'

During the first days of Pat's life I walked, talked and defecated on some strange system of remote control. My breakdown was a cause for concern for the Morrisons. They worried that their grandson, the only flesh and blood they had on earth, would be neglected.

My mother cared for the baby while my mind struggled to free itself from its fog of grief. She fed him, changed him and nursed him to sleep. Far too often for my liking, she would place him in my arms as I sat and stared and asked questions of the sky, of the trees, of the trail of a raindrop as it slid down the window.

I knew now that this attempt to keep my distance from Pat was borne of fear. Fear that I would love him – and then lose him.

Three weeks after the funeral a letter was dumped through my letterbox. It was from the Morrison's solicitor. They were suing me for custody of the baby. They didn't think that I would be a good parent. The not too subtle subtext was that they blamed me for Patricia's death.

Their arrogance galvanized me. How dare they? I raved. Who the hell did they think they were? Patrick was *my* son.

That morning, exhausted after an hour-long rant, I sat in my usual position by the window. My mother placed Pat in my arms after his feed. Full of anger at the Morrisons I was even less inclined to take any notice of him, until a burp laced with milk floated up to my nose, and his tiny hand gripped on to one of my fingers. I looked down into his crumpled face and for the first time into his eyes. They looked back at me without fear; without judgement.

I moved my hand to cradle his head and neck, feeling the heat of his skin and the silk of his bleached-gold hair. Tracing his fontanelle with my thumb, I wondered at how vulnerable he was and at the strength with which he gripped my other hand.

The first physical sign of emotion was the cool wet of a tear as it slid down my right cheek. Then there was no stopping them. I cried for what seemed hours, my shoulders shaking and my head falling forward towards Pat's. Still he continued his stare, as if trying to make sense of the being holding him, while his face melted under the force of my tears.

Even now, I can still remember that first kiss, the first time I placed my lips on the soft warmth of his forehead. That moment when I began the unfaltering process of falling in love with my son.

Perhaps the Morrisons should have received my thanks for bringing me to my senses, but the thought that they would try and take Pat incensed me. Let's see how they feel at the thought of never seeing him. Let's see how they suffer. And for four years, I made sure they did just that. Though somehow their names entered Pat's conversation.

'So why did you decide to let Pat go with the Morrisons?' asked Jim

'Anna talked me into it,' I answered. 'She made me understand how it must have been for them. Besides, I've known for a wee while that Mum has been taking him over to see them…'

'How…?'

'I'm no daft and four-year-olds are not very discreet.' I looked over at my brother, pleased and not at all surprised that he didn't try to deny it. He was wearing one of his many suits – three piece, with a shirt and silk tie that matched perfectly – and I was reminded of where we were going. This was a good sign. The fact my brother had dressed with his usual attention calmed me. The planned pranks wouldn't be too messy then.

'So, what's on the cards?' I asked, not expecting a truthful answer.

'Oh, you know,' he grinned. 'A few jars at the rugby club and then the minibus is coming to take a few of us across to Edinburgh.'

'Edinburgh?' I was worried by the weasel thought that entered my head: Anna might be annoyed. Then I dismissed it. If she was, too bad. Just because she had refused to have a hen party, didn't mean I should stint on my own evening of fun.

'I'll send her a text in the morning. From the hotel, just before we hit the bar again.'

*

At the door to the club, Jim paid the driver and we walked in. From the entrance I could see around twenty guys in suits at the bar, the deep hum of their voices audible above the jukebox.

Malcolm Kay, one of my oldest friends and a colleague from the bank, was the first to turn round. Judging by the flush on his cheeks the pint glass in his hand wasn't his first.

'There he is, guys,' he announced.

'Strip him,' the roar rushed at my ears. I turned towards the door I'd just entered as if to leave, but Jim gripped my arm.

'Best just to give in, Andy.' He smiled and nodded slowly.

'Aye. Right enough.'

I pulled at my tie. There was absolutely no point in fighting them, the end result would just be the same; me with no clothes on. In seconds I was naked, apart from my feet. No one would go near my socks.

'Hey, steady on, guys.' The sixty-year-old club secretary was the lone voice of sanity. 'What about the barmaid? Poor Senga'll have to stare at that thing all night.'

'Hold on, Dave Heaney,' said the aforementioned Senga as she placed a perfect pint on the bar. She ran stubby fingers through her cropped brown hair, stuck out her breasts, placed her hands on her expansive hips and leered. 'Is this an expression of complaint you see on this here dish? No? Well shut up and let an old girl have her fun. It's no very often I get to see any of these well-stacked young men in the skuddy.'

The rest of the evening passed in a blur of booze and banter. I eventually came to the next morning, wearing nothing but my boxers, lying on top of a bed in a strange hotel room.

4

The shower in my hotel room was like some form of magic. Hot water just a few degrees from being able to melt flesh battered my head and neck like aqueous rivets. Just what the doctor ordered to banish the last of my hangover. I turned my back to the wall and let the water massage my shoulders. Excellent. On and on the water poured, cleansing, soothing. I almost felt ready to phone Anna. I opened my eyes. Anna. Shit, what will she say?

Something registered in my brain. A colour. The water pooling at my feet was stained pink. My eyes were then drawn to my groin.

'Bastards,' I yelled. While I was comatose someone had shaved my balls and painted them bright red. I prayed no one had taken a photo for the wall of shame behind the bar at the rugby club. It was then I heard the sniggers. Jumping from the shower I ran into the bedroom. Twenty barrel-chested men were in various stages of apoplectic laughter. When they spotted the dye running down the inside of my thighs like some bizarre menses, their guffaws reached new heights.

'Who … how … what the?' I could barely speak and the more they laughed, the angrier I got. The angrier I got, the more they laughed. Weak with impotent rage all I could do was stamp my feet and storm back into the bathroom. Well, as much of a storm as a naked man with fluorescent-pink balls could manage.

Back under the shower I examined my scrotum for razor cuts and then soaped off the last of the dye. Bastards. I managed a chuckle.

By the time I got out of the shower, my bedroom was empty. Drying and dressing quickly, I phoned Patricia's mother.

'You all right, Andy? The idiots haven't damaged you in anyway, have they?' she asked. We'd barely spoken since Pat died and unexpressed emotions lingered in the space between words. Assuring her I was fine, I asked to speak to Pat.

'Daddy, I'm a good boy,' his sweet soprano filled my ear.

'Hey, buddy. Daddy misses you.'

'Ganny got me a toy, Daddy.' You're not missing me too much then, I thought, my doting smile bounced off the mirror opposite me.

'Remember you're Daddy's best boy, ok?'

'Okay,' he replied.

'Right, I'll have to go. You be a good boy, son.'

'You be a good dad, Dad.'

I had less success with Anna. The answer machine came on straight away and I spoke to the recording, told it I was fine. In Edinburgh, but still in one piece.

The weekend quickly assumed the pattern of many previous trips, minus the usual rugby match. There was Guinness, Guinness and more Guinness. Throw in plenty of food, some women to chat up, and you had your ideal stag weekend.

Thankfully the visit had been arranged with only two nights' stay and soon we were on the train on the way back across to the west of the country. The sorry sight of once-healthy, strapping men, reduced by too much alcohol and not enough sleep, assaulted our fellow passengers. Vomit, beer, bad breath and BO vied for their nasal attentions. I doubted that anyone had used up any valuable drinking time to attend to such a chore as personal hygiene.

'What a weekend,' I said to Jim. We were propping each other up, shoulders and heads touching.

'You're welcome, brother.' Jim sipped at a hair-of-the-dog, last can of beer.

'You're still a bastard.' I sat up. Looked at him for the first time that morning. Properly looked. The right side of his face was a mess. Swollen and black and blue. 'What the hell happened to your eye?'

'Yeah,' he tapped the side of his eye with care. 'You should see the other guys.'

Plural? 'Guys?'

'My brother the lightweight was in his scratcher, snoring. A few of us found one of those titty bars. The bouncers thought I was paying too much attention.' He shrugged. 'Nobody talks to me like that, mate.'

'Oh for fucksake, Jim.' I could see it all play out. It wasn't like it was a rarity. Jim gets challenged. Jim takes offence. Jim goes in swinging. 'Its guys like you that give testosterone a bad name.'

'You're just worried about the wedding photos.'

'I am not.'

'Yeah you are.'

I had another, closer look. 'To be fair, worse could happen in a rugby match.'

Mum and Anna would be worried. They wouldn't want the best man sporting a shiner in perpetuity in our photo album.

'Wanker,' I said and returned to my earlier position. My head was too sore to argue with him.

I could sense his answering grin. Then we slipped into silence, listening to the small group of guys on the benches across from us who were still going strong. Malcolm was right in the middle of it due to his unfeasible capacity for alcohol and an endless stream of jokes.

'Andy?' Jim spoke quietly. 'I know you're fond of the guy and all that, but…'

'But what?' I knew he was speaking about Malcolm.

'Have you ever known him to have a girlfriend?'

I shrugged. 'Can't say I've given it much thought. He puts in a shift out on the rugby pitch. Gets his round in. That's enough for me.'

'Just wondered,' Jim said as he looked across at Malcolm as if the thought had just occurred to him. 'Quite camp, isn't he?'

'Doesn't make him a bad person.'

'Aye. Right enough. Just so long as he's not trying to get near my arse.'

'Conceited prick. What makes you think any self-respecting gay man would fancy you?' I laughed and he grinned in response.

All energy used up, we were silent again, enjoying the jokes and laughter that wafted over on a fog of halitosis. Thoughts of Anna popped into my head. Anna and the wedding. Anna in a wedding dress.

Couldn't come soon enough.

5

From the foot of the stairs I watched her stepping up towards the bridal suite, swinging her stilettos in one hand and holding her white satin train in the other. While my eyes followed, my heart thumped each time the forward thrust of a knee pulled the white sheath dress tight across the perfect swelling of her rear. I once again thanked God, my lucky stars and my fairy godmother for sending me the perfect wife.

Number two.

'Anna,' I said, her name sounding like a prayer. Her long hair swung in a dark arc as she turned to face me.

'Andy,' she shone a smile.

'What are you up to, Mrs Boyd?'

'Just going up to the room, honey. To touch up my make-up.'

'Don't be daft. You're gorgeous enough.' She looked as if she'd just stepped from the front cover of a magazine. I looked back along the red-carpeted corridor and through the open doors of the reception suite to the throng beyond. No one appeared to notice we were both missing. Isn't it amazing what some free booze will do? Turning my back on the babble and thrum of voices, I caught up with Anna in six easy bounds. Standing on the step below her, I was still a full head taller than her.

I heard the rapid beat of small feet and a happy, high-pitched shout: 'Daddy.'

Followed by my mother's remonstration: 'Come on, Pat. Leave your dad alone for now.'

So much for escaping the crowd.

I looked back down the stairs to see my mother had my son by the hand. Mum and I exchanged glances and I was taken back to the conversation we had had at the house just before the car came to take me to the church for the ceremony.

I had been standing at the front window, scanning the street for the limo, terrified I would be late.

'Relax,' she said and walked over to me. She smiled when she reached me, looked up and brushed an imaginary piece of lint from my lapel. Then she smoothed out the shape of my tie.

'Mum,' I said, noting that even in her high heels she was still a good deal shorter than me. 'You shrinking?'

She snorted. 'You're still not too big to go over my knee.'

'Good luck with that.'

'Look at you,' she said, her expression soft with love. 'My handsome big son.'

'Got your waterproof mascara on?' I asked.

'I'm so happy for you, son.' My tie again became the focus of her mothering. 'You're happy aren't you?'

'What the hell is that supposed to mean?' My tone was sharper than I intended, but I had an excuse: my emotions were heightened. Wedding day nerves. Besides, although she was too classy to say something, I knew she had reservations about my wife-to-be.

She swallowed. Stepped back. Ran her hands down the front of her dress.

'I made myself a wee rule. Never comment on the women my boys choose…'

'But you're about to break that rule.' I trained my eyes down the street. When Mum decided she was to be heard there was little I could do about it. And this I was certain I didn't want to listen to.

'She's a lovely-looking girl…'

'Her name is Anna.'

'Pat loves her…'

'So do I.'

'But she's the first woman you've been with since Patricia died.'

'That you know of.'

She snorted. Gave me a look. She knew me too well. I was never the prolific dater in the family. That role went to Jim.

'I've been a single parent, son. I know what it's like.' She looked away from me and out of the window as if she was looking for the strength to say what she wanted. Then her eyes searched mine. 'Don't marry her out of gratitude, Andy. You both deserve better than that.'

I reached down and grabbed her hands. 'Mum, don't do this. Not when I'm waiting to go to the church.'

She looked as if she was steeling herself to say something that went beyond her self-imposed behaviour. 'I should have said something earlier. I'm sorry, son. I've got a bad feeling about this, Andy. Sorry, love … I just…'

'Mum. Don't.'

I heard a short, sharp beep of a car horn. Then Jim thundering down the stairs. His shout. 'Taxi's here, bro.'

Anna poked me on the shoulder and I was back on the hotel staircase. I sent my son a wink and turned to face my new wife.

'I think I may have to keep the new Mrs Boyd company to make sure she's safe.' We reached the top stair. 'In fact I may have to just sweep her off her feet…'

'… again,' laughed Anna.

'And throw her on to the huge four poster in the bridal suite and have my wicked way.'

'If you make a mess of my hair, Andy Boyd, I'll…'

Ignoring her squeals, I picked her up and marched towards the room. In front of the door, I stopped. Something occurred to me. I put her back on her feet.

'Eh, do you by any chance have the key?'

'Some hero you are.' Anna threw back her head and laughed, exposing an expanse of soft pink flesh at her throat. Which I just had to kiss. She stopped me by knocking the large key fob off the side of my head.

'Ow. That hurt.' I resisted the pain long enough to let her down gently, then rubbed at my temple.

'Serves you right.' Anna opened the door and marched in. She threw her shoes down and sat before a huge, mirrored dressing table. I made sure the door had closed behind us and walked over to her. Kissed the top of her head while breathing in her perfume.

'You had a nice day so far, sweetheart?' I asked.

'Yes.' The single syllable was drawn out and pitched with a note of indecision.

I looked into the reflection of her sad brown eyes and plump bottom lip.

'What's wrong?' I knelt down at her side feeling a stab of uncertainty. I was not sure whether she was being playful or if she was serious.

'You didn't turn round and look at me when I was walking down the aisle.' She picked up a brush and slid it down the silk of her hair.

Didn't I? 'Yes I did.'

'No you didn't.' Lips tight and eyes focused on my face. Accusing.

'Hey.' I grabbed at her hands. 'Maybe I didn't. I really can't remember … I was so nervous … all I could do was stare at the altar and thank God you'd actually turned up.'

Her expression softened. 'You were nervous?' She reached out and stroked my face.

'As a kitten. Never been so nervous in my life.'

'Even more than the first time you got married?'

'Absolutely.' I resisted the temptation to look up at the ceiling. We had talked the first wedding to death. Or so I thought. Time to change the subject.

'Give us a kiss.' I stretched forward, lips puckered.

She laughed, held a hand up in front of my face, a small smile of victory on her lips. 'Don't you be getting any ideas, Andy Boyd. You've a room full of guests down the stairs, including your son. Cool your jets.'

I kissed her neck. Then moved up closer to her ear. Kiss. 'Oh,

come on.' Kiss. 'Pat'll be fine. My mother has been dying to get him
to herself all day. And I've been dying to make love to you with your
wedding dress on all week. So, on the Andy Boyd scale of anticipation, I win.'

She pushed me back and tilted her head to the side. 'You know,
I've always wanted to have sex with a man in a kilt.'

I stood. Held out my hand. 'If madam would be so kind…'

'Why, sir…' she stood and took my hand. I guided her over to the
oak-framed, four-poster bed. She sat down on the foot and smiled
up at me.

'I do declare.' She fanned her face. 'The temperature in this room
has suddenly increased.'

I knelt before her as if in devotion. Soaking up the view.

She smiled. 'You can touch as well as look, you know.' Grin. 'We
are married.'

I didn't need to hear any more and, leaning forward, I pressed my
lips against hers, savouring the delicious swell of soft, warm skin. I
nibbled at her bottom lip, then the top one and then slid my tongue
into her mouth. Her tongue glided across mine and slowly circled
it. I could feel the rough tip and then the soft under-side. Pleasure
rumbled deep in my throat as her touch sparked darts of pleasure in
my groin. I pressed against her.

'Don't mess my hair,' she muttered.

'Your hair's perfect. There's so much hairspray there I couldn't
mess it up with a pitchfork.'

'You cheeky…' She punched my shoulder.

Laughing, I ignored her, picked her up and placed her seven-stone
frame on the bed. I kneeled before her. At the sight of her, my breath
momentarily stuck in my throat.

'God, I love you.'

'You do?' She made a face.

'Even now you question me?' I asked, leaning back on my heels.

'You'll always love me?'

I nodded.

'For ever and ever?' She made a mock sad face.

'Till *Coronation Street* do us part.'

'Who you kidding, mate? You love *Corrie* as much as I do.'

I grinned. 'Okay, I watch the catch-up shows now and again.'

She giggled. Grew serious. 'Anyway, what about your mum and Jim. You think they'll ever fall in love with me?'

I leaned forward and grabbed her hands. Anna had never been this needy. I put it down to wedding-day nerves.

'They'll just have to deal with it, honey. If anybody's got a problem with you, they've got a problem with me.'

I reached for her again, but a panicked knocking at the door disturbed my movement.

'Andy. Andy.' It was Jim.

'Oh for…' I stood up and, pushing down on my sporran, I went to the door and opened it slightly. Jim's smiling face appeared in the space.

'You'll need to keep it under your kilt for a wee while longer, bro. The band's signalling that it's time for the first dance.'

We danced plenty that night. In fact Anna and I were pleased that not only were we the first people on the dance floor, we were also the last to leave it.

'Why spend all this money for a party and leave early?' Anna asked as she sipped at a vodka and coke, just as Jim held out his hand and invited her on to the dance floor when the band picked their way into a Bon Jovi tune.

I watched them dance, pleased that Jim was making an effort. At one point Anna threw her head back in laughter at something Jim said. I sent him a silent, 'Good work, brother'.

Too soon, the band were going through the last bars of 'Three Times a Lady' and our evening was over. Anna and I herded those guests that were left to their taxis and then wearily made our way up to the bridal suite.

Once inside, Anna climbed out of her wedding dress and, wearing only her white lacy underwear, turned to me and gave me that look.

A look that sent blood surging to my groin.

'Anyway. Where were we?' she asked with a grin. 'It's about time we consummated this marriage, Mr Boyd.'

'Don't mind if I do, Mrs Boyd.' I replied and pushed my sporran to the side.

All the dancing, booze and lovemaking took its toll, and when we finished I rolled over on to my back, exhausted but feeling happier than any man has a right to be.

'I'm done in,' I said. 'Not sure I can keep my eyes open a second longer.'

Anna turned away from me on to her side. Gave a little snort of laughter. 'How's that for romance? Hope you're not needing cuddles after, Mr Boyd?' She reached for the lamp on the bedside cabinet. Flicked it off. 'Night, honey.'

'Night.' I mumbled, giving in to my body's demand that I shut my eyes. 'Best day ever.'

'Best day ever,' Anna repeated and reached back with her right hand. Patted me on the hip. 'Now, ssh, Andy. I'm totally done in. Sleep.'

It may have been minutes or perhaps hours later when something woke me.

I was on my back, in the same position as when I closed my eyes, which was unusual for me; I usually adopted the foetal position for sleep. I must have just conked out, I thought with a smile.

The room was still in darkness, so I judged it was still the middle of the night.

Anna shifted in the bed at my side and I felt another surge of joy that this beautiful woman had chosen me. She mumbled in her sleep. I couldn't make out the words.

She twitched and spoke louder, her voice a low moan, but her words still difficult to decipher. I turned and placed my hand on the naked curve of her shoulder. Her skin felt hot and clammy.

'Anna,' I said just above a whisper.

She twitched and spoke louder. It was almost a growl. I still couldn't work out what she said.

I turned and lightly touched the rise of her hip. 'Anna?'

She made an animalistic noise – something like a bark. She sounded distressed; almost feverish. Her feet kicked at the quilt.

I propped myself up on my elbows. 'Anna, honey. You're talking in your sleep. You okay?'

'Didn't turn to look, you bastard.'

She turned. Brought her arm up and around.

Hard and fast.

Her elbow smashed against the bridge of my nose.

I screamed.

6

The hotel staff were incredulous, Anna was abject in her apologies and the doctor on call at Accident and Emergency was hugely sympathetic.

'What rotten luck, to break your nose on your wedding night ... Dear me ... How did it happen again?' He reached up and stroked his own nose as if to check it was still in one piece.

By now we had become expert at telling everyone how I had got up in the middle of the night to go to the toilet, tripped on her train and flown head first into one of the bedposts.

'Dear me.' The doctor tutted as he examined my nose up close. At least he hadn't sniggered like the rest of his nursing staff. There was a fire in my face that licked across my checks and up my forehead with every beat of my pulse.

Anna sat by the bed, squeezing my huge mitts between her slim and delicate hands. Regret was clear in the furrows of her forehead, the rise of her eyebrows and the downturn of her mouth. She looked so sorry I couldn't feel any resentment towards her. After all, it was a strange accident.

'Now you just rest here for a moment.' The doctor smiled. He pulled back the curtain and exited the hospital cubicle that had become our honeymoon suite.

Once his footsteps had faded down the corridor, Anna spoke.

'Andy, I am so, so sorry.'

'It's okay, babe.' My voice was muffled with pain.

'No it's not. I can't believe I was so ... I mean, who's ever heard of someone hitting someone in their sleep?'

'Honestly, it's okay.' I lifted a hand to my face in a weak attempt to still the pain. 'Don't worry about it.'

My gentle tone brought tears to her eyes. She leaned forward and, resting her head on my lap, let them flow.

Just then heavy footsteps thumped down the corridor and the sound of metal on metal sang out as the curtain in the very next cubicle was pulled back.

'Oh fuck. It's the polis.' slurred a voice.

'Aye. There's no pulling the wool over your eyes, Mr Craven. What have you been up to now?'

'Just had wan too many, officer.' The voice was too loud, in the manner of drunks who lose the power to regulate their volume.

'And you just slipped and the knife just happened to cut across your wrists.'

'Aye. Lucky white heather, eh?'

'What about the black eye?'

'Oh that? I'd forgot all about that. Ma lodger took exception to being asked for the rent. On account he was shaggin' ma wife. Thinks he should have got a hundred per cent discount.'

'Did he give you the bruise on the other side of your face?'

'That … that was nuthin'.' The voice was much quieter now.

'Doesn't look like nothing to me, Craven.'

'It was just a wee disagreement with the wife. I'm tellin' ye, it was nothin'. I asked her if she was fuckin' the lodger and she took a wee swing at me with her handbag. There was a half-brick in it at the time.'

The casual, almost accepting tone of his voice as he mentioned the first acts of violence disturbed me. I was almost beginning to feel sorry for him until he mentioned the beating he took from his wife. At that point my sympathy changed. The situation seemed almost laughable.

Anna squeezed my hand again and brought me back to my own life and my own troubles, such as they were. It had been a wonderful day. Standing at the altar, waiting for my new bride to arrive, I had looked up at the crucifix suspended from the ceiling and thanked God for this new blessing.

What a difference from my last visit to this church. A day I would never forget. A day I would never allow myself to forget: my first wife's funeral.

The midwife said it was unusual, what with medical advances. She said she was sorry for my loss. She said she didn't know what to say as she knotted her fingers. Her pale lips mouthed the words as her eyes shrunk in anticipation of my reaction. I simply stood in front of her, my hands hanging limp by my side, mind suspended in a cotton-wool numbness.

It was strange that even now I could remember every detail of that young woman's face, yet I had to examine photographs to remind me how Patricia looked.

I shook my head as if to throw off these thoughts and instantly regretted it. Pain exploded once again in my face.

Anna's hand tightened on mine and I resolved to keep my head still for the next ten years if need be and to keep my thoughts on something a little more cheery. Pat's face imposed itself on my mind and a smile seeped through on to my lips. My son, Patrick. He liked being called Pat. That was what his gran called his real mummy. What a boy. He had been delighted to be a pageboy and to be wearing a kilt. He didn't sit still throughout the entire ceremony and once out of the church ran from me to Anna to his Gran and to Jim, hands waving and eyes flashing.

'I have a new mummy,' he told everyone that would listen.

I didn't have to worry about him for the next few weeks, Granny was taking care of him for me. She only had a two-bedroom place, and one was being used as a store for stuff from her previous, much larger house, but she would gladly sleep on her sofa if that meant a visit from Pat.

My mother would be upset she didn't get a chance to see if I was all right, but would she be convinced by the story of the trip and the bedpost?

7

The new Mr and Mrs Boyd left for their honeymoon ten days after the wedding, which thankfully gave my nose a little more time to heal and the bruising to fade. Neither of us spoke again about our wedding night, preferring to remember two days later when our next act of love-making as husband and wife ended with untroubled sleep. We lay in each other's arms afterwards and spoke late into the night, our words punctuated with caresses, sentences hyphenated with laughter and paragraphs bridged with slow, deep thrusting and soft orgasms.

I was like an addict, I couldn't get enough of Anna, and she never once turned me down whenever she noticed that spark in my eyes.

Before leaving for holiday, I made sure I spoke with Pat to explain why Anna and I were going away on our own. Prior to this, the longest periods I had been away from him were two nights on a rugby trip, and then the stag weekend. Now I had not only presented him with a new mother, but I was taking her away from him for a week.

'Anna and I will be back soon, buddy. We just need to go away for a few days. And before you know it we'll be back and you'll be the most important person in the world for both of us.'

His green eyes looked deep into mine.

'Is Anna my family now?' he asked.

'Yes, son.'

'Are you still my family, Daddy?'

'Of course I am, son.' I hugged him tight. 'Of course I am. I'll always be your family. You're the most precious thing in the world to me.' I had spent a lot of time with Anna that week; he must have noticed my distraction. I kissed his forehead while searching for the right words. Words that a child might understand.

'All of your friends at nursery have daddies and mummies don't they?'

He moved his small head back and forward in an earnest nod.

'Well, I needed to find a mummy for you to help me to show you how to grow up and become a good man. And I need someone to talk to late at night when you're tucked up in bed.'

He nodded again as if he understood every word. My chest tightened with the pressure of my feelings for him and I wondered if I could ever love another human being as I loved this child.

Life aboard the cruise ship settled quickly into a pattern of lovemaking, sleeping, eating and sight-seeing. We were waited on by an army of diligent waiters who seemed to anticipate our every whim. The food was dangerously abundant.

'Did you know that the average person on a cruise puts on two pounds a day?' Anna asked me as I piled my plate high at the midnight buffet. Her own plate was a sea of white china with a solitary strawberry, dipped in a chocolate fondue, in the centre.

'I need my strength,' I winked, 'for later.'

The cruise itinerary was an architectural heaven, allowing us to sample some of Europe's finest moments. The place names glided off the guide's tongue like a series of honeyed sunsets: Florence, Pisa, Rome, Nice, Monaco, Monte Carlo and Barcelona. A new port every day and each city worthy of every word of praise heaped upon them. We strolled through the living art museum that is Florence hardly daring to speak above a whisper, so awed were we by the churches, paintings and sculptures. We revelled in the contrasts of Rome: the modern apartment blocks right next to an excavation that reached back into a time before Christ; the roar of the traffic and the hush in St Peter's Basilica.

Anna's favourite was the Trevi Fountain. We approached this through a maze of tall apartments and narrow streets barely wide enough to let a car pass through. The sheer scale and beauty of the fountain hit you by complete surprise as you turned yet another corner, expecting another street. I held Anna close by my side as I immersed myself in the glory of the site. We stood like this for minutes, doing nothing but holding each other and staring. Then we snapped photograph after photograph.

Surveying the crowd, I watched a Roman teenager nuzzle into his girlfriend's neck and then turn his back on the fountain. He threw a coin over his shoulder and then kissed her. Do our teenagers in Scotland have such a romantic view of their heritage? I wondered, or is the romance of this city so strong, even its inhabitants cannot escape it?

In Nice we ambled along the Baie des Anges and then found an explosion of colour and blooms in the flower market. Anna looked as if she had stumbled on heaven as she wandered along the stalls, soaking up the scents and tracing petals with a light touch. And so the week went on, view after glorious view massaging out the kinks in our souls, soaking our spirits in calm.

The cruise ship provided a counterpoint to this grandeur with its on board entertainment. By day we had all the sights that our eyes could manage, by night, back on the boat, it was time to exercise our taste buds in the restaurant and our ears in the theatre as we listened to the ship's cabaret.

Seats were quickly taken in the lounge that hosted the main show, and on one occasion we were lucky to get a seat at all. A middle-aged woman and her teenage daughter squeezed together to allow us some room. The daughter almost shone with youth and wore the flush of early womanhood with an acceptance that would have every middle-aged woman on the ship give a quiet groan of envy. Her mother was an older version; the firm line of her jaw and her trim physique evidence of how she took care of herself. The line, *you could be sisters*, almost tripped from my mouth, but I successfully edited it before I looked a fool.

The mother began speaking to us about the cruise, telling us how much she and her daughter were enjoying it. Her daughter, meanwhile, sat side on to us and rolled her eyes as her mother spoke, probably wishing that she was back home in a nightclub in England.

As the woman talked, clearly pleased to have someone listen to her, she addressed most of her comments to me, only occasionally looking at Anna. Sensing Anna's boredom, I attempted to draw her into the conversation, but each time Anna simply smiled and deferred to me. Not a moment too soon the curtain rose and the young crew, as eager as a litter of pups, set about entertaining us.

Their energy was amazing, their talent impressive, and after what seemed only moments, the show was over. Anna stood up straight away, before we could get drawn into another conversation, and walked briskly to the door. I followed her, aiming a smile at my new friend over my shoulder.

'God, who does that woman think she is?' Anna turned to me as soon as we were out of the door.

'She was just lonely,' I answered, surprised by the irritation that flared in Anna's eyes. 'She probably just wants someone to talk to.'

'Well, she needn't think she can have *you*.' She emphasised this last word by stabbing a finger into my chest. She paused as if she regretted her response. 'Sorry, honey. Think I'm just a wee bit tired. I'm going to bed,' she said and with a wave walked towards the stairs. When she got there she turned and offered me a wicked grin. 'Coming? Or do you want to go and chat up your new best pal?'

This was the first night of the holiday that we went to bed on anything like a disagreement. Once we were inside our narrow cabin, Anna stripped wordlessly, jumped under the covers and turned to face the wall.

'We're ok?' I asked, surprised not to be welcomed into the bed by her open arms.

She turned, gave me a small smile. 'Just worn-out, honey.'

'That woman's just lonely, babe. And I'm probably the only male on board with all his own teeth.'

She snorted. 'Aye, you're a catch, right enough.' She yawned.

'Stop worrying, Andy. It's nothing. She's nothing.' She lifted a hand out from under the covers, found mine and gave it a squeeze. 'Now sleep.'

But I lay awake for what seemed like hours, going over Anna's reaction to the woman in the ship's theatre. She didn't think for a moment I was interested, did she? This was as close as we'd come so far to a cross word during a holiday that I'd determined would be perfect. Sleep eventually won me over and I knew nothing till I was woken by a pressing need to pee. Eyes still closed, I moved from my side of the bed and walked towards the toilet, which was only four steps away.

After two steps I fell over something large. My elbow hit a seat and the side of my head the dressing table. Holding my forehead, I righted myself and sent a silent prayer skyward in thanks for not bashing my nose again. Anna's tousled head rose from the pillow and she reached for the light.

'What the…' she murmured, wiping sleep from her eyes.

'Bloody cabin boy. Left a bloody suitcase right where I could trip over it.'

8

My mother's face was the first that I saw on arrival back at Prestwick Airport. It was quickly followed by Pat's as he ran at full speed and jumped into my arms.

'Whoa, cowboy. You nearly knocked me over. Don't know your own strength.' I hugged him fiercely then covered his face with kisses.

'Dad, Dad, don't,' he laughed, loving every second.

I ran my eyes over him as he radiated a smile. He seemed bigger than I remembered and we had only been gone a week. Mum and Anna kissed politely, like the strangers they were. Time would be my ally here. I was certain that once Mum got to know Anna she would grow to love her almost as much as I did.

On the way home in the car Pat chattered non-stop, one sentence rushing into the next and knocking it out of his mouth. He told us of the nice time that he had staying with Gran. They had gone to Kidz Play every day, a soft-play area down at Prestwick Beach. They'd gone to MacDonalds, Burger King and KFC lots of times as well. At this news I gave my mother a reproving look: an eloquent shrug was her reply.

It was this look from my mother that gave me a lightning flash of insight. That look said to me she was worried that, with Anna on the scene, she might not get to see as much of Pat and that she was making the most of it while she could. I made a mental note to make sure this didn't happen.

'Did you have a nice time, son?' my mother asked in an attempt to change the subject, lest Pat say anything else incriminating. I watched her as she drove with care and practised ease through the traffic and noticed again the effect that the years had had on her. Lines as deep as her laughter was warm and unforced spread from her eyes.

As usual, my mother was perfectly turned out. She rarely left the house without her mascara and lippy. Jim and I used to complain about the lipstick on our cheeks and the foundation on our collars, which earned us lots of teasing from our mates. The lines, however, I saw as a badge of her fortitude, her determination to bring up two boys without a father. My mother was one of those women that Scotland seemed to excel in. Women who face life's downpours with a raincoat of stoicism and an umbrella fashioned from humour.

My father had died at the age of thirty-five. He was an assistant bank manager who worked hard at his profession to provide for his wife and children. It was as he poured over his ledgers that he suffered a massive heart attack and died. I was five.

My memories of my father are faint. If I concentrate I can see a tall, slim man with large hands and broad shoulders. My mother tells me that I most resemble him and old photographs seem to bear this out. A photograph of him in his swimming trunks, posing beside a car, holding Jim and I, down at Troon beach was always my favourite as a child.

Mum was father and mother during those early years. From wiping away our tears and cleaning the cuts on our knees to playing football, she brought herself whole heartedly to each task and with such vigour that we hardly noticed our little family unit was missing anything.

At the age of seven my mother encouraged me to become an altar boy. I don't remember having much choice in the matter. We were Catholic and it was every mother's wish to see her son assist in the Holy Mass. Now, as an adult, I can see that what she was really attempting to give us was a male role model; a priest called Father David filled this post admirably.

He seemed to take a shine to Jim and I and would go well out of his way to say hello. A ruffle of the hair, his hand on our shoulder was often enough for us to know of his comforting presence. Once we were more used to him, he began to call round at the house and take us swimming, fishing or would even just kick around a football in our back garden.

For the first time I felt able to talk to an adult on equal terms and this I believe to have been his great strength. He used to assure us that there were no stupid questions, only stupid answers, and he would let us prattle on for hours, never correcting, never judging.

On one occasion, he had just dropped us at the house after a trip to the beach. Jim was delighted with the number of whelks he had collected and charged into the house to show them off to Mum. Father David sensed that I wanted to talk.

'Did you have a nice day, Andrew?' he asked.

'Yes, Father, thanks.'

We sat in silence for a few minutes.

'Father?' I asked at last.

'Yes, son.'

'Is it a sin to hate someone for dying?' I blurted out, staring at my fingers.

'Do you hate your Dad?' It was amazing, I remember thinking at the time – he knew who I was talking about.

'Yes,' I said with as much energy as my small frame could muster.

'Why?'

'Because he left us.'

'Did you cry when he died?'

'No.' My voice was barely audible.

He paused before speaking. 'In answer to your question, no, it's not a sin. Do you think your Dad wanted to die?'

'No.' That was a stupid question.

'Do you think that he would really rather be here with his wife and two bonny boys?'

'Probably.' *That* made sense.

'Why do you think you didn't cry?'

'Because I was angry?' I asked.

'You know, it is all right to cry. Big boys do cry. I cried when my Dad died.'

'You did?' I looked up at him, I couldn't have been more amazed if he had said 'fuck'.

'Yes, of course. I was terribly sad. I loved my father … You know when I cried it was not for my father, it was for me. He was a good man and so would have gone to heaven. I cried for me because I knew I would miss him every day for the rest of my life.'

These words spoken quietly but confidently by this compassionate man broke down the flood walls of my resentment. They collapsed under the storm of my grief. I have no recollection whatsoever of how long I sat in that car crying. I only remember Father David's shoulder and noticing how wet it was from my tears.

When we arrived home after the ten-minute drive from the airport, Mum and Anna made straight for the kitchen to put the kettle on, one to try and help and the other to assert her place as the new woman in my life. Pat, oblivious to the politics, made straight for the TV and put on a Disney movie. I carried in the suitcases, dumped them on the bedroom floor and went downstairs to drink my tea.

Anna was standing proprietarily by the kettle, holding a huge bouquet of flowers.

'Look at these sweetheart, aren't they gorgeous? Your mother bought them for us to welcome us home.'

'Thanks, Mum. They're lovely.' I leaned forward and gave her a kiss on the cheek.

At that moment, Jim walked in the door, Pat following him like a puppy. 'Did you guys have a nice time then? Or were you too busy to enjoy the sights?'

'Jim,' Mum scolded, 'Not in front of the boy.'

'I know, Mum. I'm far too young for this kind of talk,' I jumped in.

'Sorry, Mother.' Jim dropped before her feet and pretended to kiss them. Pat, thinking that this was hilarious, jumped on his back. This resulted in the two of them running into the living room, round the couch, Pat saddled on Jim's back. From there and back to the kitchen, to the dining room and back to the lounge, with Pat barely able to hold on for giggling. Jim hollered like a cowboy on ecstasy.

I looked over at Anna to check if she was enjoying the show. She was modelling a smile the Mona Lisa would have done well to emulate. During our courtship it was only on rare occasions that we were all together at the same time. Perhaps, not coming from a rowdy family, she found all of the carry-on a bit strange. Or she was simply tired after our holiday.

'Right, Jim, sit on your bum and stop winding up my son. Pat you come over here and watch the film that you asked to get put on.' The two of them walked over and did as I asked, but Jim couldn't resist one final raspberry blown on Pat's neck, which elicited a fresh gale of giggles.

'Jim,' Mum said. 'Can't you see that Anna's tired? Leave Pat alone and let him calm down.'

The talk seemed to go a little flat after that with Anna offering little by way of conversation. She's tired, I thought. The poor soul was just getting an idea of what it really meant to marry into our family. I was sure that, given time, she would learn to love the strong, male sense of fun that characterised all our get-togethers.

Anna sent me a quick smile of thanks.

I looked at my watch, 'Pat, I think it's time you had your bath.'

'Daaad.' He managed to make such a small word last a long time.

'Come on, son. It's getting late and you know that you usually have your bath before now.'

'Do you want me to do it? You two could do with a wee break,' Mum offered. This was less about us needing a break – we were just back after all – than Mum's reluctance to give up her time with Pat.

'No, no,' said Anna with a tired smile. 'You guys get off home, I'll see to Pat. Got to get into the routine of everyday life. The honeymoon is definitely over.'

'Very wise,' said Mum. 'Right.' She slowly reached for her handbag. 'I'll be off. I've got a busy day tomorrow.'

I was pleased to hear it. Jim and I were both concerned that she didn't have enough in her life.

'Oh, what are you up to then?' I asked.

'You know,' she answered vaguely, 'this and that.'

'Is that horny old goat next door taking you out somewhere, Mum?'

'Jim.' I said, 'Not in front of Pat.'

'No harm done.' Jim ruffled Pat's hair.

Pat in turn stood up and, bringing each hand up to the side of his head with only the index finger sticking up, he butted Jim's belly.

'Mr Henderson's got horns he wants to stick into Gran.'

Trying to look sternly at Jim while stifling a laugh and at the same time hoping to give Pat the impression that he had said nothing out of the ordinary, I succeeded only in looking constipated.

Anna came to the rescue. 'Right, bath, young man.'

Pat ran to his Gran and gave her a kiss. 'Night, night, Gran. Love you.'

My mother looked as if she was about to cry.

'See ye, pal.' Jim walked over and tweaked his nose. He looked back at me. 'I'll give you a phone, Andy. We'll go out for a drink, eh?'

With Pat's happy chatter interspersed with Anna's singsong voice floating downstairs from the bathroom, I washed and put away the cups. Then, enjoying the solitude, I sat on the settee with an ear on the two most important people in my life. I smiled. I was delighted to hear them clowning around together. Pat had a highly developed sense of fun and it was a joy to watch him play with the water. This was a sure way for the two of them to connect, so I decided to stay where I was and let them get on with it.

I sat forward in my chair. The laughter and splashes had stopped. Then I heard a sharp tone from Anna and an answering wail from Pat.

I was up the stairs three at a time.

'What the…?' I said as I ran into the bathroom. Anna was on her knees at the side of the bath with her hair soaking and Pat was sitting in the bath with a look of abject shame on his face.

'The wee bugger soaked my hair,' Anna said, standing up, her face heavy with tiredness and irritation.

But she immediately seemed to regret her tone. She sank on to her haunches. 'I'm so sorry, Pat. You took me by surprise that's all.'

Pat's got to his feet. His bottom lip was sticking out and was on full tremble.

'Forgive me for being a bad girl?' Anna said, holding out her hands. 'Hug?'

'Yeah, she didn't mean it, son,' I said, picked up a towel and plucked him out of the water.

'I've got this, Andy,' Anna said. Now it was her turn to look huffy.

'It's alright,' I said. 'Why don't you go down and make us a coffee. I'll be down shortly.'

'Andy…' Anna said with a look of disappointment on her face.

Pat was sitting up in my arm looking from one of us to the other. He wasn't sure who he should be looking to for guidance. Then, giving up, he lay his head on my shoulder.

'We were fine, Andy. You don't need…'

'I know,' I said. 'Sorry. I just…' Pat was mine, my responsibility and seeing Anna on the point of disciplining my son brought out a reaction that completely surprised me. If Anna was to be his new mum, she had to be able to have a part in that side of his life as well. I sent her a look of apology. 'Won't happen again.'

'I'll stick the kettle on,' said Anna.

She pushed herself to her feet and, as she walked past me, she ruffled Pat's head, offered him a look of apology and then looked at me. Her look said, you have to let me in.

The three of us. That's our family now.

'Anna…' I began. But she was out of the bathroom and down the stairs.

*

I dried Pat and helped him into his pyjamas. Then I put him to bed and read him a story.

'You okay, son?'

A small nod. Anna had never spoken to him with any edge and it looked like he was trying to make sense of it.

'Anna's just not used to little boys. She still wants to be your friend.' I smoothed the hair down on the top of his head. After drying it I had forgotten to brush it and it was sticking up all over the place. 'Okay?'

This time I received a quiet ''kay' in response.

Downstairs Anna was curled up in a chair. 'Is he all right?'

'He's fine.' Pause. 'Thought you were making the coffee?'

She stuck her tongue out and I knew we were fine. 'What did your last slave die of?' she asked.

It seemed like hours before I got to sleep, the evening's events revolving around my head. I couldn't bear to see any distance open up between Pat and Anna, and prayed that the little scene in the bathroom would be quickly forgotten by them both.

Sleep must have eventually claimed me, because I was awakened abruptly by several blows to my head.

'What the….?' I grabbed the arms of my assailant. It was Anna.

'Anna, what the hell…?' I pushed her off me, sat up in the bed and switched on a lamp. Anna was crouched at my feet, her small frame heaving with fright as she forced air into her lungs.

'What the…?' She rubbed at her eyes as if just coming out of a deep sleep. 'Why did you…' She looked around herself. 'How did I end up at the bottom of the bed?'

'Bloody hell,' I said. 'That was some nightmare you were having.' I edged down the bed towards her. 'You woke me up with a punch. You were hitting me in your sleep.'

'I what? I did what?' she asked, her eyes large with shock.

'Bloody hell, Anna. What got into you?' My irritation evaporated. She looked so small and scared I could do nothing but hold her.

Folding her in my arms, I lay back down on the bed and rocked her as she chanted a mantra of apology.

Pat's tousled head popped in the door.

'Daddy, what's wrong with Anna?' he asked.

'Nothing, son.'

'Dad, why's she crying?' he continued.

'Pat, just go back to your bed now, son.' I spoke through clenched teeth and instantly prayed that I could reel back the words and kill the tone. I rarely spoke to him like that. Even in the dark I could make out his bowed head as he turned and shuffled back to his room.

9

I awoke to the sensation that every nerve end in my groin was being charged. Something warm and wet was teasing every piece of skin. My first thought was that Pat might come in and wonder about the large bump at my waist and ask where Anna was.

'What about Pat?' I managed to squeak.

'Don't worry, he's fast asleep,' was the muffled reply. I was amazed; judging by the light that filtered through the curtains it must have been fairly late. Since Pat was born he had been an early riser, any time between six and seven o'clock being the norm.

All thoughts of my son were driven from my head by the insistent tongue, lips and hands that were building up a maddening rhythm. As I began to tighten, this beat lessened and stopped altogether and when my breathing had slowed, started up again. Anna did this several times, kissing, squeezing and pulling me to the peak before letting me fall back down again. Eventually, it became too much and I begged for release.

'Don't stop, please, don't stop,' I moaned.

Mercifully, Anna did as I asked and her rhythm took on an urgency that had me tumbling over the other side. And in an explosion of dancing nerve ends, I yelled out.

'Dad?' We heard a small voice, the drum of his feet on the landing and then he appeared at the foot of the bed.

'It's okay son,' I laughed, thankful that he had delayed his entrance. A few moments earlier and it would have been red faces all round. I made a mental note, perhaps it's time to get a lock for our bedroom door.

Anna kissed me on the lips.

'Good morning, big boy,' she whispered.

'Dad, Dad, can I go down and watch *The Lion King*?' pleaded Pat. In the mood that I was in, he could have asked for permission to play with an open razor and I wouldn't have refused him.

'Of course you can, son. I'll just have a quick shower and then I'll make you some breakfast.'

'No you don't,' said Anna. 'You have a long soak in the shower and I'll make us all a fry-up.'

'I think I've just died and gone to heaven,' I said as I returned her kiss.

I put my hands behind my head and watched as my new wife slipped out of the bed and into a figure-hugging robe. I thought I couldn't be happier. But, as the endorphins slowly drained from my body, I became aware of a faint ache on my temple, and the events of the night returned.

'One second, Anna,' I said just before she opened the door. 'Can we talk about something?'

'What about?' She appeared mystified.

'Last night.'

'What about last night?' Her tone darkened.

'Last night when I woke up to you playing the drums, with my head as the drum and your fists as the drumsticks.' I offered her a chuckle, to show it wasn't a big issue.

'I'm sorry, honey. That's never happened to me before.' She made an apologetic face. 'And anyway...' Big smile. '... didn't I just show your how contrite I was?'

After breakfast, I changed Pat out of his pyjamas and into his clothes, while Anna went upstairs to shower and dress.

In little time Anna was ready to go out. As she zipped up Pat's jacket and checked the laces on his shoes, I allowed the attention she paid my son to deepen and widen my love for her. Last night was weird, but it was a one-off. She was under a lot of stress – joining a new family when her own had been a trial. Not that I knew much about her people; none of them were invited to the wedding and any questions about them were always met with an unnerving quiet.

10

The first day back at the office after my honeymoon, I sat at my small, neat desk and one by one I ripped pages from my small calendar to bring myself up to date. October the sixth we were in Florence, I remembered. On the seventh we were in Rome. Ah well, I thought and ripped the remainder of the week in one go. Did the holiday really happen just last week?

The four other people I shared the office with all had their heads down and were quickly getting into their day's work. Beyond them a grey sky barely lit the day, the clouds leaching any heat from the sun. What would I give to be back in Barcelona? Fingering my wedding ring, I turned my attention back to my desk and to the pile of brown in my mail tray.

'God, another rainforest cut down just to give me a load of grief,' I said to no one in particular.

'Hello the groom.' A head peered in the door. '… and he's talking to himself already.'

'Hey Malcolm. How's it going?'

'No bad,' he answered, hugging the doorway. 'How was the honeymoon, then?'

'Oh, you know, wonderful,' I said. Everyone in the room looked over at me with varying levels of leer.

'For chrissake, we're not teenagers, we did manage to leave our cabin,' I said, mock-sternly. 'At least for five minutes a day,' I laughed. 'And can we get off the subject of my sex life?'

'You're the one doing all the talking, Andy,' said Jim Dick, one of our business relationship managers, from the other side of the room.

'Andy, I need a word with you,' said Malcolm. For the first time I wondered why he hadn't fully entered the room.

'Right, okay. Just now?'

He nodded, barely making eye contact.

'Coffee machine?'

'Lead the way.'

A coffee machine had been installed just down the corridor from my office and there was a small interview room beside it. Hands warmed by the plastic cups that seemed to be melting as we held them, we each took a seat in the interview room.

'I just want you to know it wasn't me,' he said.

'Eh?'

'Before this whole sorry mess breaks out. I want you to know it wasn't me. I wouldn't steal and you know how my face doesn't fit. Old Campbell's the Operations Manager now and he's always had it in for me.' The Operations Manager was responsible for the area's staffing and resources, which included disciplinary matters.

'Malcolm, take a deep breath, speak slowly and tell me what the hell you are on about.'

Holding the cup in both hands and looking as if he would rather sit on top of a lit Bunsen burner than drink from it, Malcolm fortified himself with a deep breath.

'There was a cash difference last week. We checked thoroughly and couldn't find anything.'

'How much?'

'One thousand pounds. Short.'

'Oh.' Serious stuff. 'Did you check all of the cabinets in the safe, and down the back of all the drawers?'

'Yes.' His tone was heavy. It asked, do you think I'm an idiot?

Malcolm and I had begun working for the bank in the same week fifteen years before. One month later we were on the cash together and fifty thousand pounds went missing. It was later found in a cupboard that the Head Teller had somehow forgotten to count.

'Right, let's not panic,' I said. 'Have all the day's slips been checked?'

'Yes.'

'Have all the pay-ins been double-checked?'

He nodded.

'Was the remittance to the Post Office checked?' We supplied the local GPO with its float.

'Yes, Andy. I am the Head Teller now. I do know how to do my job.' The eyes that could make most of the girls in the office swoon flared at me.

'Just checking, Malcolm. I'm going to get asked all of this by Head Office. I need to know for myself.'

'Sheila checked the cash on Friday.' Sheila stood in for me whenever I was off work.

'I'll need to do it for myself.'

'Fine, fair enough,' agreed Malcolm.

Something niggled at me. Why was Malcolm taking it so personally? We'd had cash differences before. Maybe not as big as this one, though. As we left the room and walked towards the area where the cash was held I stopped and gripped his arm.

'Is there something else?'

'Something else? What do you mean?' He looked at the floor, at the walls, anywhere but at me.

'Is there anything else I should know?'

'Oh, brilliant. You think it was me, don't you?'

'No, I don't, Malcolm.' I didn't. 'But you've had differences before and you've never behaved like this.'

He stood for a moment as if a debate was raging in his mind.

'Right, not here. In the business cash safe.'

In silence we walked to the safe. Malcolm inserted a key in the top lock from a bunch that he held in his hand and I inserted a key in the bottom lock. Once inside Malcolm opened a cupboard and acted as if he was counting the contents.

'There has been more than one difference over the last few months,' he said from the side of his mouth.

'How much?' I was beginning to worry now.

'About ten thousand in total.'

'Ten thousand?' I shouted.

'Ssshh.' Malcolm faced me.

'But how; why hasn't this come to our attention?'

'Don't know.'

'Over how long, would you say?' I had taken over as Branch Manager two months before.

'About nine months.'

'Steve Munro didn't do anything about it?' Munro was my predecessor. It was obvious from the work that I had had to do when I started the job that he had been on a long wind-down to retirement. This, however, wasn't just neglect; this was criminal.

'No. From the looks of it there is no pattern and they were all for small, different amounts.'

'There must have been a number of them to total a further nine thousand pounds.'

He shrugged in response.

I rubbed at my eyes. There was going to be one almighty stink. The inspectors would have to be called. There would be an investigation. Not a nice atmosphere to be working in; everyone looking at their neighbour wondering if they were a thief.

'Okay,' I said. 'Let's get this into perspective. There has been a series of shortages in the cash, amounting to around ten thousand pounds.' Saying it out-loud made it seem worse. 'Nobody died.' I finished weakly.

'I will.' Malcolm said, leaning against the cupboard with his head thrown back. I was hypnotised by his Adam's apple sliding up and down as he continued to speak. 'Once Campbell hears about this. I'm dead.'

'Roy isn't so bad once you get to know him.'

'He's an arsehole and you know it.' His tone accused me of being a sell-out. I would have agreed with him before I was promoted.

'Mmm.' I tried to maintain a diplomatic, managerial silence.

'So I thought I'd speak to you, Andy. Let you know before Campbell tries to sack me.'

I looked at his handsome features, contorted with worry. There was still that niggle worming its way through my brain. He was simply taking it too personally.

'Malcolm, what aren't you telling me?'

'I've looked back at the people working on the cash each time there was a difference.' He paused and picked at a nail. 'Sheila Hunter was present during all but one of them. The last big one. She's been off on the sick.' He stopped speaking, but continued to pick at the nail.

'And?' I asked.

A deep breath, 'I'll be the other chief suspect. I'm the one present during most of the cash shortages. I missed two.'

'You're no thief, Malcolm.' I chewed at the inside of my mouth. 'Mind you, it doesn't look good.'

'Thanks, mate.'

'Malcolm, I'm your mate and if there is anything you want to tell me then I will listen. But as far as this goes, I've a job to do and if it comes down to it our friendship may have to suffer. So don't put me in an awkward position and don't expect any favours.'

Malcolm narrowed his eyes, opened his mouth as if to speak and then closed it without saying anything.

'That may have been a shitty thing to say, Malcolm…'

'It was,' he interrupted quietly.

'… but it had to be said. In here I'm your boss. I knew a situation would happen where it might prove … awkward. Best to get it over with in the early days.'

Back at my desk, I tried to concentrate on the report that I would have to email to Head Office. Shock stilled my pen. Ten thousand pounds. Who could it be? Malcolm I'd known since I started work. We'd worked apart for a few years when I was on the accelerated management scheme, but we'd kept in touch and he was the last person that I would have suspected of theft. What about Sheila? I turned to one of the other people in the room: Carol Bunting, one of my management team. She was thick-set, had the fashion awareness of an aging vicar and a take-no-prisoners attitude. I loved working with her.

'Carol, what's up with Sheila Hunter?'

'Accident, Andy.' Her expression soured as she paused in the decimation of her carrot stick. 'Broken ribs, broken nose, face black and blue.' I'd noticed that Carol often spoke in bullet points.

'How'd it happen?

'Walked into a door.'

'Bloody hell,' I said, understanding immediately what she was getting at. 'That's awful. I had no idea.'

Carol raised the dark-brown fur of her eyebrows in agreement.

'Has her husband been taken in for questioning?'

'Don't know. But I hope the bastard rots in hell.' Almost a full sentence before Carol started on carrot stick number two. Her version of a diet distraction.

Although we'd grown up in the same town, I barely knew Ken. I supposed I had him to thank for bringing Anna to the club the night I met her. But I'd always avoided him. The last time I encountered him was at the wedding reception of one of the younger members of the team.

I'd said hello to him at the bar, where all the males had congregated while the women danced The Slosh. His long, lean frame was bent over the bar, as if his elbows were glued there. He barely gave me a glance. Grunted something in return. I was half-cut.

'Your patter's amazing, pal,' I remember saying. 'Who are you here with?'

'Sheila,' he said and looked over towards the dancefloor. There was something calculating about the way he searched the women there.

I studied him some more, wondering if he had changed from the teen who threw stones at the swans on the river. Small, dark eyes under the shelf of jutting eyebrows. He wore the look of a man at war with himself, while everyone within touching distance was collateral damage.

I remember a brief shiver came over me before I excused myself and joined a more collegiate companion.

'What kind of worker is Sheila?' I asked now, knowing what the answer would be, but hoping for a different one.

'No nonsense. Gets the job done. Good with customers. I like her. Takes a lot of time off work though.'

I drummed my pen on the desk. Were Malcolm and Sheila the only two possible suspects? Was Steve Munro, the previous manager, involved? It seemed strange that he had done nothing about the earlier differences. Maybe they had been too small to notice; after all, there was no definite pattern. Could Malcolm steal?

Would he? I dropped my pen and leaned my head on my hands and one further question occurred to me. Was I going to be able to handle this job?

If Lloyd Webber was ever to make a musical about weasels, he could do worse than look for inspiration from our Operations Manager. Roy Campbell was a small, wiry man with pointed features. He was hard of hearing and had an unfortunate habit of jerking his head about as if trying to catch words with his good ear. Of course, this lent to the overall weasel impression. Just as I was faxing him a copy of my report, which I had already transmitted to Head Office, his head appeared at the door. He devoured the contents in seconds.

'Kay. I knew he was no good;' his nose twitched with satisfaction; 'and a shirt-lifter if ever I saw one.'

'Roy…' I assumed my diplomatic role; badly, but I wanted to help my friend, regardless of what I said to him. 'I've known Malcolm all my career and not only is he honest but he's been with more women than…'

'Proves nothing,' he interrupted, which was a good job as I was struggling to come up with a comparison. 'If he's not gay then I'm six foot six.'

'Instead of four feet four.' I turned my head to the side and pretended to look through my drawer for something. I caught a grin from Carol.

'What was that, Andrew?'

'What was what, Roy?'

'Oh, never mind.' He smoothed his lapels, 'So have you suspended Kay yet?'

'Pleasing as that thought may be to you, Roy, we have to go through the correct channels. I've contacted Head Office and I'm sure that the hit squad will be here shortly.'

'Hrrmmm,' he issued with a bored expression. 'You've been on holiday. Have you checked the cash yourself?' Roy was being his usual warm and fuzzy self, not even a mention of my honeymoon.

'Yes, I've been on holiday. No I haven't checked the cash.'

'Well, why not? Let's go and do it now.' He led the way to the safe and barked for Malcolm and I to open the safe door.

'Right, stay there and watch, Kay, while Andrew and I show you how to check your cash.'

Malcolm crossed his arms and leant against the side of the door. His eyes betrayed nothing of his worry, but his lips were closed tight.

This'll be fun, I groaned inwardly. First day back and a major cash check; I was well out of practice. To my disappointment Roy was not. He hefted a bundle of tens on to one hand and flicked through them with the first three fingers of the other hand as if he had done nothing else for the last twenty years.

'No counting machines for me,' he sneered. 'Far better to do it the old fashioned way.' For the next three hours he counted every note in the safe while I took the details on a form. Finally we agreed with Malcolm's figures. Exactly. Roy's lips curved into a smile.

'Right. What about the transactions for that day?' he asked Malcolm.

'Checked.'

'By yourself?'

'No, one of the machinists did that.'

'Why didn't you do it yourself?'

'Well, I would assume that…'

'Speak up, Kay.' If I didn't know better I would have thought that Roy was trying to wind him up.

'I would assume…'

'Spell assume, Kay.'

'What?' Malcolm looked puzzled.

'Spell assume,' he answered, a spider laying out the silk of his trap. 'A.S.S…'

'Stop there.' Roy Campbell was wearing an expression that told us he thought this was the wittiest use of language ever. Trouble was, the delivery had been completely humourless and meant to wound, and both Malcolm and I knew it. The ensuing smile was a weak attempt to show that, really, he was joking.

'I like your tie, Roy,' said Malcolm, taking us both completely by surprise.

'Wha…?'

'Nice colour, navy blue is it?'

'Eh, think so.'

'What are those letters?' Malcolm moved closer peering at the tie. Roy picked up the bottom of the tie and read the two letters that were peppered all over the tie in a lighter colour of blue.

'F.W.' said Roy as he squinted.

'Fucking Wanker.' Malcolm barely moved his lips; not easy, given the words he was saying. He spoke in a tone that only I could hear.

I thrust the most horrible thought I could into my mind to keep me from losing the straight face I had quickly manufactured. Pat and Anna going over a cliff in a car. That should do it.

'There's no F in wanker.' Malcolm spoke slightly louder now.

'What was that?' asked Roy, suspicion narrowing his eyes.

'Just thinking aloud, something to do with bankers,' Malcolm answered easily.

'Right. Anyway, enough about my tie. Let's get on with this, shall we?' Roy appeared less sure of himself now. He had shrunk in stature, not quite as sure of his position and puzzled as to how he had lost control.

The paperwork took another two hours to check. The three of us were sitting with ties to the side and top shirt buttons undone, sleeves rolled up and, if my appearance mirrored the other two, thoroughly pissed-off expressions on our faces.

'Kay, you've done all you can do at the moment. Go and speak to Fiona Meldrum, see if she needs any help,' ordered Roy. Fiona was in charge of Personal Accounts.

'But…' began Malcolm.

I could see the sense of what Roy was saying and I thought that I should explain why this might be the more sensible action.

'The auditors will be here soon, Malcolm,' I explained. 'As the Head Teller they'll want to talk to you, go through more figures. So it's better that you go and help Fiona with some filing, or something not too long term, rather than going back to your normal duties.'

The truth was that Roy and his auditors would not be happy with one of the more likely suspects still being in a position where more money could be obtained. They tended to work on a basis of guilty until proven innocent, or at least, removed the suspect from further temptation.

Happily, that was sufficient explanation for Malcolm and he went off to find Fiona.

'You're learning the art of diplomacy,' said Roy. 'I couldn't have put it better myself.'

Or you wouldn't, I thought.

'Still,' he continued. 'I know you two are mates, but I don't trust that guy.'

11

The office was a quiet place to work for the week of the investigation. Even the customers, who were told nothing, were uncannily subdued as they did their business. The staff went about their duties with faces as long as a salary print-out for South Ayrshire Council. This was proving to be a major challenge for my budding managerial skills. To make matters worse, the atmosphere at home was less than appealing.

Every other night, since we'd returned from honeymoon, we either had a visit or a phone call from Mum or Jim. Not being used to a close family, I think Anna saw this as a threat. At the end of each visit or phone call, she would give me a look, sigh loudly or, once she'd made sure of my attention, march out of the room. I made several attempts to air the subject but each one was met with a blank stare or a complete denial.

One night, I gathered her into my arms. I was a little torn. We'd always been a close family, but I didn't want that closeness to feel like a challenge to my new wife.

'Does it all feel like a bit much?' I asked, looking down into her eyes.

'No, Andy. It's fine,' she answered with a weak smile. 'It's just…'

'They're a bit full-on?'

She laughed, looking pleased that I understood.

'They were like this before we got married and it didn't bother you then.'

'It didn't. No.'

Or maybe it did and you hid it better, I thought, and instantly felt a pang of guilt.

She stretched up on her toes and kissed me. Managed to reach my chin. 'It's fine. Really. To be honest it reminds me I never had that, any of that, with my own family. Jealous, I guess.'

At work, however, there was no room for doubt. Someone was responsible for stealing a large amount of money and that someone had to be caught. To his credit, Malcolm let the auditors know about his theory of the differences going back a few months. They would have found this out in the course of their investigation anyway.

Computer entries were checked in triplicate. Credit and debit slips going back a year were cross-checked and every corner of the business cash was scoured for the missing money. Meanwhile my staff attempted to continue with their work, but I couldn't fail to notice their change in attitude to Malcolm. Rooms went silent when he entered, and from being one of the more popular members of staff, he became somewhat of an outcast. Bravely, whenever he noticed this he would sniff at each armpit theatrically and do whatever he had come in the room to do. Quite how it became widely known about the cash shortages and Malcolm's possible recrimination, I wasn't sure, but I had my suspicions.

'Roy Campbell is an utter bastard.' Malcolm rounded on me in the men's toilet. 'He's been giving me hell.'

'What's he been doing?' I was concerned. If he was overstepping his remit, I would have to do something about it.

'Oh nothing, really.' Malcolm rubbed at his forehead. 'But seeing as you are asking…' He looked pointedly at me, his eyes saying 'at last'. '… The prick made sure that I was watching him while he walked away from a computer that had my bank accounts up on the screen.'

I raised my eyebrows in response. 'What is one of the first things you would do if you were him?'

'Check the suspect's bank accounts for any unusual pay-ins,' he admitted reluctantly. 'But, it's the way he's doing it. Rubbing my nose in it. And I swear, if I hear one more snide comment from my supposed friends and colleagues I'm going to punch somebody.' His whole body was rigid with tension.

'Malcolm, don't you think you should take some time off?'

'No way.'

'Go see your doctor, get a line, you're in a state.'

'And really look guilty? No. No way.'

I took a deep breath, ashamed of what I was about to ask him.

'Malcolm.' I looked him in the eye. 'I need to ask you this, for myself. Please don't be offended, but did you take the money?'

Without a pause, he returned my look. 'No, I did not take the money.' Each word was spoken slowly and clearly.

I gripped his shoulder with relief. 'Fine, I just needed to hear you say it. Go on, Malcolm, take some time off.'

'No, Andy. I'll not give that wee prick the satisfaction.'

As I walked into the house that night, one hour late, Anna took one look at my face and silently went off to pour me a whisky. Pat's remedy was much more holistic; he jumped into my arms. A smile softened my expression. I kissed his forehead.

'How's my best boy?'

'Dad, Dad, Dad, I watched Barney today. Daniel stole my juice.' Daniel was his friend at the nursery. It was cutely titled 'Us'n Kids'.

'Oh, and what did you do?'

'I drank his and it was nicer than mine.'

'Pat, let your Dad have a seat and relax a minute.' Anna put a glass in my hand.

'It's okay, Anna. This is better than whisky any day.'

'Oh fine. Sorry I couldn't help you as much as your son.' Her tone was jocular, but I could tell there was a slight edge to the comment.

I was about to try and reassure her when Pat tugged at my tie, distracting me. 'Take this off, Dad. Can I have a drink of your juice?'

'No you cannot. Besides it tastes horrible.'

'Why do you drink it then?' His face was about a foot from mine and cocked to the side.

'That's because adults do some very strange things, son.' I kissed his nose.

The phone began to ring. Pat raced to answer it.

He listened, then said, 'Hello, Uncle Big Nose.'

Jim said something.

'Bye, Uncle Big Nose,' Pat said before handing me the receiver.

'How's it hangin', bro?' asked Jim.

'Och, not bad.' I rubbed at my eyes.

'You sound like you need a drink.'

'Funny you should say that.' I took a loud sip. 'I could meet you in Billy Bridges at nine, once I've got Pat bathed and in bed.'

'Why don't you meet him earlier? How about straight after your tea?' said Anna, loud enough for me to hear over the voice of Jim in my ear. 'I'll see to Pat.'

'Ok, thanks, Anna,' I said; then wondered, was there an edge to her tone? Or perhaps tiredness was making my imagination work in the wrong direction.

I arranged to meet Jim at seven-thirty and hung up.

Over dinner, conversation consisted mostly of a monologue from Pat, detailing his day at the nursery. Then even he grew quiet, perhaps sensing an awkwardness between Anna and myself.

Just as I was slipping my arm into a sleeve of my jacket in the hallway, Anna approached me.

'Do you have to go, honey?' She put her hand on my waist. A light touch of promise.

'I won't be long, sweetheart.' I moved closer to her and kissed her cheek. Lingered at the press of our skin, but then with reluctance moved away.

'Okay,' she said, her expression downcast. 'Have fun.'

She turned and made her way back into the living room. Feeling guilty, I followed her.

'When was the last time I went out for a drink with Jim?' I asked. 'The stag night, and that was weeks ago.'

She sat on the sofa, pulled her feet under her and crossed her arms.

'It's fine, Andy. Honest. Go.'

'Sure?' I sat beside her. Looked over at the phone. 'I could phone Jim back and cancel?'

'Just ignore me, honey.' She gave me a small, tight smile. 'It's just been a long day and I was looking forward to curling up on the couch with you tonight.' She stretched a hand out and tapped my right cheek. 'Go have a drink with your brother. I'll see you when you get home.'

Billy's, as you would expect on a Tuesday night, was fairly quiet. Only about half a dozen people were dotted about the place, all of them regulars. Jim was leaning against the bar, facing the door as I walked in. He addressed the barmaid.

'A pint of lager for the ugly brother please.'

'And I'll have the same,' I said with a grin, 'and a whisky chaser,' I added. Jim raised his eyebrows at the extra drink but said nothing.

Armed with our drinks we sat down at a table near the back of the pub. Although we were happy to spend our money in the town's trendier pubs we always felt more at home here, with its unpretentious chipped formica table tops. The quarter of a gill alcohol measures were also a part of Billy's charm.

'Busy?' asked Jim.

'Busy.' I answered.

'What's with the whisky?' he asked.

'Busy.'

'Do you think that we'll get past the monosyllabic responses by the time you're on to your second drink?'

'Yes.' I couldn't keep up the pretence any longer and grinned.

'Smart arse.'

'So tell me,' I asked. 'You still seeing that girl you brought to my wedding?'

'No,' he smiled. It was his turn.

'Are you seeing anyone else?'

'Yes.'

'Who?'

'Morag.'

'Piss off; nobody's called Morag nowadays. They outlawed that name along with decimalisation.'

'Morag,' he repeated. 'She's a bit of a shag.'

'So what was wrong with…?' I couldn't remember the girl's name from the wedding.

'Val.'

'Oh right, Val. I should remember that name. People are going to be looking at my wedding photos for years to come and asking who was that girl? You'll have moved on to girlfriend number five hundred and no one will know.'

'Val,' he repeated.

'Right, enough,' I said. 'Mum's worried you'll never settle down.'

He snorted. 'My position as favourite son will always be safe.'

'Favourite son, my arse. You and your women are an embarrassment to her. She thinks you're a male slut. I'm the more dependable, lovable type of man. I'll get everything and you'll get nothing when Mum dies.'

'So what would you do with a collection of lace doilies then? Wipe your arse?' We both laughed and as the laughter attracted the attention of the clientele, whose numbers were growing, I allowed its music to soak into my knotted muscles and drain some of the tension away.

Jim was in the middle of a detailed, loud and probably fabricated version of why he and Val hadn't lasted when I felt a tap on my shoulder.

I turned around. Saw a familiar face.

'Malcolm.' I injected my greeting with real warmth. 'Can I get you a drink?'

'No, you're alright. I was just in with some friends.' He waved vaguely at the far end of the bar. 'When I saw you, thought I'd come over and say hello.'

'How's it going then?' asked Jim.

Malcolm looked at me before answering, probably wondering if I had informed Jim of recent events. 'Oh, eh, fine. Not bad.'

'Why don't you give your mates a shout and tell them to join us.'

'No, it's fine. They'd probably bore you two. Don't know anything about rugby.' Malcolm smiled, more like his old self, although he did seem reluctant that we should meet anyone that he was with. However, we persuaded him to join us for the duration of a drink. Once seated with a glass in his hand he soon seemed to relax. Always a witty guy he was soon giving better than he received as Jim tried to tease him. It was good to see him with a smile on his face again. Even when Jim, quite innocently, brought the subject round to work, Malcolm wasn't fazed.

'So what's it like having this prick as a boss?' Jim asked, nodding his head in my direction.

'I've had worse,' answered Malcolm with a tight smile.

We were sitting in the narrow part of the pub, just at the foot of a set of stairs that led to the toilets, so Malcolm had to move a few times to let people past. When one slim, fashionably dressed young guy tried to slip past, Malcolm lost the thread of his conversation. He even seemed quite distracted. Looking at neither of us, he excused himself.

'Listen guys, I need to go. See you later.'

As he walked away Jim looked at me quizzically.

'What was that all about?'

'Beats me.'

'Not having it,' Jim said. 'You and Malcolm were a wee bit awkward with each other there. You guys had a lover's tiff?'

'Work stuff,' I said. 'Confidential. I can't say any more than that.'

Jim made a face but didn't delve any deeper. He knew how seriously I took work issues.

After an abnormally long silence between us Jim cocked his head to the right, his eyes narrowing. 'You see that guy?' I turned to follow his gaze. 'The lanky drink of pish in the black jacket,' Jim added. 'Don't we know him?'

A tall, dark-haired man in a black jacket twisted away from us just as Jim asked the question.

'Don't you recognise him?' I replied. 'That's Ken Hunter.'

'That tosser? Barely recognised him. He's gone all gaunt and heroin skinny.'

I looked again. He was even thinner than the last time I had seen him. As I looked, he turned back, taking a toke on his cigarette. It was a thin paper stick, looked self-rolled and I wondered if it only contained tobacco. He blew out and squinted at me through his smoke. I held his gaze. Challenged him with a calm look. It said, I know what you are and, given the flimsiest of excuses, I'd be over there and showing you what should happen to wife-beaters. What kept me in my seat was how it might reflect back on Sheila, and the bank. Wouldn't do for the Branch Manager to be done for public brawling. But I imagined driving a fist into the bridge of his nose and took a small sense of satisfaction from that.

'He keeps looking over here,' said Jim 'Didn't you feel his eyes boring into your back? Don't know whether he wants to fuck you or fight you.'

I turned away from Hunter, letting him know that he was being dismissed. Then explained to Jim in a low voice that it was him that brought Anna to the rugby club the night I met her. And I also filled him in on the branch gossip. How we suspected he was mistreating his wife.

'Dickhead.' Jim took a sip of his drink. 'I always thought he had it in for you.'

'What do you mean?'

'Just. School and stuff. When we were out and about as kids. I always thought if he had a knife he'd be burying it in your back.'

'That's a bit dramatic,' I smiled.

'You didn't see the way he used to look at you.' Jim shivered. 'Never liked the prick. Want me to sort him out?' Jim pushed his pint glass to the side as if getting ready to stand.

'Ignore him,' I answered. 'I can deal with Ken Hunter.'

*

We were the last to leave the pub. The barman asked us to finish our drinks with a curt, 'Have you two no got a home tae go tae?' Once the door had been locked behind us Jim asked me if I wanted to carry on drinking back at his place. He lived in a flat overlooking Ayr Harbour a mere two hundred yards away from where we stood. Swayed, would have been more accurate.

'Naw, I'm bushed. Got work tomorrow.'

'Will Anna be waiting for you?'

I nodded.

'With a kiss or a kick?' he chuckled, 'And you keep asking me when I'm going to settle down. Not me, matee. Answer to no one. Come and go as I please. Live the life of Reilly me. In fact I think I'll change my name. Do you think Reilly Boyd would be better or Jim Reilly?'

'Here's twenty pence,' I answered. 'Phone someone that gives a shit, and get me a taxi while you're at it.'

'Phone a…' Jim checked his pockets and I realised he was looking for his mobile phone. He'd taken to that whole thing better than me. I couldn't see what the fuss was all about. Who wants to be contactable twenty-four hours a day? He looked into the distance as if accessing a memory. 'My phone's still on the charger at home. You can come over to mine and phone a taxi if you want.'

'Naw, I know that if I go back to yours we'll end up drinking to yon time. I want my bed, but a wee walk to sober up first might be in order.'

'Awright, suit yourself. Away you go to that gorgeous wife of yours. See if she's waiting up for some of that Big Boydy loving.'

With a wave of his right hand he turned and walked away from me and for the first time I sensed a note of loneliness in my brother. Perhaps for all his bluster, life was less than ideal for Jim Boyd.

12

I walked the long way home in a vain attempt to weaken the effect the alcohol was having on my body. My thought processes were fine but the signals weren't quite getting through to my lower limbs. A patch of grass looked particularly inviting. Perhaps I could just lie down there for a minute.

Dangerous thinking, big guy, I thought. Better keep moving, wouldn't want to wake up like a piece of frozen vomit. I began to run, but my head was angled several paces in front of my legs and they had to move faster to keep up.

Legs feeling a tad heavier than normal, I slowed down to a walk and, admitting defeat, looked around for a taxi. The roads were empty. If this had been a hot country, tumbleweed would be rolling down the middle of the road. Had some sort of deadly virus attacked the people of Ayr while I was in the pub? Common sense made me concede that most normal people were in bed at this time.

When I was a boy and I wanted to get home quicker, I devised a system of alternately walking and running the distance from one lamppost to the next. Now would be a fine time to re-adopt this. But I was too tired.

Where were all the taxis?

Among these thoughts the realisation that I was close to home pushed through. My next obstacle would be Anna. She had probably assumed I would have been home hours ago. Would she be up waiting for me or would she be fast asleep?

Eventually, I reached the door and with relief tried to locate my keys. As I swayed on my front step I heard a cough carry in the night air. I turned to the right. At the far end of the road a streetlamp threw shadows on to the pavement. Was there someone there?

I squinted. There was a man there. Tall and lean.

My fingers had located my bunch of keys and I glanced down at my hand to select the right key for the door. When I looked back along the street it was empty. Jesus, I must have been drunker than I thought; imagining strange men in the dark. I fumbled with the key, twisted it in the lock, tripped over the doormat and fell into the hall, my head pushing open the door. I turned on to my back, laughing at my own clumsiness while trying to focus on the door lintel above me. A face swam into focus.

'Anna, honey. There you are. Oh, there you are, no there,' I pointed three inches to the left and laughed.

'You big bastard, where the hell have you been? I've been worried sick.'

'At the pub, just havin' a few.'

'A few?' Anna's face got closer. 'A few?'

'Aye, a few. What part of those two syllables don't you understand? A feeeew.' I was getting quite comfy down on the carpet.

'Are you taking the piss?' Anna's voice was higher in pitch, but coming out in a strangled whisper. Her teeth were bared and a stream of curses splattered down onto me.

'Bastard…' she repeated over and over, and with each curse she bounced the door against my head. I tried to move out of the way and crawled a little further into the hall, which meant that my back was getting a beating. Then suddenly it stopped. Anna leant over me and pulled my head towards her by the hair.

'If you ever do this again, you're dead!' she hissed into my face, hers contorted with rage. Then she let go of my hair and my head dropped on to the floor.

'You're on the couch.'

Her feet drummed away up the stairs.

I don't know how long I lay there. My back wasn't hurting too badly, but I could feel a few bumps on the back of my head and the patch of hair that she had pulled at was still sore. What anger.

I couldn't believe the force of her fury. Where did that come from? I crawled into the living room and up on to the couch. I propped a couple of cushions on the arm rest, and tried to make myself comfortable. There was no question of going up to bed. Anna was far too angry.

Rightly so, I thought. I was taking the piss coming in so late. We were not long married for goodness' sake. I should know better than to be so inconsiderate. She did have a right to be annoyed. She must have been worried sick about me. Best to leave her to calm down. I prayed that Pat had slept through all the banging, and hadn't witnessed what an arse I was.

These thoughts accompanied the throb in my head well into the morning when sleep at last wrapped me in its bandage.

I was wakened by small fingers pulling at my eyelids, letting the light stream in. The thump in my head started up again. My skull felt as if it had tightened overnight. My fingers tested the tender part at the back. They withdrew quickly. Still painful.

'Is he sick?' I heard Pat ask.

'No, Daddy was a naughty boy last night, so he slept here,' Anna replied.

Pat's mouth formed an eloquently small circle, showing equal measures of shock and pleasure that his Dad could behave badly.

'Do we have a sore head this morning then?' Anna peered down at me with an affectionate smile. A smile that surprised me. Where was the wild woman from last evening? Had I had a nightmare? The pain in my head testified, however, that the events of the previous night really did happen.

'You go up and have a shower and a shave, Andy. I'll see to Pat's breakfast.' Anna walked through to the kitchen as if it was just another day. Not the morning after she had beaten a door off my head.

I sat up, holding my head as I did so. A couple of paracetamols would have to be first on my agenda. I looked up and saw Pat staring at me. His eyes shone with unasked questions. I ventured a smile. At least my facial muscles didn't hurt.

'Were you really bad, Dad?' he asked.

'Really bad,' I answered.

'What did you do?' he looked tiny.

'I stayed out way past my bedtime.' He nodded wisely at my answer. It made perfect sense to him.

My day at work went past in a smog of questions, self-recrimination and a little fear. Was Anna really capable of such violence?

But it was my fault. I knew that. No more socialising unless Anna was with me, I decided. But why shouldn't I go out for a drink with my brother? A loud noise made everyone in the room look over at me. I realised that I had just heaved a huge sigh. Head in my hands, I swore. God, this was enough to give me another headache.

'Woman trouble already, Andrew?' Roy Campbell entered the room.

'Why would it be woman trouble?' I answered. 'There's more to life than women.'

'Yeah, right,' he answered. 'Can't live with 'em, can't live with 'em.' He laughed far too loudly at his own joke and patted Carol Bunting on the shoulder, 'Isn't that right, Carol?'

'Yes, Roy, whatever you say, Roy, get your hand off me, Roy,' she said flatly and looked up at him with a bored expression. When he turned around in mild shock she mouthed 'Twat' at his back.

'Christ, women are touchy these days,' said Roy, 'One silly cow chains herself to the railings and the next thing we know we're not allowed to touch women on the shoulder.' In one sentence our Operations Manager trivialised a century of women fighting for their rights.

I'd had enough.

'Roy, do yourself a favour, say what you've come to say and then piss off before you alienate three-quarters of my staff.'

'Bloody hell, Andrew. I couldn't offend anyone. I'm just having a wee laugh.' He turned around and caught Carol making another face at him. 'Isn't that right, Carol?'

'Yes, Roy,' she answered with a face devoid of expression. 'You're dead … funny.'

'Right. See.' Roy opened his arms, completely missing the irony. 'I'm funny, it's official.' Then, his change of tone signifying he meant business now. 'Andrew we need to talk … in private.' He filled the last two words with the importance of a papal decree and spoke them loud enough to make sure that everyone in the vicinity heard him.

In the interview room he sat down in the biggest seat. Roy always made sure he had the biggest seat. His face read of disappointment.

'Kay is in the clear.' He clasped his hands on the desk in front of him. 'We don't have enough evidence to lay the blame fully at his door. Fly bastard. He was too clever this time.'

'So what do we do?' I sat down.

'Dunno. Make sure that shirt-lifter doesn't get near the cash again.'

'Roy, for goodness sake. Give the guy a break. One, you said yourself that there's not enough evidence; two, his sexuality is none of your business and three … we do have another suspect.'

'As far as I'm concerned Sheila Hunter is not a suspect.'

'She was present at as many of the differences as Malcolm. How's it going to look at Head Office if you haven't investigated her?'

'Right enough,' he said. The thought of not looking good at Head Office was always enough to have him reconsider his options. He looked into the distance over my left shoulder and thought aloud. 'Sheila is still off sick, but looking to come back to work. I hear her husband's been laying into her…' I recoiled at his tone; it was as if he was dismissing his violence to her as *just one of those things*. 'She's due a visit from our Occupational Therapist … why don't you go along with her?'

'Me?'

'Why not? You're her immediate superior.'

'But you're responsible for staffing.'

'Yes, but you're the more sensitive type. She'll only be uncomfortable with me.' A rare piece of sensitivity from Roy – or was he just
unable to handle people when they were not well?

A week later I was on Sheila's doorstep with Tracy Fenton, a human
resources specialist from Head Office. Both of us were trying to
assume an air of nonchalance at the fierce barking that was coming
from the other side of the door. We heard a woman's voice cajole the
dog into silence and the door was opened.

'Andy, in you come. You must be Tracy … you'd better come in.'

The yellow Labrador that sounded so frightening from the other
side of the door tried to impose death by licking once we were in the
house. Its whole body wagged and it made a few desperate lunges
with its front paws.

'Toby,' Sheila censured, 'Calm down. You'll get hair all over the
nice man's suit.'

'It's fine,' I reassured her, wondering at the childish tone she used
with the dog.

A coffee in my hand only moments later, I sat on a leather sofa in
a very comfortable, large room with a pink tongue depositing saliva
on my shoes. Looking around myself in admiration I began to doubt
that Sheila was our thief. Who, living in such a house, in one of the
most sought-after parts of the town, would need to steal? Then I
reminded myself that I shouldn't make any assumptions.

For the first time I had a good look at Sheila. Always thin, she
now looked on the edge of emaciation. She had made an effort with
her hair and her make-up, but the colour on her face only made
her look more gaunt, and the style of her hair couldn't disguise its
listless brown or its lifeless hang. Her eyes shifted around the room,
never once meeting my gaze. Her fingers supplied an endless line of
cigarettes to her thin lips, which were being bitten when they weren't
sucking on a tab.

'Thanks for seeing us, Sheila,' said Tracy. 'Before we start, I would
just like to reiterate that we are not here to coax you back to work or

to check that you really have been ill. We're here to help you get back to work as and when you are ready and not before.'

'Yes, you did say that on the phone thanks, and thanks for coming out to see me. I appreciate it. You're both busy people,' said Sheila. Her voice was so quiet, it was as if she was sitting in a church rather than her own home.

'Don't thank us.' I noticed how gruff and male my voice sounded in the hushed femininity of her house. 'It's always nice to get out of the bank.' Perhaps that wasn't the best thing to say. 'I mean that it's nice to get some fresh air,' I finished lamely.

'I know what you mean.' Sheila smiled at my awkwardness. Her smile transformed her face and even seemed to brighten her hair. Inwardly I remarked that she was actually very attractive. I had never noticed it before because she was one of those people content to stay in the background, diminishing their size and importance. Her particular tactic was to hide behind long hair while wearing clothes that were too large.

I was suddenly sure that the woman I knew from the bank was not the real Sheila. There was no way she had walked into any door. This was a shrunken woman crushed by the grip of a bully.

'So, tell me, Sheila, do you feel ready to come back to work in any capacity?' Tracy asked.

'I think so.' Sheila then considered her answer. 'Yes, I'm sure.'

'Your doctor's line is up in about ten days' time,' I added. He'd been circumspect and given the reason for her absence as 'stress and anxiety'. 'I'm sure we can arrange for you to come back, say, two mornings a week and gradually increase that over the next few months until you're back to full time.'

'Before we talk about your rehabilitation, Sheila, can I just check with you that you have not been put under any pressure to come back to the bank?' asked Tracy.

'No, absolutely not. In fact everyone has been very kind.' A tear gathered in the corner of her eye. 'I don't know how I would have coped without everyone's support.' Another tear reached her cheek before it was staunched by a tissue. 'You know, for ten years Ken ruled my life. Right from the day and hour we married ... when I could go to the toilet, what sort of jam I could eat, which of my friends I could speak too. And if I didn't do as I was told, by God the punishment was severe. For ten years I put up with it.'

This was a new experience for me; listening without any input being expected in return. It was clear from Sheila's stare into space that what she needed was to hear the words out loud and not to have any solutions or judgements offered.

'Bloody hell,' I said. 'That's awful. How can this happen without anyone picking up on it?'

I looked at Tracy to gauge her reaction. She was holding herself tight as if fighting to maintain a professional demeanour. It was clear from her expression that this was a story she'd heard before.

'Ten years.' Sheila shook her head in bewilderment. 'What kind of a fool was I? But you know what the craziest thing is? I miss the bastard.'

She stared off into recent memory. Her lower lip trembled.

'I was sure he was going to kill me that last time.' She was back in the room and remembered that she was safe, but couldn't stop wrapping her arms around herself. She looked from me to Tracey and back again. 'I knew he was capable of a lot, but that was the first time I saw death in his eyes.'

She breathed deeply. Exhaled slowly, as if finally expelling a series of anxious thoughts. 'Sounds dramatic, eh? Death in his eyes. Hark at me.' She offered a weak smile as if that might reduce the drama of her statement. 'But there's no other way to put it. I was a bug and he would relish stamping on me until every bone in my body was broken.

'I managed to get to the neighbours. While he was having a cigarette break from the hard work of trying to murder me. Called the police. But by the time they arrived he was off.' Her tissue was almost translucent with her tears. 'I'm ... I'm like a toddler. I mean Ken did everything. Everything. I'm amazed he ever let me go to work. That's why I need to get back. I need to get out of this house. I've lost ten years of my life.' She straightened her back and looked me in the eyes for the first time. 'I've lost ten years. That evil swine has stolen enough from me. It's time that I took charge of my life. Going back to work will be the first step in that process.'

'That's excellent,' said Tracy as she leant forward and patted Sheila on the hand. She retracted her hand quickly, as if she was worried her actions had breached her self-imposed conditions for professionalism. It was just in that moment she was unable to contain her empathy. They were woman to woman and she couldn't help but show her support. 'With regards to your absence from work, as far as we are concerned, the reason, as we said, is stress and anxiety. If anyone is to find out the real reason, that will come from you, not us, okay?' Tracy looked at me to back up her statement.

'Absolutely,' I said.

'Thanks, guys,' Sheila said. 'I won't be making any big announcement in the office, but I think it's long past time people talked about this. If people ask, I won't shy away from telling them the truth.' She gave a smile; one tinged with hope and not a little fear. 'Perhaps it will encourage other women to speak up.'

Silence followed her words. The courage and determination that suddenly flared in that small frame filled me with admiration.

13

With Timon and Pumba urging Simba to take life easy and Pat sitting on my lap, still enthralled with Disney's magic at about the thousandth re-showing, I pondered my work problems. Taking a long draught from my bottle of beer, I considered the options. Having met with Sheila, there was no way that I could imagine her stealing the money. But the alternative was unthinkable. Malcolm had been a friend of mine for years. He couldn't be the thief. I would bet a year's wages on it. Another mouthful eased down the back of my throat. Anyway, it wasn't my problem. Roy's audit team had come up with nothing that would secure a conviction. We would have to hope that all of the Head Office action would put the thief off for life. They would certainly not be using their previous method of stealing funds.

A shrill ring from the phone pierced my thoughts. Pat, as usual, reached it first.

'Stop that, Uncle Jim,' Pat giggled. 'You're cheeky.'

'What filth are you passing on to my son?' I lifted the phone from Pat's hand.

'Oh nothing, bro. Just saying that if he ever got tired of his boring old dad that I was the nicer brother and he should come live with me.'

'Oh right,' I smiled. 'What can I do for you, Jim? Before you rip my family apart.'

'I'm just phoning to tell you that I'm in love.'

'Yeah, right.'

'… with the most stunning woman I have ever met.'

'Jim, if I had a pound for every woman that you had ever been in love with I would be able to end world hunger.'

'I've told you a million times,' laughed Jim, '… don't exaggerate.'

'So who is this poor unfortunate?'

'The lucky lady is called Paula and I met her tonight, in Tesco after work.'

'Don't tell me you're so desperate that you're approaching women in the supermarket.'

'No, no … I met her for the first time last weekend – when I took Pat to Kidz Play.'

'So the wedding was over two months ago and you're on to someone else already? And you're using my son as a front for a solicitation service? I knew there had to be a reason for you offering to take Pat there.'

'Aye, there was. To let you and Anna have some time together. I just sort of got talking to Paula when Pat started to play with her wee boy, Daniel. I'll tell you, there are some gorgeous single mums around.'

'Bloody hell. You're unbelievable. You're really picking up women at a children's play area?'

'Man, she's gorgeous.' He ignored my reprimand. 'You should meet her. She's amazing. Long brown hair, slim, nice tits. Anyway … you're never going to believe how I bumped into her…'

'Go on tell me, I can't wait. Teach me your chat up lines O great one,' I laughed.

'You know how they have those bargain sections in Tesco? Well I spotted a trolley with some cut-price stuff, and I was looking through it when she walked over to me. It was only her bloody trolley.' He chuckled. 'Talk about a brasser. Mind you, a packet of tampons in among the onion bhajis should have given the game away. I apologised, we had a good laugh about it. I asked where her husband was. He left her last year, so I asked her out.'

'Just like that.'

'Just like that. If you snooze, you lose, my friend.'

'Well, when do I get to meet this vision, this paragon of womanhood … she of the nice tits.'

'Whenever you want.'

'Why don't you come over on Saturday for dinner? We can turn on the fabled Boyd charm and she'll completely fall in love with you and yours. How about 7.30?'

'You're on.'

As I put the phone down I felt a nip on the back of my neck. Rubbing at the pain, I turned round.

'What the hell was that for?'

'That was for not consulting me. And this,' Anna poked me in the solar plexus, pushing the air from my lungs, 'is for being a dick.'

Surprised at her anger I took a seat on the stairs. She moved closer, lifted my head up and pushed her face against mine.

'What the hell are you doing inviting people over here?' She spoke in a forced whisper.

'I just thought that it would be nice…'

'You don't think. That's your problem. You're useless.' She punched my forehead with the heel of her hand. There was a hint of a smile in her expression and for a moment I couldn't work out if she was messing with me or being serious.

'Hey,' I said, and stood up, smarting from the three different assaults. 'What the hell is your problem?' I bit down on my irritation. I was suddenly aware of the differences in our heights. I towered over her. If I had a mind to, I could really cause her some damage.

Anna was not cowed by my size. Instead, a smile teased the corner of her mouth. She pressed up against me, her hand sought my groin. Slowly she stroked. My body responded while my mind tried to reconcile the different versions of this woman who had just appeared before me.

'Honey, the next time you want to do the social bit,' her hand moved faster, 'let me know first.'

I bent over to kiss her. She gently cupped my testicles, raising an eyebrow and a smile, and parted her lips. Then her face hardened and her mouth formed a tight line. Her hand balled into a fist while holding my testicles. She squeezed tighter. Pain weakened my legs. She pulled down, forcing me on to my knees.

'If you don't,' her lips were pressed against my ear, 'I'll have you.'

Then, as if she had just been meditating with the Dalai Lama, she glided through to the living room, where Pat was still engrossed in *The Lion King*, and offered to make him a sandwich.

I sat on the stairs, balls and head aching, mind dull with worry. What was going on here? Who was this woman I married? She was so small. I was so big. Why hadn't I retaliated? I had a vision of what I could do to her with my superior size and strength, and all thoughts of retaliation vanished like a summer snowfall. My mind conjured an image of her lying broken and bloodied. That wasn't me. But what was? My mind was a fog of emotions, as competing thoughts slugged at each other in the gloom. I loved this woman, I knew I did. But was she the same woman who'd just shown herself? And why hadn't I stopped her? What would Pat think?

It had been ingrained into me as a boy: you don't hit girls. They are weaker than boys. Why was I the one in pain, then?

Women are always advised to leave their partner at the first sign of violence. Shouldn't I follow this advice? The thought of leaving Anna sat heavy in my gut, making my mouth feel dry with panic.

No, that wasn't happening. I loved her. I wanted her approval.

People, including members of my family, said we'd married too soon. I had an image of Mum on my wedding day as we waited for the taxi to take me to the church. Her expression heavy with concern.

I wasn't about to prove her right.

In the living room, Pat was face first in a jam sandwich. I slumped in my seat and pretended to be engrossed in the movie.

When the movie credits started rolling, I stole a look at my son and my wife. Pat was leaning into her as she curled up on the couch. He looked as happy as I'd ever seen him.

'Honey?' I spoke first, determined in this instance I'd be the one to broker peace. 'Do you want me to phone Jim and cancel? I'm sure I can think of some excuse.'

'Why would you do that?' She looked over at me, her hand playing with Pat's hair, an unreadable smile on her face. 'It'll be nice to have dinner with Jim and his new friend. Tell me about her.'

I regurgitated my conversation with Jim, describing Paula as he had to me while Anna cooed how lovely this was and how much she was looking forward to meeting her. Menus were discussed, as were outfits to be worn. I wondered who had been laying into me earlier on, and even questioned if it had actually happened.

As the night of the dinner drew close, Anna mentioned it regularly, saying how much she was looking forward to us socialising as a couple.

It was she who called my mother and asked her to have Pat for the night. Mum, of course, was delighted.

'She said she's really pleased to think of her two boys and their women getting on so well,' Anna said as she made up a shopping list for Saturday's meal.

'We don't do this often enough, Andy,' she said, sucking the end of her pencil. 'It's like you want to keep me all to yourself.'

Before I knew it, I was welcoming Jim and his new girlfriend in the door and the four of us were sitting around the table sipping wine.

'Jim tells me you have a lovely wee boy, Andy,' Paula said as she settled into her chair.

She was everything Jim described. Dark, slim and lovely.

'Yes,' said Anna. 'He's the cutest wee boy in the planet.' She looked across the table at me and grinned. 'He's the *real* reason I fell in love with Andy.'

I blew her a raspberry then made a face as if conceding defeat. 'Pat's my secret weapon. No self-respecting woman would look at me twice if I didn't have that kid at my side.'

'That's not fair,' said Anna reaching out to take my hand. 'Takes after his handsome and caring dad.'

'God, you two make me sick,' said Jim. 'You're married now. Is it not time to get all indifferent?'

'You've such a romantic notion of marriage,' Anna said to Jim. Then to Paula. 'You've got your work cut out with this one.'

'Ach, he acts like a curmudgeon,' said Paula. 'But he does have hidden shallows.'

Everyone laughed at Paula's comedic summing up of my brother. I gave her a look and realised there was a cool head on this one. Perhaps it might be her giving Jim the runaround shortly.

After the food had been served and eaten, we all leaned back in our seats, bellies aching.

'The meal was lovely,' said Paula. 'Thank you, guys.'

'You're welcome,' said Anna. 'It's not often we get to entertain. Andy has become quite shy in his old age. Anti-social even.' She reached over and patted my hand. 'I'd go out every night of the week, but Andy wants me all to himself, don't you honey?'

I nodded. 'Why would I want to share you with anyone, babes?' I lifted her hand up to my mouth and kissed it.

'I'd say, get a room. But you don't have that far to go.' Jim laughed.

'He just can't get enough of me.' Anna stretched over and rubbed my shoulder. 'Isn't that right, honey?'

'Absolutely,' I said. And meant it. Sure, we'd had a couple of moments recently, but as I looked into her eyes I realised that I loved her more than ever. I pushed my chair back, stood up, walked over to Anna and kissed her on the top of her head. Then I looked at Jim and Paula.

'Coffee or more wine?'

Paula said. 'Coffee.'

'Wine,' both Jim and Anna said. They laughed and high-fived.

'Oh, ok then,' said Paula with mock reluctance. 'Wine it is.'

'Comfy seats?' Anna asked and stood up.

We ushered our guests to the living room and poured the wine. Watching Jim I was reassured by his total involvement with Paula. Perhaps my brother was growing up at last? He would have wrapped himself around her if he could. He laughed at her every witticism and rarely lifted his hand from hers.

'Pat is at your mum's, Jim tells me,' said Paula. 'Must be nice to have such a willing babysitter.'

'Oh aye, Mum would have him every day if we'd let her, wouldn't she, Anna?' I said.

'Yes, but we've little need for a babysitter. We're hardly ever out.' said Anna.

'Well, we'll have to do this again,' said Jim. 'I've really enjoyed myself. Next time we'll do it at my place.'

'That would be nice,' said Anna.

The conversation then split into two. The women paired up and Jim and I spoke together.

'You playing this year?' Jim asked.

'Nah.' I shook my head. This was the first rugby season I would miss. I had retired from the team, partly because the work promotion meant I had less free time to train, partly because I didn't think my knees could take any more punishment, and partly because the need it used to fill no longer existed. After Patricia died, the Rugby Club had become my lifeline to the world. A change from the demands of a baby son and a demanding job. Now, though, I had Anna, and I felt that outlet was no longer necessary.

Of course I said none of this. Jim would have looked at me as if I had a pink dildo growing out of my forehead.

'How's the knees?' I asked Jim.

'Oh you know, fucked,' laughed Jim. 'But some strapping and I'm good to go.'

'That's cos you're a real man, bro.' I snorted. Jim had a tendency to ignore injuries. Better to take the chance on permanent injury than to admit weakness.

I heard Paula ask Anna about any plans she had for redecorating. Colours and fabrics then floated over our gammy knees and scrums. Now and again Paula would try to draw me into their conversation, no doubt wishing to assess if she had made a hit with big brother.

'What do you think? Gorgeous, eh?' Jim asked in a low voice.

'Good taste must run in the family, bro.'

Paula then tried to draw me back into her conversation.

'Have you guys made plans for any holidays, Andy?'

'No, not yet. We'll probably go to the Med. Anna's a serious sun worshipper aren't you, sweetheart?'

'What about you two, any holidays planned?' Anna asked mischievously, knowing that they had just got together.

'Nothing for me yet,' answered Jim.

'Nor me,' said Paula. 'Although I fancy a skiing holiday. Have you ever skied?' She was looking at me as she asked this.

'Yes, but not for a few years.'

'I've skied before too,' Anna joined in. 'But it was a long time ago – on a school trip. I'd love to try it again.' Had I heard a slight edge to her tone?

'Excellent,' I said. 'That's just what we'll do. Pat would love it.' I looked over at Anna and tried to gauge her mood. Everything had gone smoothly so far, hadn't it?

'Right,' Jim announced abruptly, rubbing his hands. 'Time for us to be off. Let these lovebirds get their beauty sleep.'

No doubt he was anxious to be alone with Paula. He exaggerated a yawn. 'Jeez, I'm tired. All that good food.'

'Aye, me too,' I said. But I found myself surprised by the need for them to stay longer. Anna's mood had definitely cooled in the last few minutes, and judging by the shape of her brow I was in for a hard time as soon as the door closed.

I shook off the feeling. I was tired. Stressed from work. It was no more than that.

Like the perfect hosts, Anna and I shook hands and kissed the pair goodbye. As I kissed Paula's soft cheek I was sure I felt Anna's focus on me. But then, drawing back, I saw she was in a warm hug with Jim. My mind was playing tricks with me again.

We stood, Anna's head leaning against me, her arm around my waist, my arm over her shoulder, and waved to Jim and Paula as their car drove down the road. But while one of Anna's hands waved extravagantly, the other was nipping at the flesh above my belt. My smile never wavered. But I was now certain that I hadn't been imagining things. There was trouble coming; and it was approaching fast.

As soon as they were out of sight Anna headed for the living room.

'I'm just going out for a wee walk. I need to clear my head after all that wine,' I said and quickly hopped out of the door. If I stayed out for a while, hopefully she would have either calmed down or, even better, fallen off to sleep by the time I got back.

I plucked a jacket off the coat-stand and closed the door firmly behind me. Reaching the gate, I paused, my fingers rubbing the metal catch. What was I doing? I was running away from a woman half my size. I was being chased out of my own home by my wife. A home that I had spent a lot of hours and effort in making. Avoidance was the easy option. The only way to resolve this was to face up to it.

Walking back to the door I fumbled in my jacket pocket, hoping that I had left a set of keys in there when I last wore it. I was in luck. Filling my lungs and gritting my teeth I slid the key into the lock. The hall light was out, but enough light filtered in from the street for me to see a round object speeding towards me. My arm lifted up in reflex. The sound of metal filled the room. I grunted in pain and with my other hand caught Anna's wrist as she aimed a blow at my head.

'You're useless, I hate you. I hate you,' she screamed. 'Don't know why I married you, you tosser.' She dropped the frying pan and began to flail at me with her arms and legs.

Unsure of what I could do, I wrapped her in a bear hug and held on, hoping that she would tire. Her feet aimed at my shins and she aimed her face at mine. Her teeth flashed past my nose.

'Anna, calm down. For fuck's sake, calm down.' I would not hit her, I would not.

'You're a bastard, you don't love me. Couldn't take your eyes off her. You make me hit you, you make me … it's all your own fault … your fault.' Her voice faltered with exhaustion. Her eyes cleared, she went limp as a rag in my arms, tears replacing the fog of rage in her eyes.

Her slack body slipped out of my grip, until she knelt on the floor, her head resting against the wall.

'Oh Andy, what have I done? What am I doing?' she sobbed. 'I'm so sorry, so sorry.' Her tightly wound features had melted into a puddle of guilt.

The sudden switch in mood caught me off guard. I found myself wanting to help her.

'Don't worry, it won't happen again.' I was on my knees before her now, pushing back her hair from her face. But somehow also standing above myself, as if watching from afar, confused by my own behaviour. 'You were just stressed about having visitors,' I said. I scooped her up and carried her like a child through to the living room couch, where I laid her down. I was as if she were in a faint. 'Can I get you a glass of water?'

'No, don't leave me.' She looked into my eyes. 'Please, don't ever leave me…'

'Okay, okay.' I soothed her clammy brow with my hand. 'I'll never leave you.'

'But I'm terrible. I'm a terrible woman. How could I attack you like that? What gets into my head?' She reached out for my hand, her eyes imploring me to understand.

'You're not terrible.' I was keen to calm her down. 'It was all my fault anyway, I was talking to Paula too much. You were bound to get jealous.'

The tears stopped, but her eyes translated the anguish in her mind.

'Make love to me, Andy. Show me you can still love me.' She kissed me deep and hard, hungry with need. While my mind reeled, my body responded.

'In the morning … we need to talk …. in the morning.'

'Yes … in the morning … yes.'

We didn't talk over that fight the next morning though. Anna woke up as if it hadn't occurred at all. And for my part, I had accepted her instant apology, and decided that should be the end of the matter.

The ensuing months spun past in happy equilibrium. Harsh words were distinctly absent, and caresses and kisses constituted all our physical contact.

There were no more outbursts, Anna was consistently the woman I fell in love with and we were able to relax into our marriage. It seemed that Anna had gotten over that moment of fury. She was my beautiful angel of a wife, and an easy-going, attentive stepmother, who Pat adored almost as much as I did. It niggled that we never talked over that episode, but I was grateful that there were no more signs that she might need some form of anger management. I was as happy as she was that it was over and thought that it might be better to consign that early part of our marriage to the memory bin.

It did take some time to relax fully, however. In the days that followed her attack, I found myself taking care about how I spoke, who I spoke to or where I went in case it provoked her. But we managed to have Jim and Paula over again several times without incident. And, to my pleasure, Paula and Anna seemed to hit it off. Since I had known Anna, I was the only person in her life, so I was concerned that she would focus all of her energies on me. I encouraged her to go out with her ex-colleagues, to take up a hobby, to make more friends, but she stated that she was happy with our little family and didn't need anyone else. If only we could add to it, she added with a small smile.

We were now eight months into our marriage. We had stopped using contraception almost as soon as we'd returned from our honeymoon, when Anna had first expressed her hope that we would give Pat a brother or sister. Yet, in those months we failed to conceive. The doctor said that we should give it a little more time. We were both young and healthy, if we continued to have a loving relationship, then he was sure that nature would take its course.

Pat continued to be a joy with only the odd demonstration of petulance. His energy was boundless, his sense of fun growing daily, as did his affection for Anna. A smile never failed to materialise on my face as I watched them together. The married life that I had hoped and prayed for – the family life for Pat that I'd dreamed of – all of it was happening and I couldn't have been happier.

Even work had settled down. I was growing in confidence and competence in the job. Roy Campbell stayed out of my way and the problems with the cash shortages had gone. All in all life was good. Yet a faint voice itched its way into my consciousness, a voice that warned me not to be too self-congratulatory, a voice that I placed on a shelf in the darkest recesses of my mind and ignored.

14

The first real test of our new-found domestic content came just a few weeks before our first wedding anniversary. I was asked to work in Campbeltown for a week. The previous manager was off work with a stress-related illness and they needed someone to oversee the place while her replacement took a well-earned break.

Some Head Office wallah probably looked at the map of Scotland, thought that Ayr and Campbeltown looked relatively close and decided I would be the right man for the job. They didn't take into their calculation a large body of water called the Firth of Clyde and the five-hour drive it took to negotiate.

My home for that week was the Ardsheil Hotel. The room was compact and cosy, the food was filling and tasty, and the hotel bar had as good a selection of fine malt whisky as I had seen anywhere. I phoned home every night and spent at least an hour talking to Anna and Pat.

Sitting at a table for one after work the first night, it occurred to me that eating alone in a restaurant must be the loneliest occupation that anyone could have. There were four other diners in the hotel restaurant. All men. We each nodded and grunted at the other, then fixed our attention on our place settings. Food was barely given enough time to cool by a single degree before it vanished from the plate. It occurred to me that if we'd been a group of women, we'd have known each other's life stories by the time the main course arrived.

After eating, my regime became a quick glass of whisky at the bar followed by a phone call home and an evening with one eye on some bank reports and the other on the TV.

Eventually my work was done and I was able to go home. We'd

had a week of brilliant sunshine while I was over in Campbeltown, but on the way home the weather broke, giving me a familiar taste of the wetter aspect of the Scottish climate.

I debated whether to drive up the length of the Kintyre Peninsula to Tarbert and from there to take the wee ferry across to Porta-vadie, drive across to Dunoon, where I could take the ferry across to Gourock, and then drive down the Clyde coast to Ayrshire.

Instead, I drove home the long way. It would take over five hours, but the journey up to Inveraray, past the four turrets of the fairy-tale castle and on to Arrochar and down past Loch Lomond was its own reward. A series of views that would warm the heart of any broody Scottish émigré and one that no doubt colours the tin of a lifetime's worth of shortbread. Mean, moody and magnificent is the best way to describe the hills that roll down to a full concrete stop at the side of the A80, before resuming their climb into the clouds on the other side. Draped in a lush cloth of green, accessorized with heather, pine and granite, the hills borrowed their disposition from the weather, but never failed to stir even the weariest, most jaded traveller. Snaking around sea lochs, ascending rocks and tumbling down the other side, the road eventually brought me to a gentler countryside, a greater concentration of houses, and home.

I expected Pat to jump on me as soon as the car entered the drive, but nothing. Car parked and locked, luggage in my hand, I walked past the living-room window towards the door. Movement in the room caught my eye and I paused to watch my son and wife in an unguarded moment.

Pat was holding a miniature rugby ball over his head as if he had just scored a try. Anna was mimicking his pose and they were both wearing a huge smile of triumph. I laughed at the sheer pleasure of it all, delighted they were so clearly having a great time, while a small part of me was envious. Looked like they didn't need me.

A second after I opened the door, Pat was at my feet.

'Daddy, Daddy, what have you got me?'

'Let me in the door first, son.' I picked him up. 'How's about a hug for your old man?' He rested his small head on my shoulder and patted my back.

'There, there,' he said. I kissed his head and looked over at Anna, who was standing watching us with a huge smile. She joined in the hug, wrapping her arms around us both.

'Family hug,' we all chanted as one.

'What do you want for your tea?' Anna broke the spell.

'Oh, anything, honey, I'm starving. But make it plain and simple, I've been having hotel food all week.'

'Omelette and chips?'

'Sounds wonderful.' I kissed her. 'It's great to see you. I really missed you both.'

'Me too, I mean, I missed you too,' Anna replied. 'Right, omelette it is.' She ran her fingers down the front of my trousers while making sure that Pat couldn't see. 'And wait till you see what's for dessert.'

We tucked into the food, bathed and put Pat to bed in record time. With a record number of whinges.

'But, Dad, I don't want to go to bed. Anna let me stay up late every night.' I hoped that eventually he would add the word 'Mum' to his vocabulary. Anna ruffled his hair.

'Oh, you rotter,' she smiled. 'I thought that was to be our little secret.'

'Sorry,' said Pat, head low but wearing a smile that would liquefy a stone goblin's heart.

'Bed,' I said, injecting my voice with a stern quality I didn't feel.

'Okay.' He dragged those two syllables out like a piece of gum from his mouth. The first one twice as long as the second. He trudged up to bed carrying his favourite bear, a small toy that fitted neatly under his arm and was covered with brown, matted fur. He was called Sam and Pat never went to bed without him. Pat turned at the top of the stairs and looked at Anna and I gazing fondly up at him.

'Tuck me in, Dad?'

'Of course, pal.' I bounded up the stairs, swept him under my arm and raced through to his bedroom, to the sound of his delighted squeals.

'Don't wind him up, Andy,' Anna shouted from the bottom of the stairs. 'He'll never go to sleep.'

The ritual was that I tucked the quilt tightly down Pat's sides and then placed Sam beside him with the same service being performed for the bear. This I did with an expression that said this was my most important duty of the day.

Regarding those large, bright eyes, I smoothed his soft fringe to the side.

'Well? Have you been a good boy?'

'Yes, Dad. Have you been a good Dad?'

Yes, son.' I bent forward and kissed his forehead. 'Love you.'

He reached up and mimicking my movement, pushed my fringe to the side, somewhat less smoothly than I had managed.

'Love you, Dad. Night, night.' He turned round on to his stomach, folded his arms under his body and went up on his knees, sticking his bum into the air. Since he had first gone into his own bed, Pat had adopted this position to sleep and it never failed to warm me.

Anna was waiting for me in our bedroom.

'Are you going to tuck me up in bed?' Her face was demure, her body quite naked.

'There is the small matter of this first.' I pointed down at the bulge in my trousers, amazed at the speed of my reaction.

'My god, that was quick.'

'It's been a long, lonely week.' I pulled at my clothes and then swept Anna onto the bed.

Our lovemaking was by turns tender and heated, languorous and spirited, hungry and sated. After who knows how long, I lay back on the bed, flushed, covered in a fine film of sweat and feeling like I was floating on a cushion of air. The smell of sex coated the room with a sweet musk.

'That … was … wonderful,' I managed to say, while my body sought sleep. Anna leaned over to kiss me and then sat up. She hunched forward on the bed, opened her legs and pulled up the flesh under her pubic hair.

'What are you doing?' I sat up slowly, feeling as if I had no strength left.

'I'm looking. There isn't very much.' Her voice sounded strangled.

'Much what? Gold nuggets?'

'Sperm, you useless git. There isn't very much, is there?' She rounded on me, her eyes tight with anger, 'What have you been up to?'

I was astonished at how rapidly the temperature in the room dropped. Sweat chilled on my back.

'How can you ask me that? Have I given you any idea that I have been unfaithful?'

'Yes,' she spat. 'There's not very much sperm here.' Her head ducked down again. She pulled at her vagina. 'Where is it all? You've been with some woman, haven't you.' She pushed me down on to the bed.

'No, absolutely not.' I sat back up again, 'I didn't even have a wank while I was away.' I put my arm round her and pulled her tight. My tone was conciliatory. 'Honey, how could you think I would betray you? I love you. I neither need or want another woman.' I'm sure that my eyes must have shone with sincerity for this was the absolute truth.

Anna looked up at me, and the anger in her expression dissolved swiftly into desire.

'Okay, if that's the case then make love to me again.' Her fingers cupped my half-flaccid penis.

'Give me five minutes, a man need time to recover you know,' I said.

But she ignored my words and stroked me, almost roughly.

'No, I don't want to wait. I want you again. Now,' she barked, her fingers tightening.

'Aww, come on, honey. Don't get so uptight.'

'Uptight, I'll give you uptight!' She pushed me back down on to the bed and sat astride me. 'I want your hard cock inside me now.' At the right moment this last sentence would have worked beautifully, but now the words were laced with threat.

'Anna, Anna, please.'

With her right hand she was trying to stuff my lifeless penis into her vagina.

'Are you a poof or something? I want you hard!' Her voice rose in pitch, its edge, her expression and wildness anaesthetising me to desire.

'Useless.' She cursed, raising herself above me.

And then it came. What I had been secretly fearing for months. Her fists rained down on my stomach, her eyes blazing from behind a torn curtain of hair. I tried ineffectively to deflect the blows. As her arms moved in a blur insults were spat at me. 'You useless bastard, I hate you.'

'Quiet,' I urged. 'Don't wake up Pat.'

Suddenly her shoulders dropped, she tugged at her hair, pulling it behind her ears. A strained smile pulled at her face.

'I'm sorry, Andy. I just want you inside me,' she wheedled. 'Please, just stick it inside me. Prove that you love me.'

'Not like this, Anna. Please. Not like this,' I whispered and softly placed my hands on either side of her hips.

'Why the hell not?' She had barely rested enough to catch her breath. Her hands reached down again and pulled at me. Her nails raked at the tender flesh.

I fought to keep control while pulling her hands off me. If I treated her too harshly I might hurt her, or even make her hurt me even more.

'Anna, stop it.' Despite my best efforts anger flooded my voice. Pushing her off me I stood up. 'Anna, you need help. This is crazy.'

She came at me now, launching herself from the bed, her teeth bare in a rictus of rage. She aimed a kick at my groin. I deflected it with my hand and backed away, all the time speaking to her, begging her to calm down, trying to keep my voice low, Pat always in my mind. But my words had no effect. She was rabid. Options raced through my mind. I could run downstairs, but she would only follow me. There were knives down there and I was afraid the raging, spitting monster in front of me was capable of anything.

Should I just stand and let her hit me until she cooled down? If I protected my head and my groin, the damage wouldn't be too bad. Neither of these options were realistic or bearable, I had to calm her down.

I rushed at her and caught her up in a bear grip. Her knees and feet once again aimed for my groin. Overbalancing, we fell on to the bed. Taking advantage of this I pinned her down with my knees jamming her arms to her sides. Her teeth flashed dangerously close to my genitals and her knees thumped up at my back. The teeth were clearly the worst threat so I placed my palm on her head and forced it down on to the pillow; with the other hand I tried to deflect the blows to my back.

For what seemed like hours Anna managed to maintain this effort. I was showered with her sweat and saliva, but I was determined to hold her like this until she calmed down.

Eventually she weakened, her knees barely reached my back. Judging that the dangerous part of the storm was over, I loosened my grip but stayed ready, in case she should erupt again.

When Anna eventually quietened, I heard a suppressed cry, sniff and a shuffle of feet from the door.

I turned and looked over my shoulder.

'Pat?'

Shit. How long had been there?

He wheeled to the side and ran out of view back to his bedroom. I grabbed at my boxer shorts, pulled them on and followed him. When I got to his bedroom, he was burrowing under the covers, his small body heaving with tears: trembling with fright. I tried to imagine what he might have seen.

Anna and I naked. Her eyes distant with anger. Me holding on, trying to save myself from injury.

No child should ever experience something like that. What would it do to his growing mind? How would he make sense of it? He'd bury it. That's what kids do. Until it comes back like some kind of mental acid reflux. And causes what?

I tried to pull the cover down so I could see his face. He resisted.

'Pat. Pat,' I said. 'We're fine. You've nothing to be afraid of, son.'

He turned away from me. I placed my hand on what I guessed might be his shoulder. He had stopped crying, but even through the thickness of the quilt I could feel him vibrate with fear.

I pulled the cover from him. Lifted him from his position on the bed and pressed him against my chest. Then I lay down with him on top of me, his head tucked into my neck.

'I'm so sorry, buddy.' I stroked the silk of his hair. 'I'm so sorry.' And in the slow motion of my fingertips on his head I searched for a peace I was sure I would never find again.

When Pat's breathing slowed into sleep, I turned onto my side, allowing him to fall onto his bed. Then I placed the cover over him and with one last kiss on his forehead I returned to my wife.

Anna was sitting up against the headboard, still naked, her knees pulled up to her chest. Her hair was stuck to her forehead and sticking out at crazy angles from the side of her head. She looked tiny. Lost.

I sat on the edge of the bed, my back to her.

'Andy,' she said in a croak. 'Andy.' There was pain there. In only two syllables, a world of apology and shame.

Clenching my teeth, I hardened myself to her distress. This was my wife, this was the woman I loved, yet who knew what she was capable of? I'd thought the attacks months before were one-offs. But now ... was I at risk? But of what?

Was Pat safe?

'I'm so sorry, Andy. I'm so sorry.' I could barely hear her, but in any case her apologies were weak-winged and floundering against the worry of what this would all do to Pat. I loved her, but I couldn't compete with the demons I had now seen take her over for a third time.

I stood up, pulled on my dressing gown and turned to face her. She looked as if a strong wind could lift her up and carry her away with as much ease as if she were a dandelion seed. I hardened myself to her vulnerability.

'I'm going to spend the night on the couch.'

I steeled myself and stood up, feeling the tremble in my thighs. Everyone tells you that an abuser will never change. Get out. And I knew that's what needed to happen. This would be the most difficult thing I ever had to do, but I had no choice.

I loved her. But in that moment, I knew I had to protect my son. I couldn't risk him seeing his dad attacked again. Couldn't risk him losing me, perhaps. I had to do this. For everyone's sake. For Pat's sake.

'Tomorrow I'll help you pack. This … this marriage is over.' Ignoring the plea in her face, the anguish that distorted her beautiful features into a mask of self-loathing, I walked out of the room.

15

My mother was incredulous, Jim said nothing and Pat withdrew into the world of cartoons. He only spoke to me when I spoke first or when he needed food. He had a TV, a video recorder and a tower of trusty cartoons that never let him down, what did he need his father for? I tried to talk to him about Anna, to let him know why it wouldn't work, but how do you tell an almost five-year-old that your wife and his new stepmother has such potential for violence? I told him that we were arguing too much and that we didn't love each other anymore. He asked for a packet of crisps.

'I don't mean to judge, son,' said Mum. 'But you youngsters don't know how to work at a marriage. You're not even married a year and you're splitting up? Crazy. I blame this whirlwind lifestyle you all lead. A quick fix and then move on. Things that are worthwhile don't come to you as easy as that.'

'Yes, Mum.'

'Still, at least I'll get to see more of you now.' This was the first time that my mother alluded to the fact that she had seen less of me since Anna came on to the scene. A lot less. 'Where has Anna gone to stay?' she asked

'I found a bedsit for her. I'll look for something more substantial, a flat or something.' We were talking in her kitchen. A place that we had often sat and talked over the years. We always sat on the same bone-hard seats, facing each other, cradling cups of strong tea in our hands, talking for hours. Even though my mother didn't bake much anymore, the scent of scones, pancakes, fresh bread and jams still hung in the air like a sweet cloud. These four walls had listened to the growth of our family, its joys and its torments. I used to swear that my mother dropped something into my tea whenever we sat here, because I could never hide anything from her while we talked in this room. It became my confessional. My hopes, my desires, my sins were all disclosed to my mother while sipping tea and eating cake.

Mum would just sit and listen. Sip and chew. She would only speak to ask questions, draw a little more out from me.

This time, however, I couldn't confide in her. I couldn't tell her that my wife was violent, that my penis was bruised and lined with lacerations from Anna's nails. What would she think of me? I was a man, a big man. Anna was a dainty woman, how could I have let her do this to me. This was one situation I would never be able to discuss. Shame stoked the furnace of my face. I buried my head in my hands to hide the deep flush on my skin.

Mum misread my actions.

'Don't worry, son,' she offered. 'It obviously just wasn't meant to be. You'll get over it. In time you'll be able to put it down to just one of those things and you'll move on, meet someone else.'

'No thanks,' I said vehemently. 'I've learned my lesson. No more women for me. Widowed once, almost divorced once and I'm just in my early thirties. Married life obviously isn't for me. Someone up there is trying to tell me something and I've heard them. Loud and clear.'

'Never say never, son.' Mum topped up my cup of tea. 'You're a young man yet. You've just not met the right woman.'

'Yes I have, Mum.' I said with finality. Patricia's ghost hung silently in the air between us.

Mum sipped at her cup, her eyes looking at me apologetically over the rim. Her obvious sorrow at my troubles touched me. Emotion tightened my throat. I smoothed my forehead with my fingers and waited until the threatened tears subsided.

'Besides, Mum, I have Pat.'

We both smiled fondly at the mention of his name.

'Yes,' Mum agreed, 'He's a wee joy, isn't he?'

'And I can't keep putting him through the process of meeting a new mum every so often. That wouldn't help him. I'll just have to live like a monk.' I grinned, trying to inject some humour into the sombre room. 'I'll have to tie a knot in it.'

Mum laughed, 'If you're anything like your father then that'll be impossible.'

'Mum.' I made a face. 'Too much information.'

At work, the rumour mill swung quickly into action. My fellow employees loved nothing more than a good gossip and that doesn't come much better than a marriage that has floundered within the first year. Reaction ranged from quietly spoken sympathy to people completely ignoring the subject.

Not keen on anyone knowing my business at work, I preferred the silent approach. With Roy Campbell, however, this was not possible.

'Ah, Andy, Andy.' He bounced into the room as if delighted to hear of another's misfortune. 'Sorry to hear about you and the Mrs. Still, better to realise you've made a mistake early on than spend twenty years in absolute misery.'

'How long have you been married?' I asked

'Twenty … ah, you cheeky monkey. You won't catch me out like that. So what went wrong? Not giving her enough? She spending too much of your money?'

'Roy,' I groaned. 'Do you have any idea what the word "sensitivity" means?'

'Aye.' He looked at me quizzically. 'It means…'

'It means that I'm telling you nothing and I'd rather be left on my own.'

'Fine, fine.' He looked wounded. 'Miserable sod,' he announced to no one in particular as he walked back out of the room. At least with Roy there were no surprises. You knew what to expect and he never let you down. I heard a brief conversation in the corridor and then another face popped in the door.

'Hey, how are you?' It was Malcolm.

'Oh, you know. Bloody wonderful.'

'Fancy going out for a pint tonight? Let it all hang out? Get it off your chest?'

'Nah, no thanks, Malcolm.' This miserable sod didn't want company. 'Too raw just yet. Soon though, eh?'

'Aye,' he said retreating back out the door. 'Soon.'

The truth was that I just wanted to be left alone. I didn't want to talk about it. I didn't even want to think about it, but it was in my thoughts all of the time. It was sitting right on my shoulder, a boulder crushing bone, muscle and sinew. I couldn't sleep, I couldn't eat.

I wanted her back.

Four weeks passed while I lived in this purgatory. No one could reach me, I was living in my own little world of misery. I couldn't escape the fact that I still loved Anna and that I would take her back in an instant. But every time I thought of phoning her a picture of a bowed, quiet woman would impose itself on my mind.

Sheila Hunter.

I recalled how that shrunken, emaciated figure had talked to me in her house about putting up with a violent partner. I thought of all the films, books and articles that preached as soon as the violence starts, get out. It will only escalate.

Easy for them to say.

Get out.

What if you can't? What if you are certain it will stop, despite all evidence to the contrary? You love the person, you don't want to give up on them despite everything. You just tell yourself a suitable lie, and carry on. I had given Anna some time, convinced that her first attacks had been an aberration, something born of stress, her new situation, everything conspiring to get on top of her. But, just as all the experts might have predicted, the violence had returned.

And returned again.

I had to be strong. I would just have to make do without her in my life, no matter how much it hurt.

Work became my solace from confusion. The minute I walked into the office at eight o'clock my mind closed the door to thoughts of Anna. Behind the thick doors they stayed until six in the evening when I would go to pick up Pat from my mother's.

He had now started school and seemed to be enjoying every minute of it. All the way home in the car he would chatter non-stop about what his teacher said that day and what his friends got up to. He talked of painting, of letters and of numbers, and his sweet soprano was a balm to the muddle in my mind all the way through to his eight-thirty bedtime.

It was one such night, however, that my world was thrown into more chaos. I picked Pat up from my mother's, who had herself picked him up from school and fed him. That night his chatter was about a giraffe that he had drawn. His teacher, Miss Talbot, thought that it was very good. He held it up so that I could peruse it in the car mirror, then, not waiting for my words of praise, folded it back up again. Obviously the fact that Miss Talbot thought it was excellent meant that my opinion on the subject was redundant.

Once home, he played with some toys while I heated and ate a microwave meal and then it was bath time. Occasionally I would join him in the water and that night I decided to do just that. We splashed each other, pretended to make his little rubber bath toys fly before diving into the soapy depths. We laughed a lot. There is something magical about father and son playing naked in a bath. Divested of clothes and of society's mores we were simply two humans having fun. As we splashed I considered how sad it was that people would often feel too uneasy about playing with their child in such a way.

'You're really hairy, Dad.' Pat interrupted my reverie. 'Will I be as hairy as that when I grow up?'

'Who knows, son. For your sake I hope not. Girls seem to prefer hairless chests these days.'

Dried and dressed, him in pyjamas, me in joggers and a t-shirt, we sat down to an animal programme on the Discovery Channel.

Animals, the larger and fiercer the better, were Pat's passion. He could sit and watch them all day. And if Disney caricatured and animated them, that was perfect. Soon it was time for bed.

'Aw, Dad. Can I not stay up for a wee while longer? There's grizzly bears coming up.'

'No,' I said. 'It's bed time. You can watch the grizzlies another night. Come on, bed.'

'Okay, okay. Will you read to me?' He brightened at the thought.

'Five minutes, okay?' He raced up the stairs almost before the words were out of my mouth.

I had been reading for around fifteen minutes when I heard the doorbell.

'Right. I'll go and answer that. You get to sleep, young man.' I tucked in his quilt, kissed his forehead and put on his nightlight.

'Goodnight, son,' I said from the door.

'Night, Dad,' Pat said and closed his eyes tight as if trying to convince me he was suddenly asleep.

Wondering who could be at the door at this time of night, I walked down the stairs. It would probably be Jim on the cadge for a couple of cans. Paula must have given him the night off, I thought as I pulled open the door.

And there she was.

'Anna! What the … what …?'

'Can I come in, Andy? We need to talk.' She seemed swamped by her coat, her head bowed as if too heavy for her neck.

'I thought we'd said all that needed to be said.'

'Andy, please. I'll just take five minutes and then you can fling me back out again.'

Intrigued by her tone and quiet demeanour I stood aside and let her in. She reached the living room and, as she walked, she looked around herself as if memories of happier times were filling her mind.

She faced me. Her eyes were circled in shadow. She looked thinner. She looked like she needed a hug. At the thought I crossed my arms, as if that might curb the impulse once and for all.

'How's Pat?' she asked.

'He's … he's fine. What do you want, Anna?' I wanted her out of my house quick. I also wanted to hold her and never let go.

She looked up at me. Her eyes large and moist. 'I'm pregnant.'

16

As I drove into work the next day, I pushed down the visor to lessen the effect of the sunshine on my eyes. Ten minutes later, as I waited in a queue of traffic heading up Ayr's Sandgate, I was surprised when I had to switch on the wipers to wash away the rain. My mind was just as confused as the weather. Anna pregnant. Unbelievable. A yawn ruptured my smile.

I didn't get much sleep after hearing that piece of news. I had breakfasted, dressed Pat, got him off to school, this being still only his first week, and then driven into work in a daze. Anna's voice reverberated in my head.

'I'm pregnant.'

I've often watched TV programmes and prayed that the man displayed the right reaction to this sort of news. A reaction that would bring reassurance to their partner. I was usually embarrassed to be male when they inevitably acted like the Neanderthal the scriptwriters intended. But now I knew why. Pat was planned for, prayed for. He was the product of respect, devotion. My reaction then was of exhilaration, joy and tenderness. With Anna my reaction was a classic caveman 'Ugh!' and I sat down.

So did she.

'Say something.' She had twisted her fingers. 'I didn't know how to tell you or even if I should. I mean, I wasn't the best wife. I know I screwed up. But … this is your baby and I thought you should know.'

'Are you sure?' My voice sounded as if it came from the end of a long tunnel.

'Am I sure of what?' Anna demanded. She looked stung by my question.

'Sure that you are pregnant?' The question of parentage never entered my head.

'Yes,' she said wearily. 'I bought three testers, one a day for three days. I couldn't believe it … I'm still struggling to believe it.'

Silence widened the distance between us.

'Say something … please,' Anna begged me at last. She was leaning forward, elbows on her thighs, hands before her as if clasped in prayer. Hands that had before now bruised my flesh. Hands that would soon care for my child.

'What are you going to do?' I asked her, my voice soft, frightened of the answer.

'That depends.' She examined her fingers.

'On what?' I asked, voice raised.

'I don't know, Andy. I don't know. I'm scared. I'm on my own. A child's a huge responsibility…'

I forced out the question: 'Have you thought of termination?'

'No, absolutely not.' She looked up at me. 'Is that what you want?'

'No, but there's no way I could stop you, if you really wanted to.' I paused. 'I'm sorry I asked you. I just needed to know.'

'I was thinking more of adoption.' Her nails now came under close scrutiny.

'Adoption?' I fought to keep control. I needed to show as little emotion as I could. I didn't want Anna to think she had the upper hand. But the thought was clear in my mind: no child of mine would be brought up by strangers.

'Yes, but I'd rather keep her.'

'Her? You know it's a girl?' The thought that she might have had a scan and I didn't share in the experience filled me with jealousy.

Anna didn't reply at first. She stuck her hand in her bag and pulled out an envelope.

'Here.' She handed it to me. 'They can't tell the sex at this stage. Way too early … I would love a girl though.'

I opened the envelope and pulled out a small, glossy piece of paper. I had held one before, so I knew instantly what it was.

'Is that it? Him or her?' I pointed at a tiny white dot in a forest of black-and-white lines. Anna nodded.

'Wow.'

More silence. We were both lost in the small, shiny piece of paper.

'How far gone are you?'

'Four weeks.'

'That means it was that night…?'

Anna nodded but I carried on with my question anyway.

'…The night that I came back from Campbeltown?'

While Anna was pulling and tearing at my genitals, my seed was battling through her body with only one purpose. It had succeeded despite everything.

'My God.' I stared out of the window for moment, then turned back to Anna. 'A child conceived in less than perfect circumstances.' My laugh held little humour. 'You hear couples saying they remember when they conceived their child. It's usually, oh I don't know … after a party, a romantic meal, that weekend they spent sheltering from an April shower in Paris.' I breathed deeply. Keep calm, I told myself. No point in shouting.

'I know, Andy, and I'm so sorry. I just can't apologise enough. My behaviour was shocking. But this is our child. Ours.'

She dropped on to her knees, moving forward. She reached me and held my hands tight in hers. I wanted to pull them away, but I couldn't move. I was immobilised by a bruise of emotions. Hurt, joy, fear and frustration were only the ones that I could articulate and they were painting my mind purple.

The one feeling that I didn't want to admit to was relief. But it was there, however much I tried to deny it. The baby gave me a valid reason to take her back.

'I love you, Andy. As soon as I realised I had to tell you about the baby, I knew that we had to get back together.' Her eyes were soft, the rim of her irises blurred with tears. 'This is our baby.' She gripped my hand tighter for emphasis. 'We can make it work, for her sake.'

I managed to pull my hands free. Anna took this as a negative sign, stood up, head bowed and went back to her seat.

'I need … I need to think. I need to let this soak in,' I told her.

Hope sparked fresh in her expression.

'Of course.' She stood up. 'I'd better go. Let you think. Say hello to Pat for me.' She was out of the door before I could say goodbye.

The noise of a horn tore me from my thoughts. I was sitting on the approach to a roundabout with a growing line of angry drivers behind me. I waved an apology and drove off.

What should I do? The question was rooted in my mind and shoots of thoughts were spreading in every direction. As I negotiated the final stretch of my drive to work I tried to make sense of the commotion in my mind. Let Anna go but keep the baby? Let them both go? Hold on to them both? Which was the decision that would provide the most security for Pat and myself? Could I even make such a decision?

A knock on the car window pushed these thoughts and questions temporarily from my mind. I was sitting in the bank car park, elbows on the steering wheel, head buried in my palms. Sheila Hunter was standing beside the car, peering in.

'You okay?' she mouthed.

I motioned that I was fine and, taking care that I wouldn't hit her with the door, I got out of the car.

'You alright?' she asked again.

'Yes, yes … fine thanks,' I answered. 'You?' I looked at her. 'Hey, you're looking great.' She had put on a little weight, her hair was cut stylishly and her already fine features embellished with make-up. She looked a lifetime away from the mouse of a beaten woman I had visited only weeks ago.

'Thanks.' Somewhat self-consciously she tucked a strand of hair behind her ear. 'I'm doing a lot better thanks, Andy. Sorting my life out once and for all.'

'Is that man of yours giving you any more trouble?'

'No,' she answered. 'Haven't seen or heard from him for ages. Letters from my lawyers are keeping him occupied. How's things with you?'

I took my briefcase from the car and we began walking to the staff entrance. 'Oh, you know…' I avoided eye contact. '… The usual.'

When we reached the door I rang the bell. While we waited for it to be opened I felt driven to ask her something.

'Do you mind if I ask a personal question?' I turned to face her.

'That depends,' she answered with a smile on her lips and curiosity in her eyes.

'If it's too personal you don't have to answer,' I tried to reassure her.

'Well? Big build-up, what's the question?' She smiled.

'If you were to give advice to another person … another woman…' the lie soured my tongue '… in a violent relationship, what would it be?'

'Simple. Get out.' She spoke quietly. Her eyes gave no hint if she wanted to know my reason for asking.

'What if the domestic situation is complicated? Kids etc? Things are never simple are they?'

'You're right, things are never simple. But violent people rarely change and if someone wants to hold on to their self-esteem, their confidence, their … self-worth, then they have to get out. And if there are kids, especially boys, then consider what messages they are getting. It's okay to be a bully? A slap, or worse, now and again works wonders to keep the little lady under control?' She paused as if to moderate the edge in her voice. 'No, violence doesn't belong in any home and whatever your reasons are for asking…'

I began to speak, to make up a story.

'Don't tell me. I don't need to know,' continued Sheila, having said the last thing I wanted to hear, but the first thing I needed to. 'But if you are asking on someone's behalf, tell them to get out, go to the police, social services, a woman's refuge. There are lots of places that a woman can go for advice nowadays. The situation's far from perfect, but there is help out there for women in that position.'

But, what about a man? I wanted to say, but couldn't. There was no way that I was about to admit to this. What a laugh everyone would have. I could just hear them. A big bloke like him and he can't handle a delicate wee woman. Telling them that size was deceptive or that I would rather face a wall of New Zealand rugby players than my wife would probably only result in louder derision.

The one thing Sheila said that I couldn't believe, didn't want to believe, was that people don't change. I refused to accept this. Beneath Anna's carapace of anger was a soft centre that needed to be shown a way out. I loved her, and she could see that. I could help her chip away at her brittle shell and reach the real woman beneath. I would have to. The alternative was just too frightening to contemplate.

17

We met in a restaurant in the centre of town. I thought a neutral venue would encourage a calmer discussion. Anxious to begin talking, I arrived early to find that Anna was already there.

My heart thumped when I saw her. I wanted nothing more than to take her in my arms and hold her. Instead I took a seat, leaned back in the chair and crossed my legs.

'Hi.' Her voice was quiet, unsure, even in that one syllable. Her arms and legs were crossed and a cup of coffee sat on the table in front of her like a large, brown full stop.

This display of uncertainty pleased me. It let me see that she wasn't taking me or my decision for granted.

'Hello,' I replied, trying to get a view of her stomach, which was of course a waste of time as it was far too early for her to be showing. But the future of the child floating in that amniotic sea could depend on the course of the next hour or so, and I needed a quick reminder of the reason that had opened up this opportunity to talk.

Anna was looking her usual beautiful self. Hair sleek and groomed; clothes, fashionable and freshly laundered; make-up precise and flattering. The only sign that pregnancy might be having any effect on her was a slightly darker pink under her eyes.

'How are you feeling?' I picked up a menu and held it between us as if to prevent my affection for her leaping across the table.

'Okay … Mind you I could do without this morning sickness malarkey.'

'Have you told anyone else yet?'

'No, no. I need to know what you … what *we* are going to do.'

'I think I'll just have a coffee, I'm not hungry.' I avoided a direct answer until there was no way a waitress would interrupt.

We were silent as if by mutual consent while I attempted to attract the attention of the waitress who was much too interested in a magazine that was spread out on the counter in front of her. Tired of waiting, I walked over to her.

'Could I have a coffee, please? White.'

'Sure.' She didn't take her eye off the latest himbo that was draped over a sun lounger.

I returned to our table and we waited in silence until my drink arrived.

'So.' I dropped a teaspoon of brown sugar into the coffee. 'Let's talk.'

'What's your decision?' Her face was inscrutable, but she fidgeted with her wedding band, twisting it round her finger. For a moment I wondered if it was a deliberate action.

'I don't want a child of mine to be brought up by strangers. I want to be a large part of their lives, and if we have to get together to make it happen then that's the way it has to be.'

'Not because you love me?' Anna pulled at an ear lobe.

'Let's not be mistaken, Anna. I do love you. But the only thing that's brought me here is the tiny clump of cells growing in your womb. I'd force myself to live without you otherwise. I have too much respect for myself to allow you to hit me again.' I took a token sip from my cup. 'For the sake of the baby I want us to give it another go.'

Anna's face revealed nothing of how she was taking this news.

I made sure she was looking into my eyes. 'But I have one condition.'

'What?'

'That you go to your doctor and you get help.'

'Already done that.'

'When?' This was encouraging.

'Just after we got married, after the time … you know.' It was too difficult for her to continue, but I knew she was referring to the time she repeatedly banged my head with the door.

'And what did he say?'

'Oh, he said that I was probably still uptight from the stresses of the wedding and not to take it too seriously.'

'What? That was it? Years of medical training for that?' I was incredulous. 'Right, in that case I think we should go and see a marriage guidance counsellor.'

'Fine, that might help.' She bowed her head as if willing to accept any conditions I might impose.

'You're happy with that?' I asked.

She nodded.

I needed to know why she had reacted the way she had. What made her turn violent? A flash of memory and there was a taste of blood in my mouth: a dull heavy feeling on the side of my head.

'Why did you do it, Anna? Where did all of that anger come from?'

She shrugged in response. 'Don't know.'

'That's a cop-out. Of course you know, you just don't want to admit it.'

'I love you, Andy. Believe me I'll make this marriage work, but there are things that you don't need to know.'

'Of course I need to know them. I want to help you. I want to understand.'

'Are you finished with that coffee?' Anna was looking over at the waitress.

'Eh?'

'Let's go somewhere more private. The waitress has decided eavesdropping is much more interesting than her magazine.'

Dodging the rain, we were soon in my car. The windows fogged quickly, giving me the impression that we were alone in the world within the confines of the small metal box. I wished I had thought of this earlier. The confessional of a car is something I have experienced often. Put two people in such close proximity for any length of time and they have to communicate. Silence in such a small space begs to be filled.

I turned off the radio and, facing Anna, repeated myself.

'I need to know why you get so angry. In fact, I know so little about you. You've never talked about your family, your friends, any of your life before you met me. Wouldn't that strike you as being a little odd if you were me?'

Now that I had asked this question out loud the strangeness of my own behaviour struck me anew; I wondered why I hadn't asked before. Perhaps I had sensed that this was a no-go area, that this was hazardous ground. But with a new air of openness surrounding us, I thought that Anna would find it difficult to fudge an answer.

'S'pose.'

'I've often thought of asking you, but never did because I thought you'd open up to me in your own good time.'

The windows were completely misted over now. Anna breathed deeply. A long, slow breath that seemed to seep right down to her toes. She exhaled slowly and loudly.

'You're right … as usual. I should talk about it, about my past, but I … I … can't.' A tear slid gracefully down her pale cheek, leaving a shiny trail. 'I'm afraid that if I start speaking … I won't be able to stop screaming.' She finished in a whisper.

'Look, I'm no expert but even I know that if something is causing you so much upset then you need to talk about it, get it in the open. Only then can you deal with it. Better out than in, my pal's Dad used to say. But that was his excuse when he farted.' We both smiled weakly at my poor attempt at humour.

'I don't know. I'm afraid that if I say it out loud then it must have happened. I can't pretend any more that it's all a horrible dream.'

What on earth could she have been through to say something like that?

'Talk to me, please. Tell me what happened.'

Until now I had been holding in my love for her, like it was stale breath. Now, seeing her so upset, I couldn't stop a little leaking out. I leaned over and gripped her hands.

'My childhood was a war zone,' she began, holding on to my

hands tightly. 'Everybody fought. Nobody won. I was the young-est.' She stared at the misted window as if looking at a replay of her past, a stately procession of tears flowing down her cheeks. 'I had … I *have* two brothers and one sister. My parents had us all in the space of six years. There were another two pregnancies that ended in miscarriages. At least that was the official excuse.' She looked at me. 'Both my parents were alcoholics. I come from a long line of alco-holics. How's that for a pedigree?' The window reclaimed her stare. 'My parents fought like … not like ordinary parents – they fought like animals. They were both about the same height, five feet two. Sometimes it was a slugging match. They would stand there swaying with the drink, only feet apart, fists aimed at the other's head. Often in total silence. They would run out of insults. Either that or their brains were so pickled that they couldn't think of anything else to say. We … the kids … we'd hide behind a couch.' The words were becoming difficult to decipher now as great heaves convulsed in her chest.

'Here.' Rather ineptly I handed her a hanky. 'Give yourself a minute to calm down.' Emotion thickened my voice. I didn't know if I could listen to any more without my tears spilling over hers. 'Do you want to stop? We can carry on some other time. You could wait and speak to a…' Somebody else but me, was what I wanted to say. I didn't know how to help with such pain. '… A professional.'

'No, I'd like to carry on. I've started…' She straightened her shoulders. 'More often than not Mum would start it, calling him names, flinging things at him. Oh, they would get tanked up first, as if getting ready for the main event. But he never backed down, he always rose to the bait. It became so that we almost saw their behaviour as normal. I rarely brought friends home because I knew what would happen. One time I brought a wee pal home. She lived just round the corner. Mary … Mary something. Anyway, Dad came in the door having forgotten to bring home the *Ayrshire Post* for the second time of asking, and Mum just launched herself at him. She jumped on his back and pummelled the back of his head. He fell forward onto the floor. Mary just stood there, frozen. She couldn't believe it. I'll never forget the expression on her face. For the first time, I saw their behaviour through someone else's eyes and I realised just how crazy it all was.'

'Did they ever hit you?'

'What do you think?' She turned her gaze to me. 'Me and my sister, Angie, didn't get it as bad as the boys did though. We were … we were girls. We were sugar and spice and all that crap. But the boys got leathered regularly. Then they would take it out on us, give us a battering, pull out clumps of our hair. Mind you, when we were younger we could give as good as we got. The boys, to their credit, were apt to hold a little bit back. We didn't. We just went crazy. Then, when the boys reached puberty, they got stronger than us so we had to use different tactics. We'd wait until they were sleeping, or defenceless in some way before attacking them.' She smoothed the damp hankie between thumb and forefinger. 'I remember one time I caught my oldest brother masturbating over a Page 3 girl. He nearly broke my nose and threatened to give me some more if I told anyone that I had caught him. I vowed that I would stop him from ever hurting me like that again. I waited until he was asleep that night … and stabbed him in the ear with the steel handle of my comb. He's deaf to this day on that side. I'll never forget his screams.' She paused, mind replaying a film from the past. She laughed briefly, mirthlessly. 'He never came near me again. We told Mum it was an accident, he had fallen out of bed in the middle of the night. She was the more sober of the two on that occasion. Dad was unconscious, in the kitchen. We used to come down in the morning and find them in the weirdest places. Angie and I used to help them to bed once in a while. We didn't want them to hurt themselves. Then we gave up. As soon as I could, I got out. Married my neighbour's son at sixteen.'

What the hell?

'You've already been married?' Why didn't I know this? Then, absurdly, a worm of jealousy curled in my gut. Who was this guy?

Where was he? After all I had heard, Anna still had the capacity to surprise me.

'Oh yes.' She smiled apologetically. 'Lasted four years. It ended the day he kicked me so hard I lost ... my baby.' Her fingers were in a row before her mouth as if she wanted to push the words back in. 'I lost my baby.' She began to rock. 'My baby.'

Open mouthed, I could only stare at her. I couldn't even begin to imagine the amount of hurt and anguish she had suffered over the years. I took her in my arms and rocked with her.

'Anna, Anna,' I intoned like a mantra.

'It's the only way I know to love, Andy, and it terrifies me,' she said, her voice muffled by my shoulder. 'I don't know what I'm capable of. When I go into one, I just can't control it. I barely even know what I'm doing.' She stopped rocking and looked up at me. 'And I do love you, Andy. You've got to believe it.' She looked desperate for my reassurance.

'I believe you.' I gave it willingly.

'I'm terrified to love you and I'm terrified to lose you. It's just ... when I feel even a little bit like I'm not in control, I lash out. I know you're a good man and you won't hurt me. I know that in a way I'm safe, so I suppose I just try to push you. See if I really am as safe as it seems.'

In that damp, warm little space, it all made so much sense. I held her again, regretting I'd ever pushed her away.

'And what about the baby?' she asked through sobs. 'I don't know what I might do to her?' She stopped speaking and then started again as if she was being crushed by the weight of the silence.

'The funny thing is, the worst of it wasn't the physical violence, the cuts and bruises all healed. But the things that my mother said to me all of those years ago still hurt. What if I turn out like her? She used to call me and Angie sluts, laugh at everything we tried to do, call us stupid and ugly. She said that she was just preparing us for life, trying to make us tough.' She shifted in her seat. 'I don't want to be that kind of mum, Andy.'

'You won't be, love. I won't let you. Between us we'll get you through this.'

I don't know how long we sat in the car hugging, but it was dark by the time that I dropped her off at her flat to pick up her belongings.

I was confident that we could work out our problems. Anna needed me. She needed my patience, my broad shoulders, she needed the love of a good man. One who wouldn't hurt her with words or fists. A man who could teach her the true warmth of affection. Whatever it would take, I was determined to do it. She looked so vulnerable cradled in my arms that I couldn't resist the plea in those eyes.

This confidence was, however, tainted with fear. In eight months Anna would have my baby. The last woman I loved died while giving birth to my child. If the same thing happened again, I didn't think that I could take it. The logical side of my brain protested that the chances of such an event happening again must be remote, but in the deep recesses of my mind, atavistic fears crouched like hungry griffins, growling dire words. You weren't meant to be happy, they rumbled. Death and unhappiness will haunt you for the rest of your life.

First, your father, then your wife, could it be your child next?

18

The first month or so of Anna's pregnancy was in her words 'a dawdle'. Her eyes, hair and skin seemed to catch every spare mote of light and reflect it a thousand times over. She was more energetic than ever and had an even larger appetite than normal for sex. I managed to overcome my reluctance about sex while Anna was in this delicate stage, when she produced a book on pregnancy. The author maintained that when a woman became aroused the womb was moved in such a way that even the longest penis would be hard pushed to harm the foetus. The mechanics of this were a bit of a mystery, but it was there in black and white, and that was good enough for me. Pat was regularly packed off to his gran and uncle over these few weeks while Anna and I lost ourselves in a feast of corporeal delights.

Then a period of sickness and fatigue followed. At the time I was amazed to see that Anna seemed almost relieved that this happened. On one occasion while her head was stuck down the loo, I held her hair out of the way as her stomach heaved, and each time she surfaced there was a small look of satisfaction overprinting the fatigue on her face.

'How can you be happy when you're heaving your guts up every morning?' I asked.

She leaned back on her heels and took a breath. Wiped some saliva from her lips with a sleeve and said, 'I never thought I could have a baby after…' A cloud of memory slipped over her expression, '… after what happened. So this…' She pointed at the toilet bowl and grinned, '… reassures me that I am actually pregnant.' She grabbed my hand and rested it over her still-slim belly. 'There's really a baby in here, Mr Boyd.'

I leaned forward and kissed her wet forehead. 'There really, really is, Mrs Boyd.' We exchanged grins.

'Any more thought about names?' I asked as I sat on the edge of the bath.

'Theodore, if it's a boy. Storm Puddleduck if it's girl.'

'Nice,' I smiled. 'I was thinking Biggus Dickus for a boy and Fanny Bigpants for a girl.'

Anna laughed. Loud and throaty. Her shoulders moving up and down in an exaggerated fashion. Putting a hand on my knee she used it as leverage to stand up. I stood before her. She leaned into me and put her head on my shoulder. I could feel her head moving there as her laughter continued.

She looked up at me. 'Toss you for it.'

'Race you for it,' I replied. 'First one down to the living room wins.'

'That's not fair, Boyd,' she shouted at my retreating back.

Down in the living room, she slumped on to the sofa beside me and rested her head on my shoulder.

'I needed that,' she said. 'Can't beat a good laugh.'

I held her tight, feeling treasured and loved and wishing that this moment would stretch out for the rest of our lives.

As Anna's belly expanded she seemed to become mellower. Sickness aside, she was happy to loll around on the settee and watch the world go by. Her needs were minimal: warmth, shelter, affection and a towel to wipe her mouth after another bout of retching. Nothing bothered her. It was as if being part of something bigger than she could previously imagine meant now everything else was mere trivia.

Pat was initially reluctant to be alone with Anna when she moved back in, but he was soon caught up in the happy atmosphere and the love that flowed between us. He was open-mouthed with awe when we told him that Anna had a baby in her belly.

He sat back on his heels and pondered this for a few moments.

'A baby what?' he asked.

'We're not sure yet,' I said. 'We'll find out in eight months' time.'

'I hope it's a baby puppy,' he said and went back to his toys.

That night at bath time the questions began in earnest.

'What kind of baby is it?' Pat asked as he brought two dinosaurs crashing together across a sea of bubbles.

'A baby sister or a baby brother,' I replied. Anna grinned from her perch on the toilet, relieved that the puppy was no longer in his thoughts.

'How did it get in there?'

Anna looked at me as if to say, over to you, pal.

I explained about eggs and seeds, and how I had put my seed inside Anna's belly and one of her eggs caught it. Pat nodded as if that made perfect sense. He looked over at Anna's midriff and assessed.

'How does it get out?'

'You know how Anna doesn't have a willy like we have? She has a vagina. The baby comes out there.'

Pat mouthed the word vagina as if practising, looked down at his willy. Plopped some bubbles on top of it. Looked over at Anna. And went back to his dinosaurs.

I looked over at Anna. She grinned as if to say, well that wasn't too difficult.

The next day was a Saturday and we were queuing up to get into the soft play area at ten o'clock. A young couple joined the queue behind us. The mother had a boy by the hand about the same height as Pat. The father had an infant strapped to his chest. It's head was thick with dark spiky hair and it's face almost folded in on itself as it dreamed.

'Wow, beautiful,' said Anna as she turned and noticed the baby. 'How old?'

'Four weeks,' said the father with evident pride.

'Beautiful,' repeated Anna, her face bright with appreciation. She reached out and with care stroked the top of the baby's head. 'Look, Pat,' she said. 'A baby.'

Pat had been craning his neck to see past the queue, past the doors and into the play space beyond. Anna's voice tore him from his fun imaginings and he looked at the infant with interest.

He looked at Anna. Then at me. Then his mind whirred back to the conversation we'd had the previous evening.

'Wow. Your vagina must be huge,' he said to the woman with evident admiration.

It was a late spring morning when Anna uttered the immortal words. Strong sunlight framed the curtains and birds competed outside for the highest decibel count of the year so far. Anna was on her side, facing me. She prodded my shoulder. I turned to face her, rubbing sleep from my eyes.

'Andy, I'm all wet.' There was a glint in her eye. A look of suppressed excitement.

'Wet? What do you mean wet?' Sleep was pushed aside like a weightless quilt as I propped myself up on a pillow.

'Wet, you know, wet. Down there.'

'Is it your waters?' I was now fully alert but keeping my voice calm and even.

'Well people tend not to leak indiscriminately. So I've either peed myself or my waters have broken,' she said. 'Could you phone the midwife for me?'

'Sure.' I jumped out of bed, paused and looked over my shoulder, 'Mind you, the midwife did say that she'd rather speak to the mother, to save her having a three-way conversation.' Anna struggled to push herself up from the bed.

'I'll get the phone, you lie there.' I said.

Instructions from the midwife were simple: go straight to hospital. Once the waters had broken there was a risk of infection, Anna reminded me, having momentarily forgotten herself.

'Bring a glass of water and let's make a detour into Mothercare,' she grinned.

'Eh?'

'Any expectant mothers who break their waters in the shop get all sort of goodies.'

'Aye, like a slap on the chops for ruining their good carpets,' I said.

We laughed, it sounded good, helped to stem the flight of nerves that were beginning to build up momentum in my stomach.

'My bag is already packed: nightie, breast pads, disposable knickers, extra-large sanitary towels, the lot.'

'Extra-large what?' I asked wondering how women seemed to automatically know about these things. I hadn't missed any of the ante-natal classes and not once did they mention sanitary towels. Did the women hold a mini-conference in the loos? I strained my memory for similar details from when Pat was born. Remembered the crash cart being brought into the maternity ward. Being thrown out into the corridor while the medical staff fought to save her life. I beat a hasty mental retreat. That was a place I did not want to go.

'Don't ask. Conjures up too many painful pictures. Let's go. I'm desperate to get rid of this lump.' Anna struggled straight-backed to push herself off the chair that she was sitting on. 'Bet it's a bloody boy, all the grief that it's given me over the last nine months.'

'Talking about boys, I'd better phone Mum, see if she can take Pat,' I said. 'I hope she's not got something arranged.'

I needn't have worried, Mum was on stand-by.

The drive to the hospital was relatively calm and I even managed to stay within the speed limit.

'Any contractions yet?' I asked as I drove.

'No.'

'Sure?'

'Yes I'm bloody sure.'

'Fine, just asking, sweetheart.'

'You've "just asked" about a dozen times.' She looked over at me. 'Just you concentrate on the road, Andy Boyd.'

We were ushered into a small room with one bed and various

implements dotted around the space. Implements that I imagined would not have looked out of place in a twenty-first century version of the Spanish Inquisition. Anna calmly lay on the bed and let her head sink into the pile of pillows.

She looked over at me. Read the pale of my skin and reached for my hand. Thoughts of the last time I was present at a birth rushed to fill my mind. Please, God, let everything be ok.

'It will be fine, Andy. Relax.'

'Shouldn't I be the one reassuring you?' I somehow managed a smile.

Patricia died. The same thing couldn't happen to Anna.

Two nurses then bustled into the room and while one took Anna's details the other attached her to a blood-pressure monitor. They applied a gel to her abdomen and took a scan. Due to work commitments and the fact that Anna hadn't wanted me there I had not been present during the previous scans and I was fascinated by the black-and-white screen and the life pulsing within its lines. So much so that I almost missed the ensuing conversation.

'So, you're about two weeks early?' one of the nurses said.

'No,' Anna said with a firmness that was at odds with the question. 'I'm late, I'm bloody late.'

'Anna, calm down, love.' I held her hand, making every attempt to hide my surprise at her outburst.

'It was always the same when I went for the scans. Bloody NHS doesn't know what's going on.'

The two nurses looked at one another and shrugged. The shorter one smiled at me and smoothed down the front of her uniform.

'Whatever it is, it's about to be born,' she said.

'Fine,' Anna said. 'But I'm not early, I'm late.' I turned away determinedly from any thought that the tone she used was anything like that which had preceded her rages.

Things then happened in a blur. Without me noticing, the room was suddenly full of people. A midwife was introduced to us. Names thrown at us in an effort to suggest normality, which I'm sure felt anything but to Anna, whose legs were thrust apart and her feet placed on stirrups.

Hospital staff bustled. Anna screamed and panted and sweated and squeezed every cell of blood from my hand. The next two hours passed in a haze and were only brought into sharp focus by the sweetest sound: a baby crying in protest at being torn from the warmth and relative dark of its mother's womb. The pressure on my hand eased as Anna finally relaxed and I sat down. While waving my hand about in an attempt to restore the circulation, I craned my neck for a glimpse of our new baby, who was being cleaned up, and fingers and toes counted.

'You okay?' the midwife asked me.

Emotion robbed me of speech and I could only nod.

'So, what are you guys going to call your son?' she asked.

BOOK TWO

1

Several voices were tunelessly, but happily raised in song.

'Happy Birthday, dear Ryan,
Happy Birthday to you,
Hip, hip, hooray,
Hip, hip, hooray.'

The Birthday Boy himself, perched in my arms, looked around at the smiling faces. The light in his eyes danced with pleasure at being the centre of attention, although he didn't quite understand why.

'Presents, presents,' he chirped in my ear.

'That's right, son. You've got lots of presents,' I parroted.

'Cake, cake.' A chubby finger pointed.

'Yes, that's right, son. And what's that on top of it?' I asked while stretching out my smile for the benefit of the video camera that was hanging only feet from my face.

''s a candle,' Ryan said proudly. I mouthed 'Piss off' at Jim, who had been walking around with the camera all afternoon. Looking for a moment that could earn him some cash if sold to a TV programme, he informed me with a mercenary smile.

'And what number does the candle say?' I asked Ryan, colluding with Jim but with a different aim in mind. I wanted to be able to show this video to Ryan when he was a teenager and have a laugh with him.

'Two,' he said after some prompting from his brother.

When I say prompting, Pat was actually standing on a chair, his face inches from Ryan's, shouting at the top of his voice. 'Two, two,' he was roaring. Then he looked at Anna and me. 'Ryan's stupid,' he said.

Everyone laughed.

'Time to blow out the candle, sweetheart,' said Anna.

'Fire, fire,' chanted Ryan.

'You were never this cute, Andy,' said Jim. At last he had the camera down and was holding Pat's head under his arm in a wrestling grip. Pat was helpless with giggles.

'You go and jump on the bouncy castle with Pat, Jim. See if you can get rid of some of his energy.' I suggested.

We were in Kidz Play and had commandeered a row of tables for Ryan's party. We had invited some of the children from Ryan's mothers and toddlers group or there would have been more adults that kids.

An assortment of parents hung around the tables and tried to get to know everyone else. A little girl caught my eye. She had very fine, shoulder-length hair and an expression of constant surprise, her eyebrows almost meeting her hairline. Dressed in head-to-toe pink, she charged after a boy who had dared to jump in her plastic car when she wasn't looking. Anna noticed the direction of my eyes.

'Wee cutie,' she said.

'That's a bonny wee thing,' agreed my mother.

'Would you do me a favour, Mum, and make sure that everyone has a piece of cake?'

One of the mothers homed in on the offering. 'Was on a diet,' she said. 'But I always end up fatter at the end than I was at the beginning.'

'Been there,' I admitted. Weight had piled itself on my midriff in the last couple of years. It never seemed to shift. I patted my belly. 'Oh well,' I said. 'Doesn't make you a bad person.'

'Have you been in the wars?' the man at her side asked, motioning towards my eye. He was the first of our guests to mention it.

'Kind of,' I smiled while pretending to look around for my sons. 'Slipped coming out of the shower.'

I turned and made my way over to another couple. While doing so I noted that Anna had taken over Jim's job with the camera, Mum was having a quiet moment with a cup of coffee and Jim, Pat and Ryan were nowhere to be seen.

*

Our two hours were soon up. People started gathering their children and making to leave.

'You okay, son?' Mum was behind me as I walked to the car laden with presents.

'Aye, fine.'

'You're getting clumsy in your old age.' She looked at my bruised eye.

'I know, felt so stupid when I did it. Some of the bank's customers have been giving me some odd looks through the week.'

'You'd tell me if there was something wrong, wouldn't you?'

'Course I would. Anyway what's all this about? I'm fine.' I struggled to contain the irritation in my voice.

'Okay, okay. You're fine,' Mum said. 'Just letting you know that you can come to me.' She walked away. Anna joined me.

'What was all that about?'

'Mum just wanted to make sure that I was okay.'

'It's your son's birthday party. Why wouldn't you be okay?' Anna screwed her eyes up.

I shrugged and pulled her into a hug. She rested her head on my shoulder and then stretched up to kiss my cheek.

'My big handsome man,' she said. 'Love you, baby.'

'Happy with how it's turned out?' I asked.

'Yeah,' she said, touching my arm and looking around the place with a smile. 'Pat's having a great time and Ryan's done nothing but smile all afternoon.' She slipped one palm off the other. 'Job's a good 'un.'

'Yeah,' I said, pleased with how much fun the boys were having. I smiled and as my cheek bunched up I felt the swelling and ache under my right eye. 'Let's scrape Pat and Ryan off the ceiling before Jim completely wears them out.' I said.

A boot full of presents and with Ryan fast asleep in his chair, we drove the short journey home.

After all the excitement Ryan was changed into his pyjamas. His head lolled against my chest. Try as he might he could not keep his eyes open. Pat, on the other hand, was wide awake.

'Do I always have to go to bed at the same time as a two-year-old?' he protested. His forehead furrowed with resentment. 'I don't want to go to bed yet.'

'Now, Pat, don't…' I began, trying to reason with him.

'Tough!' Anna held the collar of his pyjamas and started to march towards the stairs. 'Bed.'

Pat knew not to argue with her when she was in this sort of mood and with his head hanging like a cow's as it moved towards the abattoir, he dragged his feet up the stairs.

Anna followed him, 'I'll just tuck you up.'

'Night, Dad,' his flat voice floated down to me.

'Night, son,' I replied and walked into the kitchen to see what I could have to eat. My stomach was protesting that all I had eaten all day was sandwiches, sausage rolls and birthday cake. A bowl of cornflakes would go down a treat, I decided, and, placing a bowl on the worktop, I reached up to a cupboard and pulled out the box. A rush of air cooled my ear and a cup crashed the cupboard door shut. Pieces of crockery fell to the worktop. I spun round.

'Who the fuck do you think you are?' Anna stood at the kitchen door with her fists planted on her hips.

'Anna. What the…?'

'Don't you ever contradict me again.' Her eyes were huge and the muscles in her jaws pulsed dangerously.

She reached for another cup. I ducked. A shard from the cup bounced off the door and just missed my nose.

'If I say we are not going, then we are not going.' Her voice was all the more chilling when she spoke this quietly. I preferred when her rage was loud.

'Okay,' I answered, not sure what she was talking about.

'That fat couple asking us to the party for their fat son. Not happening.'

'Fine,' I said. I was struggling to place this conversation. Couldn't recall anyone inviting us to a party. As I did this my feet were wide apart and I was on my toes trying to judge where I should move next. 'Fine,' I repeated. Noticing that the lay of her jaw had softened, I straightened my back from the protective half-crouch I had adopted.

'Just ask me about these things first,' said Anna, her mouth now spreading into a smile, 'You know how shy I am. All I ask is that you consult me before making any arrangements. Okay honey?' She turned and walked out of the room as if we had just cheerfully discussed what to give Pat in his lunchbox.

Sweeping the shattered cups into the bin, I reflected on the events of the last two years. Other than the first month after Ryan was born, despite all the promises, the tears, the protestations of love, Anna still hadn't managed to control her rages. Now, however, leaving her or throwing her out were so far out of the question, they weren't even in the quiz book. The Marriage Guidance Counsellor had never even merited a second mention.

Trying to second guess what would set her off was difficult in the extreme. Interpreting what she wanted was nigh on impossible. To say that her mood swings were erratic would be like saying hyenas have a tendency to scavenge. From one hour to the next I never knew what to expect. Something that would spark that dangerous light in her eye one day would raise a smile the next. No longer hungry, I put the cereal bowl back in its place and the cornflakes back in the cupboard. With elbows on the cool surface of the worktop, I placed my head in my hands. I was so tired. Moving my head up and down, I rubbed at my forehead with my fingers. What choices did I have? I couldn't see any. I would just have to make my life as easy as possible amidst the difficulty. Try to keep Anna sweet, while making sure that the boys were okay.

As long as they were not being ill-treated I could put up with anything.

About a week later I received a call from Jim. Before Anna and I reconciled, Jim and I spoke every other day. These days, we were lucky if it was once a month. And I had no idea how we had fallen out of that habit.

Yes I did. Anna's look of displeasure when the phone rang. The huffs and sighs. The nips and punches that followed. It became easier just to let the phone ring out. Eventually Jim got the message and tried less and less often.

'Fancy going out for a pint, big guy?' he asked. His voice was bright.

'Eh…' I stalled, looking over at Anna.

'Don't knock me back again, Andy. I've phoned you regularly over the last I don't know how many months. Say yes. You must need a night out.'

Guilt sat heavily in my stomach. I knew I was neglecting my family. Mum was kind enough never to mention it, but I didn't want them even to detect a hint of what my life was really like. He was right, I thought, desperately trying to ignore the surge of acid in my stomach, I did need a night out. I would just have to deal with Anna's mood later.

'Right, you're on. Where and when?' I quickly asked before I could change my mind.

'Yeah?' asked Jim, surprise heightening the pitch of his voice. 'I don't know, you tell me.'

'How about tomorrow lunchtime?' My resolve was weakening and I was trying to think of a way of seeing Jim without annoying Anna.

'Lunchtime? Naw, we're male, Scottish and I would like to have a good chat with you. Alcohol is therefore a prerequisite, big man. Tomorrow night. I'll see you at seven-thirty in Bridges.' He hung up before I could say anything.

I put the phone down and looked over at Anna. She was sitting on the settee with her feet curled under her, watching one of the soaps on TV.

'What was Jim wanting?' Her eyes didn't move from the flickering screen.

'Nothing,' I answered, wondering what I was going to tell her. Don't be pathetic, I told myself. She's your wife, you shouldn't be this afraid of her.

'Actually, he wants to have a word with me. Sounded like something important.' I pretended to watch events unfold on the screen, thinking that a lie might help the situation.

'Yeah?' Anna asked casually, her tone requesting further information.

'Yeah, no idea what it was. He wouldn't say. Only that he wanted to tell me over a pint. Tomorrow night.' I leaned back and waited for a reaction.

'Good,' she said as the character on screen walked away from his tearful wife. 'You guys should see more of each other. Be sure and tell him I was asking for him.'

The remainder of that night passed by without incident, we even made love before going to sleep.

Work the next day, however, was not quite so calm. Three separate customers came into the branch to complain that unauthorised withdrawals had been made from their accounts. Each of them was for ten pounds. Sheila Hunter – who had done so well since her rehabilitation from her abusive husband, she was now Head of Personal Accounts – presented me with the facts.

'It's weird,' she said, looking down at me as I sat behind my desk. Paper was piled before me. 'Three unrelated people come in on the same day and complain about the same thing.' She stopped speaking. 'Are you okay, Andy?' Her eyes creased with concern.

'Yeah, yeah. Why do you ask?' I smiled. Realising my smile was too big, I adjusted it, somewhat self-consciously.

'Don't know. You just reminded me … oh it's nothing. You just look tired.' She held her folder up against her chest and looked as if she was suppressing a shiver.

'So…' I needed to draw the conversation away from me, ' … have you checked the paper entries that relate to the complaints?'

'Not yet, thought I should let you know first. I'll get Malcolm to look into it.'

'Fine, tell him to let me know what he comes up with.'

As she left the room my eyes followed her out. She was one lovely woman. Roy Campbell was sitting across from me.

'No fraternising with the staff, Boyd.' He pointed his pen at me.

'What?' I asked all innocence.

'I saw the way you looked at her.'

'Nothing wrong with window shopping. Besides, I'm a married man. A quick knee-trembler wouldn't be worth the risks.'

'Hasn't stopped me,' Roy said with a smirk.

'Yeah, right,' I said under my breath. 'In your dreams.'

'What was that, Andy?' he asked. I jumped, wary of a confrontation.

'I was just complaining,' I said just a little louder. 'I have reams and reams of paperwork here.'

'Oh.' Not quite hearing what I said, but too proud to admit it, Roy went back to his work. Staring into the screen of my computer I wondered when I had become so mousy. I used to love getting a rise out of Roy, and here I was frightened in case he heard what I was saying.

Late in the afternoon, Sheila popped her head back in the door.

'Andy, you'd better come and see this customer.'

'What is it?' I asked, mentally cursing all customers. I had too much to do without this.

'It's Mrs More.'

'Oh.' Mrs More was one of our high net worth customers. To make matters worse she was the widow of a former bank manager. When she barked, and bark she did, we jumped, through paraffin-sodden hoops if need be.

She stood at the reception desk, feet planted shoulder-width apart, ready for battle. Close up, powder gathered in the creases of her skin and lipstick outgrew the seared, thin line of her lips.

'Mr Boyd.' Her voice soared in the banking hall. 'I have a complaint.'

At the magic words every other customer and quite a few of the staff stopped what they were doing and looked over. I was amazed to feel heat rise in my face.

'What can I do for you?' I tried to ignore the flush in my skin and to appear calm under the approaching onslaught. Mrs More and I had had several 'discussions' over the years and I liked to think that she respected me because I didn't immediately back down, as everyone else she came across undoubtedly did.

'You can tell me what the blazes is going on!' She banged the steel pin at the end of her umbrella on the floor for emphasis and with the other hand waved a bank statement under my nose. 'There is an entry in my statement for ten pounds, one that I have not authorised. My husband told me that banks often make mistakes. And he was right.'

'Erm, let me see.' Under the guise of examining the piece of paper she handed to me I attempted to restore my calm. I couldn't believe that I would suddenly fold under pressure from this woman. 'Erm … there's no reference against the entry … I'll … eh … have to…'

'Stop stuttering, man and tell me what is going on.' Deep lines grew straight up from her top lip as if someone had tried to draw in an extra set of teeth while she slept. Sheila, who had been standing by my side, entered the conversation.

'Would you like to come through to the office? I'll give you a seat and a coffee while we look into this.'

'Cream and one sugar,' Mrs More said, chin thrust forward.

While Sheila mollified Mrs More I went through to what was fondly known as The Machine Room, to find out what Malcolm had discovered. From the name of the room, it would seem that it was wall-to-wall machines; instead there was only one, plus a postage-franking machine. Here, Malcolm was bent over a desk, with several towers of pink dockets in front of him. He looked up and saw me approaching.

'Hey, Andy. Looks like some people have been charged in error for items held in our safe.'

I handed him the statement. 'Find out if Mrs More is one of them,' I said.

She was. And after eating several of our bourbons and recounting to Sheila for over an hour what it was like to be married to a bank manager, Mrs More declared herself happy that she was being refunded with the errant amount.

'Thanks for dealing with that.' I caught Sheila by the arm before we both went back to our respective desks.

'Oh, that's fine. She's really just a very lonely old woman. Needs someone to talk to.'

'Well, thanks again.' I turned and walked into my office. Berating myself as I walked. What the hell was wrong with me? I used to have Mrs More eating out of my hand. I could feel Sheila's eyes follow me. I was sure that if I turned and stepped back out of the room, she would still be there. Her eyes bright with a knowing look.

2

When I walked into Bridges that night, Jim was standing at the bar with a full pint moving towards his mouth. Eyes heavy-lidded with expectation, he opened his mouth. I reached him and slapped him firmly on the back.

'You bastard,' he spluttered and wiped the foam from his nose with his sleeve.

'Hey, nice to see you too, bro,' I said with faked heartiness.

'A pint?' he asked.

I nodded. 'Would be rude not to.'

'Damn right.' Jim smiled at the barman and ordered my drink.

After taking a large mouthful of beer each we moved over to a seat.

'What's fresh?' asked Jim.

'Nothin'.'

'How's work?'

'Fine.'

'How are the boys?'

'Fine, fine.'

'Christ, this is like drawing teeth. Have you given up speaking in long sentences for Lent or something?'

'No. You need to let me get warmed up,' I smiled. 'I'm a Scottish male, I need more than one mouthful of beer to enter into a conversation.'

'Very funny.'

'Besides, your questioning technique is crap. You need to ask me open questions. Questions that will make me give long, detailed answers.'

He thought for a moment. 'Tell me how work is, how the boys are and what's fresh.'

'Fine, fine and nothin' much.'

'Piss off, ya prick.'

We both laughed. I hid the pleasure I felt at this simple moment by taking another long drink from my glass.

'You hungry?' Jim asked. 'I've had nothing to eat yet and I'm starving.'

'I've had my tea, but if you want to go up the road to that new place in Newmarket Street, I don't mind sitting with a drink while you stuff your face.'

'Good man.' Jim slapped me on the back, aiming to get me with my face close to the glass, in retaliation for my earlier joke. He mistimed and I successfully negotiated a sip.

Soon we were seated in The Wine Bar with Jim's face shoved into the menu; mine was hovering over another pint.

'I hate eating on my own,' said Jim. 'Do you not fancy joining me?'

'What're you havin'?'

'Lasagne, probably … and some garlic bread.'

'Order me some garlic bread.'

'Are you sure?' asked Jim, his voice full of sarcasm. 'We wouldn't want you getting too heavy now.'

'Aye, okay. I'm a skinny bastard.' I faked a laugh.

'You're letting yourself go, mate.' He looked down at my stomach stretching at the fabric of my shirt. He was right. In my rugby-playing days I would never have let this happen.

I didn't want Jim to question my lack of condition any further, so I changed the subject. 'So, tell me about you and Paula. Still in love?'

'What can I say? We still fuck like rabbits.'

I paused theatrically before I spoke. 'Do rabbits use vibrators and watch pornos?'

He had the good grace to smile, but only because the waitress was standing at my shoulder. With my face going a delicate shade of pink I turned to face her. She was smiling too.

'Eh, sorry about that,' I managed to say.

'Don't worry about it. I hear a lot worse in this job.'

I took the opportunity of the conversation to appraise her, while trying not to look like a lecherous old man. She must have only been about nineteen. Her skin was luminous with health and youth, her eyes shone with intelligence and her uniform strained in just the right places.

'What will it be, gents?' Her pen was poised above her pad.

'I'll have the lasagne with garlic bread,' said Jim, his eyes frank in his appraisal.

I moved my eyes back to the menu, suddenly ashamed of my thoughts and hoping that the girl was not uncomfortable under our gaze.

'I'll have the same,' I said. forgetting that my intention was only to go with the bread.

She wrote '× 2' on her pad, smiled and made as if to walk away.

'I haven't seen you here before,' said Jim.

'Just started last week,' she replied and crossed her arms.

'Things are looking up,' said Jim and flashed his best smile. 'I'll need to come in here more often if they're employing girls as gorgeous as you.'

Her smile in reply was her best I'm-just-being-polite-to-the-punters version.

'She seems a really nice girl,' I said when she was out of earshot.

'She seems like a really nice girl.' Jim mimicked me with a clichéd gay voice. 'God, if that's what marrying does to you, I'm going to stay single. She was fucking gorgeous.'

'The problem is, she thinks we're a pair of old wankers.'

'Speak for yourself, bro. If I wasn't shacked up with Paula, I'd be right in there.' His confidence was unaffected by my comment.

Soon our waitress was back with our food. The lasagne was just the way I like it. Plenty of meat and not too much sauce.

'So what are the boys up to?' asked Jim while chewing on a mouthful.

'Pat has gone ga-ga over Star Wars,' – this was a safe subject – 'and Ryan' – I loved talking about my boys – 'demands that we watch the Teletubbies every day.' From the moment that I began to work with the public I realised that one sure way to seem like a nice guy was to ask people about their kids. They were bound to be their pride and joy. I was no different from anyone else and would bore people into a religious retreat given half a chance.

'And Anna? How's she?'

'Och, you know, gets fed up being at home all day.'

'Who wouldn't?'

'Yeah, it's not easy.'

'Mum's asking for you. When was the last time you saw her?'

'Don't start, Jim.' I was instantly on the defensive. 'I'm busy, all right.'

'Just asking, bro, just asking. You get married, Ryan comes along and suddenly we hardly see you. I mean, over the last two years I can count the number of occasions we've been out together on two hands. Used to be we were never apart. What's happening, Andy?' I could see he had been itching to say this all night. Probably for a lot longer than that.

'Nothing's happening, Jim.' I fidgeted with the salt dish. 'I've a lot on, two kids and a demanding job.' An image of a furious Anna flashed in my mind. I flinched at an imaginary blow.

'I could handle it' – he grinned – 'if I never saw your ugly dish again. It's Mum, she misses you and the boys. Ryan's birthday was the first time that she'd seen you all since Christmas.' He looked deep into my eyes, trying to read my expression.

He wasn't being accusatory, was just full of genuine concern. I felt like shit. But I couldn't tell him the truth. I couldn't tell him that every time I saw him or my mum, Anna and I would fight and I would end up with several bruises. Even a phone call could be enough of a spark. I missed Jim and Mum, but it was far easier for all concerned if I pleased Anna. The boys wouldn't have to listen to us screaming at one another if I kept my contact with my family to a minimum. Anna had agreed that I should go out with Jim tonight, but I was sure that the ferryman would take his toll later on. Her good intentions were bound to evaporate under the heat of her insecurities. As I sat eating, I knew that she would be pacing up and down the living room, wild thoughts populating her brain.

'I'll make more of an effort, Jim. I will.'

'So you'll go and see Mum?'

'Yes, and I'll take the boys.' And then I'll pop a few arnica pills for the resultant bruising.

'Mum thinks that you and Anna aren't happy and that's why you're keeping your distance. In case we get wind of what's going on.'

Startled by the accuracy of this statement, I gave a laugh that sounded weak even to my ears. 'Tell Mum not to be silly, Anna and I are fine.'

Just then the waitress came over to remove our dirty plates.

'Can I get you guys a dessert?' she asked.

'No thanks,' I said.

'No,' said Jim, 'I'm sweet enough.'

'I take it you don't want cheese either then?' she asked with raised eyebrows. I slapped my hand on the table and laughed, impressed by her quick mind. Jim joined in, acknowledging the waitress's wit with a large smile.

'You must get a lot of tossers in here,' he said.

'Goes with the job,' she grinned.

After we'd eaten, we decanted down the hill to Billy Bridges, planted our elbows on the bar and set about a few more pints. A few hours later, feeling pleasantly pissed, we left the bar and ambled down towards the bridge, where Jim could make his way to his flat and I could hopefully wave down a passing taxi.

Jim stopped at the bridge and looked over the side, down to the water below. I joined him in peering over the side and realised we were standing just as we had been at the bar, like binge-drinking bookends.

'Wonder how cold that is,' Jim slurred.

I bent down, reached for his right leg and pulled up. 'Why don't you go see?' My head was spinning too much to put more effort into the joke, so I released him.

He cuffed me across the back of the head. 'Funny guy.'

I stuck my tongue out and resumed my earlier position, with elbows on the cool brick.

'Water's low tonight,' I said.

'Yeah. There's not been much rain recently.'

I laughed. 'Listen to us. Pair of wankers.'

Jim snorted a laugh. 'Yeah, the Boyd brothers and the art of conversation.'

Silence settled over us again. The night air, sailing in on the coastal breeze, was a salty, balmy caress across my face and the back of my neck. Far below, the dark slick of fresh water was about to merge with the sea just beyond.

Jim turned and leaned his back against the bridge wall.

'You happy, brother?'

I turned to him, surprised at the question. Jim and I had always been close. But it was a closeness born of a shared experience and of the certainty in our affection for each other. We didn't share feelings very often, nor did either examine his navel in the presence of the other. And if we did, it was at the wrong end of a drinking session when we were fairly sure the other would never remember what we said.

My stomach gave a lurch. Did he know something? Was the acrimony between Anna and me evident? Was Mum in on his concern?

My answering smile started as fake, but then I thought of my sons. 'After what happened to Patricia, sometimes I feel like the luckiest man in the country.'

'I envy you, Andy,' he said and studied his hands as if unsure how his honesty would be received.

I fought back an automatic, sarcastic response. 'You've got a good life, bro,' I said at last.

'Looks like it, eh?'

I said nothing, leaving him a silence that he could fill himself. Or not.

'It's all a bit empty. I've got a nice flat, all the clothes I could want, a nice car … But I'd swap it all in a heartbeat for what you've got.' He smiled into the distance. 'Those two wee boys? I'd do anything for them, bro. Love them to bits.'

I felt the heat of my love for the boys build in my chest and swell in my throat. I coughed, pushed the emotion down. If I let it rise there was no telling how this conversation would end.

Then.

'Bullshit,' I said. 'Jim Boyd the mad-shagger wants a life of domesticity?'

He turned back around and faced the water. Looked into the distance where the river flowed into the Firth of Clyde. When I started work in the bank in the early eighties, this area was a fishing port that bustled with hard-working men intent on nothing more than a good life for their families and a wee drink or two with their mates. While others in the houses around them were waking to the sound of their alarm clock, they'd have finished a three-day stretch out in open water and would celebrate the fact that their wallets were full of cash and their lungs empty of seawater with a pint and a whisky chaser in any one of the pubs that lined the harbourside.

I looked at Jim's profile and tried to read what was going on in his mind. He was bulkier than me, square jawed with defiance at the world, but I could see the man I saw each morning in the mirror in the cast of his eyes and the thin spread of his nostrils.

'Feels like I'm playing a role, you know? Chase the girls. Buy the latest BMW, spend a couple of grand on a watch…'

'What about Paula? I thought you and her were…'

'Treading water, mate. She says I'm an easy man to fall in love with, but would be a difficult guy to marry.'

'What the hell does that mean?'

'I can see what she means. I've heard it before. I brood, apparently. Go quiet for days…'

'You do?' He couldn't have surprised me more if he said he was into cross-dressing and he had an alter-ego called Desperate Denise.

'Seems I hold back, and women sense that shit.' He offered a shrug to the distance and all the women he was feeling he had let down. He turned to me. Cupped the back of my neck with a strong hand. 'You've got it, mate. Hold on to it for all you're worth.'

By the time I arrived home I had sobered slightly, was weak with the need for sleep, but full of brotherly bonhomie. Jim's words echoed in my mind and I wondered how he would feel if he knew the truth.

The house was quiet. All of the lights were out. Hugging the wall, I climbed the stairs. The boys often played with toys there and I had nearly tripped on them more than a few times.

Flicking the bathroom light on, I used it to illuminate the boys' rooms. Ryan was in his favourite position, on his front, propped up on his knees, his bum sticking up in the air. Pat was on his back, his quilt wrapped around his legs. Both of them were in a deep sleep. Standing over each of them in turn I was amazed at what I had helped produce. They were breathtakingly beautiful. Did every parent think that of his child? Tenderness for each of them almost brought tears to my eyes as I lightly ran the back of a finger over two small foreheads. They were worth everything that I was going through. They kept me coming back for more and I couldn't bear to contemplate life without them.

A shadow blocked some of the light from the bathroom. A harsh whisper reached me.

'What time do you call this?'

3

The first time Pat called Anna 'Mum' was a moment I didn't think either of us would ever forget. For all her faults, Anna loved both of the boys and did her best not to favour her own child. Pat eventually allowed himself to reciprocate.

Perhaps Pat became tired explaining to people that Anna was his dad's wife, perhaps Pat wanted to feel that, as a family, we were complete. Whatever his reason, he slipped the word into a conversation so casually it felt like he'd never used any other name for her.

Just the day before, he asked me if he could look at some photographs of his mum. They were hidden in the loft, I didn't quite trust Anna not to do something with them when she was in a mood.

With his little body perched on my knee, my cheek resting on his soft, apple-smelling hair, we ventured into the past. The dim light and the way the ceiling angled down to the floor added a special flavour to the photographs and the stories. This was our space. This was where Pat and I could have some time on our own.

Our journeys up to the loft were frowned upon by Anna. Not because she felt that Ryan was being left out, but because any place that held the threat of a spider was to be avoided. This of course made this small, bare room the ideal place to store such memorabilia.

As soon as he was aware of the difference between him and other children, Pat was hungry for details of his mother.

'Other boys and girls have mums,' he told me one day. 'Why can't you be a mum?'

'Then who would be your dad?' I asked attempting to work with a child's logic.

There was a stage that lasted for about three months. He could not go to sleep until I told him stories about his mother. Stories that would have made little sense to a three- or four-year-old, but stories that were punctuated with the words 'your mum'. Two magic syllables that could make his life complete.

All of the photos we looked at were well thumbed, some even wore chocolate and jam stains like medals. Each of them came with a story that Pat, by now, knew by heart. Nonetheless he insisted I tell them all over again.

After I completed my repertoire Pat turned his gaze on me.

'Mummy's watching me, isn't she, Dad?'

'Of course she is, son.'

'Do you think she likes Anna?'

'I'm sure she does,' I answered. So far I had managed to keep the reality of my relationship with Anna from Pat. Pride was a factor in this, but I also wanted him to feel secure within our little family.

We were eating breakfast when he said it. Ryan was in his highchair chanting, 'Mummy do it, Mummy do it,' meaning that he wanted Anna to spoon him his Weetabix. Normally, no one could 'do it' but Ryan himself.

Pat sat down in his chair and poured some Sugar Puffs into a bowl.

'Could I have the milk, Mum?' he said.

Anna opened her mouth as if to say something, left it hanging open and pushed the milk over to Pat. Without looking at her, he spooned the cereal into his mouth like it was the last plateful on the planet. Anna's eyes were large and bright with moisture as they met mine. Her smile of joy threatened to spill completely over into tears. She leaned forward and kissed Pat on the head.

It was moments like this that I clung to, evidence of her vulnerability that I thrust to the front of my mind whenever Anna bore down on me.

'I said, what fucking time is this to be coming home?' Anna's whisper was now a low growl.

Without even looking at her, I walked past her into our bedroom. She chased after me, feet drumming on the carpet.

Thrusting her chin up at me she said, 'Well?'

'Well, nothing.' I stood in front of her. The last argument we had I had cowed down to her in an attempt to see if passive behaviour would deflect her fury. It didn't. Tonight I would give as good, verbally, as I got.

'You useless prick. You leave me all night with the boys and then you come in at midnight and expect a smiling wife.'

'I expect nothing, Anna. But a civil wife would be nice.' My alcoholic fog had all but dispersed.

'I'll give you fucking civil.' She ran at me and drove her fist towards my groin. I managed to get my knee up in time.

'Just leave it, Anna.' I pushed her away from me. 'We're both tired. Let's just get some sleep.' I spoke through clenched teeth, trying to keep a hold of my irritation.

'Don't fucking tell me to leave it, you arsehole.' A few more expletives were hurled at me. 'I don't mind if you go out with your precious brother, but I expect you in at a decent hour.'

I began to undress. But I didn't turn away from her. I had learned early on in our marriage that was a foolish thing to do. Wearing only boxers and a t-shirt I padded over to her. Before we got married I always slept in the nude. The night clothes I chose to wear now were a precautionary measure. It kept a further layer between her and my skin.

'You're a liar. You do mind that I go out with Jim. You hate it. You're jealous that I have a decent relationship with my family. That there are people who love me. Who have you got? Nobody, cos you've scared them all off.' I braced myself for her reaction. For a moment there was none. It was the first time that I had ever been so unkind to her. Her stunned expression backed my theory.

She quickly recovered. Her right hand shot up and grabbed a chunk of hair. With a speed that surprised me she tugged my head down towards her. Satisfaction that I had obviously stung her alleviated the pain that crowded the back of my head.

'Ya big bastard,' she spat. Her other hand raked at my face.

I pushed her away from me, lost my balance and fell onto the bed. She jumped on me. Her knees drove into the small of my back while her fists flailed at my back, neck and head.

'Get off me you mad bitch,' I shouted. Until now, concern that we would wake the boys had quietened my voice. This was too painful. 'Get off.' I pushed up off the bed, throwing Anna from my back.

I heard her fall onto the floor. She grunted. Then her voice took on a pitiful whine.

'Andy, I've hurt my back.'

Guilt punched anger out of the way and feeling that I had gone too far I leaned over the bed to see if she was alright.

'Wanker!' she laughed, and drove a fist into my face. Her blow caught me on the chin. I fell back but managed to keep my balance.

'I had two brothers,' she crowed. 'I learned every trick in the book.'

My fists clenched inadvertently by my side as I took a step towards her. One punch and I could take her out. She read the furious look on my face.

'Just try it big boy,' she said defiantly. 'The police will be down here sooner than you can pack an overnight bag.'

I knew she was right. Any violence on my part would result in me being locked up. God knew what would happen to the boys then. Or even my job. I would be labelled a wife-beater and I was sure the bank would take a dim view of that. I slunk out of the room, fully expecting my turned back to become a target of more blows.

In the bathroom, I examined the welts on my face. They had begun to smart. My chin was only faintly bruised. Fortunately Anna's nails had not broken the skin. So I would only have to explain away some red lines instead of scabs.

Her fist slammed into my right kidney.

'I haven't finished with you yet.' She was beside me. Her eyes those of a stranger, her nostrils flared and her mouth drawn in a tight, white line of hate.

I screwed my eyes shut against the pain that blossomed in the small of my back. How long would this go on for? How long could I take it before I hit back? What sort of damage would I do once I started?

'Daddy.' Pat appeared at his door, rubbing sleep from his eyes. 'What's happening?'

'Nothing, son.' I brushed past Anna. 'C'mon, we'll take you back to bed.'

'But you and Mum are shouting. We don't like it when you shout.' He was wearing his Darth Vader pyjamas.

'Mummy and I are fine, just you go back to bed.' I patted his behind and led him back to bed.

Closing his door, I turned to face Anna, fury simmering in her expression. She followed me into our bedroom, punching at my kidneys as we walked. The only ploy available to me now was to pretend she was having no effect. Teeth clenched in pain I walked to the wardrobe. I plucked my coat from its hanger, a thick wool coat that Patricia had bought me the Christmas before she died. It would keep me warm as I slept on the couch

'Where the fuck are you going?' demanded Anna.

'I'm going to get some sleep. On the couch.'

'That's what you think.' She ran out of the room.

Kicking my feet into my slippers I followed her. When I walked into the living room she was pouring the contents of the kettle over the couch. She faced me and almost purred with satisfaction.

'So where are you going to sleep now?'

'Fuck you, you mad, sad, bitch.' I drove my arms into the sleeves of my coat and walked at a furious pace out the front door.

Huddled against the chill night air, I don't know how long I walked for, my mind chanting 'bitch, bitch, bitch' until the word lost meaning.

What the hell was I doing? I had allowed a woman half my size to chase me out of my own home.

What kind of a man was I?

As I passed a shop door, it opened and the shopkeeper propped an advertising board for a newspaper against the wall. He looked at me as if he recognised me. Smiled and then went back inside. It was already morning.

Eventually – I have no idea how long I was walking for – I returned to the house. Anna had obviously fallen asleep waiting for me. She was in the armchair. The quilt from our bed was pulled up tight under her chin. Her pale cheeks looked scarred – streaks of mascara showed where furious tears had flowed from her eyes.

As I stood there, I imagined my hands around her throat. Felt the thrill of revenge as her imagined face turned red and she fought for breath. With Anna dead we could get back to a normal family life. I'd get some sleep. Wouldn't be woken up in the middle of the night with her knees kicking into my kidneys, her nails tearing into the back of my neck.

My boys wouldn't grow up to accept violence; to see their father as a bent and broken man.

Then I saw Anna at my feet with staring eyes, as still as the grave.

I almost bent over with the horror of the thought. My breath caught. My gut torched with the pain of it.

Despite everything, I couldn't hurt her.

There had to be another way out of this situation.

If I left Anna, she would certainly get custody of Ryan. All she needed to do was claim I had hit her and she would probably get Pat as well. Then she would deny me access. I knew how petty she was. Concern for the boys would be the last thing on her agenda; pain for me the first. What kind of a mother would she be to the boys without me to deflect her anger? How violent could she be with them? I had to save my two beautiful boys from the fate of being brought up solely by Anna.

Looking down at her sleeping form, I could see nothing of the deep well of anger that could drive her at me for hours on end. All I could see was the small, slight woman I had fallen in love with.

And God help me, I realised standing there, with my muscles slowly thawing, I loved her still.

Dragging myself up the stairs, I looked in on the boys before heading for a shower. They were both stirring from a deep sleep. Planting a kiss on each of their foreheads I vowed once again to protect them.

Hot needles of water offered some refreshment to my tired muscles. I turned away from the shower-head to let the water work its magic on the dull ache in my lower back. My kidneys had taken a bit of a bashing and I was beginning to notice their protest. Arching my back I let the water drum on my flesh. The pain eased only slightly. Perhaps if I peed, that would help. Looking down at my feet I noticed a pink taint in the water. Shit. Blood in urine was not a healthy sign. Anna must have done more damage than I first thought.

At work that day it was all I could do not to flinch each time I moved. Staying alert was also a problem. Thankfully, subsequent visits to the toilet showed no signs of blood. I wouldn't have to try and explain that to a doctor.

That evening, once the boys were safely tucked up in bed, the onslaught began afresh.

Anna waited until we were in bed this time, sleep demanding my full attention.

'Useless prick,' she shouted in my ear.

My eyes felt as if they were glued shut. But her fist slammed into my kidney and they shot open.

'Owww,' I moaned.

'Listen to me, when I'm talking to you, arsehole.' She pulled at my hair.

'No, we are not going through this again.' I climbed on top of her and using my superior weight advantage pinned her arms and legs down. Her teeth flashed dangerously close to my nose. Then she stopped struggling.

'Honey, get off me,' she moaned. 'I can't breathe.'

'Well, I need to sleep. Do you promise to leave me alone?'

A coquettish look appeared on her face. 'Well, that depends.' She pressed her groin up against mine, 'That depends on what comes up.'

'What?' I couldn't believe the change in her. Although I had witnessed her rapid changes of mood before, they never failed to catch me off balance. She continued to rub against me, her fingers stretching under the waistband of my boxers, kneading at my buttocks.

'Ooh,' Anna cooed. 'Somebody is enjoying this.' Her eyes pierced mine. 'You want to fuck me don't you? You want to fuck me till I bleed, don't you.'

I kept my expression blank lest she should discern my distaste at her choice of words. 'No, I don't want to fuck you.'

'Liar,' she smiled with triumph. 'You've never been so hard.'

It was true that the traitor in my groin was showing definite signs of life, but I was far too tired to do anything about it.

'Just let me sleep, Anna. I'm shattered.'

'No way. I want you and I want you now.' Her voice was low, quiet and chilling. The warning was clear in those bright, beautiful eyes.

'Anna.' I tried unsuccessfully to keep the pleading tone from my voice. 'Please. I'm tired.'

She reached under the waistband of my shorts and grabbed my penis. It didn't fill her hand as well as she hoped.

'Get harder.' Her voice was a muted growl.

Her hand began to move. I felt myself harden again, surprisingly quickly. No, I said to myself.

'No,' I said aloud. 'No.' I pushed her away. 'Just leave me alone. I want to sleep.'

'No sleep for Andy until Anna gets her pole,' she chanted in a singsong voice. 'No sleep for Andy.'

'Fine.' I jumped out of bed. 'Then I'll just walk the streets again.'

I was going to make a stand. I was not going to be bullied into having sex. No matter how much she wanted it. Or my Judas prick, for that matter.

As my slipper-clad feet slapped the pavements of Ayr once more, I wondered at my energy, that I could cope with this for another night. As I congratulated myself and considered whether or not my rugby training had given me this much grit and endurance, a question thrust itself to the forefront my mind. Why didn't I just let her fuck me? In every other aspect of our lives she was doing that very thing.

What could I do? How could I get out of this horrible situation?

I thought about how I might react the next time she attacked me. Shook my head as if to disperse the terrible imaginings provided by my mind. Each answer I came up with was discounted until all I could think about was Anna dead at my feet, by my hand.

4

Life at home was becoming more and more of a strain; I had to look for ways to keep my sanity. Anna didn't know what she was doing, I reasoned. She was a victim of her past. I drove her to it. It was *all* my fault.

It was *my* fault.

It *was* my fault.

These were the legends that coursed through my mind. Flames of self-doubt licking hungrily at any suggestion that I might be blameless; that I might have any control.

While at work, there were times that I could barely read the charts and reports in front of me. My brain was disorientated from lack of sleep. I could see the numbers, I could follow the line of figures, but they made as much sense as if they had been written in Sanskrit. All of this made escaping into work futile. Besides, I didn't want to give any clues to my colleagues that things weren't quite what they should be at home. In the past, I had myself participated in office gossip sessions where people questioned the marriages of those who were overly conscientious at work.

The Rugby Club was a contender as a distraction from my problems. But it was ruled out after a suggestion of a night out there received an answer in the form of a knee to the groin. I deserved it. I should have known not to mention the club.

Another woman was definitely not an option. Anna was particularly zealous in checking for signs that I was being unfaithful. I was having enough problems with one woman. Two, was two too many.

The boys were a constant source of joy to me. Their trusting, beautiful faces offered up to mine every day in a rainbow of grins. I would have been lost without them. But I couldn't rely on them to be my rescue party, my cushion against the blows.

I had also begun to realise that my boys were much more aware than I thought possible. They might not have the vocabulary to articulate what they saw and felt, but they might note the tension and translate whatever was going on as their fault. For this reason, I had to try and make their lives as normal as possible. Even if this was at a cost to me.

While I waited for some other possibility to occur to me, I could just go and get pissed.

If I was going to endure a beating anyway, I would be as well as to take it like a drunk. Inebriation would be my anaesthetic. And in my darkest moments I imagined that final irrevocable act.

With a deep, burning shame, and in great detail.

'You look like shit,' Roy Campbell said as he entered my office.

'Thanks,' I muttered. Keeping my head up was using all of my energy. A witty riposte was nowhere near the agenda.

Sheila Hunter walked in with him. I managed a smile when I saw her. What a transformation. One divorce and two promotions later, she continued to look every inch the modern professional. She was now Roy's assistant and handled his particular brand of 'humour' with irony warmed with the suggestion of a smile. She had known a real hard man. Roy Campbell was a pet mouse by comparison.

The smile with which she greeted me had concern laced around the edges. 'Hi, Andy,' she said, the smile turning into a slight frown.

I mumbled something in reply and moved my attention back to my sales figures. A blush heated my ears and I wondered at my discomfiture. Why would a woman I liked and one that I admired make me feel so uncomfortable? Even as I asked, I knew the answer. I envied her composure and her strength. I also wanted to tell her everything that was going on, because I knew that, of everyone I came into contact with, she alone would understand. She alone would be able to offer advice.

But I would never be able to admit to anyone what was happening. What self-esteem I had left was wrapped up in the torn linen of the thought that I at least had the appearance of a strong, confident, capable male.

'We're on our way down to Girvan,' said Roy, 'for a wee inspection.' He rubbed his hands together, no doubt at the thought of catching some poor member of staff out. 'And just thought we'd pop in, say hello.'

'Hello.' I didn't look up from my work.

'How's the family?' he asked.

'Fine.'

'Right … good. Staffing levels okay? Not having too many cash differences?'

I considered these questions for a moment. 'Yes and no.' The truth was that I wasn't sure. I had lost track a little over the previous weeks.

Whatever Roy was, he was no slouch and he had asked these questions for a reason. When he had gone I would make my own enquiries.

'Right, better go. I'll just go to the wee boy's room before we head off.' He left the office.

'You okay, Andy?' Sheila asked, after making sure that Roy was out of earshot.

'Aye, fine.' I met her eyes for as long as it took to blink.

'You sure?'

'Aye … aye. No problems.'

'I should warn you – ' she craned her head to look down the corridor '– we got a complaint at Regional Office that you were coming in, stinking of drink and that you were leaving your work to junior staff.'

'Has no one at Regional heard of delegation?' I bristled.

'Andy, I'm on your side.' Sheila leaned towards me. 'Remember, I've been there.'

These last five syllables were uttered quietly, conspiratorially. Could she know? How? I was hiding it, wasn't I?

'Don't know what you're on about,' I said, more harshly than I intended, while checking that my tie was on straight.

'Sorry. Just thought that I should warn you. Roy's been sent down here to check up on you.'

'Well it's a waste of his fucking time then, isn't it? Cos there's nothing wrong.'

Sheila took a step back, her hands up, palms facing me.

'What's this?' Roy re-entered the room. I caught the look of warning he flashed at Sheila.

'Nothing,' she said with a smile. 'I was just asking Andy about the kids. I'd heard that Ryan was down with chicken pox, and Andy was just telling me that there was nothing wrong with him.'

'Good, excellent,' said Roy, seemingly satisfied with this explanation. 'Terrible thing that for kids. Could be worse; mumps – now, that would get Dad where it hurts.'

'Goodbye, Roy. Got to get on with this.' I pointed at the sheets of paper in front of me.

As soon as they left the room, I buried my head in my hands. Shit. I thought I was keeping up appearances. Everyone must have known what a mess I was in. I always prided myself in keeping a tight team. The fact that I'd driven someone to complain about me made me burn with embarrassment. I would have to get my act together. But I couldn't until I got some sleep.

Sleep. Sleep…

'Andy, Andy.' I was roughly awakened by Malcolm. 'What the fuck are you up to? Sleep for elevenses?'

'Eh … oh … Ryan had nightmares last night.' I surprised myself with that one. I must have been sleeping for about an hour. 'Took me ages to get him back to sleep.'

'I just wanted you to sign this off. Safe Custody charges. I need your initials.'

'Fine.' I took the batch of slips from him and quickly initialled them all. There was quite a bundle of them and Malcolm stood before me quietly as I did as he asked.

'Cheers, boss,' he said as he left the room.

Better get your act together, Boyd, I told myself. Things had obviously gotten pretty bad if Roy Campbell was on the sniff for trouble. Sleep was my solution. I had to do whatever it took for Anna to let me get a good night's sleep.

Short meetings with various members of my staff were able to satisfy me that my rudderless ship was staying on course, thanks to the excellent team I had. But I could discover no clue as to who might have complained about me to Regional Office. The day slipped past quietly, with only a few menial tasks at hand. This afforded me the luxury of a few more cat-naps.

The boys greeted me at the door that night with their customary zeal, each trying to outdo the other. Pat easily reached me first, sending Ryan into a sulk.

'There you go, son.' I gathered him up with my left hand, Pat was perched on the right, 'There's plenty of room for you both.'

I looked for Anna, while acid threatened to scorch my gullet. For the boys' sake I forced some gaiety into my voice. 'Sweetheart, that's me home.'

She appeared at the kitchen door wearing an apron over her jeans with her hair tied back from her face. She blew at a stray lock of hair that tickled her cheek.

'Hi, honey. Tea's nearly ready,' she smiled. This was the first friendly sign I'd had for weeks. 'Boys, give your Dad some peace,' she said. 'Give him a chance to get in the door.'

Although I was more than happy to have the boys climb all over me, I allowed Anna to shoo them away to their toys.

'I'll just get you a cup of tea while I give your steak another couple of minutes under the grill,' she cooed.

A cup of tea? Steak? Anna's mood swings had proven to be mercurial in the past, but this was beating all records. With some trepidation I held my hand out to accept a hot mug of tea. It was offered with a warm smile. I waited for hot liquid to scald my scalp. Instead, hot china filled my palm.

'Thanks,' I said.

'Welcome.'

Emboldened by this gesture I asked, 'Are ... are we okay?'

'Of course, hon.' She leaned forward and kissed my forehead. I disguised my flinch. 'But we do need to talk.' Her eyes shone with affection. 'As soon as the boys are in bed, okay?'

Nodding in agreement, I was temporarily bereft of speech at this turn of events. Anna wanted to talk. Usually anything out-with her comfort zone was added to the large heap under the carpet.

Pat protested that we were putting him to bed a little earlier than normal, but did as he was asked nonetheless.

'Will you read me a story, Dad?' He was going for the usual delay tactic.

'Just a wee one, Pat.' With my mind elsewhere, I raced through part of a tale of a boy and a dragon.

Soon I was downstairs and waiting for Anna to begin.

She sat beside me on the settee. Her small hands seemed to envelop my larger ones.

'Things haven't been too good between us recently and...' Even such a small sentence was like magic. She still loved me. She still needed me.

'Anna, it's okay.' I was almost down on my knees before her. Every muscle in my body sagged with relief. 'It's okay, sweetheart. It's all my fault. If I wasn't so obstinate ... if I wasn't so self-centred...' With every word I brought myself down, with every sentence I accepted the burden of blame. While logic screamed that this was ludicrous, all I could think of was that Anna still loved me. She hadn't actually said so yet, but the mouse that the man had become was nibbling greedily at the smallest morsel of reconciliation offered.

'Don't be so hard on yourself,' Anna offered. 'It's not *all* your fault. You do drive me wild at times.' She punctuated this statement by holding my cheek between finger and thumb and giving it a squeeze. 'But I shouldn't go off the rails like that.' She gathered my head to her breast and I could feel the heat of her face through my scalp.

'I do love you,' she said. Letting me go she looked deep into my eyes. 'Pals?'

If I'd been a dog, my tail would have been lustily sweeping the floor. I nodded.

'Come on.' She stood up. 'Let's go to bed. I've not had my big man for a while.'

After we made love, exhaustion threatened to pull me into a sleep from which I would never wake. I was on the rim of oblivion when Anna spoke.

'Your mother called just before you got in from work.'

'Mmmm.'

'She said to say hello. She was full of questions. She asked how were the boys, how were you, how was I, what had we been up to. Hope you haven't been saying anything to her.'

Several weeks passed in which peace reigned in the Boyd household. Not one word spoken between us came pre-heated with anger. No gesture from Anna even hinted that she was struggling to contain herself. She was quite simply in a good mood.

This truce was evidenced by the carefree behaviour of Pat. Ryan was, of course, too young to take note of any difference, but Pat laughed louder, played harder and smiled much more than he had for months. I was able to charge my depleted 'good-time' battery up for the leaner times to come. Come they would. I was certain of it. Anna had shown too much evidence of lack of control for me to think that in just a matter of weeks she had changed. No, it would take much longer than this before I would let my guard down.

It was one of those late-summer days when nature attempts to make up for the cold weather ahead. Or perhaps she was trying to persuade us that winter would be delayed indefinitely. Whatever her intentions, the garden was a melée of colour and the sun was stout in the sky.

Tanned and smiling, the boys raced around me after a ball. Ryan could hardly run for giggling while Pat egged him on. No doubt he was hoping for a repeat of the previous evening. Ryan had become so excited he fertilised the plants in the border with his dinner.

'Pat,' I warned, 'don't get your brother so het up.'

'Dad…' I am always impressed by how long a child can make that one syllable last. 'We're just havin' a laugh.'

'I'll just have a laugh, my boy.' I picked him up and, holding him tight in my arms, ran round the garden. This of course pushed Ryan's giggles to further heights. Pat joined him in mirth.

'Daaaad.' He stopped giggling to groan. 'Make me stop, it's sore.'

'I'll make you stop alright.' I let him fall to the floor, bent over him, pulled his shirt up and blew raspberries on his stomach. While I was doing this, Ryan, using my outstretched foot as a step, climbed on to my back.

'Me, me, me,' he chanted.

'Happy to oblige.' I pulled him off my back, lay him on top of Pat and went from one soft belly to the next, blowing laughing raspberries.

'Careful, Andy.' Anna's head was leaning out of the kitchen window. 'You know what happened last night.'

Ryan heard his Mum's voice and scampered to the back door shouting, 'Mummy, Mummy, Mummy.' Anna had been away at the supermarket for the weekly shop. She had only recently stopped taking Ryan everywhere with her and he was taking it hard.

'Dad.' I was on my knees before Pat, tucking his shirt into his trousers. His eyes were on Ryan's rapidly receding back. 'Do you think *my* Mum is watching me?'

'Of course she is, son.'

The question surprised me. Watching Pat over the last couple of years I had convinced myself that he had accepted Anna as his mother. With my hand resting on his shoulder I realised that I had seen exactly what I wanted to see.

'Can I look at the photos of her again, Dad?' He paused. 'I don't remember her face.'

'C'mon. We'll go up to the loft.'

'Yes!' he squealed and ran into the house.

Under the harsh light of a bulb with no shade, Pat stared at one photograph in particular. It had been taken on our wedding day. Patricia was on her own and the photographer had snapped her unawares. I knew that off camera, I had been swapping insults with Jim, with Patricia as our audience of one. Whatever I was saying, Patricia's face was vivid with joy. Her cheeks were pushed out by her smiling mouth into those dimples that I used to love so much.

After she died, I would look at this photograph and try to remember what I'd said to Jim that was so funny. For days I would sit with it in my cold hands and try to dive into the memory. I would come up gasping for air, remembering nothing.

I looked over at Pat. Infected by a moment that happened before he was even considered, he sported identical dimples to his mother's.

'Andy?' Anna's voice rose up the ladders. 'What are you guys doing?'

'Nothing, sweetheart. Do you want to join us?'

'No way. The place is crawling with spiders.' She sounded like a little girl. 'How can you go up there?' I heard the shiver in her voice.

'Be down in a second.'

When her footsteps retreated down the stairs Pat tore his gaze from his mother's face.

'Dad, I saw Gran yesterday.'

'Oh.'

'She came to see me at school. She was waiting outside at playtime.'

'That was nice.' Inwardly, I groaned. How could I have allowed things to deteriorate to such an extent that my mother felt she had to sneak a visit with her grandson.

'How come we don't see her as much?' he asked.

Startled by his question I could only mumble a weak reply and hope that he would be satisfied with it. 'Dad's just been too busy recently. I've had a lot of things to do.'

'Like what?'

'Oh, this and that. Do you miss her?' Guilt forced the last four words from my mouth. I needed evidence of how I had let my son down.

'Well, she is nice, and she did bring me some sweets.' A typical Scotsman in the making, he avoided the admission of emotion. Or is that typical of all males?

'Don't worry, Pat.' I reached over and squeezed his knee. 'We'll meet up with Gran soon.' Concern over how Anna would react to this led me to modify this assertion. I whispered, 'But we'll just make it our little secret.'

That evening passed without event. The boys were tired after their day of play in the sun, Pat was a happy little boy after his time with me in the loft, and the pair of them submitted to bath and bed time with only a token protest. Anna and I had a couple of hours in front of the TV and then followed the boys' example and went to bed at an early hour.

I woke some time later. Disorientated in the dark, my first instinct was that something was wrong. I sat up in bed and listened.

Anna's breathing was slow and even beside me and there wasn't the slightest noise from the boys' room.

Just in case, I walked through to their room and peeked in. Both boys were fast asleep, each body a warm disarray of limbs, quilts tossed to the side. I felt a surge of love and sent them each a silent kiss.

Wondering what had disturbed me I walked on the balls of my feet down the stairs and into the kitchen. I opened the fridge, pulled out the milk and by the fridge's light I located a glass and poured.

As I knocked back the cold drink, something snagged my attention. I looked out through the window. Was there someone out there? I bristled. Felt a surge of adrenalin. Then I closed the fridge door to help me see better in the darkness.

I moved closer to the window and stared.

And relaxed.

There was no one there. I turned and leaned against the sink to finish off my drink. An image of a shape thrust itself into my mind's eye. It was there, indistinct in the weak light and strong shadow, but clearly human shaped. There, by the boys' swing.

Dropping the glass into the sink, I walked over to the kitchen door, unlocked it and stepped outside. My bare feet shrunk from the cold paving, but I ignored the chill and walked out into the garden.

'Who's there?' I asked in a harsh whisper.

The night settled around me. The breeze stippled my skin. A car moved somewhere off to my right.

'Who's there?'

I heard something behind me.

I whipped round. Anna. She was coming out of the kitchen, pulling a dressing gown round her to ward off the cool night air.

'What the hell are you doing, Andy?'

'Thought I saw someone.' I turned away from her and searched the shadows of our garden. I stepped over nearer the swing and viewed the garden from there.

Nothing.

'Andy. What's going on?' Anna stayed by the door as if afraid to venture too far out into the dark.

I looked up at the house. At Anna, and then back at the house. My boys' bedroom. Everything I cared about, right there. If anything happened to either one of them, I didn't know how I might cope.

My feet were cold in the damp of the grass. I moved. My right sole felt a different texture, something faintly warm. I lifted my foot up, balanced and picked at the something that had adhered to the pad under my big toe.

A cigarette stub.

Where the hell had that come from?

Anna reached me, looked around herself. 'Come on in, Andy.' She shivered. 'It's freezing.'

'Someone was here,' I said. 'Look. A cigarette.'

We both looked at it. It was about an inch long and homemade. I gave it a sniff. I didn't know what I was trying to decipher. I wouldn't know tobacco from weed.

'Look at you, the great detective,' laughed Anna. 'It's nothing.'

'So where did this come from?' I demanded and held up the stub for her to see.

'One of the girls was over this afternoon. Jean Given.'

I knew Jean. She was a part-time teller. Had twin boys around Ryan's age.

'I didn't know Jean smoked.'

'You don't know everything,' Anna said and put a hand on my arm. Then she stepped in towards me and leaned her head on my shoulder. I felt her laugh. 'My hero.' She moved back slightly and looked up into my eyes. 'C'mon My Protector. Let's get you back to bed.'

5

The next morning, while we were still in bed, I told Anna she needed a rest. She was surely due some time to herself, I said, and insisted that I do her a favour and take the boys out of her way on a Saturday morning, so she could have a long lie-in.

'Thank you, honey,' she replied, turned on her side to face me, pulled the quilt up to her chin and burrowed into her pillow. 'That would be lovely.'

The cigarette stub we discovered during the night was still on my mind, but I decided against bringing it up. Besides, if she was sure it was Jean's, why should I argue?

The shadow was probably just in my imagination.

I told her that I was taking them to Pet Corner at a local farm park, where they could feed the deer and rabbits. I worried that Anna would renege on the deal and join us, so, instead of the farm park, I took them to Kidz Play.

Where their Gran was waiting.

Joy flushed Mum's face as I walked towards her. She was holding her handbag tight against her body, as if practising the hug she would give the boys. Guilt scorched my gullet. I felt like the worse son alive to have deprived her for so long of their company.

'How are my lovely boys?'

She walked towards us with her arms outstretched. Her handbag fell to the floor. If I had been nearer, I would have been included in that embrace, but I held back, content for Pat and Ryan to receive my mother full beam. There would have been far worse things to endure at that point than an embrace from my mother, but I was afraid that my emotions might be too near the surface.

'How are you, son?' She reached up and touched my cheek.

Inadvertently, I stepped back, but immediately regretted my response as a little of the heat was dissipated from her joy. Somewhat self-consciously, I bent over and picked up her handbag and passed it to her.

'Shall we get a seat?' I asked.

She nodded and turned to face the bombardment of questions from Pat. Ryan, who hadn't shared his gran's company so much as Pat had, held onto my hand. His little fingers held me tightly, showing his alarm at his brother's response to a relative stranger. Mum answered one of Pat's queries and then turned to Ryan.

'And how's my favourite two-year-old?' she beamed.

Ryan's answer was to hide his head behind my knee.

'Don't pretend you're shy, Ryan Boyd.' I picked him up and he buried his head into my shoulder as I remembered the last time that these two had met: six months ago at Ryan's birthday party.

'Gran, I can climb all the way to the top of that,' said Pat, trying to reclaim some of the attention. He pointed at a large climbing structure that inhabited most of the space within the large, hanger-like building.

'You are a clever boy,' she cooed.

'Pat, why don't you take your brother into the ball pit and play with him for a while. Gran and I have a lot to talk about,' I said. There was an inquisition coming and it would be better to get it out of the way.

'Daaad.' Pat let me know that he wasn't completely enamoured of this idea.

'Go and play for a wee while and when you come back we'll have a Coke and some chips.'

'Okay,' he smiled. The parents' official last resort: bribery. Worked every time.

We sat within viewing distance of the boys at play.

'Ryan's really coming on,' said Mum, 'and Pat is turning into a wee heartbreaker.'

'Yes,' I agreed.

'You must be very proud of them.'

While I agreed with every fibre of my body, I considered Mum's words. Her statement was something that a stranger might produce. I felt that it was something that a salesman might say after reading the How To Get On with Parents Guide. Had I driven her so far away?

'Jim says hello.' Her eyes didn't leave the boys. 'I told him that I was spending some time with you today.'

'Right,' I said noncommittally, as if I had just read the Parents' Guide to Handling Salesmen.

I watched her watching the boys. She hungrily took note of every action and I was struck by the thought that she looked like an expensive wool cardigan that had been put through the wrong cycle in a washing machine and come out slightly smaller and slightly faded.

I prayed that concern about me wasn't wearing her down. No, my mother was tough, she had come through a lot. Surely less of me in her life wouldn't have such repercussions.

'So.' She faced me. I noticed the small but sharp intake of breath as she did. 'What's been happening with you, son? Tell me all your news.'

'Nothing much, Mum. You know, work, nine to five-ish. Come home, play with the boys, sleep, work…' I let my voice trail off. The washing machine's cycle must have been tougher than I thought; the lines on her forehead were deeper than I remembered. My hand fell onto her forearm and rested there for a moment. 'Just the usual stuff.' I attempted a smile.

'As long as you're happy, son.'

'Oh, I'm happy alright.' Realising that I had taken my eyes from hers as I spoke and with the further realisation of how that might be translated, I continued, 'How could I not be, with two such beautiful kids?'

'I notice you didn't include your wife in that.' Her eyebrows were raised in sympathy.

'Mum, Anna and I are very happy.' My tone was harsher that I intended. I tried to soften the line of my shoulders. Relax, I told myself.

'What has Jim been saying to you?' I continued in the same vein.

'Don't get all defensive, Andy. Jim has said nothing. I do have eyes in my head and this brain might not be as sharp as it was, but I'm not a fool.'

'What do you mean by that?'

'Where's your wife today, Andy? Why isn't she with you?'

'I don't know what you're getting at.'

'Didn't want to be in the same room as the in-law, is that it?'

'Is that it? You think Anna doesn't like you?' I could handle that objection quite easily. 'Anna thinks you're great.'

'Of course she does.' Mum's voice leaked sarcasm. 'Don't patronise me, Andy. I'm not in my dotage yet. I couldn't care less what Anna thinks of me. What I do care about is why my son, after remarrying, doesn't want me to be part of his life.'

Ryan chose this point to fall and hurt his head. Hoping this would deflect my mother from the conversation, I rushed to him and spent more time putting him together again than I normally would. He was struggling to get out of my arms to join his brother, while I was still kissing his forehead and saying 'There, there.'

'Tea and a biscuit?' I joined Mum at the table.

'Please,' she said quietly. 'Andy, I'm sorry…'

'Don't worry about it.' I turned and walked over to join the queue at the food counter. When I returned, my tray was laden with tea and cakes for Mum and I, and soft drinks and fries for the boys.

'I really am sorry, son,' Mum said as I poured her tea.

'It's okay, Mum,' I said, trying to hide my relief that she was going to drop the subject. Nothing short of a thumbscrew-wielding Spanish Inquisitor would make me divulge to my mother the mess that I was in. Mrs Boyd's sons should be self-confident, capable, well-adjusted men. She hadn't raised her son to be a weakling.

'It's not okay. I should know better than to interfere. I've always believed that I should let you both make your own lives.'

'You haven't interfered, Mum. You're concerned about me and rightly so…'

Alarm at what I said halted her cup about a centimetre from her mouth. 'I'm right to be concerned?'

Shit, I cursed inwardly. I shouldn't have been so keen to appease her. 'I mean … I would be concerned if one of my boys suddenly stopped coming to see me…' Damn, I was shovelling myself quite nicely into a rather large hole.

'You *have* stopped coming to see me and I *am* worried.'

'You know how it is, Mum. Life just gets busy, it gets in the way.'

'You've been busy before, Andy. You didn't stop seeing me then. You've been married before. You didn't stop seeing me then either.'

'I thought we weren't getting into that.'

'What is there to get into?' She leaned forward.

I leaned back on my chair. 'Nothing. Jesus, will you back off.' The fact that she was stung registered somewhere at the back of my mind, but I had tapped into a well of frustration and couldn't quite stop. 'What is it with everyone? I'm fine, we're fine, everybody is fucking fine!'

'Fine, FINE!' Her tone rose to meet mine. Then she pulled her lips tight and controlled herself with a deep breath. Now composed but undeterred she continued. 'I'm sorry but you don't look fine, you are not acting fine and as far as I can see everything is far from fine. You put on lots of weight – now you've lost it; you look … grey, and you've got shadows under your eyes that could block out the sun. All I want is for my sons to be happy and to play a part in their lives. If that makes me a bad mother then sue me. And don't ever use that language to me again.'

Her eyes locked fiercely onto mine and I felt that I was twelve years old again. She placed her cup on the table and moved her hand to grip mine. I couldn't move it away.

'This job's for life, Andy. Don't expect me to stop caring just because you're with another woman. I *know* that there's something not quite right. You don't want to tell me what it is? I have to respect that. What I don't have to do is bow out when my son is in trouble.' She applied more pressure to my hand. 'My door is open to you any time, day or night. Let me help you.'

The honest and raw emotion in her plea, nearly unmanned me. Salt stung my eyes and muscles bunched in my jaw as I fought to control myself. A deep, quavering breath filled my lungs before I could speak.

'I'll be fine, Mum.' I could barely hear myself. I'd have to do better than that. I cleared my throat and went for the Oscar. Smiling, my words were much louder. 'I'm fine, Mum. The truth is…' I built myself up for the lie '… we haven't been getting on that well recently.'

'I knew it.' She leaned forward.

'The thing is … Anna wants another child. She's desperate to try for a girl.' She had mentioned that it would be nice, but only in passing. The most convincing lie is one that strays just a little from the truth.

'Aww, pour soul.' Mum sat back in her chair, her tension dispersed by my words. 'I can relate to that after having you two big lumps. So why is that causing so much strain?'

'It's in the bedroom, Mum.'

She flushed a little. 'Right,' she said as her eyes slid from mine.

'I'm afraid to let things get too far in case…'

'All right, all right,' she held her hand up. 'Enough information, thank you. Goodness, what are you like? One extreme to the other. First you don't tell me enough, then when I get you to open your mouth, you can't stop. A mother shouldn't have to hear what goes on behind her son's bedroom door.'

While grinning at her discomfort, I congratulated myself on my story. Mum wouldn't dare to ask me any more questions on the subject.

'Well, that's you sorted. Now I need to deal with Jim.'

'What's up with him?'

She stuck a teaspoon in her coffee and stirred. 'Don't know if I should tell you, if he hasn't.'

'For God's sake, Mum.'

'Alright,' she said quietly. 'For two brothers who're close, you tell each other nothing.'

'What's going on?' I felt a shimmer of fear on behalf of my brother.

'Oh, he says he's fine now that he's on the happy pills…'

'Happy pills?'

'Prozac. Agnes at number thirty-two is on something similar. She says it's calmed her right down.'

'You talked to Agnes at number thirty-two about this?'

'No,' she replied, looking as if I'd slapped her. 'Course not. I'm just saying that she—'

'Enough of Agnes whatsername. Tell me about Jim.'

'He's fine.'

'He's clearly not fine if he's on Prozac.'

'Says he feels a bit lost. Says he'd love to just give it all away and join a monastery.'

'A monastery? Jim?'

'Yeah, I know,' she smiled. Grew wistful. 'You know, when I look back at him, Jim was a thinker. He always was the deep one.'

'Deep?' I laughed. 'Are we talking about the same guy?'

Mum dismissed me with a look. 'See you when you boys talk? Do you ever actually, you know, *talk*?'

For the remainder of our time together that day the conversation was occupied by less contentious issues: the boys. Mum wanted to hear every little detail of the last few months: what they were eating, how Pat enjoyed having a little brother. While I answered her questions a weight on my shoulders gorged on the guilt that I was feeling and grew heavier with every word. I did want Mum to be in my sons' lives, I did want to see her more often, but the truth was that each visit was punctuated with a slap or a punch from Anna. She wanted me all to herself, I reasoned. The best thing to do was to limit those things that might cause a fight, and if seeing less of my family meant a happier, less threatened Anna, then that's what would happen. The problem was seeing less of eventually became seeing nothing of. My mum didn't deserve such shabby treatment. I would have to do better and I would.

I just wasn't sure how.

*

On the way home in the car, I worried that the boys might let it slip just who we had spent time with that morning. Sneaking behind Anna's back would not be received well. Ryan would be fine, I was sure he hadn't grasped just who paid him all that attention. Pat would have to be warned to say nothing.

'Pat…' I looked in the driver's mirror into the back seat.

'What, Dad?'

'Do me a favour, son. Don't tell your mum that you saw your gran today.' Pain thudded just where my neck met my shoulder. I didn't want to include my son in my lies, but it would make life easier for us all.

'Why not?' His nose lifted up closer to his eyes as he squinted quizzically.

'Because Gran and I are planning a surprise for Mum.'

Just then Ryan began to chant, 'Ganny, ganny.' He was still having problems with his r's.

'Don't worry, Dad,' said Pat, reading my worry that Ryan would give the game away. 'Mum won't know what he's saying.' The pain became sharper. Just how much was Pat aware of? 'I know, I know, we'll say my friend, Danny was there,' he continued, excitement at helping us in the 'surprise' heightening the pitch in his voice. 'Say "Danny, Danny".' He leaned over his little brother.

'Ganny, ganny,' was Ryan's response.

'Leave him, son,' I said wearily. 'We'll just have to hope for the best.'

'Wee brothers are stupid,' Pat said, folding his arms in disgust.

Feeling drained, I didn't have the energy to correct him and we drove the rest of the way home in silence.

Anna was waiting at the open door as I parked the car. My stomach lurched as I noted the set of her arms, folded tight against her body, and her legs, shoulder-width apart. Even from the car I could see the rage simmering in her expression. The acid content in my stomach raised another pH as I realised that she must have gone to the farm park to meet us.

'Where the hell have you been?' She waded down the path, her elbows punching the air behind her as she walked.

'It was raining, so we went to Kidz Play. Why? Did you go to the farm park?'

'Rain? What rain? And yes, I went to the bloody farm park. No bloody husband, no bloody sons.'

'Relax will you, we're fine.'

'What bloody rain?' She tilted her head back to peer at the cloud-less sky.

'Honey, this is Scotland. We are talking about two or three hours ago. Plenty of time for the sky to dump its load and then clear.'

'Oh, so you're a bloody weather man now?' Her voice was barely audible. I was sure I could see some of the neighbour's net curtains twitching on the periphery of my vision.

'Let's go inside and carry on this discussion.' I herded the two boys up the path towards the front door. Anna followed.

'What have you been up to, Boyd?' she demanded. Once we were inside, I closed the front door and answered her.

'Nothing. I took our sons to the soft play because it looked like rain at the farm park.

'Oh, so it *looked* like rain. A moment ago the sky dumped its load.'

'What's with the third degree? The boys were at a different place than I told you. You weren't even meant to be out there. You were supposed to be having the morning off. Last time I try and do you a favour.'

'And it'll be the last time that I let you have the boys on your own. You can't be trusted to do what you say you will.'

As Anna spoke, Ryan was tugging at her trousers still chanting, 'Ganny, ganny.'

Pat was leaning against the far edge of the settee, staring at the silent TV. He looked as if he was trying to fold in on himself.

'Let's not argue in front of the boys, love.' My tone was conciliatory.

'Why the hell not?' Anna was winding herself up even further,

'Let them see what an arse their father is and how he can't be trusted to take his sons out for the day. Can't be trusted to tell the truth.' Her saliva sprayed my face. She moved closer to me. So far she had never struck me in front of the boys and I was confident that she wouldn't start today, so I stood my ground.

'Liar,' she hissed. 'You men are all the same, fucking liars.' Her hand snaked out and struck my cheek.

Pat stood facing us with his eyes as large as his open mouth. Ryan ran to him, crying.

'Anna, control yourself,' I shouted. 'Can't you see that you're frightening the boys?'

'The boys, the boys,' she mocked. 'All you fucking care about is the boys. What about your fucking wife?' Another slap. This time on the other side. 'What about me? I'm the one you tell lies to. I'm the one who goes looking for you and thinks that you're all dead in a car crash.'

'I'm sorry, Anna.' My head hung in shame. 'I'm sorry, I should have phoned you.'

'Too late for sorry now, you lying scumbag.' Her knuckles connected with the side of my chin, a foot missed my kneecap and collided with the meaty flesh of my thigh.

'Stop it! Stop it!' Pat's small body was between us. His face was twisted with fear, yet he stood his ground. 'Dad took us to Kidz Play and we met my gran. He didn't want to tell you because they were planning a surprise for you.'

'Oh.' Anna's eyes bored into mine. 'And what surprise is that, Andy. Do tell.'

Inwardly, I groaned. Now I was really going to suffer. 'Pat take your brother up to your room and watch a video,' I said. The boys had to get out of the room before it got too nasty.

'No,' screamed Anna, 'Stay here, both of you and I'll show you what I do to liars.'

'Pat, take Ryan upstairs now.' Any authority I had was in my voice.

I watched gratefully as Pat quickly grabbed his brother's arm and pulled him up the stairs. Ryan was screaming.

'Look what you've done,' Anna said. 'My son is traumatised and part of your lies, all because you wanted to see your precious cunt of a mother.'

'You're twisting things. And don't call my mother that.'

'Aye, you're right. My apologies.' She bowed mockingly. 'A cunt's a useful thing.'

'How can such a beautiful woman be so ugly?' The words were out before I could stop them. I backed away from her. 'I'm sorry, I didn't mean that.'

'I'll make you sorry you piece of scum.' That dark light was in her eyes. The light that signalled there was no way to stop her. All I could do was curl into a ball and take my punishment. Like a man.

After what seemed hours, the blows ceased. With caution I looked up. I had to protect my eyes. Anna's fury had dissipated. The tide of her rage had gone out, leaving her as limp as piece of seaweed on the beach. She hunched forward, fighting to catch her breath.

'See … see … what you make me do?'

'I'm sorry.' I shouldn't have driven her to this.

'You … lie. You … meet people behind my back. Am I such an ogre that you don't want your mother to be in my company?' Her face was twisted with anguish.

'It's all my fault. I'm sorry.'

'Am I so awful, Andy? Do you really hate me?' A tear began its silent trail down her pale cheek.

'I don't hate you…' I began to try and reassure her and stopped myself. What the hell was I doing? Just a moment ago she was bent on breaking a few of my bones and now she was making me feel sorry for her.

'Don't hate me, Andy. I need you. If I didn't have you…' Her voice tailed off as she let me imagine what she was capable of doing if I wasn't with her.

'Don't … don't,' I said and stepped forward. Then paused. A stew of conflicting emotions swirling in my mind. She needed me, but she couldn't stop herself from hurting me. Despite myself I stepped forward and took her into my arms. I just couldn't stand by and watch her pain. Not when I was the cause of it.

'This is too much, Anna.' I stroked her hair, trying not to wince as pain flared in my side with each movement. She was tiny. Vulnerable. Her head bent forward, hair falling to either side of her face. I could see the row of vertebrae on the back of her neck.

I could break her like a twig. I imagined my hands round her throat. Squeezing for all I was worth. In my mind I saw her face go red and her eyes bulge with the agony and the desperate need to suck in some air.

Then it would all be over. All of this misery.

The image was so vivid, I brought my hands to my sides, as if part of my mind was worried I would actually carry it out.

Fingernails digging into the palms of my hands, I took a deep breath. And another. Enough about her pain. What about mine? Did I deserve this? Was I worth more?

I wasn't sure I was.

Finally I managed to speak. 'I need to go and see to the boys.'

Upstairs I knocked on the door first.

'Can I come in?'

'Yes,' was the soft reply. They were on the bed and Pat was propped up against some pillows while Ryan was curled into his side. The TV screen was black and silent.

'Thought you were coming up to watch a video.' At the sound of my voice in the room Ryan jumped up. Fresh tears flowed down his face.

'Dad.' He ran to me, arms wide. I pulled him to me and studied his brother. Pat stayed on the bed, pulling his knees up to his chin. He had the air of an octogenarian.

'Didn't want to watch a video,' Pat said, his face as blank as the TV screen.

'Do you want to come back downstairs? I'll make us some lunch.'

'No, I'm not hungry.' Something imposed itself on his face, then disappeared as quickly as it arrived.

As I trudged wearily down the stairs with Ryan tight against my chest, I tried to decipher Pat's expression. Was it disappointment? Was it pity?

6

Following the 'ganny' incident, we had a couple of weeks of calm. Anna apologised several times for 'punishing' me in front of the boys, and I vowed not to drive her to such an extreme ever again. In fact I steeled myself to do whatever I could to placate Anna. Whatever it took to help her keep control of her temper, I would do. My motivation was not fear of the pain that she could and would inflict, but the mental image of me with my hands round her neck. That and the look on Pat's face after the fighting had died down.

The following evening, I shouted through to Pat in the bedroom to bring me a towel while I bathed Ryan. He ignored me and continued to watch *Scooby Doo*.

'Pat. Will you bring me a towel, please.' I wasn't the most patient person that day. Still he ignored me. Bundling Ryan, dripping wet, into my arms, I walked through to the bedroom, stood in front of Pat's eyeline and switched off the TV.

'Daaaad.'

'Will you go and get me a clean towel?' I couldn't control my wife but I there was no way I was going to let my son walk all over me.

'I was watching Scooby,' he protested.

'And I asked you to help me. Now go and get me a towel or the TV stays off for the rest of the evening.'

When he brought me the towel, he threw it at my feet.

'Can I put *Scooby Doo* back on?' he asked, his eyebrows drawn tightly together. Without waiting for my reply, he walked back into the bedroom and the cartoon noises filled my ears.

For the remainder of that evening and over the course of the next few days, this behaviour was repeated each time our purposes crossed. He would defer to Anna but completely ignore any requests I made of him. Friendly queries became shouted demands, became lost causes. My son seemed to have lost all respect for me.

Talking to him won nothing but silent reproval. He quickly became articulate with face and body language: crossed arms, a glance to the floor, and other signals became his mode of contact with me. Words were used only with Ryan and Anna. At a loss as to how I could win back his affection, I did nothing, hoping that time would return the real Pat to me. A fight with his younger brother, however, made me act.

The boys were in the back garden playing. Anna had popped out to the shop to buy dessert for our dinner, and I was in the kitchen peeling potatoes. Any parent can quickly recognise the message loud in their child's cries: hunger, boredom, I want attention, can eventually all be recognised by their pitch and intensity. The cry Ryan issued that afternoon was about pain and lots of it. Dropping the knife, I was out the kitchen and in the garden as fast as I could move.

'What the…' was all I managed to say before Ryan flew into my arms. His small face was purple and dripping with tears. Teeth and tonsils were exposed as he fought to show me just how upset he was.

Pat stood defiantly over Ryan's bike.

'He wouldn't let me sit on it,' Pat said.

'It is his.' I was bewildered at the change in him. Normally where Ryan was concerned, he displayed the patience of a she-lion as its cubs trampled all over it.

'I just wanted to sit on his stupid bike…'

'Go to your room, Pat.' I controlled my anger.

'All he kept saying was 'mine, mine'.'

'Go to your room, Pat.' Ryan was still screaming in my ear.

'I don't want his stupid bike…'

I lost it. 'Pat, go to your fucking room.'

Stunned, he was silent for a moment. I had never spoken to him like that before. Then tears swamped him as he ran into the house and up to the bedroom. This display of tears from Pat quietened Ryan.

His screams were now quiet sobs. Just then Anna's face appeared at the door. Her expression was one big question mark.

'Honestly, I'm out of the house five minutes and World War Three breaks out. What's going on?' she asked.

Ryan heard her and freshened his sobs. More sympathy from Mum was what was required obviously. I handed him to her and, feeling like a spare pair of underpants at a wedding where all the men wore kilts, I stood and watched as Anna rocked Ryan, his face returning to a healthy pink.

What had happened to my adorable eldest son? I couldn't just let this go on any longer, I needed to speak with him.

He was in the foetal position on his bed when I entered the room.

'Can I speak to you, son?'

'Go away.' His voice was muffled by a pillow, but his meaning was clear enough.

'We need to talk, son. You know that it's not fair to hit your wee brother.'

'He hit me first.' He sat bolt upright, like an exclamation mark.

'Was it sore?'

'Yes.'

'Pat, Pat.' I sat beside him. 'Look at the size of him compared to you. You're twice as big as him.'

'It was still sore. Look…' He rolled up his trouser leg. His shin was an angry red and looked badly swollen.

'How did that happen?'

'Ryan hit me with a stick.'

'It does look sore,' I thought aloud.

'So I was right to hit him back.' Pat seized on my words.

'No, no, no. You could do him some real damage if you hit him hard. He's only small.'

His eyes met mine for the first time. He said nothing, but his expression betrayed that he was processing my argument. He looked as if he was about to speak. Changed his mind.

'What?' I asked.

'Is that why you don't hit Mum back?'

'Yes.' My heart was a lump of stone. 'Compared to me she is only small.'

'And you could really hurt her if you hit her back.'

'Yes.'

'But was it sore when she hit you?' I saw this as one last attempt at vindication of his own actions.

'Yes, it was sore, really sore.' I rubbed the side of my face as remembered pain echoed there.

'But you didn't hit her back because you could hurt her more than she could hurt you.' He affirmed and crawled onto my lap, where he curled up, thumb in his mouth.

7

Friday morning and there was a memo on my desk. Anna wasn't going to like this. My presence was requested in the Campbeltown branch. It was from the Regional Manager's office; I could no more disobey it than I could choose Pat over Ryan.

Anna would not be happy.

There had been an emergency, the staff couldn't cope, it was a flagship branch for the area, it couldn't be allowed to get any worse and I had performed so well on my last visit ... Some emergency, I thought. A phone call was the usual method of communication in this event. The memo filled the page with inanities and corporate clichés that were supposed to motivate and impress. A curling lip was my response.

Who wrote this drivel? The word 'clearly' prefixed every statement and the phrase 'going forward' indicated, several times, that I was needed to help build a branch for the future. A snort erupted from my pursed lips at 'show the staff there what good looks like'. I would have to do all this in three weeks.

I was to be accompanied by Sheila Hunter. Flight tickets were included. The shrill ring of the phone interrupted my reading. Sheila's voice filled my ear.

'I take it you've spoken with Roy about Campbeltown?' she asked.

'No, was he supposed to call me? I've received a memo about it though. What the hell's going on? And why did I have to find out about it in a bloody memo.'

'I'm sorry, Andy. Roy was supposed to phone you at the beginning of the week. Probably too busy.'

'Probably couldn't be arsed.'

'You were over there a couple of years ago, weren't you?' Sheila asked.

'Yes.'

'Well, the guy that you helped get organised…'

'Sandy?'

'Yeah, him. Well apparently, he's had some sort of a brainstorm. He's informed the local press that he's setting up on his own; some sort of consultancy for business customers to help them get the most out of the financial market place. He told the local rag that the bank were happy for their customers to shop about and that he was the right man to help them do it.'

'What?' I was astounded. What a strange thing to say. And to hope that the bank would hear nothing about it. 'I didn't think Campbeltown was known for its wacky baccy.'

'Well, he's certainly been taking something. Mushrooms maybe.'

'And you and I have to clear up his mess.'

'Looks like it.'

'Why the memo?' I thought aloud.

'Dunno,' said Sheila. 'A phone call's the way we usually do things.' She paused; something had just occurred to her. 'Anna won't be too happy.'

'What do you mean?' I asked – too quickly.

'Well,' Sheila answered, 'she'll be on her own with two boys. That's a lot of work.'

'I know.' I groaned inwardly at my defensive response. What must Sheila think?

'Anyway, I've booked us in at The Ardsheil. Is that okay with you?'

'Aye, that's fine. It's a nice wee hotel. Has one of the best selections of whisky you're likely to find.'

Knowing how negatively Anna would react, I waited until the boys were asleep that night before telling her.

'Bloody bank,' she said. 'Why you? Is there no one else in that shit organisation?'

She was standing facing me wearing one of my t-shirts. I was sitting up in bed. I shrugged in response to her question. When I saw her standing there, anger tight in her jaw, the idea of going away for a few weeks was quite appealing. She folded her arms.

'You didn't ask for this did you?' Suspicion filled her hard stare.

'No. No of course I didn't.' I'd better make this convincing, I thought. 'Why the fuck would I want to go to that shit hole?' The lies dripped easily from my tongue. 'It has one pub, the hotel's a dump, and the folk there are the unfriendliest bunch you're ever likely to meet.'

She was on the bed quickly and tugged at some of my chest hair until she elicited a response. 'If I ever find out that you volunteered for this…' The threat was stark in her tone and all the more frightening for going unsaid. How would she react, I wondered, if she knew that I was going over with a female member of staff – an attractive one at that?

The flight to Campbeltown was at the ridiculously early time of 6.55 a.m. Sheila admitted her unease at the first sight of our aircraft.

'God, it's tiny. I hope you're not frightened of flying.'

As I climbed the half-dozen stairs into the plane, I answered, 'No, not at all.'

Bending over to avoid bouncing my head off the roof and noticing that it looked even smaller inside, I considered that I may have to review this opinion. The craft had two seats lining one side and one seat on the other. When I sat down on a two-seater, it was obvious that only a two-year-old could accompany me with any degree of comfort.

Sheila and I were the only passengers and we received the full attentions of the flight crew, who were equal in number.

'First time flying to Campbeltown?' asked the pilot. He was sitting at the control stick, looking over his shoulder at us. The knot of his tie was all but concealed by the right wing of his collar and his hair obeyed its own set of rules as it skewered in the air around it.

'Yes,' I answered, confidence falling as the door was shut. The last time I went there I drove and at this point the pleasures of the road were definitely calling.

'Don't worry, old son. These wee planes have a great safety record.' He beamed at me. 'Right.' The pilot clapped his hands. 'We'll soon be in the air. There's the exit.' He pointed over our heads at the way we had just come in. 'And your lifejacket is under the seat. Any questions? No, good. Enjoy the flight.' He turned around and strapped himself in.

'This should be fun.' Sheila smiled. She had chosen the seat in front of me. We could both see every move the pilot made.

We were quickly airborne and I looked around me, trying to get my bearings. Wings cutting through the crisp early-morning sky, we followed the River Clyde through Glasgow's urban sprawl, out to the Firth of Clyde and the sea. From there our flight path was Bute, Arran and down the length of Kintyre to Campbeltown.

When we arrived at the branch, the staff were almost pathetically grateful that someone with authority was there to help out. The erstwhile manager had obviously been planning his escape for some time; it looked like he had done nothing for months. Some borrowing propositions were dangerously late, cheques had been paid that were piling some customers deeper and deeper into debt, and his customer files were a disgrace.

There was a lot of work to be done and I, apparently, was the man to do it. The bonus was that I was free from the distractions of home and able to get a full night's sleep, and subsequently do a full day's work.

There was one distraction from home, however. Every evening at around nine o'clock, once the boys were in bed, Anna would phone. She insisted that she phone me as it would save on my hotel bill. I didn't have the energy to point out that the bank would be picking up the tab for the telephone. Besides knowing how jealous Anna could be, I was fairly certain that she wanted to phone me to make sure that I was where I said I was.

'Is the pub shut, then?' was her typical greeting.

'Been chatting up the local slappers?' was another.

The first weekend at home flew past and we were back in Campbeltown for week two. While at home my thoughts were often drawn back to the previous week: Sheila and I poring over printouts; Sheila and I discussing the day ahead over breakfast; Sheila and I ... Several times I had to mentally rattle my brain as if to dislodge the growing affection I had for her. At odd times my thoughts would stray to her. While bathing Ryan, her laugh would play its song in my ears; while reading the newspaper she walked across the page; and while making love with Anna, Sheila's smile radiated from the pillow.

Stop it, Boyd. You're a married man, with two boys, I told myself. I would have to fight to maintain a professional distance. But, with a thrill that surprised me, I found myself looking forward more and more to sharing the flight back to Campbeltown with her.

The next week back in Kintyre flew by. We worked from eight in the morning till eight at night, grabbed a quick meal at the hotel and then went off to our respective rooms to pore over some more files and then get some well-deserved sleep – and for me to anticipate Anna's call. On the Tuesday her call was a little later than usual.

'Hi, honey,' she said. Her pleasant tone took me by surprise.

'Hi. You're a wee bit later tonight,' I said without thinking.

'What are you trying to say?' I could almost see her shouting at the mouthpiece. 'I've had enough of your accusations.'

'Anna. I just commented on the fact that you're phoning a wee bit later than you normally do.' I heard a deep voice in the background. 'What's that? You got the telly on too loud?'

Anna cleared her throat. I was too busy thinking how I could calm her down to notice the way she did so. If I had been as paranoid as she was, I may have thought it sounded like she was warning someone.

'Aye, some documentary...' a strange noise, like a stifled giggle '... about dinosaurs.'

'Since when did you watch documentaries?'

Anna's TV habits were soaps and movies.

'Since tonight. Is that alright with you?' she snapped.

'How are the boys?' I thought it best to change the subject.

'They're fine. A handful. They miss their Dad. Christ knows why.' She laughed, and I forced a smile into my voice.

'Ha, ha. Give them a kiss for me.'

Placing the phone on the receiver, I gave no more thought to Anna's weird behaviour. I had more pressing matters to consider: Sheila. Having recognised my attraction for her, I forced myself to speak to her only when she spoke first, and then I would only be drawn on work matters. Several times I caught a glance, a partially opened mouth, as if she was about to say something. At this I would feel awful, but steeled myself with the thought that it was for the best. I just couldn't afford to let my attraction grow.

One evening as I ate in silence, Sheila decided to say what was on her mind.

'Andy, what the hell is wrong with you?'

'Uh?' I looked over at her while drawing a string of spaghetti up into my mouth.

'You've been off-hand with me all week.'

'I haven't,' I said when I had swallowed my mouthful.

'You have, and I want to know what I've done.' Her beautiful eyes drilled into mine. 'Have I said something? What?'

'Nothing, nothing.' I felt uncomfortable. I couldn't admit my feelings and I couldn't just leave her feeling like she'd somehow offended me. 'It's me…' I finally answered. 'Things at home…'

'Oh.' Silence. 'I don't want to pry. Just thought I'd … never mind…' More silence. 'Have you finished with the Borthwick report yet?' Sheila moved onto safer ground.

'Yes. Do you need it? I left it in my room last night. I can go and get it for you if you want.'

'No, no,' she answered. She had finished her light meal by this point. 'Give me your room key and I'll go and get it while you're still eating.'

I passed the key to her. 'It's on the dressing table.' As she reached the door, I jumped up. It was almost time for Anna's phone call. I looked at my watch. 8.45. Calm down, Boyd I told myself. It's still a wee bit early.

Just as I was wiping at the bolognaise sauce with a slice of crusty bread, Sheila returned with the file under her arm. She ordered some coffee and sat down sliding my key over the table.

'Did you ring for me just there?' she asked.

'No.'

'Oh.' She looked puzzled. 'Your phone rang while I was in the room and I answered, thinking it might be you. There was no one there. Odd, isn't it?'

I gripped the fork in my hand and fought the urge to groan. Anna. Shit. She couldn't have phoned at a worse possible time. No reasonable explanation would please her; her only thought would be that a woman was in my bedroom and I was surely sleeping with her.

'Is something wrong?' Sheila asked, 'You've gone all pale.'

'Must be something I've just eaten.' Nausea pulled at the food I'd just swallowed. I was in serious shit. I stumbled to my feet. 'See you in the morning, I'll just go and lie down.'

Safely in my room, I paced the floor. Should I phone home? No – better let her calm down first. But if I didn't phone I would be damned for sure. She would know that I knew she had called. In the end I settled for doing nothing. Whatever reaction Anna planned would happen regardless of any assertions I made. I would just end up digging myself a larger grave.

Sleep evaded me that night and I was able to plead sickness the next day when Sheila showed some concern. All the while thoughts of Anna's retribution filled my mind. Muscle tightened at imaginary blows and my self-esteem curled up at the thought of the slurs to come. The truth of what happened that evening would simply not be believed, so I had to think of some story that would appease Anna, but none came. Her reaction was too large in my imagination.

*

That night, back home, while the boys jumped all over me in competition to out-do the other, Anna maintained a chill distance. She kept this up until the Sunday night.

'What's wrong, honey?' I dared to ask. Like a convict whose execution had been postponed by an hour, then another hour, then another hour, I needed to know what was going on. I couldn't stand her silence any longer.

She was in the kitchen, I was standing in view of her in the living room, my hands deep in my pockets, my shoulders almost level with my ears. She stopped what she was doing and walked towards me, her hands behind her back.

'Who was she?' Each word was spoken crisply, quietly.

'Who was who?' I moved back.

'I'm not an idiot, Andy.'

Silence can be a very effective way of forcing someone else to speak and Anna's lips were sealed tight. She would not speak again until after I had spoken. My nerves drew tighter and tighter. Sweat popped out on my forehead like an admission of guilt.

'Okay, okay,' I burst. 'I know you called. My colleague went to my room for a file that we were working on.'

'You were working in your room, on this file, with this woman?' She was preternaturally cool. The blast must be on its way.

'No. I was working on the file, on my own in my room. This … colleague needed it once I was finished with it.'

'Why are you sweating, Andy?'

'I'm not sweating.' I lifted my arm and wiped my forehead on my sleeve while wondering what she was holding behind her back. She moved closer.

'You're sweating because you've been fucking some bitch behind my back.' The sentence started off quiet and clipped, but ended with a high-pitched squeal. 'You bastard.' Her hand shot out, connected with my solar plexus. Air bulleted from my mouth.

'Uhn.' I fell to my knees, bent forward, struggling for air. 'Anna, please … I didn't do … anything.'

'Prove it to me!' She held my head back by the hair.

'What?'

'Prove it to me!' Her other hand moved from behind her back. Light reflected on whatever she was holding. Realisation of what it was made me try to struggle to my feet, but her grip on my hair was too tight, too painful.

'Anna.' I tried to keep the desperation from my voice. 'What the fuck are you doing with a knife?'

8

The airport on Monday morning was mercifully quiet. Not many people around to see the mess I was in. Sheila, however, couldn't hide her shock. Anna was normally careful not to make any visible marks. But this time she had really lost it.

'Oh my God.' Sheila's hand hid her mouth. 'What on earth happened to you? Have you been in an accident?'

'Yes,' I mumbled from the side of my swollen mouth. I motioned to Sheila that it was difficult to talk. 'Car,' I said. 'Steering wheel.'

'You poor thing.' Sheila lifted her hand to the side of my head as if to caress the bruising. 'Look at your eye.' She didn't touch me and pulled her hand back to her side. 'Are you mad? You should be at home in bed. Or better still in the hospital.' She paused. 'You did go to the hospital?'

'Of course I did,' I lied. 'Only bruising. Looks worse than it is. I'd rather be at work.'

'Fine by me if that's the way you want it. It's your funeral.'

I tried to laugh at Sheila's flippant remark. The thought that she was closer to the truth than she would ever know cut off my strangled laughter. Even now I could feel the iced steel pressing against my neck, Anna's breath hot on my face as I knelt before her on the floor.

'Prove it to me,' she had demanded.

'How the hell can I do that?' A fist connected with my eyebrow.

'You know how,' she hissed in my ear.

'I don't. I haven't a clue what you're on about.' A knee shot up to my chin. I bit my lip. Pain surrounded me, pain and a growing certainty about what Anna wanted me to do: state my own punishment. Because then my humiliation would be profound.

'Remember the last time,' she whispered. I recalled that time when, after we had made love, she checked herself for the volume of my emission.

'No,' I cried, 'I won't do it.'

The knife moved in the air in front of my eyes. It caught every available beam of light and reflected it at me with menace. She pointed the knife at my groin.

'Prove to me that you haven't been fucking about or I'll get busy with this knife. Take your trousers down. And your pants.'

'Anna, please, stop it,' I begged. My mind screamed at me, why aren't you running? But I went nowhere and with wooden limbs I unbuckled my belt, allowed my trousers to drop to the floor and then I pulled my underwear down to my knees, exposing my genitals.

'You should have thought of this while you were screwing around.' She flicked the knife at my pubic hair. 'Or do you want to be like that guy Bobbit in the States?'

Utterly defeated, I started to tug at my shrunken flesh, willing it to expand, willing the blood to flow.

'If you're not hard in thirty seconds…'

I pumped my hand faster. Nothing.

'You can't get it up, you arsehole because you've been screwing someone else. I'll fucking kill you if you don't prove me wrong.' The knife was back at my neck. Something wet trickled down into my chest.

'Anna.'

'Keep wanking. Prove to me that I'm the only one.' Her eyes were an inch from mine. Madness swirled in them like black wings. She could do it, I thought. Right at this point she could quite easily push the blade through my flesh, seeking the vein.

I couldn't have believed it possible, but fear for my life fired blood into my groin and semen spurted out of my penis.

'Catch it in your hand you messy bastard,' she ordered. 'Don't let any fall onto the carpet.'

Anna then grabbed my wrist and examined the contents of my hand. Like a scientist peering over a petri dish she peered at the milky fluid strung over my palm. With a grunt she acknowledged that the volume was satisfactory.

'Look at you, you're pathetic.' The scorn in her voice was sharper than the blade at my throat and infinitely more painful. 'Go and clean up, you wanker.' Finding her choice of words amusing, she laughed. 'Get out of my sight.' She kicked at my shoulder and I fell to the floor, my humiliation complete. But she wasn't finished yet.

'What would your precious mother make of you now, your bare arse stuck up in the air, your hand full of spunk?'

'Leave my mother out of this.' I spoke into the carpet, hoping she couldn't hear me.

'What about that brother of yours? Eh? He probably wanks himself comatose every night. I'd bet Paula is sick of him.'

'Leave Jim out of this,' I said louder, pulling myself to my feet, while simultaneously trying to dress myself. I'd been naked in front of Anna countless times but for some reason in this situation I felt deeply uncomfortable. Like a choirboy naked before a row of nuns.

'And what about the boys? How much respect do you think they would have for you right now?' She was building herself up nicely.

'Don't you dare bring the boys into this.' I fought for control. She knew my weakness and, not content with the humiliation she had already delivered, she was going for more.

'Those poor wee boys, having an excuse like you for a father. What would they think if they saw you grovelling there?

'Shut up.'

'They love you as well. I'll just have to put them right. Tell them that their father is a worthless piece of scum.' She moved closer.

I couldn't take any more and stepped towards her. Delight softened her expression. She wanted this, but even knowing it, I couldn't stop myself. I grabbed at the hand holding the knife and squeezed her wrist until she dropped it. With the other hand I swung at her head. The connecting slap, flesh on flesh, rang out. The world slowed and Anna seemed to glide through the air until she crumpled against the far wall.

Rage ran unfettered through my mind, a rage that was fuelled by years of frustration. Moments of pain and humiliation were dark beads strung on a line of barbed wire that ran from this point in time, through my past to the day we got married.

And in that moment I was caught up in the release. Enough. No more.

Anna was at my feet begging.

'Andy, don't.'

The words reached my ears, but their meaning didn't register. She needed to know what I had been feeling like. She needed a flavour of what she had put me through.

I stepped towards her. Mind dark. Fists solid.

She would understand how it felt and I didn't care what the consequences were.

'Daddy?' A sweet soprano broke through the fog. Again. 'Daddy?' It was Ryan. He sounded terrified.

I turned to him and saw the pale of his face as he emerged from the shadows in the hall.

Closing my eyes, I took a breath. Somehow forced the anger down.

'Bed,' I said and wondered where I had found a tone that was almost normal. 'Back to bed, son. Everything is fine here.'

I turned away from him and looked down at my guilty hand as if it belonged to someone else.

Sense broke through. I could hardly believe my own strength or that I had broken one of my own commandments. I sobered up. I had done exactly what she wanted.

Anna climbed to her feet, holding the side of her head. Bruised but triumphant and looking almost disappointed that I had managed to make myself stop.

'You've gone and done it now, sunshine,' she crowed. 'You're mine.'

'Anna, I'm so sorry.' I crumpled. Fell to my knees, my fists pressed against either side of my head. What would she do now? Call the police?

'Look what you've done to me.' She limped over to the mirror and examined her face, 'I'm all red.' Wincing, she then pulled at her shirt, baring her shoulder. 'I'll be a mass of bruises in no time.'

'Anna, I'm so sorry. I'll never hit you again.'

I didn't think it was possible to feel any worse than I did five minutes previously, but I did. I had broken the one rule that had kept me sane thus far. I had clung to my belief that the stronger should never strike the weaker. In a fit of temper I had thrown away my lifesaver and was about to go under.

'Anna, please forgive me, I'm so sorry. I didn't mean to hurt you.' My own hurts were completely forgotten. How could I have lost control like that? She walked slowly into the hall. Despite myself, I followed and watched her adding drama to her limp as she moved up the stairs.

She stopped halfway up. Her voice drifted down, a penetrating hiss. 'Stay out of my sight. I'll have to think about what I should do with you.'

Summarily dismissed, I slunk back into the living room and sat on the floor before the TV.

Events of the evening ran through my mind. An image of my erect penis in my hand was superimposed on the TV screen by my imagination. Cold steel burned my neck. Fear that Anna would carry out her threat had stripped every voluntary thought from my head. I was thankful that filling your lungs was an involuntary action or I would have probably stopped breathing as well. Adrenaline stripped fur from my arteries and filled every vein to bursting point. All of this and yet I had managed to ejaculate. Was this self-preservation at its keenest? Had the mechanics of my pumping hand been enough?

Or was I as sick as she was?

Sleep eventually claimed me, my anxiety reduced by the thought of my hands round my wife's throat. Squeezing.

Squeezing for all I was worth.

*

'Andy, are you sure you're okay?' Sheila asked once again.

I nodded. 'Let's get to the plane.'

We agreed that I would do most of the donkey work that week, out of sight and hearing of the customers. With a pen in one hand, a mug of coffee in the other and piles of folders around me, I spent the remainder of my time in Campbeltown in the staff room. Working as many hours as I could, I tried to forget about striking out at Anna. What damage could I have done if I hadn't stopped? A movie played in my head while I crossed off lists of erroneously paid cheques: Anna bloodied and lifeless at my feet, me being handcuffed to a policeman and the boys being taken into care.

That series of events just couldn't be allowed to happen. There had to be a way out of this mess. What terrified me most was that I would eventually snap and murder would be the result.

Sheila couldn't do enough for me that week. She brought me morning snacks, lunch and dinner, made sure the kettle was never empty and continually asked how I was. My resolve to keep a safe distance between us dissolved under this barrage of solicitude and I found myself anticipating her next kindness, waiting for it like a pup waits for its ear to be scratched.

Each evening we would work until eight or nine then return to the hotel. Sheila would invite me to the bar for a nightcap, and, torn, I would refuse. The idea of sitting at the bar nursing a whisky and chatting with her was just too delicious to contemplate; besides, I knew if I wasn't back in my room to take Anna's phone call, the consequence would be severe.

The first phone call, on the Monday night, was surreal. No mention was made of my violence the night before; instead Anna talked about the boys, how much fun they'd had that day, how Ryan was starting to ask for the potty at last. While one half of my mind enjoyed the thought of the boys having fun, the other was bracing itself for the aural onslaught. It didn't happen.

Tuesday night, an almost identical talk took place. My nerves were in shreds as I waited for an outburst. Nothing. Wednesday's conversation was the same, until just before she hung up.

'Oh, by the way, I registered a complaint with the police today. They'll be waiting for you at the airport on Friday. I'm going to bed now. Don't call me back.'

Stunned, I sat on the edge of my hotel bed for what seemed hours with the phone up at my ear. Eventually the insistent tone made me put it back on its cradle. Oh my god, the police. What would they do? They would never believe that Anna had struck first. I was already healing. She'd probably enhanced her bruises with a little purple make-up. They'd take the boys away from me. I'd lose my job, my house.

Why the hell did you hit her, Boyd? You've lost everything.

Sleep was a stranger that night as dire scenarios filled my mind. I made it in to the office the next day, dim with fatigue and grey with worry. Sheila, sensing that I was not really present, kept her distance. The hours passed in a blur of figures and files. I probably made enough errors that day to ruin our work of the previous two and a half weeks. At six o'clock, I threw my pen across the desk.

'I've had enough,' I stated. I needed to get out of this building. I needed to drown the voices in my head with as much alcohol as possible.

'Do you want to go for something to eat?' asked Sheila.

'I'm going to the pub.'

Walking down the hill from the bank, I entered the first licensed premises I saw.

'A large whisky,' I demanded of the barman and took a stool at the bar. Alcohol would numb my brain, stop the march of destructive thought. Three doubles later I was still in a fog of worry.

'Fuck.' I slammed the glass on the bar and held my head in my hands.

'Could I ask you to mind your language, sir?' the barman said firmly but politely.

I grunted an apology. Looking around me for the first time since

I entered, I noticed the place was all but empty. A couple sat in the far corner as if they had nothing left to say to one another and their only shared pleasure was booze. A small, thin man sat in the middle of the room toying with a cigarette. There was no sign of a lighter, he simply turned the cigarette end over end with his fingers. To my right sat another man, his head sunk into his shoulders. His face was lined and all sharp angles, his eyes dark caves. He looked like a man at the end of his road. He wore a tie the same as mine. It looked as if it could easily swing around to form a noose. He looked like me. I sipped at my drink, so did he.

I was looking into a mirror.

The stranger beside me had my sympathy before I knew who he was. Could I sympathise with myself? What mistake had I made other than to love the wrong woman? Was it really my fault, the violence? Had I really jumped willingly into the whole mess or had it sneaked up on me while I was simply trying to be happy? Overriding all of this was the image of me on my knees with a knife at my neck and my dick in my hand. Humiliation pushed its way to the front of the throng of confusion in my mind.

How could I get out? How could I leave this situation with my sanity and with my two boys? If I divorced Anna, she would see to it that I never saw the boys again. She would twist the facts and end up twisting my boys. But, I couldn't stay with her. All I could think of was murder.

The first person the police suspect is always the husband or boy-friend. I would never get away with it and the boys would end up in care, knowing that their father was a murderer. No, murder wasn't a solution.

Unless I made it look like a convincing accident.

Anna didn't drive, so that ruled out tampering with the brakes. Poison would leave trace evidence.

For chrissake, Boyd, I thought. Get a grip of yourself. You're actually sitting here contemplating murder.

'Another double, barman.'

'You sure you've not had enough, sir?'

'I'll decide when I've had enough, you officious little prick.' I laughed when the word officious blurred into something nonsensical. 'That's easy for me to say.'

At the sound of my laughter the barman relaxed slightly, obviously experienced, he quickly calculated my menace factor and considered it not worth his concern.

'Just get me a drink will you?' I said. When I saw the couple in the corner ease out of the room I realised I'd said that louder than I intended.

'No chance, pal. If you're not out of here in five seconds the police'll see to you.'

'The police, bunch of wasters…' I felt a tug at my sleeve. 'What good are they? Bunch of lazy…' My sleeve was being pulled and someone was calling my name. I looked around. It was Sheila. I calmed down instantly.

'C'mon you,' she said, 'I'm taking you out of here.'

More than anything, it was the look of pity in her eyes that drew the anger out of me. 'Sorry, Sheila. I was just about to make an arse of myself…'

'It's time you were back at the hotel.' She led me to the door and out into the street.

At the front door, the cool air had me shivering. 'Sheila, you're a darling, but if you think I'm going back to the hotel then you're sadly mistaken. I'm going to drink myself into a stupor.'

'Well, I'd better make sure that you don't come to any harm. I'm coming with you.'

'Won't be a pretty sight.'

'Don't worry, Andy. I've seen it all before. Right, where are we going?' She stood with her hands on her hips. Nothing I could say would dissuade her.

'Okay,' I laughed. 'You're on. But you better be joining in. I hate drinking on my own.'

'I can see that. You're awful shy, aren't you?' We both laughed.

*

Sheila ordered a round at the first bar we entered. It was only marginally busier than the one we'd just left. The barman, while looking every inch the local, had an Australian accent. He placed my pint on a brass-coloured spill-tray.

'Get your laughing gear round that, mate.' He grinned.

'Don't mind if I do.' His grin was infectious. I could hardly believe that only minutes ago I was about to get into one with a different barman. Sheila was clearly good for me. We choose a table and sat down.

'Thanks for calming things down earlier on, Sheila. I really was about to lose it,' I said, feeling my face heat with shame.

'Why?' She took a sip. She'd ordered a pint as well. 'What did that poor guy do to you?'

'You wouldn't understand.'

'Try me.'

'He laughed at me,' I answered, as honestly as I could without going into too much detail. 'And I do not need someone laughing at me at this point.'

'Andy,' Sheila's face was creased with concern, 'what's happening to you these days? You're not the Andy Boyd I know.' She stopped talking, looking as if she'd said more than she planned.

'And…'

'No. It's none of my business.'

'I'd really like to know what you think.' I found it easier to let other people do the talking. If there was too much silence, I might say too much.

'Okay.' She took a long drink and set her glass to the side. 'You've lost a lot of weight. You look gaunt. You always look as if you're ready for bed. You've let things slip back in Ayr.' She looked deep into my eyes. 'You know that there were complaints not long ago.'

'Aye, and I've sorted things out.'

'Have you, Andy? I wasn't going to say anything, but I feel it's not fair.'

'What isn't?' Acid bit at my stomach lining as I registered her tone and her expression. 'What's going on?'

'There was another reason why you were chosen to come here…'

'To get me out of the way?'

'Yes. They wanted to look into what's happening in Ayr and thought it best to get you out of the road. This Campbeltown thing gave them the perfect excuse.'

'Bet it was that bastard Roy's idea. What's your involvement in all of this?' I demanded.

'Don't worry, I'm not their spy. You did need help over here and I was the right woman for the job. Nothing more devious than that. Believe me Andy, I'm not here to set you up.'

'Bastards.' I slammed my glass down on the table.

'You all right, mate?' the barman shouted over.

'Piss off, *mate*,' I said.

'We're fine thanks.' Sheila drowned me out and grimaced. 'Keep it cool, Andy. You don't want to get chucked out of two places on the one night.'

'I can't take any more.' I stood up. 'I can't take any more.' I fought for breath.

'Andy sit down.' Sheila looked up at me. 'Tell me what's going on. What can't you take?'

'Anything, the whole fucking world's out to get me. First my wife, then my colleagues … and then you,' I spat. In a deep corner of my brain, I knew that Sheila wasn't complicit in any of this, but I needed to lash out and she was conveniently placed.

'Andy, I told you, I've nothing to do with any of this.'

'Yeah, fucking right. You're just as bad as the rest of them. I thought you were special, Sheila. But you're as poisonous as they are.' Months of ingested bile threatened to spill over onto the surface. The barman walked over to us.

'Is everything all right, folks?'

'Fuck off, you Aussie twat.'

'Andy.' Sheila stood up.

'Right sir, I'll have to ask you to leave.'

The barman gripped my arm. He shouldn't have done that. I

reacted quicker than I could have believed. My fist exploded into his jaw. I couldn't hit a woman, but I could happily hit a man.

The trouble was, once I started, I didn't know if I could stop.

9

The police cell was just what I imagined it would be like. Small, cold and sparse. The thin blanket provided barely any heat, the insubstantial mattress little cushion. Sleep was some distance away for the whole of the night. This gave me more time to think than I needed. The events of the day before reeled through my head: the insults I threw at the barman; the locals in the bar jumping on top of me to calm me down; Sheila's face wide-mouthed with shock. The soundtrack to this movie was my own voice. A scream that seemed to go on and on.

When the police arrived, I was exhausted. I had barely enough energy to hold my hands out for the cuffs. They decided that, although I had calmed down, based on what everyone was telling them, I needed to spend a night in a cell. Make sure I sobered up before I did some harm.

The cell door opened and a policeman walked in carrying a tray.

'Here's your breakfast, big guy. Bacon roll and a mug of hot tea.'

'Thanks,' I muttered. I was having trouble accepting I had acted so badly that I had been locked up. I'd never been involved with the police before. I'd never had so much as a parking ticket. Where was my shame going to end? Standing up and walking over to accept the tray, I noticed my trouser belt had gone and my shoes had no laces. The policeman followed my gaze to my feet.

'Do you not remember we took them off you last night? To save you from hanging yourself.'

'With a pair of shoe laces?'

'We get some pretty determined people in here.'

I digested that. 'When do I get out?'

'Don't know. Someone will be along to speak to you shortly. Your fingerprints were taken last night along with your statement' – I couldn't remember this – 'so you should be able to get out sharpish.' The tea was sweet and strong, but the thought of the bacon roll was too much. With both hands nursing the mug, I sat down on the bed and leaned against the wall. What kind of a mess have you got yourself into now, Boyd? I hoped the barman was okay and that I hadn't roughed up any of the locals. The bank would not be happy. Anna would not be happy. I hoped Sheila was still talking to me.

I received confirmation of this shortly after seven. The day shift wanted to clean out the cells and Sheila, unable to sleep, had arrived first thing to make sure that I had done nothing else.

Feeling like a wayward teenager, I walked over to where she was sitting in the reception area.

'You okay?' Concern was evident in her face. It was quickly quashed when she could see that I was still in one piece.

'Listen, Sheila. I am so sorry about last night. I don't know what got into me.'

'I suspect you do know, Andy. But if you don't want to talk about it…'

'Let's get out of here.' I walked briskly to the door. 'I don't want to spend another moment in here.'

'It's a beautiful morning. We'll walk back to the hotel and you can freshen up.'

We walked most of the way in silence. The early-morning light promised much for the day ahead, but the sea breeze held a chill. Our heels clipping the pavement sounded out a regular rhythm beneath the staccato cries of the gulls wheeling overhead.

'Thanks for coming to meet me.' I broke the silence just as the hotel came into view.

'No problem. I had to make sure you were okay. So I could report back to Regional Office,' Sheila replied.

I shrunk further in size. I must have really hurt her.

'Sheila, I didn't mean what I said. I was just angry and you were…'

'Convenient?' Her expression was conflicted. She wanted to show she was on my side and yet she also wanted me to know that she no longer put up with anyone's shit.

'Sheila, I am so sorry.' I stopped walking and held her hand, forcing her to stop. Her eyes were as cool as the breeze.

'Okay, you've apologised. Can we go now, I'm freezing.'

'Sheila, listen to me. I really am so sorry. You are the one person in my life right now who I can talk to, so please don't shut me out.'

'The one person you can talk to? If this is you talking, I would hate to see you mute.'

'Okay, maybe I can't talk to you either, but I enjoy your company. You make me feel … good.'

I was saying too much. While lying awake in the police cell, I had examined my feelings for Sheila and found that they had not lessened. I had prayed that hers was the first face I saw on my release. But I couldn't admit to this. Complications of that sort were dangerous, possibly for both of us. Who knew what Anna was capable of once she warmed up?

'How can I convince you that I'm sorry?'

'Mmm.' Sheila held a finger to the corner of her mouth. What I would have given for the freedom to bend forward and kiss her right where her finger was pressing. 'Kiss my feet.'

'Okay. Madam's wish is my command.' I knelt down and leaned over as if to do as she asked.

'Get up you big lump.' She giggled and pulled ineffectively at my upper arm. I continued to aim my mouth at her feet. 'Okay, okay,' she laughed. 'You're forgiven. Get over to that hotel and get yourself a wash.'

As I drove home that night from the airport there were two things on my mind. The first was Anna. What had she said to the police? And what would they do about it? Also, she would have phoned the hotel at just about the time I was punching a barman. Her imagination would apply a different set of circumstances to her unanswered phone call. This time, however, the truth was just so outlandish that she would believe it.

The second thing on my mind was Sheila. Frightened as I was of Anna and what her reaction might be, Sheila's smile as I pretended to kiss her feet was there in my mind, like a small window tucked in the corner of a computer screen. I would just have to wait until Monday before I spoke to her again.

I would have to work out what was going on here. Did I have genuine feelings for Sheila? Or was this a case of transferring my affections onto someone who seemed to care about me? She was at the police station as I came out, so she must, at least, like me. Then the picture of me as I sat in the first pub came to mind. My defeated reflection staring back at me. What woman would be attracted to that? She would only laugh at me. There was no point even contemplating an affair with her in any case, because if Anna found out, someone, probably me, would end up hurt.

The boys bowled me over as soon as I entered the house. They'd been sitting by the window waiting for my return. Was it my imagination or were they more than just pleased to see me? I briefly considered each homecoming over the past few weeks. Each of them resulted in a similar display. I mentally shrugged off my concern as paranoia. Anna adored the boys. I was the focus of her aggression, not them.

She was standing by the kitchen door in her apron. She had pinned her hair up but locks here and there defied the clip. One eye was partially obscured and at the other side a long, thick strand decorated her shoulder. She was lovely. I searched her expression for a clue as to how I should behave. It was blank.

'Change out of your suit, Andy. Dinner'll be ready in five minutes.' No mention of the police, what was she playing at?

'Have you got a present for us, Dad?' asked Pat as I walked towards the stairs. Turning round I was presented with two eager faces.

'Oh, silly me. Forgot all about my two best boys. See this plastic bag in my hand. What do we have in here?' I pulled out some chocolates and some collectible cards that every child in the know had to have.

'Yeees,' they chanted in unison as they held out their hands. Ryan, wasn't really sure what he was cheering about but he was happy to follow the lead of his big brother.

Having changed into a pair of jogging trousers and a t-shirt, I entered the kitchen and approached Anna. Aware that the boys could see us from their vantage point in front of the TV, I put my arm around Anna's waist and kissed the side of her head. My kiss would have been aimed at her face had she allowed, but she was refusing to play the role.

'Where were you last night?' She stirred the pan of bolognaise vigorously.

'Oh, there's a good explanation for that.' I shuffled to the other side of the room. Out of reach.

'There'd better be. Could you get me a spoon out of that drawer?'

I was puzzled. It was easily within reach.

'Andy, that drawer, a wooden spoon, please.'

Wondering what was going on, I moved over to her side and opening the drawer, put my hand in for a spoon. Anna slammed it shut, jamming my fingers.

'Ow. That hurt!' My fingers pulsed with pain.

'It was meant to,' Anna hissed. Louder she said, 'Silly Daddy, catching his fingers in the drawer.' Her voice quietened again. 'So where the hell were you? I must have phoned that hotel a thousand times.'

I moved as if to go back to the other side of the room. Like a disobedient dog, I was ordered to stay. So I did. This was not a battle I needed to win.

'I was in jail,' I answered.

Anna stopped stirring. Her mouth opened and closed.

'What do you mean, in jail?' she eventually asked.

'I assaulted a barman.' It was difficult to even say it out loud. 'So the police locked me up for the night.'

'And the bank? What are they saying about this?'

'I don't know. But it won't look too good.'

Anna swept her eyes up and down my frame, as if seeing me for the first time. 'You're a real man after all.'

'You're not angry?' I was amazed at her lack of reaction. I had expected her to go crazy.

'No, why should I be? You got in a fight. Big deal. Is this other guy going to press charges?'

'Don't know how it all works.'

'We'll get you a good lawyer. Say it was the pressure of work. When will your case come up?'

'Not sure. The policeman thought it could be anything from three to six weeks.' With the reference to the police hanging in the air I paused. I needed to find out what the hell was going on, so, with my heart wedged somewhere in my throat, I asked her. 'What are the police going to do … you know … about your complaint?'

'Nothing,' she continued stirring. If cordon bleu depended on use of a spoon, Anna would be a top chef.

'Nothing?' I asked, keeping the relief from my voice.

'You deaf? Nothing. I didn't tell them.'

'Oh.'

'Yes, I changed my mind. I was going to cos you don't know your strength. A big man like you shouldn't go around hitting women. But next time…'

In the normal course of events, my work provided some sort of respite from my problems, but it was with some trepidation that I went to the office that Monday. I could detect nothing different in the usual greetings from the staff. Even the brashest people in the office had nothing out of the ordinary to say. Word had obviously not reached Ayr yet.

'What, ten to nine and a caffeine-break already?' asked Carol from Personal Accounts when she saw me at the coffee machine.

'Yeah. I need something to help me face this place of a morning,' I answered.

'Not the positive message we like our managers to provide,' a familiar voice at my ear said. I turned round as if scalded.

'Roy. I didn't know you were in this morning.'

'Evidently,' he crowed. 'Once you've finished motivating your staff, could I have a word with you in private.'

'Sure.' Shit, I thought. 'We'll use my office.'

From the satisfied expression on his face, I could have bet my life savings that he knew everything. But had he already informed the Regional Director's office?

'Word has reached Sam Hyslop at Regional Office,' he began before we even reached my room, 'of an unsavoury event in Campbeltown.'

'Oh.' I sunk into a chair.

'Oh?' He remained standing. 'Is that all you have to say for yourself? What's going on in that head of yours, Boyd?'

I shrugged, I had no defence. He sat on the side of my desk and looked down at me.

'I've to provide a written report for Sam. He wants to know if you're being charged and if it has hit the local press over in Kintyre.'

'Yes I'm being charged. I've been told that my case could take up to six weeks before coming before the local Sheriff.'

'And when it does,' Roy said, 'you can bet the local journalists will have a field day.' He took a deep breath as if what he was about to say was at some personal cost and a great deal of emotional pain. 'I'm to offer you every support. If there are … issues you're struggling with … then I'd like to help you.' He looked as if he'd rather chew on a hand grenade.

'Thanks for the offer, Roy. There's nothing wrong, but I'll come to you if I have any problems.' As I spoke I realised how far I had fallen. Only a matter of months ago I would have thrown him out of my office and told him that I'd rather air my problems on a crass chat show than tell him. That day, I sat bowed on my chair, fingers laced together as if in desperate prayer. My mouth was dry with the dirt of the thousand apologies I'd uttered that weekend. I could no more speak up to him than I could Anna. Lost in a haar of uncertainty, I waited for direction from the foghorn of his voice.

'You've to carry on working' – that meant they'd already considered suspending me – 'until we conduct an investigation. We will then estimate how much damage you've done to the bank.'

'Could I lose my job?' The thought burst from my lips.

'Who knows what will happen? Sacked or demoted? We'll just have to wait and see. I don't mean to be rough on you, Andy. But it's better that you know the truth.'

I sipped at my coffee, more from a need to do something than from thirst.

'Thanks for being honest with me, Roy.' In some recess of my mind the other Andy Boyd recoiled at my passivity, but there was nothing else I could do. I had no excuse, or none that I cared to admit. It was bad enough to confess that I had drunk too much, but how bad would it sound to everyone that I lashed out at a stranger because I couldn't handle my own wife?

'Too much alcohol,' I mumbled.

Once I had provided Roy with an account of what happened, excluding my motivation, he left me to reacquaint myself with the current state of affairs in my own branch. Each of the section heads reported that all was well, apart from the usual moans about sales targets and staffing levels.

Steve, the team leader at one of the Personal Banking units, provided me with my only problem of the morning. A customer had come in late on Friday and demanded a refund on an erroneous charge she had noticed on last month's statement. The narrative on the entry read 'Safe Custody'. The customer had never used that particular service. Steve had investigated, verified the customer's claim and found a debit slip, initialled by me. The writing was not mine and I could not therefore offer an explanation as to why the customer had been charged. I authorised a refund and dictated a letter of apology.

The stack of mail on my desk was daunting and with little enthusiasm for the job I started to read. Two hours later, having absorbed very little indeed, neck sore, eyes sore, I decided to give myself a break. A coffee and a wee chat with a friendly face was in order. Although I had very little to say for myself, I would be more than happy to listen.

'Where's Malcolm?' I asked Sandra at the reception desk.

'Don't know, Mr Boyd.' Sandra was very much of the old school of banking. Managers must still have worn bowler hats when she joined the bank for no amount of cajoling would encourage her to call me by my first name. Today, however, any reminder that I could wield some power was welcome.

'His mother phoned in for him. Said he was sick,' someone said.

'That's pathetic,' someone else said.

'What is?'

'That a guy in his mid-thirties is still getting his mum to phone in for him.'

'I've always wondered about him.'

'Yeah, living with his mother at that age. Must be a poof.'

Another member of staff swivelled on their chair to talk to me. It was Sadie Banks. She and Anna had been friends of sorts at the last branch they worked together, or so Sadie thought. She was a quiet girl, keeping pretty much to herself. I thought she saw a similarity between her and Anna.

'How's Anna?' she asked. 'Haven't spoken to her for a while.'

'She's fine,' I answered. 'You should give her a call. She'd be delighted to hear from you.'

Leaving the staff to their speculation, I went back to my office. I had lost count of the times that I had overheard variations of the conversation about Malcolm. At times I butted in, defending him, saying that it was a shame that people felt they had to speculate on his sexuality based on such a cliché. So much for living in more enlightened times. Or I would cite simple economics: the guy couldn't afford a house of his own, the bank didn't pay him enough. Today, I didn't have the energy.

10

Sheila continued to inhabit my thoughts. I scanned my brain for any excuse to call her. Each one I rehearsed sounded more pathetic than the last. Why was I bothering? She would want nothing more to do with me. She'd witnessed what kind of a man I really was. I was a sham, an embarrassment to my gender. She'd had enough problems with men in the past. A bully and a drunk were what she had seen in action. I was simply a taller version of what she was used to.

Anna should have been enough reason for me to put Sheila out of my mind. But her image persisted. Like a child with its comforter, I would imagine pulling Sheila to me. Strangely, not once was the thought sexual. Each time I held her in my imagination, I was seeking comfort, trying to borrow strength.

Sheila phoned me.

'Andy, I heard about the investigation. How are you?' she asked.

'Oh, you know. Shite.'

'Don't worry about it. Everything will blow over.'

'Although I don't agree with you, the thought is appreciated. Where are you?' I asked, grateful for the call. It heartened me to know that there was someone on my side. There was no way that I could explain to Sheila what was going on but the hope that she might understand, if I did tell her, was a help.

'I've been sent to Troon, to do an audit.'

'Someone else been naughty?' The petty thought occurred to me that if someone else was in trouble it might take the spotlight off me.

'No, just routine stuff.'

Silence sang in my ear as I thought of something else to say. Sheila spoke first.

'So how are you, Andy? Really?'

'Worried about my job.' A part-truth was a safe answer.

'If you need a chat, any time, give me a call. I'll be happy to listen.'

'Thanks.' I hung up. As far as I was concerned the offer would remain on a shelf like a forgotten memento. Occasionally, I would pick it up, blow off the dust, think 'what if…', but ultimately put it back in its place, unused.

Only lunchtime and it felt like I'd been back at the office for a month. One more customer complaint about an incorrect Safe Custody charge arrived on my desk. Again, I wrote an apology. Again, the monies were refunded.

I wasn't hungry. The thought of putting anything into my mouth was enough to make me nauseous. Instead, I bought myself a news-paper and sipped at a coffee while I skimmed over the major events of the previous day. A cat in Kazakhstan could have triggered a nuclear explosion and I doubt if I would have really noticed.

After lunch, there was another complaint. The member of staff on the reception desk was so frustrated at having to field another unhappy customer's comments that she came and demanded that I speak to them.

'I mean, it's not as if it's even my fault,' she said with a sniff, arms crossed tight. 'I think a manager should deal with this.'

'Okay.' I stood up slowly, 'Who is it this time?'

'Mrs Johnson-Smythe. She emptied her Safe Custody items out the year before last and is about to close her account after further evidence of our ineptitude. I mean, I don't even know how to spell that word. Anyway, the snooty cow is in one of the interview areas.'

Mrs Johnson-Smythe was another of my old adversaries. She and I had had various discussions over the years. Her accounts with the branch were rather impressive, so we normally did as much as we could for her. She had struck me as someone who realised the value of a loud voice when issuing a complaint, especially when doing so in person and particularly in public. The interview area would suit her just fine, it was little more than a three-sided cube with five-foot-high partitions. Our other customers would have no trouble at all in listening to what she had to say.

She was standing beside one of the three seats when I approached. Obviously she felt that her voice could carry further when her lungs were not constricted by a seated posture.

'Mr Boyd,' she announced. 'So glad that you could join me.'

'Mrs Johnson-Smythe, I am so sorry about this small error…' I began, willing energy into my voice, but she interrupted.

'A small error, Mr Boyd? This is a matter of thirty pounds. Not a sum to be sneezed at when you are a poor pensioner.' No one standing in the vicinity would have believed that the voice they heard came from a 'poor pensioner'.

'I meant small from the point of view that it could be easily fixed, Mrs Johnson…'

'I hope it will be easily fixed. Because if the money is not in my account before I leave this office, then I will be leaving this office with every penny I own.'

'The money will be in your account immediately.' I prayed that I did not sound as if I was grovelling. 'I will just go and see that the entries are made and…'

'… and I will wait here until you provide me with proof in black and white that matters have been rectified.'

By the close of business that day I had refunded a further three such complaints. Each customer had been charged thirty pounds, each was as indignant as the last. Forehead resting on my palms, I tried not to look at the evidence on my desk. Six dark-pink slips punctuated the wood like warning signs. Stop. Look no further. They all bore the same handwriting – Malcolm's – and they were all authorised by me. I had no recollection of having initialled them.

I couldn't understand how Malcolm could make such an elementary error. When writing out the debits for such a charge, the member of staff quite simply copied the names and account number from the Safe Custody register. Not one person who had complained was even on the register.

'What else is going to go wrong?' I asked the empty room. I'd had enough. Time to go home, I could investigate this further in the morning, when I had a clear head.

Having slept very little, with the worry of everything happening in my life, I was back in the office at eight-fifteen the next morning. The pinks slips sat where I had left them. The cleaner must have only aimed the duster at the desk and gone on to something else. Foreboding hung at the edge of my every movement that morning like a border of heavy cloud. Something was not right and I was going to be implicated in it.

The first thing I looked for was the processing report for the day in question. This was a paper printout of every entry made on any given day. I scanned the pages for the entries relating to the pieces of paper in my hand. Nothing. This was very odd. Each and every debit or credit slip had to have a corresponding entry on the report. I checked again. Still nothing. I looked at every batch of entries on every page, slowly and carefully, to no avail. But then I noticed a strange sequence of entries.

What began as a list of debit entries, all for sums varying from twenty pounds to forty pounds, ended on the following page with a run of cross-entries. Essentially every item on these pages was part of a cross-entry. Some had two debits and one credit, others had numerous credits and one debit. The problem I had noticed was a line of debits was missing a corresponding credit to balance them off. The machinist who processed this page could not have finished her work without it. So where was it? A quick search showed that there were no pages out of order. Then a small rag of paper round the elastic rope that bound the pages together caught my attention. That explained it. Someone had ripped out the pages.

By now the office was beginning to fill up. Staff were staring at me as I shot through the office, mumbling to myself. Where would the pages have gone and would we have another copy? The fiche copy. Yes, that was it. A copy was sent to the branch each day on a small piece of plastic that could be viewed on a fiche. But as I walked to the cupboard where the fiches were stored, I became certain that the day I was looking for would be missing as well. Whoever was behind this would have also known about the fiche copy. Sure enough, there was a blank space in the folder where it should have been. I ran my finger down the folder to check if it had been misfiled and noticed that another couple of days' reports were missing.

'Has anyone seen Malcolm come in yet?' I asked in the main office.

'His mum phoned in sick for him yesterday,' someone said.

'I know that,' I snapped. 'Has he turned up today?'

Blank faces all round me was the answer. I went back to my office but not before I heard a couple of comments.

'Somebody got out the wrong side of bed this morning.'

'Maybe his wife kicked him out.'

Stifled laughter followed me into my room. I closed the door.

'Malcolm, what the fuck have you been up to?' I asked the four walls. It had to be him. He had written all of the entries. Pity I couldn't remember authorising them. Then I remembered previous questions being asked about Malcolm's honesty. Money had gone missing from the cash. To compound matters, I had defended him at the time. I sank into my chair. What was I going to do? I could simply do nothing and hope that the matter would not come to anyone else's attention. I could stifle matters here at local level. No one else need know. Excellent, that was it decided, I would do absolutely nothing.

But what if there were others? This thought nagged me as I opened my mail. Why would he go to the trouble of stealing thirty pounds from six customers? It was hardly worth the effort. That was what made me certain that there must be more.

'Could I speak to Sheila please?' I had picked up the phone and dialled almost without conscious thought. Sheila would know what to do.

'Have you reported this yet?' she asked once I had appraised her of the detail.

'Are you off your head? I'm implicated here. This is the last thing I need after my boxing match at Campbeltown.'

'But if you don't report it then it could look even worse for you. I agree with you, Andy. It looks quite likely that there are more customers being debited than just these six. You're bound to get even more complaints.'

Sheila was telling me what I already knew. It made it easier for me to face up to things hearing her say it.

'Where's Roy?' I asked.

'He's in Glasgow.'

'Right, I'll phone him right now.' Before I could change my mind, I punched in his number. I could almost hear the acid hissing in my stomach as I spoke to him. It raced up my gullet as he told me that he would be at the office within the hour.

'It's not looking good, Andy.' Roy perched on the edge of my desk. 'First, your writing is on each of these slips. Second, you kept this to yourself for a full day before informing Regional Office. Now this is not my opinion, but there are those who would say that this gave you plenty of time to dispose of any evidence.'

'Roy, surely…'

'I'm not saying that you're involved, Andy. Just that it doesn't look good for you. You and Malcolm have always been close. Then there's this business of you assaulting people while at another branch.'

'Shit, Roy, I would never steal…'

'I know that, Andy, All I'm saying is that it doesn't look good.' He stood up. 'I think it would be best if you went home for the day.'

'What?' I couldn't believe what I was hearing.

'Make it a week. We'll have to have a full investigation and you can't be around to tamper with any more evidence. Not that I think you would,' he hastily added. 'We just have to be careful, that's all I'm saying. Why don't you stay at home until I contact you? Just think of it as an opportunity to catch up on those odd jobs around the house.' He smiled. 'Spend some time with that lovely wife of yours.'

11

I left the office that day without saying a word to anyone. With briefcase in hand, I walked out of the front door, trying to look as if I was going about my normal business. Shame and confusion spat fire in my stomach. Inadequacy and worry flicked at the muscle of my heart. My pace was slow and measured, yet I felt out of breath. By the time I reached my car I was panting.

At about the fifth attempt I managed to insert the key into the lock and gratefully sat in the driver's seat. Looking around me, I was relieved to see no familiar faces. Automatically, I turned on the engine and clicked in my seatbelt, but I couldn't quite concentrate enough to drive. I stared out of the window, seeing nothing. What was I going to do? And how many times was I going to ask that question? First, I hit Anna, then I assault some poor stranger, then I become implicated in a fraud for God knows how much? Could my life get any worse?

Closing my eyes, I forced my breathing into a slower rhythm. But just before each breath was fully exhaled, I felt panicked into inhaling. It was only two-thirty in the afternoon, far too early to go home. I couldn't face Anna just yet. How was she going to react when I told her I was suspended? Because, whatever way I looked at it that was what had happened. I wasn't on 'gardening leave', nor was I on an unplanned vacation. I was suspended, plain and simple. My breathing was faster again. Slowly I filled my lungs and dropped my shoulders as I breathed out. Again, I had to breathe in too quickly.

By now I was becoming accustomed to the strategy of inertia. If something happens, do nothing, was my new motto. Plainly, it wasn't working; but it was much easier than the emotional cost of having to act, or even worse, react. My new course of action therefore was blindingly simple: each day I would leave home as if going to work. Instead I would go to the town library and pass the day reading newspapers. Before too long had passed, the powers-that-be would realise that I couldn't have stolen any money and they would reinstate me. This would take no more than a week. Anna, therefore, need know nothing. This episode of my life would then be filed under 'bad dream'. I could concentrate on the important stuff, like making Anna and the boys happy.

On most days, nine to five in the office seemed to pass in the single movement of a clock's hand. In the library, each tiny movement of the same hand had the pace of dripping treacle. By lunchtime each day, I had read every newspaper. Thursday was a poor news day and I read most of them twice. In the afternoons, I picked up magazines, on any topic. It didn't really matter, because very little that raced before my eyes reached my brain. As long as it contained the written word, it would do. As long as it provided the illusion that I was keeping my brain active then I was happy.

I lost count of the times I would get to the edge of a page, turn over, then turn back, wondering what I had been reading about. On a couple of occasions, I mercifully fell asleep. Despite myself, I wakened with a start, hoping that hours had passed. The clock showed that it had been barely minutes.

Otherwise, the reading room of the library had a curious but beneficial effect on me. Whether it was the general sense of peace in the room or the shared hush of its occupants, I wasn't sure, but it was the only place that my breathing returned to normal. At home, I felt as if I was continually out of breath. At night, I would fall asleep only to wake up moments later as I fought for air. I knew this was not normal, but to do anything about it would be too difficult. Besides, if I went to my doctor, he would only laugh. No, I would wait and, like everything else, it would go away. It became so that the library was my sanctuary from the world. Each day as I drove there, I anticipated the calm I so needed and pressed my foot on the accelerator.

Once inside, serenity flowed from the rows of books until my breathing slowed and my posture eased. The events of the real world could not touch me here. I was unable to forget them, or to stop worrying, but their cold grasp didn't tighten muscle or shorten breath. By the Friday of that week, I was able to sustain this composure almost until I reached home. Only when I parked in front of my house that afternoon did the calm recede.

The front door opened in time with me closing the car door. But instead of waiting for me to walk up the path, Anna turned and walked back into the living room, leaving the door open. What was all that about? I wondered as I moved up the path.

'Where the hell have you been?' Anna shouted as soon as I entered the room.

'Eh ... at work. Where else?' My breathing quickened, my limbs leaked energy into the carpet.

'Liar.' Her fist was a blur, then pain bloomed at the right corner of my mouth.

I fell onto the couch and brought my knees up to protect my genitals. There was a noise issuing from behind me. It sounded like a dog in pain. Then I realised it was Pat and Ryan. Without even looking, I could see them in my mind, knees pulled up to their chests, Ryan leaning into his big brother. This was no life for a child.

'Pat, Ryan, go up to your room.' At the sound of my voice, they shot from behind the settee and ran for the door.

'Stay where you are.' Anna's voice halted their run as if they had slammed into a glass door. 'Stay and see what a disgrace your father is.'

They edged along the wall towards the corner of the room that was furthest from us. Once there, they huddled together, each seeking comfort and strength from the other. The displaced observer in my mind appreciated how my two boys looked to each other for help. The father wept silent tears into a well of self-hate. How had I managed to reduce my beautiful sons to this?

Anna continued to fling words into the room. Words of poisoned steel with barbed edges. Edges that tore at the lines joining each of us. Edges that shredded any mote of self-esteem we may have clung to. She hit me once more. Her hand was cupped and aimed at my ear. The pain was immense. What had she done? I held my hand to the side of my head and willed the ache to stop. Streams of syllables, acrid with hate, continued to shoot from her tortured mouth. Even her lips curled away from their intent.

'Please, Anna. Leave the boys out of this. Don't you see what you're doing to them?

'I'm letting them see what an excuse for a father they have. It's better they find out now. It's better they learn while they are still young. Then they won't get let down. Don't you see, boys? I'm doing it for your own good.' Her head was pointed towards them and was about ten inches in front of her feet.

Eyes huge with uncertainty, the boys looked first at her, then at me. At such an early age Pat was clearly aware of the politics of the situation. Anna had the strength. He had to do and say what pleased her. But he struggled with the betrayal of his father.

'You see it boys, don't you? You have to see what an utter waste of time your father is now, before he lets you down. Don't you?' Her eyes snapped from one to the other, demanding an affirmation of her claim with her eyes.

Pat stole a glimpse at me, as if begging for permission to let me down. With the slightest nod of my head, I tried to show my eldest that he had to save himself.

'Yes.' His voice was a whisper.

'See.' Anna faced me triumphant. 'Even your precious first-born can see what a stupid, worthless cunt you are. What are you?'

'A stupid, worthless cunt,' I admitted, head down at my knees. 'Can the boys go to their room now?'

'Okay, boys,' Anna said. 'Go upstairs. Leave me and your father alone. We have things to discuss.' Their feet drummed out of the room.

'Look at you. Pathetic. I should get myself another man. A real man. Right, before I throw you out...'

'What?'

'Before I throw you out, I want to know what is going on.'

'You're throwing me out?'

'Of course I am. Look at you. You're a mess. You're not fit to be a father. You're a drunk, a bully, you've stolen money from your employers…'

'You know about that?' My head shot up.

'What's more, you're a wife-beater and I've got the bruises to prove it.'

'You know about the missing money?'

'Of course I know about it. Do you think I'm stupid? Where did I used to work, Andy?'

'In the bank.'

'In the bank. Right. And I still have contacts there. So what I want to know is how much you stole, where it is and where that boyfriend of yours is. You know I must be blind. All this time, I've been thinking you've been sleeping with another woman, while it's really another man. Is that where you've been all week, shagging the arse off Malcolm Kay?'

'Anna…' Where was she getting all of this?

'Don't you "Anna" me. You can tell me where the money is and then you're out of here.'

'You can't throw me out.' My voice was a flat-line on a heart monitor. I had no strength, no will and no opinion. Any fight I offered was merely a token. I was crushed and I knew it.

'I can and I will throw you out. No court in the land will let you stay or keep the boys once they know what kind of man you are.'

Anna had just given sound to the thought that worried me above all else. I didn't know one man who had been granted custody of his children. If Anna and I separated, there was little chance that I would get the boys, especially now I had a history of violence.

'You can't throw me out.' My voice was as lifeless as the rags that put together a scarecrow. I couldn't lose the boys. I needed them in my life. I needed to see them develop in size and stature; to see their first game of football for the school team; to mop up tears at the end of their first love affair; to hold their shoulder as they opened their exam results. The job of Sunday father was not for me. I'd noticed other guys with their kids in McDonalds or at the bowling alley, trying hard to maintain some form of a relationship, but, judging by the expressions of the bored children, failing abjectly.

I had to form part of the fabric of their lives. I had to be on the thread that led them to their first day at the High School, woven into the cloth that bound them when they fell and hurt themselves. The steps that Anna was about to take would unravel all of this and turn my life into a shapeless, colourless rag.

'I'm not going.' A voice issued from a well of strength I didn't know existed. Its reserves were almost gone, but enough remained for one last fight. I stood up and faced her.

'I'm not going,' I repeated. Louder. 'The bank will soon realise that I've done nothing and I'll get my job back.'

Anna opened her mouth as if to speak and stopped, jaw wide. Her expression changed as thoughts occurred to her. I could read them as easily as if she had projected them onto a wall. The change in my demeanour surprised her. She didn't know I had it in me to fight back. She couldn't let me fan the spark of my fightback into a revolution. I was almost dead and buried and she had to finish it now.

Her scream reached me only seconds before she did. Hair, teeth and knuckles blurred before me like a grotesque Spirograph. My balls were her usual target so I doubled over to protect them. Her fists were everywhere, my kidneys, my ears, my ribs. In a foetal position, I submerged the pain and cloaked her blows with images of the boys. I was taking this for them. This reminder served to keep my anger under control. It could seethe and rage within the confines of this conscience-cage, but I couldn't, wouldn't allow it freedom again. Because then I would be the loser. After what seemed hours, the blows stopped. Anna stood beside me, panting.

'Prick. I want you out of here.'

I stood up slowly, testing for breaks. I breathed slow and deep to check my ribs. They were sore but unbroken.

'Anna, I'm not leaving you or the kids.' I grimaced at the pain.

'No? We'll see about that. I'll just phone the police. They'll get you out of here.' If we had been living in a cartoon, a light would have appeared above her head, while an axe hung above mine. 'That's what I'll do, phone the police.'

'Do what you like, Anna, I'm going upstairs to see how the boys are.'

In a weak attempt to inject some routine into the day, I was dressing the boys for an early bed time when I heard the scream from downstairs.

Panicking, I ran down, taking three steps at a time, my pain forgotten. Anna was screaming insults at someone, but using my name. My steps slowed as I realised what was going on. I walked into the room just as Anna replaced the receiver. Her face was lined with pleasure. Had it been anyone else, I could never have believed the noise that had issued from this room had come from the same woman.

'The police,' she smiled, 'will be here shortly.' She then walked over to the kitchen door and turning her head to the side and slammed it against the bridge of her nose.

'What the … are you crazy?' I sank onto a chair.

Blood bloomed from her nose and sent its garland curving over her lip and down her chin. She made no effort to staunch its flow. Shaking her head wildly, she posted drops of blood all over the room.

'Anna, stop it.' I ran for a cloth and amazed at how much blood could stem from a nose bleed, began to clean. A knock at the door interrupted my endeavours.

'That didn't take long,' grinned Anna. 'Plod must be quiet tonight.' Then she began to scream. 'Help, help, somebody help.' She sank to the floor.

'Anna, get up and stop acting the fool.' I stood over her, the stained cloth in my hand. Footsteps. I was roughly pulled to the side. Turning to my assailant, the first thing I noticed was the uniform. Two uniforms. One belonged to a female, the other male. It was the male, about the same height I was, who held onto my arm. He looked about the same age as me, his once-handsome features softened by too many beers and curries. Anna began to sob pathetically.

'Thank God, thank God you're here. I thought he was going to kill me.'

The female officer went over to Anna to console her. She was tall and slim, with blonde hair tucked under her cap. Her finely drawn features were clean of make-up and her eyes sparked with intelligence.

'Let's get you a seat and sort out this mess.' She led Anna to an armchair.

'Fuck the seat,' Anna raged. 'Arrest this bastard and get him the hell out of here.'

'I know this looks bad, but I can explain everything,' I said, trying to appear calm. The grip on my arm tightened. The man under the rim of the police hat stared at me with loathing. 'You prick,' he said, just loud enough for me to hear. I could easily see what he was seeing. A large man, bent over a much smaller, beautiful and bleeding woman. Case closed.

'I'm Constable Jane Orr and this is Constable Ian Russell,' said the female. The gorilla at my side grunted. 'We need to ascertain the problem here before any corrective action is taken.'

'The problem is that horror show is still in this house. Get him the hell out of here.' Anna spat.

'If Mrs Boyd would calm down and tell us what happened then we could settle matters.'

'What? You're not going to arrest him?'

'Tell me what happened.'

'His dinner wasn't on the table when he came in from work and he went mental. Chucking furniture around the room, breaking plates and everything.'

Orr looked around the room as Anna spoke. Her expression seemed too say, if there had been such a melée why was the room looking so tidy? Anna realised her mistake. She had gotten carried away with her performance and needed to reign it in.

'He made me tidy it all up, before he started to hit me. Look. I think he's broken my nose.'

'It's all lies. You're not going to be taken in by this performance are you?' I looked at Russell and then Orr. Russell's face was an essay in disgust as he met my eyes. He had seen it all before. Too many times to count. He looked as if he would love to take me outside and rub my face along a barbed-wire fence. Orr had questions in her eyes. She didn't look as convinced.

'Mr Boyd, what's your side of the story?'

'I came home from work and was assaulted by my wife.'

A snort exploded in my ear. 'Yeah, right!' A case of two positives making a negative. Officer Russell looked pointedly at Anna and then at me. 'Who's telling the porkies now then?' He said. 'I think you need a night in a cell to cool you down, Mr Boyd.'

'Em, I think we need a little more corroboration before anyone is locked up,' said Orr, quietly but firmly.

This young lady was no stooge and I was immediately grateful for her presence. If two male cops had come to the house, I would be in handcuffs and on my way to another night in a police cell. Her colleague shot her a glance; it promised a few words once they were on their own. It also admitted that she was in the right. I relaxed a little.

'So are you going to lock up this bastard or not?' demanded Anna, thrusting her face into Orr's.

She didn't back off and held Anna's stare. 'We are here to calm things down, Mrs Boyd,' she said.

'Yes…' interrupted Russell. 'And it looks like the only course of action we have at the moment is to remove Mr Boyd from the premises.' He smiled in celebration of his little victory.

'Do you have anywhere to go, Mr Boyd?' asked Orr.

'Uh … yes, I mean … I think so,' I answered, stunned. I was the victim here, yet I was being evicted from my own home. But that wasn't enough for Anna. She wanted more, she wanted an arrest, she wanted a conviction.

'You're sending him away?' she stormed. 'Look at me, fucking look at me you pair of inbreds. He's broke my fucking nose.'

'You did that yourself you sad bitch,' I roared at her. 'I'm the one covered in bruises.'

'Right, the pair of you shut up,' Russell bellowed over our raised voices. From the expression on his face now, he wasn't quite as sure as he had been. 'We'll lock up both of you for a breach of the peace if you don't calm down.' We both fell silent. 'Right, Mr Boyd, grab some things and we'll escort you from the premises.'

'Why do I have to go?' I demanded.

'Because I fucking say so.' Russell was losing what remained of his professional detachment.

'Because…' Orr's bulleted a warning stare at her partner, and then continued to address me in her now-familiar resolute tone '… because, you're the man. Because you look much more able to look after yourself. Because' – she looked around the room at children's videos and books – 'the children will need their mother.'

'The children need their father.' I fought to keep my tone reasonable. I knew from friends in the police that it wouldn't be too difficult for them to lock me up for the night. A breach of the peace charge was easily fabricated. 'The boys *need* their father more than they need this excuse of a mother.'

Anna lunged at me, knocking off Orr's hat. Orr held her off and glared at her.

'We could as easily decide that the mother has to find somewhere else to go.'

'But I have nowhere else to go.' Anna crossed her arms under her breasts and sat down. Both movements had the effect of reminding everyone in the room just who was the smallest. 'I have no friends or relatives here. Andy's family live about ten minutes away.'

Both police officers looked at me.

12

Sleeping in a car is not a comfortable experience for a man of my size. But I had no other option. If I hadn't left my home of my own volition, I would have left in handcuffs and spent another night in a cell. A second criminal charge against me would not go down well with my employers.

There was no way I was going to knock on Jim's door or my mother's. That would have meant either facing up to the truth of my marriage or telling them more lies. Neither option sat well with me. I simply couldn't handle the shame of admitting my situation to the two people in the world who knew me best. Correction: who thought they knew me best. The Andy Boyd they knew would not have sunk so low. No, I would have to rough it for a while until I could think of a way out.

With a ski jacket as my quilt, I half sat, half lay in the backseat of my car, in a car park near the beach. I had forgotten that this was a favourite place for local lovers to park and have a quick shag. Being a week night, it was fairly quiet, but those cars parked alongside me were skewers in the gut of my loneliness. Each sweep of headlights as another car drove in or out, each high-pitched giggle, each note from a squeaky suspension, reminded me of how unlucky I'd been in love. It seemed as if the whole world was happy apart from me. I could have moved and parked elsewhere, but I couldn't think of another spot that I would not have been moved on from.

I looked at the clock on the dashboard: 10:05 p.m. It was still quite early. Not yet closing time over at Bridges' Bar. I stepped out of the car and locked the door before realising what I was doing. Five minutes later I was leaning against the bar, with a pint of lager in my hand.

*

I was onto my third or fourth pint within the hour when a man nudged past me. Just a little too heavily. It was clearly with a purpose. I turned to face whoever it was. It was Ken Hunter, Sheila's husband.

He pushed his face into mine. 'You shagging my wife?' he hissed.

The wall behind us was three paces away. It took me a second to push him up against it. My hand at his throat. My teeth millimetres from his nose.

'Ho, mate you cannae do that in here,' someone shouted.

'If you wankers are going to fight, take it outside,' another voice shouted. Good suggestion, I thought and pulled at Ken's jacket collar until we were out the door.

The next few moments were lost in a fury of punches and it only registered what I was doing when three men pulled me away.

One man said, 'He's had enough, mate.' I tried to fight against the hands that were holding me, but they were too strong. 'He's had enough.' The same voice. Quieter this time.

My vision cleared enough for me to see Ken curled in a ball under the window of the bar.

'Prick put his wife in the hospital,' I said.

'Well, if you carry on, he'll be in the bed beside her,' one of the men said.

Now that the danger of more harm was over, Ken pushed himself up to a sitting position and leaned against the wall. Chest heaving, he managed a smile. Wiped blood from his mouth with a sleeve. The expression on his face surprised me. He looked like someone who had just done something immensely satisfying. Mingled there was the fresh thought that he had a new enemy. He couldn't have looked any happier if someone handed him the keys to a new car.

He blew me a kiss. 'This isn't over,' he said.

'Great. Any time you need your arse kicked, just give me a shout,' I replied. I wasn't spooked by his attitude. I knew I could take him anytime.

Back in the car, feeling my knuckles ache, I accepted that sleep was not happening. I sat up, pulling the jacket tight around me, and I considered the night's events. I discounted Ken Hunter and concentrated on Anna. Could I have expected any other solution? Could I have done better? The police were adamant that I was the one to go. If I'd been in their position I wasn't sure that I would have decided any differently. They did allow me to say goodnight to the boys before I left. When I entered their room the sight of them nearly undid me. I sagged to my knees, stifling a sob. How could I leave them in this house? I needed them with me.

The light shone in from the hall and it lit upon their two angelic faces, pressed together. Pat was in Ryan's bed and was holding his little brother to his chest. He must have climbed in beside Ryan to offer some consolation. Judging by his posture, Pat would have been sitting up when he fell asleep, possibly determined to make sure that his father was all right before falling asleep. Sleep, however, had other ideas, and had caused him to slump, his head coming forward so that his cheek rested against his brother's head.

Thoughts raced through my mind. I could take them both with me. My mother would take them in. I could slip Ryan into my big sports bag, but Pat would not be so easy to hide. Perhaps I could wake him up and tell him to sneak out later, when Anna was in bed. Get a grip, Boyd, I told myself. It was painful, but I had to admit that it was in the boys' best interests to have as little disruption in their lives as possible at this point. But was I abdicating my responsibility by leaving them here? Never. I would fight with my last breath to make sure that my boys were safe.

'Mr Boyd.' A voice came from the stairwell, forcing me from my reverie. 'I think you'd better go now.'

Feeling like I'd left part of my soul in that room, I walked out.

Constable Orr was at the bottom of the stairs. She read my expression. 'I am sorry,' she whispered with an eloquent shrug.

Although I could understand her view and I appreciated the sentiment, I was in no mood to be polite. I managed a small nod of thanks and walked past. With my car keys in one hand and a suitcase in another, I walked out of my home. Anna's stare burned into my back, but I didn't acknowledge her presence. I wanted to scream at her; I wanted her to see how much pain I was in; I wanted her to count the tears that were sliding down my cheeks. But she would only have fed on them.

The Carnegie Library was but a book's throw across the River Ayr from the bank. As I read the newspapers the next day my thoughts made the journey over the water several times. With inky fingers I rubbed my unshaven jaw. I couldn't even go over there to find out what was happening. For one thing I was a mess and for another I wasn't exactly their pet project. The thought occurred to me that I could run over, hang around outside and watch who came and went. I might learn something that way.

I walked up Sandgate, keeping to the opposite side of the street from the bank. The doorway of a bookshop might prove a good vantage point. It was at a bus stop, so people wouldn't question why if I hung about for a long time. Propped against a wall, I waited.

My feet were sore, my back ached and my stomach thundered. I needed a seat, a wash and a feed, but I couldn't move. I had to wait and see if I could judge what was going on.

Two hours later and nothing of consequence had happened. Just a steady flow of the usual customers. It was just as well I was out of sight, for they might have thought I'd lost my mind.

Eventually, the sounds and sensation coming from my midriff won the war. I would have to find something to eat. There was the baker's shop back down the hill or the sandwich shop across the road, two doors down from the bank. I decided to risk the latter. It was closer and I would miss less if I went there.

Just as I was about to enter the shop I heard a familiar voice.

'Andy? Andy?' It was Sheila. Shit. I didn't want her to see me in this state. It was too late, I couldn't pretend I didn't hear her, she would only follow me into the shop. I turned round.

'Hi, Sheila. How are you?'

'Fine, Andy. More to the point, how are you?' She looked me up and down, her eyebrows tight with alarm at my appearance.

Noticing that we were causing a bit of a jam in the doorway, we stepped to the side.

'Andy, I am so sorry about what happened.' For a moment I thought she was talking about Anna and me. She continued speaking. 'That bastard Campbell, I can't believe he treated you like that. You're worth ten of him. How dare he?'

Sheila's indignant words worked on me like a talisman. I straightened my back.

'Does everyone know?'

'I'm afraid so,' she answered. 'Mr Tact and Diplomacy made sure of that. I swear, that man should be shot.'

'What's the general consensus among the staff?' Any occurrence of wrongdoing in any of the branches I'd worked in had always caused a queasy atmosphere. Trust in your colleagues was paramount where a good deal of money was concerned and any theft would create an atmosphere of disquiet and ill-feeling. Particularly if the person involved was management.

'No one can believe you were involved. Everyone thinks that you were somehow taken in by Malcolm.'

'Malcolm. Where the hell is he?'

Sheila shrugged. 'No one knows. His mother said he was away down to London to see some friends.'

'What does Regional Office think?' Their opinion was the crucial one; my future at the bank would hinge on it.

'I'm not so sure. They reckon that about five thousand has gone missing. They know you and Malcolm were involved…' She let the implicit consequence of that hang in the air.

'I've done nothing. Believe me, Sheila. Nothing.' My stomach let out a rumble that not even a passing bus could mask.

'Hungry?' Sheila asked with a smile.

I nodded. She looked me over again. Her eyes taking in my unshaven chin, my creased clothes and no doubt the shadows under my eyes.

'Try not to take it so hard.' Sheila reached out and held my forearm. I winced as she inadvertently pressed on a bruise. Pulling my arm back, I looked away, trying, but failing, to hide my discomfort.

'There's more isn't there? Andy, what's going on? You're a ... mess. You look as if you've slept in the back of a van.'

I said nothing, I just stood staring at the ground, wondering what I should say. Wondering what sort of lie I could come up with.

'There are two things men tend to get in bother with. Booze and women. I can't smell any booze, so it must be...' She paused. 'You had to find the truth out eventually.'

'Find out? Find out what?' What a strange thing for her to say.

Her hand flew to her mouth, 'Oh shit, you haven't ... something *else* has happened.'

'Sheila, you'd better tell me what's going on.' My voice sounded harsh, even to me.

'You shouldn't find out this way.'

'Sheila?' I stepped closer.

'Right, but don't shoot the messenger. There's a rumour going round the branch that Anna's been seeing someone else...' Sheila was staring at her shoes.

'No ... no ... nonsense.'

'Everyone thinks that's why you haven't been yourself recently.'

'Crap, absolute crap. When would she have the fucking time? Who started this shit?'

'Toni Rodgers is friendly with one of your neighbours and she said she saw a man coming out of your house late one night and it wasn't you.'

'No. Don't believe it. Toni Rodgers is a gossiping wee cow. I know Anna's guilty of lots of things but sleeping with another guy? She wouldn't do that. Especially with the boys in the house. And where was I? Watching I presume.'

'It would have been around the time we were in Campbeltown.'

'Sheila, how could you listen to this crap? You don't believe it do you?'

'Andy, I'm just repeating what I heard. I saw you looking a mess, put two and two together and thought it was all true. I'm really sorry. You've got enough on your plate without this. C'mon, I said I was sorry.' She held my arm, her face pointed up at mine.

'No, I don't believe it. Anna wouldn't do that.'

'Okay, okay. But something is definitely not right between you.'

I opened my mouth to speak.

'No,' Sheila said. 'You don't need to explain anything. Unless you really want to. But you're coming home with me to get some food, a good wash, a long sleep.'

'What about your work?' I took a step back from her. She didn't need this. Me.

'Don't worry about that. I'll just put some food on a plate for you, and then I'll go back to work. Leave you to shower and sleep.' From her tone, she would brook no argument, so I gave in. Besides, everything she offered sounded extremely welcome.

Steam billowed from the plate of soup Sheila placed before me. Sandwiches too many in number tumbled off another plate. Sheila watched me eat, a smile of pleasure on her face.

'What?' I asked self-consciously.

'Nothing … I've just never seen anyone attack a plate of soup and sandwiches with such relish.'

'Starving…' I mumbled through a mouthful of bread and ham. Realising that I was probably looking a little odd, I slowed down.

'Anyway,' Sheila stood up, 'I'd better be going back to work. There's a clean towel in the bathroom. You can have one of my disposable razors; no foam I'm afraid. I've put the dog in the kitchen so he doesn't pester you. Help yourself to the couch.'

Her kindness moved me. Nearly choking on another mouthful, all I managed to say was 'Thanks.'

I was awakened by the sound of Sheila's key in the door. It felt as if my head had just rested on the cushion for a moment. The light on the VCR read 17.20. I'd been asleep for hours.

'Hey sleepy.' Sheila entered the room. 'Sorry I couldn't be here sooner. Things got a bit hectic this afternoon.' Barking sounded from the kitchen.

'Better go and get him first,' said Sheila with a smile. She returned with the dog winding itself around her legs. He noticed me and came over for a sniff.

'Was anything said about me today?' I patted his soft fur.

'No, nothing. Roy knows we're friends. He wouldn't tell me anything unless it was to your detriment. So things can't be too bad.' She smiled, hoping to pass on some reassurance. 'Hungry?'

'No, I'm fine thanks.' I couldn't quite relax now that Sheila was home. This was her refuge from the world; she didn't need me cluttering it up.

'Oh.' She looked genuinely disappointed. 'That's a shame cos I've brought home a Chinese for us.' I noticed a white plastic bag in her right hand.

'Well, if you've gone to the bother…'

Our meal was peppered with the occasional sentence. For the most part we ate in silence. Sheila would offer titbits from the office and I listened, with only the odd grunt to signify that I was taking part in the conversation.

After one long silence, Sheila asked, 'How are the boys?'

'Fine.' I'd been trying not to think about them. Pat would have realised by now that something was not quite right, unless Anna had come up with a reason for my absence. Ryan would mercifully be none the wiser. Normally, it was on my return that Ryan would notice that I'd been gone, judging by his ebullient welcome.

'Sorry.' Sheila realised that she'd said the wrong thing.

'It's okay,' I rushed to reassure her. 'I'm just … It's … I miss them.'

'Don't worry about them, Andy. You've got enough on your plate. They won't know anything about what's going on. They'll be fine.'

'I know. A Disney video, some toys, some junk food … who needs a father, eh?' I closed my eyes, fighting back the emotion. 'I can't let them down, Sheila … I can't.' I could feel a tear slide down my cheek.

'Andy,' she said softly. I swallowed. Her kindness was not what I needed right now. I stood up.

'Please, Sheila. I'll be fine.'

I felt warm, dry skin envelop my hand. Sheila was holding it with both of hers. Her eyes shone with empathy. I slumped onto the table. My head in my hands, years of sorrow, fear and shame flowed onto the heels of my palms. My shoulders shook. Now that I'd started I didn't think I could stop. Resting my head on the table top, I crossed my arms across my stomach and rocked. The pain threatened to engulf me. Instead of fighting it, I went into it. I gave myself up to the hurt, accepted my part in the whole sorry mess and realised for the first time that I was not wholly to blame. And then I wept for Anna. For the love we had. For the stranger she had become.

The love that still flickered deep in my heart.

As I rocked and wept a part of me looked on, disjointed from the experience. He felt that this was happening to a stranger. He saw Sheila's hand on my shoulder and ordered me to stop. To calm down. I ignored him. As sure as rain washes silt from the land, I knew that I needed this release. I knew that I wouldn't move on without it. Time then, to put aside years of conditioning, to cast them off like a cloak of concrete and admit my failings. Because I wouldn't get my life back unless I did.

None of this, though, made it any easier to meet Sheila's gaze.

I rubbed at a cheek with the back of my hand. 'I'm sorry. Don't know what got into me there.'

Sheila raised her eyebrows slowly. 'I think you do and it doesn't make you any less of a man for admitting it.'

I smiled weakly. 'I can't remember the last time I did this.'

Sheila handed me a hankie. 'Do you want to talk about it?'

I nodded, not quite trusting myself to speak yet.

'Take your time.' Sheila squeezed my shoulder.

I looked at the meal, managed a laugh. 'Sorry about the food, looks a bit waterlogged.'

'Forget about the food, I wasn't really hungry anyway.' She pushed the tinfoil containers to the other side of the table and turned to face me. Her silence urged me to speak.

I told her everything.

Every beating, every slur, every act of humiliation.

As I talked I questioned why I had put up with Anna's behaviour. Hearing the words out loud made her actions more repugnant and I wondered at my own sanity and how I had not realised before now the damage Anna was causing.

'My wife beats me.' I looked at Sheila. 'Do you understand the importance of me saying that?'

Sheila nodded. 'Who more than me could understand that, Andy?'

'I … I can't believe I put up with it. What kind of man puts up with that?'

'One who's aware of his own strength. One who doesn't want to stoop to that level. Don't blame yourself, Andy. Anna is manipulative, scheming and very clever. Lots of people would have been taken in by her.'

'But I convinced myself it was my fault. My fault.' I punched my chest for emphasis. 'Anna only beat me because I fucked up, she only beat me when I deserved it…' I looked at Sheila, she was nodding. 'You?'

'Yes, it was just the same for me. He … I can't even bring myself to say his name. He made me feel it was all my fault. He was very clever. Just like Anna.'

'What makes people behave like that?'

'It's power, Andy. Look at any form of abuse and it's one person asserting their power over another.'

'But what makes people do that shit?' And in my imagination I heard my question echo through the mind of every bruised soul in the country.

'Who knows? Perhaps they were victims once themselves; perhaps they are just plain evil.' Silence. We each absorbed what the other said.

'How did you get out?' I asked.

'First, I saw sense. Realised that unless I got out one of us would die.' This last sentence reverberated around my skull. How close had I come to that? How close could I still come? 'Then I called a women's refuge, called the police, got him chucked out, went on the Prozac and got on with my life.'

In just a few words, quietly spoken, Sheila had described a series of actions that must have taken immense courage. If I wanted out, I would have to find the same strength.

'But I can't walk away. What about my boys? The mum always gets the kids, doesn't she? I leave Anna and I say goodbye to them forever. The bitch knows how much they mean to me. She'll do everything in her power to keep them from me. And what about the house? That's my home. Why should I leave that? I've been there for years. First with Pat and then with … What am I going to do?'

'Andy, you can't let yourself get bogged down. You were doing so well a moment ago. Breathe slowly.' I breathed slowly. 'Right, I'm a firm believer in action. Action replaces worry. You have to concentrate on the solution, not the problem. Concentrate on a solution. What can you do to make things better?'

I could see where Sheila was going with this. Hope sent an extra pulse through my veins.

'What did you do? The police: been there, no help. Phone a refuge. They might not have a place for a man, but maybe they could tell me where to go. Then I could see a lawyer, see what they've got to say.' I stood up and walked around the table. Sheila was right, action was the key. 'Where's your phone?'

'Up there on the wall.' She pointed to a space above the fridge.

'Where's the number of this refuge?' I asked. Sheila pulled a small book decorated with flowers, from a drawer. She flicked through some pages and showed me a number.

It was answered quickly.

'Em,' I began nervously, 'I wondered if you could help me.'

'Yes,' a female voice answered.

'Well, I'm staying with a friend at the moment and I need to know where I can go for help.'

'Yes?' Suspicion heightened the woman's tone.

'You see…' Swallowing, I forced myself to admit my source of shame to a stranger, 'My wife has been beating me…'

'Fuck off you sick bastard.' The woman raged in my ear. 'Do you think you're funny? We have women here with real problems. Go on, piss off and don't bother us again or I'll report you to the police.'

Dazed I hung up.

Sheila grimaced, she'd heard every word. 'I should have realised.'

'Realised what?

'You're a man. She sees abused women every single day of her life. You're the root cause of every catastrophe that woman has ever experienced or heard. No wonder she gave you abuse.'

'But all I want is help.'

My newfound energy had been consumed by the woman's anger. Crushed, I limped over to the chair and sat down.

'Don't fall at the first obstacle, Andy. What else can we do?'

'Don't know. The police don't want to know. The refuge doesn't want to know…'

'You can try a lawyer in the morning.'

'Yes, I'll probably need one for work anyway.'

'And what about work?'

'What about it?'

'What solution can you come up with there?' Sheila spoke more forcefully now.

'Don't know.'

'Come on, Andy. Don't let the bastards beat you. Who's the root of the problem?'

'Malcolm.'

'And?'

'No one knows where he is.'

'That's because no one has made any real effort to find him. Do you know where he lives?'

'Yes.'

'Well I suggest you get round there in the morning and wring the wee shit's neck until you get a confession.'

13

Malcolm lived with his mother in an ex-local authority house in the Castlehill part of the town. When his father died a few years before, Malcolm took advantage of the generous discounts on offer for council tenants and bought it for his mother. His father would never have agreed to it while he was alive. Anything that could be attributed to Maggie Thatcher's government would not be a good thing, according to his way of thinking. No matter how many figures Malcolm showed him, he would not change his stance.

I'd met Malcolm's father only once. He was a small, bald man with a ready smile and a cauliflower ear, who would call a spade a bastardin' shovel. You were never in doubt as to what was in his mind for it played from his lips before the thought was fully formed. He liked to test anyone who came into the house, see how they reacted to his direct and forceful words. If you looked him in the eye and answered back, you were a good man. If you couldn't meet his gaze and flustered a reply, he would never trust you.

'You another one o' these poofy cunts that work in the bank?' he had challenged me that first time.

Malcolm had warned me what he was like, besides which, I was used to having frank and often brutal exchanges with the guys at the rugby club.

'Nice to meet you too, you ol' bastard,' I replied, softening my answer with a grin. He wheezed with laughter and patted me on the back.

'Thank fuck,' he grinned. 'Our Malcolm's got a pal that's a real man for a change. Have a seat, son. Can I get you a beer?'

Sitting in a plush armchair, feet barely touching the ground was Malcolm's mother. She tutted disapprovingly at our exchange.

'George,' while addressing her husband, she winked at me, 'don't be talking like that in front of your son's guests. This man's a banker...'

'That's a hard word to say with your fingers in yur mouth, int't?'

'George.'

'Only teasing, Joan. The fella doesnae mind. Do ye, son?'

'Not at all, George. What happened to my can?' While playing to George, I grimaced at Joan in apology and hoped she would understand this wasn't my normal behaviour.

George laughed, 'A man after my own heart. Can you no' teach that son of mine to be a wee bit more like you. Him with his vodka and all that nonsense.' He walked into the kitchen, but we could still hear him talking. 'Never trust a man that doesn't like his beer.'

I only swapped insults with George a few more times, each of them on the phone. It was more likely that Joan would answer.

Since I'd married, my outings with Malcolm had lessened until we barely met up at all. I reasoned, therefore, that if I spoke to Joan to ask for Malcolm's whereabouts, she'd be less suspicious if I spoke to her in person. A voice down the phone would not win her trust.

Standing at her door, my hand poised to announce my presence, the wind snatched a child's cry and whisked it past my ear. It sounded like Ryan. With a twist of pain, I knocked at the door, wondering what he was doing right at that moment.

Malcolm's mother answered the door with a huge smile.

'Andy. How are you, son? Come in.' Her effusive welcome surprised me. I didn't think that she would remember me that well. 'God, I haven't seen you for ages. Malcolm's not in, by the way, but you're welcome all the same.' This last phrase let me know that whatever Malcolm was up to, his mother knew nothing about it.

'Right, let me put the kettle on and you can tell me everything that's been happening to you. I was sorry to hear about Patricia, she was a lovely girl. Only met her the once but I could see she was lovely. Lovely looking too. Beautiful hair. I can remember beautiful hair. Sit down, son. Sit down.' She pointed to an armchair then ambled to the kitchen.

Noises from the kitchen suggested ceremony and organisation. A ritual of welcome that was performed in almost every house I'd ever visited. A kettle was filled, a teapot emptied and biscuits rung onto a plate. China issued a perfect note and hot water rushed into a pot in a melody that brought an answering flush of saliva into my mouth.

'I don't get that many visitors now that George is dead.' Joan walked into the room holding a tray. She placed it on a low table. Her back almost squeaked as she sat down. 'I'm getting old, Andy.'

'Nonsense,' I answered. 'You look as young as the day I first met you.'

'Aye, and I was an old crone then.' She laughed.

'I was sorry to hear about George,'

'Aye, son. It wasn't nice.' The smile wavered while she remembered. 'Prostate cancer. He had trouble with his waterworks for years. Refused to go and see a doctor. Said nobody was sticking a finger up his arse. Silly bugger. A wee cup of tea, son?' She poured into a small, china cup. I picked it up carefully. It looked like a child's toy in my hand. Satisfyingly hot, it moistened my mouth.

'Oh, that's lovely. You can't beat a good cup of tea,' I said.

Joan beamed. 'Aye, George always said I made a cracking cuppa.' Silence.

'You're no' lookin' so good, son.' She studied my face. 'I don't like to say anything…'

'I'm fine,' I said and recognised the sharpness of my tone. Offered a small smile of apology.

'Have a biscuit, Andy. They'll only go to waste.' She read my smile, backed off and changed the subject.

'Thanks.' From the multitude on offer, I chose a Kit-Kat. She must have emptied her biscuit tin. There were enough biscuits to keep a child's playgroup fed for a day.

'So…' She sipped at her cup and set it down on its saucer. 'You've not visited this old lady just to sample her tea. What's our Malcolm been up to?'

'I don't know if he's been up to anything,' I said through a mouthful of chocolate. 'I just need a wee word with him.'

'You cannae fool me, Andy son. A mother knows when something's up. First Malcolm comes in here in a sweat. Tells me nothing. Packs a bag. Says he going down to London for a couple of weeks and asks me to phone in sick for him.' The lines on her face seemed to deepen as she spoke. 'Andy, tell me. I've been worrying myself silly the last few days. What's he up to? Is it drugs? You young ones are all into drugs these days. What is it? Marijuana?' She pronounced the name of the drug as if she'd only ever come across it in print – 'maridge-a-wana'.

'Joan, don't worry yourself. As far as I know Malcolm's not into drugs, other than the socially acceptable ones.' I thought about what I should tell her. 'I can't really tell you what it is. I'm sorry, that'll have to come from Malcolm himself. Do you know how I can get in touch with him?'

'Sorry, Andy, I don't. He phones every night, just to tell me he's okay. But he won't tell me where he is. London was all he said. Could be Timbuktu for all I know.'

Joan then steered the conversation onto, for her, less contentious ground. I had to give her every detail of Ryan's birth, tell her how Pat was doing at school and describe Anna.

'Want a fresh pot, son?' she asked.

'No thanks.' I saw my opportunity, with this break in the conversation. 'Honestly, I'll be running to the loo all day now. Thanks, Joan. That was lovely, but I really have to go.'

'Okay, Andy. Thanks for listening to an old woman and her problems. I'm sorry that boy of mine wasn't here to talk to you. But I'll tell him you were looking for him when he phones tonight.'

Disguising my disappointment behind a smiling mask, I went to the front door. I'd hoped to leave with something more concrete than a phone message. My name was not going to be on the branch information board at the bank for much longer unless I spoke to Malcolm. All the bank had was me, and in his absence I feared that would be enough. And if I lost my job, I could surely say goodbye to the boys. Any slim chance I had of winning custody would be blown away like tissue in the teeth of a gale.

As the door closed behind me, Joan's farewell clipped off by the wood, I felt rather than heard someone approach. Footsteps could soon be heard, the walker hidden by a high hedge.

'Malcolm.' I knew it was him even before he appeared in my line of sight.

He stopped at the top of the path, his face blanched with surprise. 'Oh. Andy.'

'You and I need to talk.'

'Aye, aye.' He put his bag on the ground and stuck both hands in his pockets. He looked anywhere but at me.

'Why don't you go in, say hello to your mum, dump your bag and we'll go for a drink.' I stood aside to let him pass.

'Aye, right. Back in a minute.'

A few minutes later, Malcolm opened the car door and got in beside me.

'Somebody been using you as a punch bag?' he asked, in a half-joking tone.

'I doubt there'll be any pubs open yet,' I said, ignoring his comment. 'The Coffee Club do?'

'Aye.' Malcolm slumped into the seat, his chin tucked into his chest.

We drove off in silence. I didn't want to speak to him until we were face to face; he just didn't want to speak.

At the Coffee Club, Malcolm was first in and chose a seat near the door. For a quick exit, I thought. In silence, we waited for the waitress.

'She's had one too many helpings of chocolate fudge cake,' Malcolm said unkindly after she had taken our order.

'Right, Malcolm. Suppose we start at the beginning…'

'Aye, well. I was in some bother. So I filled in a couple of slips at the bank…'

'A couple of slips?'

'They were all against folk who had plenty money in their account.' He studied the menu, despite the fact he'd already ordered.

'So that makes it alright does it?' I barely stopped myself from shouting. 'That excuses your theft does it? They had plenty of cash in their account?'

'No it doesn't,' he answered, his face long with shame. 'I was being flip. Anyway what's eatin' your gusset?' He looked me up and down. 'And why are you not wearing a bank suit?'

'What clown initialled and authorised your bogus withdrawals?'

'You did.' He flinched as the implications of this registered.

'Aye, and who do the bank think is your accomplice?' My face was only inches from his. He leaned back, to recover his space.

'Andy. I am so … I am so sorry. I had no idea they would try and pin it on you. I'll hand myself in tomorrow.'

'Will you fuck. You'll do it today.' I grabbed his arm, which was resting on the table. I squeezed it, hard. He pulled away and rubbed at the pain.

'Right, right. I'll do it today.'

'And I'm coming with you.'

'What? Do you not trust…' he changed his mind about asking that question. 'I suppose not. Andy believe me. I am so sorry. I never imagined…' He paused while the waitress set down our steaming cups.

'What's happened to you?' he asked while rubbing at an invisible stain on the table top.

'I've been suspended, pending an investigation.' I poured sugar into my cup, 'Since they thought I was involved they didn't want me around in case I tampered with any evidence.' I took a sip and burnt my lip. The coffee was too hot. 'What on earth were you thinking, Malcolm? Did you think the customers wouldn't notice? Did you actually think that we wouldn't trace you once they did? Did you actually think?'

'I've made a mess of things haven't I?'

'You got that fucking right.'

He leaned forward and rested his forehead on his right hand. His eyes fixed on the table as he spoke. 'Someone,' he began slowly, 'had some evidence, photographic evidence of me in a compromising situation. They threatened to send it to Head Office.' He ran a finger round the lip of his cup. 'And they were going to send stuff to my mum. I couldn't allow that. My mum would have had a heart attack. I didn't give a fuck about the bank, it was Mum I was worried about.'

'This someone was bribing you then?'

He nodded. 'Ten thousand the first time, fifteen the second.'

'There was a first time?'

'Afraid so. The bastard lied to me. Said he destroyed the photos. Then he came back for more.'

'Where were you when Dallas was on the telly? They always come back for more. What was in the photos?'

'I can't tell you.'

'Can't or won't?'

'Does it matter? I don't want you to know. I don't want anyone to know.'

'Where did you get the money from the first time?'

Malcolm said nothing, his concentration deep in the sugar bowl.

'Oh, Jesus.' It came to me. 'Those cash differences. That *was* you! You fucking idiot, Malcolm, how could you? I spoke up for you. I trusted you.'

'Sorry, sorry, *sorry*. If I could undo it, believe me I would. I was a clown to think I could get away with it.'

'You said this last time you handed over fifteen thousand. We could only account for three and a half?'

'I actually managed to take five. The rest…' he ran a finger along his lips, '… the rest I took from my mum.'

'Oh, Malcolm.' This was too much. 'Your own mother?'

'I couldn't let her find out, not like that, not ever.'

'Malcolm what's so bad that you'd steal from your own mother?'

'I can't tell you.'

'Did you murder someone?'

'No, of course not.'

'Did you rape a ten-year-old?'

'Andy.'

'What? Cos it must be something downright fucking evil for you to steal all this money.'

'I'm not telling you.'

'Why did you run away to London? Why did you then come back?' I was relentless, I wanted answers. This was something I could have an impact on.

'What is this? Why don't you just shine a torch in my eyes and get it over with?'

'Believe me, if I thought it would work, then I would.'

'I ran away because it was all getting to me. I couldn't handle it. Taking money from my mum was the last straw. I knew I'd reached bottom. Then I got another letter from the blackmailer.'

'He wanted more?'

Malcolm nodded. 'So I ran away. I couldn't go on stealing.'

Looking at Malcolm as he spoke, I could barely believe that this was the same guy I'd known all these years. His famous sense of humour, crushed under the weight of his problems, his long fingers never still as he fidgeted with every item on the table, his eyes searching the face of everyone who came in the door.

'What made you come back so quickly? You've been barely gone a week.'

'I knew that the blackmailer would carry out his threat when I didn't give him the money. After all, he'd got plenty from me already. Each day I was away I spoke with Mum, I knew from her voice that she'd received nothing. So I thought, if I came home I could intercept the mail before Mum got to it. The bank, I would just have to take my chances. I know that if there is any potential of embarrassment

they don't bring a case to trial. I hoped that they would just sack me.'
He started playing with the salt cellar.

'You'd be as well telling me what's in these photos if they're going
to be sent to the bank anyway.'

'Andy, I can't tell you. Not face to face. I've known you too long.
I don't want to see the expression on your face when you find out.'

'Okay.' In the face of Malcolm's contrition, I suddenly felt
ashamed of myself for pressing the point. 'So what do we do now?'

'Will you take me into the bank to face the music?'

'Sure. If you want me to.' Now that he was going to own up to
his actions, my anger at him had dissipated and I was keen to offer
my support.

'Who's conducting the investigation?'

'Roy Campbell.'

'Fuck.'

Conversation and noise hit the brick wall of our appearance in the
banking hall. Heads looked up from printouts, fingers hovered over
keyboards as everyone watched our progress through the hall and
into my office.

'Ah. The very man.' Roy Campbell was sitting behind my desk.
His eyes were on Malcolm as he spoke.

'Malcolm's here to tell you everything. Including the fact that I
had nothing to do with any of this,' I said.

'We know,' answered Roy, still staring at Malcolm. His expression
a mixture of loathing and disgust.

'What do you mean, you know? Why the fuck have I been suspended then?'

'We've just only worked it out. This was handed in, over the
counter this morning.' He opened a large brown envelope and threw
the contents across the desk at me. 'The police are on their way.'

'Oh no,' I heard from behind me, then felt a gust of movement as
Malcolm sprinted from the office.

'Malcolm,' I shouted and turned to go after him.

'Leave him. We don't want to see the disgusting animal in here again.'

'Roy, what the…'

'Andy, look at the pictures.'

I followed the line of his accusatory finger.

'Oh … shit …'

14

When I reached my car, there was no sign of Malcolm. I'd hoped that he would wait to speak to me. Roy followed me out.

'So what happens now?' I asked him

'This,' he waved the photograph in the air, 'we burn. Malcolm ceases to exist as far as the bank is concerned.'

'They won't charge him?

'What do you think? The press would have a field day with this. I can just see the headlines. I mentioned the police to only give him the frighteners.'

'What about me?'

'You go home, put your suit on and get back to work.'

'Oh, you think so.' I stared at him, cooling down the heat of my anger before I spoke. 'I want a written apology from you and from the bank before I even think about it. I feel a few days on the sick coming on, after all the stress I've been put through. There might even be a case for compensation.'

'There's no need to be like that.'

'No need?' I shouted at him. 'No need?'

His expression changed as he realised he was in a deserted car park with a very angry and much bigger man than him. And one with a recent record of violence. He took a few steps back.

'Andy…' His tone was placatory, almost subservient. 'I was just doing my job.'

'Just doing your job? What a prick. All kinds of nasty people have used that as their justification.' I stabbed him in the chest with a rigid finger. 'You couldn't wait to suspend me. You probably danced around my office after I'd gone.' I stepped towards him.

'Andy, calm down. Hitting me won't undo any of this.'

Fortunately, I was not so angry that his words couldn't reach me. 'Aye, but it would make me feel a whole lot better.' I poked him again. He took another step back and came up against a wall. He cowered, trying to merge with the brick.

'Look at you, you're pathetic.' As my words sounded in my ear, I heard them in Anna's voice. Not so long ago she had thrown the same words at me and here I was asserting my power over another, weaker person. I was no better than she was.

I thrust my hands into my pockets and backed off.

'Stand up and come away from the wall, Roy. I'm not going to hit you.'

'Of course you're not.' His laughter was just short of hysteria and filled with uncertainty.

'No I'm not. But I do want a letter of apology and I'm going to take the rest of the day off. Give the letter to Sheila. She'll get it to me.'

I drove to Malcolm's house. He would have gone straight home to try and stop his mother from opening the envelope that was surely there. I had to speak to him, to offer him my reassurance. What I had seen depicted in that photo was going to take some getting used to. The truth that Malcolm was gay was neither here nor there as far as I was concerned. But it was obviously an issue for him. Hadn't we got over all that? Clearly not. Shame had driven him to the theft, just as it had driven me to physically attack someone. Shame was something that I was on intimate terms with. Perhaps I could be of help to him.

Joan opened the door to me as I walked up her path.

'Andy, what's going on?' She twisted her fingers. 'Can you tell me, cos that boy of mine is saying nothing.'

'Where is he?'

'I heard a commotion out in the street, opens the window and there's my Malcolm wrestling in my front garden with another guy. This fella's shouting at me. Look at this envelope missus, he shouts.

I thought Malcolm was going to kill him. I've never seen him so angry.'

'Where's Malcolm now?'

'He's up the stairs in his room.'

'I'll go and speak to him.'

'Will you son? I'm worried sick. Don't know what's got into my lovely wee boy.' She started to cry.

Putting my arm round her shoulder, I led her into the living room.

'You have a wee seat here, Joan. I'll go and speak to Malcolm and see what's going on.'

'No need, Andy.' A voice carried from the door. 'He's here.' Malcolm's clothes were dirty and torn, his hair dishevelled and his eyes shone with defiance. His whole body was rigid with it. Like an animal that had been backed up against a wall, he was turning to fight.

'Have you come here to gloat? To tell me how much I disgust you? Well you can save your breath, cos I couldn't give a fuck anymore.' He looked at his mum. The anger that was keeping him upright lessened a little. 'Here you go, Mum. This is what all the fuss is about.' She caught the envelope, her expression fearful. Whatever was hidden within the brown paper, she didn't want to see.

'On you go, Mum. You might as well know what your son is.'

'I don't want to look at this, Malcolm.' She looked tiny in her chair.

'Well you're going to have to.' He reached her, opened it up and thrust the photograph into her hand, 'The bank will soon be charging me with theft and this'll be all over the papers.'

A small sound escaped from between Joan's lips. She didn't want to look at the photograph but simultaneously was unable to tear her gaze from it. In it she saw her son playing a prominent part. He was naked, bent over an office desk, while another naked male was poised to take him from behind. The bank's highly recognisable logo was on the wall behind them.

'Malcolm, the bank won't charge you. They're afraid of the negative publicity it would attract,' I said.

He looked at me. The anger in his eyes died. It was replaced with deep, burning mortification.

'Oh no.' He reached out and tore the picture from his mother's hands. He fell to his knees in front of her. 'Mum, can you forget you saw this?'

His eyes searched hers for a clue to her reaction. Several emotions vied for the stage of her face. Disgust and disbelief bowed before the curtain for mere seconds. A mother's love for a son in turmoil then took centre stage. I could see she wanted to hug him, but her repugnance at the images held her arms down by her sides.

'Son, I don't care if you're gay, straight or if you wear garters under your suit. But this is something a mother doesn't want to see…' She closed her eyes against a flow of tears. Malcolm's shoulders heaved as he gave in to his.

'Listen, I'll go and wait outside…' I felt I was out of place.

Sitting in my car, I searched my memory for clues as to Malcolm's sexual identity. People had continually, over the years, questioned me as to his preference. They cited his lack of a long-term girlfriend and his continued habitation with his parents.

For me, all of that was a big, fat so what.

There was a knock on my car window, the door opened and Malcolm sat in the passenger seat. His eyes were puffed red with spent emotion, but otherwise, he looked lighter, easier.

'Thanks.' He offered me his hand. 'Thanks for seeing this thing through with me. You're not disgusted?'

'If I'm to be completely honest, I've always kinda known that you were…' I was unsure if I would offend him by saying the word. He helped me out.

'Gay,' he said.

'But you weren't talking about it, so I wasn't going to bring it up. Anyway…' I shrugged. 'Who cares?'

'Yeah, we like to *think* we're living in enlightened times.' He shook his head. 'Besides, it was my call. I didn't want to admit it to myself, never mind tell anyone else.'

'But why didn't you just tell everyone as soon as you were faced with this blackmail? People are a lot more understanding nowadays.'

'Are they? Really? Sure, in the big city, there's safety in numbers and anonymity. But in a town the size of Ayr? Folk give it all this tolerance crap in public, but in their own home it's a different story. Besides, you have no idea what it's like growing up, knowing you're different. All I wanted was to be the same as everyone else. Dad screamed at the telly every time Boy George was on it. When we were kids, the worse thing you could call anyone was a poof. I wanted no one to know. I would have hid it from myself if I could. So, knowing that every ounce of me was screaming "liar", I carried on with my life as a hetero. I went out with girls, got drunk with the guys and hoped that I would be happy.'

'Were you?'

'I couldn't have been more miserable. Eventually…' his fingernails came under close scrutiny '… I cracked up. Either I would continue to live as a fraud or I would end it all.'

'You thought of suicide?' I was shocked.

'Yes.' He stared at his own private movie somewhere beyond the windscreen. 'I couldn't handle it anymore. I was something that disgusted me, something that disgusted everyone I knew. I couldn't live with it.' He looked at me. 'Can you imagine what my dad would have done if he'd lived to see this? He'd have kicked my arse out. Never wanted to see me again.'

'What did you do?'

'I wanted something painful, something that would punish me for taking the coward's way out. Each time I walked to work, I thought of jumping in front of a lorry. Every time I walked over the railway bridge, I thought of jumping onto the power lines. But I couldn't do it. I was such a coward, I couldn't even do that.'

'Don't you think you're being a bit hard on yourself?'

'I do now. But at the time … Anyway, I phoned the Samaritans. Spoke to some woman for hours. She was brilliant, should have got a medal. She gave me a number of a gay helpline. I phoned them.

That was even more difficult than phoning the Samaritans, it was tantamount to an admission of guilt.

'So some guy at the end of the line arranged to meet me in Glasgow and take me to a gay club.'

'What was that like?'

'An eye-opener. It was like … you know those horror movies where the stupid victim walks down into the cellar when you know they shouldn't. Well, I could almost hear the violins screech as I walked in the door of that club. I was nervous as hell. Anyway, this guy was really nice. Told me there was nothing to be ashamed about, that he knew exactly what I was going through and there was loads of people like me. So there I was, knees knocking, ordering a pint at this bar, with all these people around me. Some were normal looking, some were outrageously camp, but they all disgusted me. I disgusted me. I ran straight out the place and threw up all over the pavement outside. Came home on the train.' He laughed. 'I tried to pick a fight with this big bruiser on the same carriage, hoping that he would kick the shit out of me. He just ignored me. And I was back the next night and the next.'

'Did you meet someone?'

'Aye, I met loads of someones. There was one guy in particular. He was so good-looking, so confident. I wanted to be him. Other guys warned me about him, said he was dangerous, slept with everything with a pulse. But I was like a love-struck teenager.'

'Was this the guy that was blackmailing you?'

'Yup. But first he had to corrupt me, and boy was I up for a spot of corruption. Once I got started I was obsessed. Couldn't get enough cock.'

Ineffectually, I tried to conceal my grimace at his words. I shifted uncomfortably in my seat. It was so alien to me to hear those words being said by another man.

'Sorry.' Malcolm looked over at me. 'Am I making you uncomfortable?'

'No, well … yes.' I felt that I should at least be as honest as Malcolm. 'It takes some getting used to. Don't worry. I want to hear

your story. I want to understand what it was like for you.' I could
see the parallels between us. We were both fighting with our own
images of masculinity, we were both trying to overcome our self-pity
and shame. In this fight I was able to put to rest my old version of
masculinity. I was able to see that its true definition is in any act,
gesture or quality that ennobles the state of being male. Perhaps
hearing how Malcolm faced up to his personal monster would help
me face mine.

'The younger guy in the photo?'

Malcolm read my expression. 'Don't worry. He's seventeen. Looks
a lot younger, to be fair. The rest you know about. He talked me
into the scenario you saw in the photographs, then he manipulated
the situation to get some money from me.' His laugh was basted in
irony. 'The bastard must have seen me coming. He must have rubbed
his over-moisturised hands with glee when he saw me walking in
that club.'

'What now?'

'Now, I try to get on with my life. Hope that my friend will
forgive me.' He smiled at me. 'Hope my mother can live with a
gay son. Try to be happy with who and what I am. And no I'm not
going to burst into a Gloria Gaynor song.' His laughter this time was
unadulterated good humour. 'And what about you?' he asked.

'Me?'

'Yes, you. You know how us gays are noted for our sensitivity, as
well as a fascination with all things Streisand,' he added *sotto voce*.
'But I wasn't drowning so deep in my own shit that I couldn't see you
struggling in yours.'

Taking a deep breath, I told him everything.

By the time I finished talking, the sun had all but disappeared
below the horizon and the distant clouds were painted an optimistic
red.

Malcolm listened without interrupting. Without judgement.
Without laughing at me.

'So what now?' he asked.

I offered him a smile in reply, impressed by the change in him. A simple acceptance can be a huge help. I felt a boost from his courage.

'Well, if my poofy pal can do it...' I laughed.

'Hey.' Malcolm swiped at my arm, pretending to be offended. His grin showed otherwise.

'Seriously, if you can get through what you have, then I can give it a go. No more bowing down to that bitch. And there's no way she's going to keep my sons. I've no idea what I'm going to do or how I'm going to get them back. But I've got to do something.'

15

Sheila had prescribed action. Concentrate on a solution, not the problem, she said. My feelings for Anna had changed, irrevocably. My mind raced over the events of the last few years, reading the manipulation, the beatings and the verbal abuse and seeing them for what they really were. The text in my mind was clear. No more self-delusion.

I had to find a solution. I struggled to believe that at one point I had considered murder. Would I, or even could I, find myself returning to that as a possibility? Bile rose from my gut at the thought. I'd have to keep a tight rein on my emotions when dealing with Anna. Ultimately, if that were to happen, she would win. I would end up in jail and the boys would be taken into care, knowing their father was a killer.

So what about separation, divorce? From watching men I knew who had separated from their wives, I witnessed two things. First, I didn't know any men who successfully fought for custody of their children. Second, their relationships with those children, without exception and for whatever reason, suffered. Neither of these outcomes were acceptable to me.

Life without my boys would be as meaningless to me as a scroll written in a lost language. A life in which Anna got custody of them would be unbearable, she would make sure of it. However, Pat was not even her child. I could not conceive of a court ruling that she keep him. Ryan would be another case entirely. I might be able to argue that the brothers should not be split up. But, if I could, then so might she.

All this supposition was getting me nowhere. I had to speak to someone who knew. I would contact a lawyer in the morning. First, another night on Sheila's couch.

Driving up her street, I recognised a car at the end of her drive:
it was Jim's.

He was leaning against a tall breakfast chair in the kitchen when I
walked in. The dog stared up at him with a look of adoration.

He must have just arrived. A disc of brown liquid steamed at the
lip of his mug. Sheila was standing by the kettle. A mixture of trepidation and apology tightened her features.

'What are you doing here, Jim?' I tried for jollity in my voice and
failed. I was irritated by his presence, but at the same time relieved
to see him.

He obviously knew something was wrong or he wouldn't be here.
The time had come for me to tell him everything. I had wanted to
keep Mum and Jim in the dark, but that wish was driven by my old
version of what a man should be. The new Andy Boyd was gaining
power and his ideas of how a man should act and react were radi-
cally different. Misery had tempered a new steel to my backbone;
a new steel alloyed with the realisation that admission of weakness
and acceptance of emotion made me a stronger person. Just like
Malcolm, facing the reality of my life was, I hoped, making me a
better man.

But I was still at the early stages of my transformation. The old
me struggled to mask my features with a 'is this the face of concern?'
look, and ordered me to say nothing.

'Sorry, Andy,' said Sheila, 'Jim phoned the bank looking for you.
Just after you left this morning.'

'Aye.' He stood up. 'You okay, bro?' I smiled at what Jim considered to be a term of endearment.

'Why did you phone the bank?' I asked him.

'Looking for you. I phoned Anna last night and asked to speak
to you.'

'Oh. What did she say?'

'She said, why are you phoning here, then? That was a bit of a
shock. I asked her where you were. She said, fucked if I know.'

'Does Mum know any of this?'

'Jesus, no. You mad? I don't want to make her worry until it's absolutely necessary.'

'Good, let's keep it that way. How much has Sheila told you?'

'Just the bare minimum,' Sheila answered. 'Anna chucked you out because you got suspended from work.'

'And about the bitch having another man.' Jim shook his head with disgust. 'What kind of woman is she? Two wee boys, a good man and the first sign of bother she's got you out on the street and another man in her bed.'

'The other man is just hearsay.' I was still struggling with that one. Not because I was worried about being the cuckolded husband, but because the thought of another man dealing with my boys gave me chills.

I stepped toward the door. Righteous anger surged to every extremity; I could feel it spark in my fingertips.

'Where are you going?' asked Sheila.

'To get my boys. They're not spending one more moment in that witch's company.' I stabbed the air in front of me with a forefinger. One stab for each word.

'Andy, think about it first,' said Jim. 'You go round there all fired up. You frighten the boys, she phones the police … you get the jail.'

'He's right, Andy,' agreed Sheila. 'Especially now you've got a history.'

'A history of what?' Jim looked puzzled.

'Violence,' I answered, my energy weakening. 'I've got to get my boys out of there.' I could feel salt sting my eyes. I blinked back the tears, I couldn't let them see this getting the better of me.

'What violence?' asked Jim.

'You two go in to the living room and talk. I'll make us a fresh pot of coffee,' said Sheila.

Passing her as I followed Jim out of the kitchen, I sent her a smile of appreciation. She smiled in reply.

Jim sat down and leaned forward in an armchair. His arms rested across his lap, his face a large question mark. Quietly and without a trace of self-pity, I told him everything. Right from my broken nose on my wedding night, to the fights that followed any night out I had with him. I ended with the more recent events surrounding my time at Campbeltown – the thefts, my suspension and how I had ended up sleeping on Sheila's couch.

Once I finished, I was exhausted. Exhausted and relieved. Both Malcolm and I had discovered the true weight of deceit. A lie could slip out as easily as a feather from a torn duvet. But a ton of feathers was still a ton. All it would take is one last feather, one last lie, and you would collapse under the strain.

The relief of casting this load aside was immense. Once I'd stopped speaking I flopped back into my seat.

'My God,' said Jim. 'I had no idea. Absolutely none,' He looked as if he'd picked up the weight I just dropped. 'I mean, I knew you guys weren't really suited. But this? What is she, deranged? Do women behave like that? I've never heard anything like it.'

'At least you didn't laugh.'

'Laugh? Why would I laugh?' He looked horrified at the very suggestion.

'Because that's the usual reaction, isn't it? Look at the size of him. Let's a wee woman kick shit out of him. What kind of man is he?'

'No. I admit it's difficult to imagine, but laugh? No.' He looked at me. 'So that black eye at the wee man's birthday?'

I nodded.

'Bloody hell. What a bitch.' Jim stood up, fists clenched. If it was a man who'd hurt me like this he'd be straight round there with a baseball bat. But this was a woman and he clearly didn't have a clue how to react. 'This is fucking unreal.' He paced back and forward, his face getting darker and darker. 'I could just go round there. Tell her what I think of her...'

'And how on earth would that help?' I asked.

'Don't know,' Jim replied and sat down. 'It would make *me* feel better. God...' he stared off into recent memory. 'To look at her, butter wouldn't melt.'

I could only nod in agreement.

'I'm going round there.' Jim stood up so fast I thought his upward trajectory would continue until he hit the ceiling. 'Bitch isn't going to keep the boys for one more second…'

'Best sit down, Jim,' Sheila said as she came in with the coffee and sat a mug in front of each of us. 'You going round there in a rage won't help any.'

'But…' Jim ran his right hand through his hair as if he wanted to pull a clump out. Took a step back. Then forward.

'But nothing,' I said. 'Sit on your arse.'

Jim sat, but he was wearing a determined look that had me worried. 'Jim, you'll only make things worse…'

'Aye,' he said. 'I get it.'

We sipped our drinks and sat in silence for a few minutes, each of us lost in thought.

'Right, what are we going to do about you, big brother?'

'*We* are going to do nothing. *I* am going to get my boys back.'

'What about a place to sleep? You can't go on pestering Sheila.' Jim looked like he was getting control of himself, but there was a distant cast to his eyes. It wasn't beyond him to go round to Anna and kick off some kind of shouting match.

'Oh, I don't mind,' said Sheila, a little too quickly.

'You're right, Jim. I need to find somewhere else to sleep. Mum has plenty of room, but I don't really want to involve her yet.'

'You can come to mine,' said Jim.

'What about Paula?'

'Paula,' he answered pointedly, 'is no longer. We've been finished for months.'

'You never said,' I said and felt a quiet burn of shame that I had become so out of the loop that I didn't know what my brother's current situation was.

'You never asked. Anyway, I've got a spare bed. You need to give Sheila her space back.'

I looked at my watch. It was after eight p.m. 'Why don't you go back to yours, Jim. Freshen up the spare bed and I'll go over to my place, grab a few things, give the boys a goodnight kiss and come over.'

'Fine. Don't do anything daft when you speak to Anna.'

Jim revved his car up to the end of the street. The house seemed emptier with his departure. It was as if it had taken his presence to illustrate that Sheila and I had been here alone together. I didn't need to go deep into my mind to find my attraction to her. It was there, like a new suit hanging on the front of a wardrobe of old clothes. But it was a suit I couldn't afford to try on for size just yet.

'Thank you, Sheila. For everything.'

'You're welcome,' her smile warmed me. 'You take care of yourself.' She walked towards me without a trace of awkwardness, her arms wide. 'C'mere.'

I stepped forward and gave in to her embrace. My cheek resting on her head, the perfume from her hair filling my nostrils. Despite my attraction to her, there was nothing sexual about that embrace, just two people sharing strength. My arms were around her shoulders, hers round my waist.

'Andy,' she said. The word was laden with meaning. Like a warning shot, heat raced into my groin. As if burned, I stepped back.

'Andy?' She looked offended.

'Sheila, I…' Should the new Andy Boyd be honest and declare every one of his emotions? Perhaps if I hadn't been in such a mess. '… Maybe if this was a different time…'

Her eyes shone, then the colour dipped with a mix of pleasure and confusion.

'You're right, Andy. Another time, another life maybe,' she said quietly.

Hope danced in my veins, I tried to hold it in check. Here was a woman I could love. I took a step forward. Arms wide. Paused. Stepped back. Allowed my arms to drop to my sides.

This couldn't happen. Not yet. My heels were still dangling over a precipice, my toes stretching for a stronger hold. I wasn't safe. Until

I was, I couldn't risk Sheila's affections. The boys were my number-one priority. Nothing else could interfere until they were with me.

Sheila's goodbye kiss still warmed my cheek as I parked outside my house. Her words of caution sounded in my ear. Remembered pain tightened muscle as I walked up to the door. Every animal instinct I possessed urged me to turn and flee. Behind the wooden door I knocked on was a walking ball of fury and a mountain of pain. I felt like a frightened mutt, my tail curved up between my legs and reaching along the length of my stomach.

No. Steel was in the set of my jaw now. I would allow no more of Anna's abuse. The one thing that had held me in her thrall had died. She could no longer use my love for her as a weapon. But I would have to be careful. She was not stupid and would know that the one weapon remaining in her arsenal was the most potent of all. My love for my boys. She would have no problems in drawing that sword and skewering me with it.

'What do you want?' was her welcome as she opened the door.

'Some clothes,'

'Oh,' she walked into the hall, looking smaller than I remembered. 'I hope you don't think you're going to get much more.' The warning was clear. She was going to fight to keep the boys.

Acid roiled in my stomach. Fighting back was still new to me. I couldn't let her smell any fear.

'You're all right. I'll just fill up a bag with some clothes. I'll be back for the boys some other time.' Defiance sparked in every fibre.

'You wish. You've no job, no permanent residence. I've already spoken to a lawyer. The boys will be mine and any request for access will be denied. Permanently.'

16

As Anna spoke, her face was contorted with hate. For the first time I wondered who the subject of that hate was. Was it me or was it actually herself? Words that once had the power to invoke my inadequacy, were now just sounds. Streams of sound that could no longer wound. The power I had given her to hurt me, I had now taken back. And this realisation was my shield.

Her arms waved, her once fearsome mouth hurled ribbons of sound at me and I looked on, amazed at my own detachment. Her eyes betrayed a spark of insight; my reaction wasn't the usual one. Something was not quite right here. She continued her attack on my eardrums, on my sense of self-worth. I could see the thought impose itself on her brain. It had worked beautifully before; she would just have to raise the bar a little.

I leaned against a doorway, as if we were discussing where to go on our next holiday together. Her lips whitened as she drew them across the rictus of her mouth, displaying perfect teeth. She would not allow her uncertainty to show. The stream of invective continued to flow. She was unaware that she was now adding strength to my determination to win.

Words that had once been nails hammering into my psyche now drove into the lid of a coffin. A coffin that held any affection I ever felt for her. All I saw before me now was a frightened little girl. A little girl who had grown into a woman who wore her fear like a shroud. What she wanted all along was to be loved, but she didn't know how. She didn't know what love looked like. Her experience had been formed at the hands of men who knew only about power and how to abuse it. This was the cloth with which she bound her heart and her fists.

'Are you even listening to me?' she demanded.

'I've heard it all before Anna. It means nothing. You mean nothing.' I took relief in the truth of my last statement.

'We'll see if I mean nothing.' She stepped towards me and raised her fist as if to strike. I stood my ground, opened my arms and smiled.

'You mean nothing, Anna. You have no substance. You're just a sad, wee girl who used to pull the wings from wasps and soak up all the poison they could sting you with. The problem is it toughened you up too much. Now you don't know what love is, you don't know what happy feels like.'

'You think you could have made me happy?' She moved back, her eyes never settling on the one surface. 'You gave me nothing. Apart from a roof … and a lovely wee boy.' She scored with that one; a small smile of victory was her reaction as the barb bit. 'Two lovely wee boys. I need them. I'll be a good mother to them. I just won't let their father near,' she spat.

'The only reason you want them is to spite me, you sad bitch.'

'Oh, hark at the name-caller now,' she crowed. Mentally I gave myself a shake. I'd forgotten rule number one in any skirmish with Anna, she fed off negative reactions the way hyenas feed off a dying animal. Always circling, feet and mind never still. Looking for a sign of weakness. Darting in for a nip, a bite; tearing flesh with razor teeth.

'Do you really love the boys, Anna?' I asked.

'Of course I do,' she hissed. 'What do you take me for?'

'Someone without conscience. Someone without regard for herself or others, unless there was something in it for her.'

She sagged a little. 'Andy, I'm tired. Why don't you get what you came for and just go?'

'I'll get my clothes now, but I'll be back for my boys another time.'

'Dream on. You've lost them forever. Deal with it. You've no job, no fixed abode. No life. What judge is going to give you the boys? You won't even get Pat. The boys shouldn't lose one another. As little disruption to their family life as possible, that's what the judge will order.'

'That's where you're wrong. Pat isn't your biological son. I've looked after him on my own right up until the last few years. Right up until I picked you, thinking you would be a good mother to him.'

'I am a good mother too him.' Her nostrils flared.

'Aye, right. What good mother would deny her son access to his father? And let me inform you of my circumstances, so the next time you speak to your lawyer, you'll get it right. I still have my job. The real thief owned up. And I do have a "fixed abode". I'm staying with Jim at the moment. I'll move in with Mum shortly. She's more room in her house. Enough room for me and the boys. A nice house with a built-in babysitter. What judge in his right mind would deny that when faced with the competition? Anyway, we could stand here all night scoring points off one another. I'll go get my stuff and the next time I'll see you will be when I come to pick up the boys.'

I walked up the stairs. Anna followed.

'What're you doing?' I asked.

'I'm coming to make sure you don't take anything you shouldn't.'

I shrugged.

Our bedroom, her bedroom, looked as if I'd just stepped out of it for a moment. Nothing had changed. My clothes were all in their drawers or on their hangers. Anna must have caught my look of surprise.

'Everything's here. I moved nothing. Didn't even take a pair of scissors to your ties.'

'Good.' I reached under the bed and pulled out a suitcase. The symbolism didn't escape me. This really was the end.

Nor did it escape Anna. She sat on the bed. Her body language of someone calm and full of reflection. More like the Anna I'd fallen for.

'How did we get to this, Andy? We were good once. How did this happen?' she asked.

I pulled some suits from the wardrobe and dumped them in

the case. Tidying sleeves and trousers, I answered, 'Well, I seem to remember it starting on our wedding night. Then there was the beatings, the manipulations, and let's not forget the humiliations.' I faced her. 'How could you, Anna? I loved you and you treated me worse than an animal.' Ghosts of beatings past, memories of insults upon insults threatened to weaken my resolve. How had I let the woman in front of me treat me in such a way? Sat on the edge of the bed, I couldn't detect one ounce of threat from her.

'I couldn't help it, Andy. You drove me to it. I couldn't control myself.'

'Aw, for fucksake, Anna. Crap. You just chose not to.'

'Ssssh, Andy. You'll wake the boys.'

'Tell me something…' I lowered my voice. 'If we had been the subject of one of those fly-on-the-wall documentaries. If we'd a camera in here twenty-four hours a day, broadcasting live on TV our every move, would you have been able to control your anger then?'

'Of course I would.'

'Well don't you see? You simply chose not to control yourself. You had all this anger, all this … hate, and you let me have it. That's what happened, *sweetheart*.' My often-used endearment was sullied with irony.

She bit her lip as if fighting back tears. 'I'm sorry, Andy. Why don't you stay for a while? We could talk this thing through.' She folded her arms and crossed her legs. She looked smaller, frightened, more vulnerable and exhausted by our fighting.

I fortified myself against my rising feelings of sympathy. 'You just don't know when to stop, do you?'

'I don't know what you mean,' she looked up at me.

'Don't give me the eyes, the face … the legs. Stop with the manipulation, Anna. I don't love you anymore. Congratulations, you killed it. Stone dead.' I pushed the last of my belongings into a bag. 'We're over, finished, history. Now, I'll be happy to be civil to you for the sake of the boys.' I walked out of the room carrying my luggage. 'I'll just see that they're tucked in.'

Using the light from the hallway, I walked into their room.

'Dad. Is that you?' Pat squinted from his bed. 'Mum said you were still in Campbeltown.'

'Ssssh. Watch you don't waken up your brother.' I sat on Pat's bed and ruffled his hair. Bedtime was always my favourite time with the boys. They were at their cutest. Hair combed after their bath, cheeks shining with health and just a little too tired to remind you how they could misbehave. I pulled Pat from his position and wrapped him in my arms. His hair was satin against my cheek; his small body warm with spent energy.

'Love you, son,' I whispered. I couldn't trust my voice. Breathing deep, I fought to control myself. Everything had to be as normal as possible. He was used to raised voices coming from our bedroom. Me in tears would definitely not come across well.

Anna cleared her throat from the door. Her presence broke the spell.

'I've just come back for some clean shirts, son. But I won't be away long.' With as much tenderness as I was capable of, I lay him back down on his bed and straightened his sheets. I traced the silk of his cheek with the back of a finger.

'You look after your brother,' I said.

He nodded, half-smiled, still fuzzy with sleep. 'Love you, Dad.' He then turned and burrowed down into his pillow.

I turned to Ryan's bed. His small body formed an exclamation mark of peaceful ignorance. He'd kicked off his covers. He always got too hot. He was on his back, one arm thrust up behind his head, as if stretching for a toy. A toy that would remain out of reach all through his dream. Frightened I would disturb him, I kissed the fingertips of my right hand and lightly touched his forehead.

'Sleep tight, son.'

Outside the room, I closed the door behind me. I faced Anna.

'You cause harm to one hair on their heads and I will kill you.' I knew the threat was unnecessary but I let the emotion of the moment get the better of me.

'Andy,' she admonished me. 'I would never hurt them. How could you say that?'

The emotion was too raw to apologise even though I knew I was wrong. Anna chased me down the stairs.

'Andy, you've got to believe I would never harm the boys.'

'Yes, yes. I know. You reserved all your punishments for me. I'm bigger than you are. I needed taking down a size or two. Your power over the boys is assured, taken as read, they're no threat to you. Yet.'

She flinched, as if she'd read my real feelings for her for the first time. Strangely, this small sign of weakness didn't thrill me. It saddened me.

'The boys are my chance to get things right,' she said in a tiny voice, and I knew she was being genuine. 'Please don't ever doubt that I have nothing but their best interests at heart.' A single tear shone like a torch on the alabaster of her cheek. And I could see that here there was no agenda, no attempt at manipulation.

Just the loneliest expression of emotion I'd ever witnessed.

'Anna, the next wee while is not going to be the easiest for any of us. Let's try and make it as easy for the boys as we can.'

'Okay.' She caught the tear on a hankie before it spilled on to her cheek. She walked towards me and reached out for my hand.

'Andy, I'm truly sorry for how things turned out between us.' She bit her lip. Closed her eyes tight. Opened them and looked at the floor. Eventually her eyes met mine. 'You deserved better than me.'

I looked down at her hands and wondered at the damage they could inflict. What could I say in response?

Nothing.

She breathed deep as if bracing herself. 'Go on, get out of here.' Her tone was not unkind.

'Right.' Now that the moment had come I wasn't sure how to behave. What is the protocol for leaving an abusive spouse? They don't teach you that in the marriage manuals.

'Come here, give us a hug, you big lump,' she said. There was not a trace of rancour in her voice. Only an acceptance that events had finally taken a turn that they had to. If both of us were to retain our sanity than we would have to let them play out.

As we held each other, I thought of chances lost and lives warped by a cycle of despair that had begun before either of us were born. One abuse of strength led to another, to another, to another. Until here we were, saying goodbye, knowing we had no other option.

I felt the heat of her. The softness of her cheek on my neck. Noted a feeling of affection and quashed it.

A small voice filled the hall. It came from the doorway. I hadn't heard the door opening.

'Dad, are you staying?' It was Pat. Hope was a prayer filling his expression. Ryan was by his side holding his hand.

Love surged from my chest to my throat, constricted my breathing. 'Hey, guys.'

I walked over and knelt in front of them. Ryan jumped into my arms, while his older brother kept his distance in what I judged was an attempt to protect himself from disappointment.

Ryan's little body was warm and compact in my arms. His hair smelled of bath time. I savoured his presence and realised I couldn't walk away now without them. I couldn't leave them here. One more moment away from them was unthinkable.

I took a deep breath. Girded my spine for the fight I was about to instigate. I turned to face Anna just as Pat came to stand by my side. Something in him knew what the situation was and it pained me to see him turn to Anna with an expression that begged. He wanted me to stay, or he wanted me to take him with me and he didn't know how he could make this happen.

The phone rang, breaking the spell.

Anna walked through to the hall to answer it. I could hear only her mumbled replies and moments later she returned. She looked at me. Then looked at the boys. There was a strange light in her eyes. A rare softness.

'When did we become my parents, Andy?' she asked, her voice distant and winsome.

I could only shrug

She bit her top lip as if she had just reached a painful decision. 'You put your bags in the car and I'll get the boys ready.'

'Eh?' This sudden turn of events threw me completely. I looked at her as if she had just spoken to me in Swahili.

'Go on.' Her smile was weak and laced through with pain and a thousand unspoken apologies.

'Who was that on the phone?' I asked.

'Nobody,' she said. 'It was nobody.'

It took a matter of minutes to get the boys into their coats and put a collection of their clothes and toys, along with my clothes, into the car.

'You be a good boy, Pat.' She stuck her hand in the car and ruffled his hair. 'Never give your dad any bother, okay?' Then she opened the back door and leaned over to kiss Ryan. He didn't stir as she pressed her lips against the cushion of his cheek and held the kiss for a few seconds.

'Anna.' I leaned back and spoke over my shoulder. 'I … thanks.'

She dismissed my gratitude with a flick of her hair, 'Just you look after my boys. They're all I've got. Tell them I love them.'

17

Mum's face was a study in confusion when I arrived at her door with one sleeping and one almost sleeping child.

'Andy, what's going on, son?'

'I'll tell you later, just help me in with the boys and their stuff.' I stopped on her doorstep. 'You okay if we spend a few nights with you?'

'What a stupid question.' She adjusted the sleeves of her jumper and beamed. 'Of course it is.' She bent forward to look at Ryan.

'Right,' she said. 'The boys can have my bed. You have the spare room and I'll take the sofa.'

'What? No way am I putting you out of your bed.'

She just looked at me. On this occasion her word was law and would be obeyed. 'Look at the size of you. That sofa is no bed for a man.' She shook her head. 'It's decided.'

'Mum,' I protested and then gave up. The no-nonsense way she was taking over made it appear as if our nocturnal visit was completely normal and had the effect of calming me down.

'You tuck your boys in, I'll bring in the rest of the bags and make us both a wee cup of tea,' she said.

My mother's bedroom was as she always kept it. A large bed with a mattress on it that made you feel you were lying on a cloud. I could barely see the boys for the mound of pillows and the thick, pink quilt. Climbing roses adorned the wallpaper and their dark-pink heads winked out from behind the many photographs and paintings that crowded the walls. There was a new addition on top of the dresser: a portable TV.

Removing some of the pillows, I re-arranged the boys so that they wouldn't smother each other. Pat turned on his side and Ryan registered nothing of my ministrations.

'They sleeping?' Mum asked in a whisper when I reached the living room.

'Mum, why are you whispering, when the TV is on so loud?'

She looked at me dryly. 'Are your sons asleep?'

'Yes.'

'Right, there's a coffee and a biscuit. I'll turn off the TV and you can explain to your old, befuddled mother what the hell is going on.'

For the second time within a matter of hours, I explained to one of those dearest to me what my life had been like over the last few years.

My mother, for her part, gave a definitive performance of how to listen properly. She only spoke when my explanation required clarification and prompted me only when emotion threatened to overcome me and halt my speech. She didn't judge or pass comment, she only listened.

'Do you see what an idiot your son has been then?'

'Not at all. I see a brave man who gave, gave and gave. I see a man…' she dabbed at her cheek with a white, linen handkerchief '…who, if his father were alive today, he would've been very proud of. Oh, son…' she cried. 'Why didn't you tell me? I could have helped you in some way. I could've done something.'

'Mum.' I sat on the arm of her chair and hugged her. 'The only person who could do anything was me. I had to come to my senses. No one could have done it for me.'

We hugged in silence for a moment. A moment when touch transcended words, a moment when words were as effective as an ocean without the pull of the tide.

'Right, no more tears, as the song goes. What a day. And to think it ends with me getting my boys back.'

'Isn't it marvellous, son?' She reached up and kissed my cheek. 'I'm so happy that things have worked out.'

'Let's not get too excited, Mum. It's early days yet. I can't explain what got into Anna that made her let the boys go so easily. She definitely wasn't herself, though. She'll be on the phone first thing in the morning demanding them back.'

'You guys have to sort all of this out with the boys' best interests at heart.' Mum's face sagged with concern. 'Sue at number thirty-three – she hasn't seen her grandson for over a year.'

'Jeez, that's awful.'

'Her son's wife refuses to let them anywhere near them. Ignores court orders.' She shook her head. 'She even pretended the boy was autistic, needed a strict routine and that his father would only disrupt that.'

'Surely the system wouldn't let that happen?'

Mum shrugged. 'Thankfully, that ploy didn't work, but she still forgets play-dates with Dad. She even goes away for weekends when it's the dad's turn and there's nothing he can do about it.'

I understood Mum's fears. I shared them. The boys were a major part of her life and she dreaded any cessation of that.

'Grandparents are often the forgotten ones in these scenarios. While the parents score points off one another, Granny loses contact with her grandkids.'

'I get it, Mum. I'll do whatever I can to make sure the boys stay in both our lives.' I placed my hand on hers. Felt the dry warmth of it.

'It's not up to you though, is it? I've heard some horror stories of the family courts. Mums tend to hold all the cards.' She pursed her lips and sat back in her chair, crossing her arms as she was bolstered by the cushion.

'Right, Mum.' I shook my head. I didn't want to go there tonight. 'Let's just enjoy having the boys for now, and worry about all that stuff later, eh?'

'Aye, right enough. Anyway, you must be shattered after all this excitement.'

'Tired?' I felt as if muscle was sagging from my bones. 'I could sleep for a fortnight.'

'Right.' She bustled out of the room and returned with a pair of pillows and a thick quilt. 'I'll camp out here.' She forced a bright tone. 'The bed in the spare room is already made up.'

*

My bed for the night was a single and my feet hung over the end. I considered going in to join the boys in my mum's bed, but knew from experience that I would get no sleep. I'd shared a bed with them on many occasions and something always held me back from full sleep mode. Perhaps in a deep part of my mind I was scared I would turn over in the night and crush one of them.

Common sense told me a good night's rest was required if I was to get things back on an even keel, so I stayed where I was.

I lay on my back, hands under my head, eyes searching the dark of the ceiling. The moment when Anna suggested I take the boys played over and over in my mind. What had prompted that? Was she tired of fighting? She mentioned her parents. Did she remember an old promise she'd made to herself – that she would have a happier home than her parents did? Recognise that she'd failed in this and decided to start afresh?

Whatever it was, I was grateful.

I sat up in bed.

I should go to her. Talk. See how she was. If she didn't have me or the boys, what kind of state would she be in? For all her faults she loved the boys. When I was forced away from them I felt their absence like an ache in my gut. She'd be the same.

Without giving it too much thought, I kicked my feet off the bed and located my clothes in the dark. As quietly as I could, I dressed and left the house, aware of my mother's eyes on my back as I tip-toed through the living room.

Mum reached me as I put my hand on the door handle. She flicked a switch and the hall light came on. Her hair was sticking up all over her head and her eyes were shrunken with lack of rest.

'Andy, son, is this wise?' she asked in that tone that was just above a whisper.

'I need to see her, Mum.'

'It's two a.m. What can you possibly talk about now that can't wait until morning?'

'I have to know, Mum. Is this a blip or is this a change for the better?'

She pulled her dressing gown tight and searched my eyes for a clue as to my mood.

'Will you stay calm? If she doesn't say what you want to hear, can you stay calm?'

'I'll say and do whatever it takes to keep my boys in my life, Mum.'

My former home was in darkness. I parked on the street instead of the drive, climbed out of the car and stood on the pavement studying each of the windows as if they might give some sort of clue to Anna's state of mind.

The air was balmy and by the light of the streetlamps I could see that the front garden I'd toiled over in recent years was in a good state: the lawn trimmed, the borders free of weeds. To the neighbours nothing would look out of place. Nothing outwardly changed. Anna was all about appearances.

I heard a cry. Sharp and high, it faded on the breeze. What was it? I cocked my head. A fox? A pair of battling cats?

I listened some more.

The night air calmed around me and returned to silence. Whatever it was, it had moved on.

As should I, I thought. I took a step back from the garden towards the car. It would be silly to try and talk this over with Anna in the middle of the night. Some time on her own might just be what the doctor ordered. Give her a chance to gain some perspective. I could give her a call in the morning. Arrange a meeting in which we could discuss how we kept the boys in both our lives.

But something held me there, staring at the house that had been the scene of so much pleasure, and ultimately so much pain. Resentment and anger was a weight that held me to the spot. It was all I could do not to bellow out at the windows every expletive my mind could think of.

I deserved none of her anger. None of her abuse. I was a good father. A good husband.

You didn't deserve me, bitch, I wanted to shout out, without caring who heard. But the new Andy Boyd didn't scream out in pain. The new Andy Boyd took action.

I stayed standing where I was for I don't know how long, anger stiffening my fists.

Small fingers woke me as they paraded along the bridge of my nose and across my forehead. No, no, I heard myself mumble. Where was I? What was happening? Did I just have my hands round Anna's throat?

'Daddy. Sleeping.' Ryan whispered in my ear.

'What…' I struggled up from the fog of sleep, an image lingered from my dreams. Anna's face red as she fought for breath.

I shook my head as if that action might rid my head of the picture.

'Daddy, wake,' said Ryan.

I opened one eye, carefully, in case he decided that his fingers should take a walk inside the lid. Ryan's face was so close his button nose was pressing against mine.

Whoa, it was only a dream, but I could still hear Anna's panicked fight for air.

'Daddy, wake.' Ryan pushed off my back and sat by my side. He smiled when he saw me focus on him and his face changed from merely beautiful to angelic. I turned over onto my back and replied with a smile of my own.

'Give Daddy a cuddle,' I ordered, and Ryan, with a contented sigh that echoed mine, obliged.

'What about me?' Pat leaned over from the other side and blew a raspberry on my face.

'Right, boy.' I jumped up, grabbed him and tickled him until he begged me to stop. Ryan, not quite sure of the technique, joined in. His efforts received a few grunts of pain from Pat.

'Ryan. That's sore.' So I switched my attentions to him.

The sound of a child in mid-giggle has to be one of the most pleasing sounds known to man. I defy anyone to keep their expression stern when they hear that sound.

'Boys.' Mum spoke from the door. 'Your father has to get to work.

Come and get your breakfast.' They were off the bed in a flash of pink skin and cotton. 'Andy, there's a clean towel in the bathroom and the shower is on.'

'Did you…?'

'Slept like a log,' she interrupted, the lie of her statement proven by the tired cast of her eyes. Probably stayed up all night worrying. I felt terrible and promised myself that this solution would be temporary.

By the time I had showered and shaved the boys were hunkered before the TV. Their mother and I normally only allowed half an hour of TV in the morning, but Gran said they could watch it for as long as they wanted this time, because it was special.

With a mouthful of cornflakes, I spoke to my mother quietly. 'Are you okay to watch the boys today?'

Without taking her eyes from them for even a second she answered, 'Just you try and stop me.'

As I chewed through my rushed breakfast, I considered what had happened the night before. Why had Anna changed her mind? Was it anything to do with the phone call she received?

'Nobody' was her answer when I asked who'd called.

Mum interrupted my thoughts. 'Jim's delighted to hear about the boys, by the way. He phoned while you were in the shower and I filled him in.'

I spooned in another mouthful of cornflakes. Nodded.

'He said you should have told him cos he went round there last night to have a word.'

'He did what?' I stood up so fast I became light-headed.

'S'all right.' Mum held out a placatory hand. 'He said the house was in darkness. No one answered so he went back home.'

'I fucking told him…'

'Andy.' Mum looked at the boys, who were both looking up at me wide-eyed. I rarely swore in front of them. 'Nothing happened. He didn't speak to her. And don't worry, I already told him he was an idiot.'

'And I'll be telling him as well.'

A quick brush of my teeth and it was time to go to work. Scooby Doo was running away from another stupid man in a stupid monster costume when I said goodbye to the boys. I leaned down and kissed them both on the forehead.

'You boys be good boys for your gran today, okay?'

Pat nodded his head but didn't move his eyes from the screen.

Ryan turned to me. 'Dad, you be a good dad.' Then he stood up and followed me to the door.

Before I left I knelt down to speak to him. 'Daddy will be home soon. I just need to go and make us some pennies, okay?'

He nodded his assent, his large eyes grave with understanding. 'Pennies,' he repeated. 'Where's Mummy.'

'Mummy's gone away for a couple of days, so Dad and Gran are going to look after you.'

He nodded again, but this time he was not so happy. His face lengthened, his bottom lip curved into an arch and his face coloured bright red.

'I want Mummy,' he squealed. 'I want my Mummyyyyyy.'

Mum rushed to his side. 'There, there. We can't have this lovely wee boy in tears this morning. Let's go and see the birds in the garden. Let's watch them feeding off the table.' She motioned with her head that I should go and mouthed that it would be all right.

By the time I'd straightened my tie and put on my jacket I could hear Ryan's sweet soprano from the kitchen.

'Oh, wow,' he said. 'Big birds, lots birds.'

I hurried from the house, his sugared tones and trusting eyes haunting me as I thought of the lie I had told him.

At work, people fell over themselves to offer thanks that I was back at work. No one ever believed I was guilty, of course, and no one could believe that Malcolm had been so devious. The real reason for his deceit was not yet public knowledge and if I had anything to do with it that would remain the case. I was surprised at Roy Campbell not supplying the information, but perhaps after our little head-to-head the previous day, he knew what reaction he might get from me.

Sheila was in the branch. Roy had left her to finalise the audit on Malcolm and to tie off any loose ends. She smiled her support from the other side of the room, content to let everyone else say their piece.

When the doors opened for business on the dot of nine, two men in dark suits, with matching dark expressions, were the first people inside. I blinked and held onto the counter as I read the purpose in their movement and realised who they must be.

The oldest of the pair showed me his police warrant card. 'Mr Andrew Boyd?'

I nodded.

'Could we have a word in private, sir?'

'Of course, officer. Follow me.'

My eyes swept over the pair of them. The older man had a thick brush of grey hair. His face was long, thin, well lined and bereft of expression. His eyes were luminous with intelligence. They bored into me and I was immediately struck with the worry that this man could read my thoughts the moment they occurred to me.

The younger policeman was blond, his hair cropped fashionably. His eyes wore the same intelligence, but were seasoned with conceit; he accepted all the admiring glances from the female members of staff as we walked through the banking hall and into my office.

As soon as the door was shut, Grey-hair wasted no time.

'Mr Boyd, your wife was found in the early hours of this morning. I'm afraid she's dead.'

18

The radar of familiarity found me a chair, stopping me from collapsing onto the floor.

'Dead?' I mumbled to the room. 'Who … are you sure? Anna Boyd?'

Blond-hair nodded, 'Yes we're sure.' His voice was quiet and respectful, but his eyes wore another badge. He intoned our address, saying that a neighbour had alerted them when they saw that the front door was open, stuck their head in and saw something they'd never forget.

'But how?' I was beyond tears, beyond shock. 'But I was with her early last night. She was fine.' Blond's eyes were on me like a pair of magnets on a fridge.

'Can you tell us where you were in the early hours of this morning, Mr Boyd?' asked Grey.

'Anna. Dead. How?' I asked, unable to process Grey's question.

'We're still waiting for the full forensic report,' replied Grey. 'Would you like anyone with you at the moment?'

'Anna. Dead,' I repeated like a mantra, like a spell that would prove the last few minutes to be a lie. This was all a joke, a horrible joke. Anna wasn't dead. She was lying in her bed as we spoke, reading *Hello* magazine and sipping her third coffee of the day.

'I'll just phone her.' I reached for the phone. 'You can speak to her.' My eyes darted from one man to the other. 'Then you'll see that this is all a terrible mistake.' My voice rose into a yell.

Grey put his hand over mine to replace the receiver. 'I'm afraid this is no mistake…'

'What's going on?' Sheila walked into the room, no doubt alerted by my shout.

'Sheila, tell these men. Tell them. Anna's not dead. She's sitting up in bed reading. Go on phone her, phone her.' I could hear the hysteria in my voice, but I didn't care. They had to believe me.

'Anna's dead?' Sheila whispered. Her hand moved to cover her throat and an image from this morning's dream was displayed in my mind like a still from a movie. Like this morning, I again shook my head as if to dislodge it. That was a dream. Only a dream.

Wasn't it?

'Can you account for your presence last night, Mr Boyd? Between the hours of midnight and six a.m.?' asked Grey.

His voice came towards me out of a tunnel. His mouth moved, the words arrived seconds later.

'What?'

'Do you know of anyone who would want to harm your wife, Mr Boyd,' asked Blond.

'Eh? Harm? Sheila, tell these men. Tell them.' I stood up. Felt a charge of guilt as I remembered the moment I was standing outside Anna's front door. Once again I heard the cry I had dismissed as a fox.

Could that have been the moment when Anna died?

If I had gone in, could I have saved her? My legs gave way and I stumbled back onto my chair. Sweat sparked cold and wet the length of my spine.

Oh my God. Anna.

Sheila rounded on the policemen, 'I think Mr Boyd has had enough to take in for the moment, gentlemen. Why don't you give him some time to come to terms with this before you ask any questions?'

Blond made as if to say something but was silenced by a look from his colleague.

'Mr Boyd, we *will* have to intrude on your grief. If not now, then later. There are questions we need to ask.' Grey looked at his colleague. They seemed to come to some silent agreement. 'We'll be back.'

They walked out.

'Andy, what the hell happened?' asked Sheila.

'They said Anna's dead,' I repeated. 'She's dead.'

I stared at the wall. Pictures of Anna filled my mind, a montage of her smiles, laughs and kisses. Blink. I told myself, blink. Strangely, no thought of the violent side of her nature corrupted this gallery of images. It was as if my brain was already trying to sanitise her memory. Anna pregnant and shovelling chocolate into her mouth, Anna cradling Ryan just moments after he was born, Anna playing with the boys.

My hand shot to my mouth. 'The boys. Oh my god, the boys.' Only when I thought of the consequences to the boys did my emotion crash through. A sob escaped my mouth.

I can remember sliding forward on my chair and landing on the floor. I can remember thinking that the pain was as much physical as mental. I can remember rocking on my knees as I tried to soothe it.

Sheila knelt by my side, 'Oh Andy.' Her arm rested on my shoulder.

We rocked together for what seemed hours. It may have only been minutes, for the place we crouched in held no sense of time. There were no clocks, no machines here. We were two animals, one trying to assuage the other's pain..

'Andy. C'mon let's sit up. My knees are killing me.' Sheila said at last, leading me to a chair.

Gradually my motor functions returned. Coherent thoughts pushed through the haze in my mind.

'Can I get you a drink?'

'Coffee, please.' No sooner, or so it felt, than the words issued from my mouth, hot ceramic was placed in my hand.

'She was okay last night, when I left.' My mind began to question the events of the proceeding evening. 'I left around nine. We talked, she let me have the boys…'

'You have to go and speak to the police. Tell them everything.'

I heard the tension in her voice. 'Why would I go and tell them? If they want me they know where to find me.'

'Do you not watch TV? The husband is usually the first suspect. If you don't take the initiative here you could look guilty.'

I stared up at Shelia, my mouth hanging open as I chased this thought down to a horrifying conclusion.

King Street Police Station is only a short walk from the bank. I ran. One phrase imposed its rhythm on the fall of my feet – I thought about it, I thought about it, I thought about it. I had actually considered murder as a way out of my predicament. Does that make me nearly as bad as the man who did do it? After all, there is only a short step from intent to action. A short step that only a sick and evil person could take, I reassured myself. Besides, my intent was never concrete, it was only the thought of a desperate man. Wasn't it?

Grey and Blond showed me into an interview room. It was stark in its simplicity. One table, four chairs and one double tape recorder. The regularly spaced holes in the soundproofed tiles were the room's only decoration. It was a room that would encourage confession. Knowing that I was almost certainly the prime suspect did not aid my performance.

'I was at my mother's last night. All night,' I asserted.

'We will just put on this recorder, Mr Boyd,' said Grey. Blond sat back in his chair, his arms crossed. His eyes staring, always staring.

Grey pressed record and then announced who was present in the room.

'Can you tell us for the record where you were between the hours of midnight last night and six a.m. this morning, Mr Boyd.'

'Yes, I was staying at my mother's.'

'Was your mother there?'

'Yes. She slept on the couch.'

'Why were you not in the marital home?' asked Grey.

'Because the marriage is over.'

'And how happy are you about that?' asked Blond.

'Things happen, people change, and they learn more about the other than they ever wanted.'

'Interesting that you say "things happen", Mr Boyd. Were you not, only several nights ago, forcibly removed from your home?'

'Yes, but…'

'Did your now-deceased wife not complain about your violence towards her?'

If I was worried before, I couldn't begin to explain the state my mind was in then.

'I would like to speak to a lawyer.' I said. After all that's what you heard people saying in the movies.

'You can speak to a lawyer in due course, Mr Boyd. We just want to ask you a few questions,' said Grey.

'I want a lawyer. You guys are clever. You could try and trip me up,' I said.

'Is there something that you don't want to say, Mr Boyd? You can only be tripped up if there is something at your feet. A dead body perhaps? A guilty conscience?'

'No guilty conscience, no dead body at my feet, I just want a lawyer. Do you not have to let me speak to a lawyer when I ask for one?'

'Not necessarily. In Scotland, if we believe that justice will not be served by the introduction of a lawyer then we don't need to grant your request.' Blond smiled. In my present state of paranoia, I was certain he was convinced of my culpability.

'Let me reassure you, Mr Boyd. Think of this as an early question-ing session,' Grey said, his tone fatherly. I could read the intelligence in his eyes. He wouldn't just go for the easy option.

'Sorry.' I breathed deep. 'Ask me anything you want.'

'Tell us about the night the police were called to your house at your wife's insistence.'

'We've had a difficult relationship over the years,' I began. 'But the violence … that was my wife.' And so the sorry tale spilled from my lips, like milk soured by my tongue. I finished by telling them about Anna letting me have the boys last night. Just as I stopped speaking, someone knocked at the door.

The two men rose and a hurried conference ensued in the corridor, out of my hearing. Grey and Blond came back in and sat resumed their seats.

What the hell was that all about?

'Mr Boyd, you were the last person to see your wife alive and you have a record of violence towards her. She was brutally murdered last night – stabbed thirty times.'

I covered up my ears as if hearing the words would damage the fine mechanism within.

'It was a frenzied attack, Mr Boyd.' Blond's voice was heavy with disgust. 'Blood was everywhere. A man of your height was spotted running away.'

'No, no, no.' Poor Anna, I thought, to die in such a way. My mind fought with both the idea of Anna pierced with tens of cuts and the insinuation in Blond's statement.

'Would you like something to drink, Mr Boyd? Some water?' asked Grey.

I could only manage a nod. My mind was full of an image of a blood-soaked Anna.

Once Grey fetched a drink the questions continued.

'Tell us again about last night.'

'Tell us about the fight you got into in Campbeltown.'

'Tell us where you stayed the night you were evicted from your house.'

'Tell us about your relationship with Sheila Hunter.'

'Tell us about your relationship with your wife.'

On and on the questions went. While one spoke the other watched and then shot in, questioning one of my answers, telling me that I had contradicted myself. The only thing that kept me going was knowledge of my innocence. An innocence stained by the intent I once shared with Anna's eventual killer.

19

The next day at work, Roy Campbell was sitting behind my desk.

'What are you doing here?' he asked.

'I'll ask you the same question, Roy.'

'Your wife died, Andy. Shouldn't you be at home grieving? Looking after the boys?' Was that sympathy in his tone? Sympathy served up to disguise the question running through his mind: was I guilty?

'I'll go nuts if I stay at home,' I replied and walked round the desk as if expecting him to vacate my seat. He stayed where he was.

'Andy. Really,' he said. 'You shouldn't be here.'

I came to a stop and towered over him. 'Shift your arse.'

He snorted. Stood and stepped to the side. If I hadn't been suffering there was no way he'd have let that slip by without comment. 'Have a serious think about it.' He walked to the door. 'Nobody will think any worse of you if you go home.'

Roy left and I took my seat, feeling a little shame that I'd spoken so harshly to him.

A knock at the door. It opened and Sheila stepped inside.

'Hey,' she said. Didn't need to say anything more. That one syllable was somehow laden with unquestioning support.

'Good to see a friendly face,' I said and managed a half-smile.

'Nobody thinks you did it,' she said as she took a seat across the desk from me. 'Not really.'

'That means the staff are already talking about me.'

'Of course they are, Andy.' She shrugged. 'Human nature.'

I plucked my diary from the top drawer on the right of the desk. Opened it at today's date. Shapes and letters filled the pages, none of which made any sense whatsoever. I rubbed at my eyes in an attempt to focus my sight. It made no difference.

'For once, Roy has a point,' said Sheila. 'This is not the place for you today, Andy.'

'You don't think I did it, do you?' I asked.

'Course I don't,' she replied and as she did so she leaned across the desk and took my hand. 'I've spent enough time with evil to know when it's absent.'

I felt myself bristle at her touch and withdrew my hand. I didn't deserve her sympathy. After all hadn't I been a few moments away from killing Anna myself? I sat back in my chair. Crossed my arms.

'I wanted to.' My voice was just above a strangled whisper. 'God help me but there were times I wanted her dead.' I bit my top lip in an attempt to hold back the emotions that were only a heartbeat from spilling over.

'Go home, Andy,' Sheila repeated. 'Be with your boys.'

'I haven't told them anything yet. I don't know how to…'

A loud knock came at my door and the detectives stepped in without being invited.

'Detective Holton,' said Grey.

'Detective Bairden,' said Blond. 'Mind if we have a word?'

'What?' I asked from my cotton-wool mouth. I could barely hear myself speak; I was suddenly weak with fatigue.

Sheila got to her feet and with a nod in my direction she left the room.

I licked my lips. Forced moisture into my mouth. 'What can I do for you, officers?'

'We just want to go through a few things with you,' said Bairden.

'Shouldn't you be inviting me along to King Street?'

Holton looked around the office. 'This is private enough.'

I looked beyond the door that he'd left open, spotted the harassed and worried face of Roy Campbell and understood what they were up to. This was two days in a row they'd spoken to me at my place of work. They were sending a big signal to everyone in the building.

My wife had been murdered and they thought I was guilty.

'When did you last see your wife?' Bairden asked, again, in a repeat of the questions from the previous day.

'I told you. When I picked up the boys.'

'And that was the last time you were at the house?' asked Holton, and I was aware of his scrutiny. Forced myself not to shift in my seat.

'I picked up my boys and that was the last I saw of my wife.' I couldn't tell them I'd stood outside the house and stared up at her window in the dark.

They asked pretty much all the questions they'd asked me the day before, obviously looking to see if I would keep to the same script. After about fifteen minutes of this, at some silent signal they both stood and walked to the door.

'Oh, before we go,' said Bairden. 'Could you let us know where to find your brother, Jim? We need a word with him.'

I gave them his work address, wondering what on earth they'd want with him. When they left, I dialled Sheila's extension.

'Know any good lawyers?' I asked her.

20

On automatic, I headed straight home and went through the motions of pretending that everything was okay.

As I tended to the boys and parried any questions about Anna, all I could think was, Anna is dead.

Once the boys were settled and watching cartoons, I managed to grab a few minutes with Mum in the kitchen.

'Dead?' Mum's face went grey and she all but collapsed onto a chair. 'How?'

I told her. The words scarcely managed to push out of my throat.

She held my hand in hers. 'Oh, my God.' Her eyes bored into mine. 'Do they know who did it?'

I shook my head.

'You went round there last night…'

'Yeah. I stopped at the kerb. Realised you were right, that this would achieve nothing and got back into the car.'

'You didn't go in the house?'

'No.'

'Did anybody see you?'

'Not sure. Why?'

Her face lengthened. 'Estranged husband seen outside the house on the night of the wife's murder?'

'I didn't do it, Mum.'

'Of course you didn't,' she said with just a little too much haste. Did she actually doubt me? 'I just meant that if someone saw you and mentioned it to the police, it wouldn't look good.'

Mum and I fed, bathed and put the boys to bed in record time that evening.

'When do we tell them? How do we tell them?' I asked Mum when we were safely out of earshot, back in the kitchen.

She could only shrug. 'Wee lambs.' She held a hand to her mouth as a thought hit. 'And Pat. That's two mums he's lost now.' A tear slipped down her face.

I moved to comfort her but stopped when I realised I had nothing to offer, my emotional well was completely dry. I had nothing to give.

Karen McPherson had bags under her eyes that could have carried the laundry from a small hotel, but the laser focus and the friendly smile that flirted across her lips suggested that she was a lawyer I could work with.

She leaned forward in her chair, pushed a filing cabinet's worth of blue folders to the side of her desk and asked me to tell her everything.

I talked for what felt like hours. She nodded as I talked and stopped me occasionally to elicit further understanding and to fill a new blue folder with copious notes.

'And you say they asked you for your brother Jim's address?' she asked once I'd almost run out of words.

I nodded.

She narrowed her eyes. 'From what you just told me he isn't an alibi.' She pursed her lips. 'Could he also be a suspect?'

'No,' I answered. But I said the word with a long, drawn-out note of contradiction – a thought had occurred.

'What is it?' Karen asked.

'He told Mum that he went over there that night.'

'Why would he do that?'

I sat back in my chair as I remembered talking to him in Sheila's kitchen. The anger in his face. His balled fist. 'I told him about the abuse and how Anna threatened to keep me away from my boys. He didn't react well. Said he'd go round there and put her straight.'

'Hardly helpful,' she said and for a second looked even more tired than when I walked in. 'And what happened?'

'He told Mum the house was in darkness. No one came to the door, so he left.'

'Any idea what time?'

'She didn't say.'

'So, on the night your wife was killed both you and your brother went over there at different times?'

I nodded. Crossed my arms. Didn't tell her that I'd lied to the police about being there. Bit the inside of my mouth. It didn't look good. If I was a detective, why would I want to look anywhere other than me and Jim for the killer? Will they hear about this and think we colluded?

I felt a chill. Jim wasn't capable of murder, was he? Could he have lied to Mum? He had a temper on him, but I was all but certain he wouldn't hurt a woman. An image of Anna in full battle mode jumped into my head. If she came at him, would he defend himself? Retaliate?

If I knew my brother, that is exactly what he would do.

'Tell me what you're thinking,' Karen ordered.

'Nothing,' I replied. 'He said he didn't get an answer and left. I've no reason to call him a liar.'

Karen drummed her pen against her desk. Stopped, and then twisted the barrel of her pen off and on. 'If the police had enough evidence to put you in front of the Procurator Fiscal they would have done that already. So the visits to your office and sitting outside your house are fishing trips. They want to rattle your cage. See how you react.' She twisted the pen so that the nib shot out of the end and took some more notes. Once she finished, she looked up at me. 'We'll lodge a complaint. Say you're being harassed at your place of work.'

'What will that do?'

'Probably nothing, but it will make them think twice. Maybe rein them in a little. Meantime, let me know if it happens again.' She smiled to signal that the meeting was over.

I walked to the door. Hand on the handle, I turned to thank her for her time.

'If Jim decides he needs legal advice, I can recommend some good people,' she said and pulled a different file from the pile on her right.

Mum was bug-eyed with worry. I'd barely got one foot in the door before she was tugging at my sleeve.

'Those detectives were here,' she said.

'Right,' I replied, forcing calm into my voice and expression.

'They asked about Jim. I had to tell them. I had to,' she said as she twisted her fingers.

'Ganny,' Ryan chanted from the living room.

'In a minute, son,' she said over her shoulder. 'Be there in a minute.' Then to me. 'What have I done? Have I put them onto him? Do they think one or both of my sons are murderers?'

'Mum.' I took her by the elbow and led her to the kitchen. She sat at the table. 'When did you speak to them?'

'About eleven.'

'They were in my office just after nine and they asked me how to get in touch with him, so they already had him on their radar before they spoke to you.'

We both sat with that for a moment.

'Do you think a neighbour might have seen him?' she asked.

'Who knows,' I replied and thought of the Stewarts across the street. They had Neighbourhood Watch stickers on every window and their net curtains were on permanent twitch.

'Phone him,' I suggested.

'I have,' she replied. 'No answer.' She went back to twisting her fingers. 'What is happening to my family?' A solitary tear slipped from her right eye.

I gripped her hands. 'We'll be fine.' I offered a reassurance I didn't feel.

'You don't think…'

'What? No fucking way,' I half shouted. 'Jim's been in a few scraps in his time, but he would never hurt a woman.'

'I know. I know.' She pulled her hands from mine and held them to her throat. I could see the skin there, like pale-pink crêpe paper, and was reminded of her age. 'It's just that you hear stuff. People stare, make comments and you start to think. Start to doubt…'

'Who's saying what, Mum?' I prayed she would give me a name. Then I'd have someone to focus my anger on.

'Oh, nothing. Nobody.'

'Who was it?' I stood.

'Och, it was just … I was in the supermarket. Saw Jean Campbell and she couldn't wait to ask me about Anna. Said she'd heard that both of you were round there that night.'

'Jesus fuck…'

'Daddy said a bad word again,' said Pat. He'd appeared at my side as we were talking. 'What are you saying about Mum?'

'Go back and sit with your brother,' I said with more anger than I wanted to.

'But…'

'Go,' I shouted and pointed in the direction I wanted him to move.

He ran from me, crying, and I felt even worse. 'Pat,' I shouted after him, my tone an apology. Too late. The living room door slammed shut.

'Poor wee lamb,' said Mum. 'He knows there's something wrong. They both do.' Her subtext was that we needed to tell them. I needed to tell them.

'I can't go there just now, Mum.'

The kitchen door slammed open and Jim stalked in. He was wearing a suit, but the top button of his shirt was open and the knot of his tie was at mid-chest level. His hair looked like it was no stranger to a hedge.

'What the bloody hell is going on?' he demanded of us both. 'I've had the polis round my work asking all sorts. And everywhere I've been today it feels like everyone is pointing and staring.'

'It's gossip and speculation, Jim,' Mum answered.

'Do they actually think that between us we killed Anna?' Jim asked, his eyes large and bright. 'Are they fucking nuts?'

'Killed Anna?' I heard a small voice at my side.

Oh no.

'Pat. I'll…'

He ran.

Mum looked at me, her face a model of disgust that this was the way he'd found out about Anna's death. 'Go to him, Andy. He needs his dad.'

It was dark by the time I re-joined Mum and Jim in the kitchen.

'How are they?' Mum moved to the edge of her seat as if to go to the boys.

I stretched my neck to the side as if to iron out a kink in the muscles there and shook out my hands, willing the blood to return. I'd been lying on the bed for hours with both boys in my arms. Ryan didn't have much of a clue as to what was happening, but he read his brother's weeping and got caught up in it.

'Ryan's upset cos his brother's upset. Pat is inconsolable.' I looked back over my shoulder. 'He's sleeping at the moment, but I need to go back to him in a moment.'

'We're trying to work out who could have done it,' said Jim. 'We know you couldn't hurt a fly, and it sure as shit wasn't me. So who murdered your wife, Andy?'

I looked from Jim to my mother. Read the confusion and concern in their eyes. How do you deal with such an event? How do you take such a violent, irrevocable act and give it sense or meaning? Murder is something that happens on the news or in a book or TV drama. Not to someone you knew and loved.

'The cops have got you and me in their sights, Andy,' said Jim. He ran his right hand through his hair. 'Why the hell did I go over there? What was I thinking?' he asked no one in particular. 'Somebody in this town just committed murder.' Jim shivered. 'Who?'

We sat in silence for a few moments, each lost in terrible imaginings. I saw Anna's face as it was two nights before, when I went to see her. Read the contradictions in her behaviour from the distance of time. At first she'd been hateful, angry, but it was almost as if she was playing a part. Then the phone call and she switched completely. Told me to take the boys.

What one earth had been going on in her head?

Jim stood. Moving from a seated position to standing in a blink. The feet of the kitchen chair squealing in protest.

'I can't handle this,' he said, his eyes on a fixed point in the distance. He looked at me. 'Got to go.' He made a tiny movement with his head, telling me he wanted to talk to me outside on my own. He kissed Mum on the cheek and without another look at me he left.

I counted to thirty and followed him outside.

He was sitting in his car. Drumming on the steering wheel with rigid fingers.

'Jesus,' he said when I sat in the passenger seat. 'This is fucked up.'

I twisted in the seat to face him. There was something more here. This wasn't just about my dead wife and police suspicions.

He turned to face me. Eyes large. He wiped a hand over his mouth. Returned to drumming. He looked into the driver's mirror at my mother's house behind us.

'Those wee boys,' he said. 'These beautiful wee boys.' His smile was tortured but full of love. 'You know, I wouldn't blame you if you…' He paused. 'Whatever happens, those boys have to be looked after.' His eyes searched mine as if looking for some sense of my culpability in the death of my wife.

21

Next morning, Ryan was full of energy, but Pat hung onto my shirtsleeves as if he was worried I might disappear and never return. I read the haunted expression on his face and tried to reassure him with smiles, a hand on his shoulder and regular hugs.

'Take them to the park, Andy,' said Mum as she served up some toast for breakfast. 'Some playtime is just what the doctor ordered.'

'Good idea,' I replied. We had to aim for some version of normality for the boys' sake.

An hour later and we were in Belleisle Park, walking past the deer enclosure on the way to the swings and climbing frames. Ryan was zipping about. His movement like the flight of a bluebottle, he didn't spend more than a moment in one place. He moved quickly and at random, as if as soon as something snagged his attention, something else replaced it.

Pat was by my side, but I was relieved to note that his grief was temporarily being elbowed aside by the fresh air, the greenery around us and Ryan's infectious movement.

My youngest son reached the play area first. As he ran, he kicked up little clouds of the bark the council had used to cushion the ground. I took a seat on a bench and was followed by Pat.

Despite the early hour there were already several children in the playpark; parents dotted the area, holding jackets, keeping guard.

'On you go,' I said to Pat, using the tone I might with a pup with a sore paw. 'I'll hold your jacket.'

He looked from me to Ryan. Eased one arm out of its sleeve. He looked at me again. His eyes large, the pupils like bruises.

'I'm not going anywhere, buddy,' I said and leaned back in the seat. The sun peeked out from behind cloud. I felt its warmth and leaned my head back and closed my eyes, hoping my relaxed posture might help.

'Pat. Daddy,' Ryan shouted over. 'Swing.'

Without opening my eyes I spoke to Pat. 'Go push your wee brother on the swing.'

I felt the light touch of his jacket land on my lap and heard him turn away and walk over to the swings.

Ryan let out a high, excited squeal and I sent a note of thanks for his sunny disposition and lack of awareness. He'd asked several times for his mother, but didn't dwell on her absence, moving on to whatever was interesting him at the time.

I crossed my arms and legs. Exhaled. Felt a stab of grief. And then a note of relief – I wouldn't need to justify anything to Anna when I got home. Then came a shock of shame that my thoughts had gone there.

In my imagination I was back in Jim's car and listening as he spoke, my hands tucked under my arms as if that might stop me from punching him. His words had haunted my sleep, running over and over in my mind.

'She was alive when I left her,' he had said. 'Believe me.'

'Wait a minute,' I replied. 'You said to Mum that you didn't go in.'

He looked at me. Quickly moved his eyes away as if looking at me caused him pain.

'I was furious, Andy. That witch battered you and then tried to keep your sons away from you. I couldn't just stand by.'

'What did you do, Jim?'

'Fucking vicious,' he said. He rolled up his sleeve to display two red lines on his forearm. One wound through the thick hair there for about four inches. The other was about an inch shorter. Both looked like they'd torn off a good layer of skin. I recognised the shape and intent of them. Anna had inflicted those on me on many occasions.

'Why didn't you go straight to the police, Jim?'

He looked at me as if I'd asked him to lie down in front of a train.

'A woman dies. You might well be the last person to speak to her. An innocent man would help the police and cross himself off their investigation.' I couldn't keep the anger from my voice, but I didn't know who I was angry at. Him, her or me.

He pushed at me. 'Andy, how could you think…' Disappointment and anger vied for attention in his tone. He cut off his question as if he was telling himself that I was confused and bound to be looking for someone to hit out at. The confusion lingered in his eyes as if he was processing our conversation and everything he ever believed about me.

He rolled his sleeve back down. Buttoned it with his usual precision as if in this action he was closing off that part of the conversation.

'Went round there like I said. She was in and got annoyed that I'd just walked in without knocking.' He looked at me. 'She said you'd just picked up the boys, which kinda took a wee bit out of my steam.'

'Jim, what were you thinking?' This wasn't good. When the police got the details of his visit it wouldn't look good for either of us.

'I'm an idiot. What can I say? Anyway, we got into it. I told her she was a bitch and if she did anything else to hurt you she'd have me to deal with.'

Footsteps approached and I was back in the present. I opened my eyes, expecting to see Pat.

It was a woman with shoulder-length brown hair, a red fleece jacket that struggled to contain both her and her expression of disgust.

'How dare you,' she hissed at me. Judge, jury and social-executioner. She crossed her arms under her bosom and glared, her small, dark eyes telling me she found my very presence to be harmful. Then she turned away from me. 'Chloe. Ashley,' she shouted. 'Come on. We're leaving. You are not playing anywhere near those boys.'

I was on my feet before I knew it. Took two steps and towered over her.

'What the hell is your problem?' I'd wear any kind of criticism, but involve my boys and I'm a she-bear protecting her cubs.

Everyone around us stopped what they were doing to watch. A man who was a matching pair for my accuser, wearing an identical fleece, inched closer. It was clear from his movement that he didn't share his wife's disgust, but felt pressure to back her up.

'You're sick,' she said. 'Everybody knows what you've done.'

She spat at my feet. Actually spat. I was so stunned I could do nothing but look up from the white glob on the tip of my right shoe to the righteous, tight expression on her face.

'We're leaving.'

She turned and walked away to the side, gesturing at her children, and sending looks that demanded solidarity from the other parents. A couple of other women made a point of walking close to me as they left.

'They think it was him and his brother,' said one.

'Police don't have enough evidence yet or they'd be locked up.'

'Hangin's too good,' said the first one as she looked me up and down.

As they passed me they both looked at me as if they were daring me to strike out at them. As if they'd take courage from standing up to me and use that as a force field for the rest of their lives.

Within minutes the play area was empty apart from my two boys. Ryan was completely oblivious. Pat had paused in his play when he noticed people were all leaving at once.

'Dad, why did everyone leave?' he asked as he ran to me.

I fell back down on to the bench as if my knees had been taken from me. Throughout my life I'd always been popular. People liked me. They gravitated to me. My mum used to say it was a combination of my size and benign expression. According to her it said trustworthy and helpful. And now for the first time I was the object of scorn and hate.

Pat tugged at my sleeve. I looked at him. His face held a twist of fear and love. 'Did you and Uncle Jim kill Mum? Are the people lying?'

I couldn't answer him. My job was to protect him, not be the source of his pain. I'd found him a mother to replace the one he never knew and we'd both let him down grievously.

'Son.' I turned to face him, loss a suffocating weight in my throat and chest. I heaved at it. My breath in gasps. And tears took me for the first time since that moment the police broke the news.

Not sure what to do, he placed a hand on my shoulder while I cried, as if he was too frightened to come any closer.

22

I dropped the boys off at Mum's and headed back out. Jim said he didn't do it, that she was still alive when he left the house, and I had to believe him.

My conscious mind was elsewhere but memory kept me on the right track as I drove and soon I was parked and walking up a familiar path. I knocked on the door. It opened quickly.

'Andy, what are you doing…?' Sheila Hunter asked. She was wearing black leggings and a tight pink t-shirt as if she was just about to go to the gym.

'Are you heading out?' I asked, taking a step back.

'It's all right,' she said with a smile on her lips and a question in her eyes. 'Come in. What's up?' She stepped to the side and I was greeted by her dog, who wound himself in small circles, wagging his tail as he showed his pleasure at seeing me again. I reached down and patted his head then made my way into the kitchen.

'I'll just put the kettle on,' Sheila said as she bustled in.

I sat at the small pine table, taking in the space around me, spotless save for a couple of dirty plates and mugs in the sink. A small radio was sitting on the window sill. An advert sounded out followed by the opening bars of a Michael Jackson song.

'So you're one of them?' I asked with a smile. 'One of the people who does actually listen to West Sound Radio.'

'Shut it,' she laughed. 'It's not that bad.'

'Did you have a visitor last night?' I asked, my gaze returning to the dishes in the sink. The words were out of my mouth before I could consider that the question might be impertinent.

'Just one of the girls,' she smiled and turned from me with the kettle in her hand. She filled it and put it on its cradle. 'What's up,

Andy?' She looked at me as if it was the first time that morning. Concern at what she saw was clear on her face. Made me think that I must have looked like shit.

'You said that you heard Anna was having an affair?'

Sheila sat down in the chair in front of me and studied my expression. 'Why do you ask?' Then, when the thought struck, her mouth opened a little.

'You'll have heard the gossip?' I asked.

She made a small face of apology. 'You don't want to listen to…'

'Jim didn't kill Anna. If he didn't, the only person I can think of … I mean, they say that most killers are known to their victim…'

'And if it wasn't Jim…'

'It could be this mysterious guy who Anna had an affair with.' I sat back in the chair and crossed my arms, struggling to keep the desperation out of my face and voice.

Sheila made a dismissive sound. 'Office gossip. You know what folk are like at the bank. When would a woman with a house to run and two small boys to look after find the time to have an affair?'

'You didn't ever hear a name?'

Sheila shook her head, but her eyes slid from mine.

'If you know anything, Sheila, please tell me.'

'If I thought it was worth telling you I would, Andy.' She reached across the table and held my hand. I felt the heat of her and took reassurance. Everyone else, it seemed, was running from me. I sent her a look of thanks.

But.

Maybe I was misreading her, but it felt like she was hiding something.

The dog pawed at the back door, stopping my train of thought. Sheila stood and opened it for him. In a flash of tail and yellow fur he was outside. I pushed myself off the chair and followed him outside.

There was a small patio area with red flagstones and varying sizes of plant pots at regular intervals around it, as if Sheila had wanted a low wall and this kind of planting was an affordable alternative.

The dog walked over to the fence that bordered the back lawn and cocked a leg.

I spotted a couple of cigarette stubs at the side of one of the pots.

'Didn't know you smoked, Sheila?'

She coloured and tried to hide that with a smile. 'I don't. My friend likes a puff now and again.'

I looked away from her as I tried to work out why she was so uncomfortable. Did she have a new boyfriend and didn't want me to know in case I was disappointed it wasn't me? Normally, I would have let it pass, but that morning social niceties weren't high on my list of behavioural skills.

'If you've got a boyfriend, Sheila that's fine. You don't owe me anything.'

'A new boyf…' She tailed off and I mentally rewound her words. Heard the stress on the word 'new'. Then I looked over again at the white stubs. They each held a twist of paper at the end as if they'd been self-made.

A memory swooped in and I was holding a cigarette stub in my back garden. I saw a shadow. Then a tall, lean man hunched over a bar. And my brain made a connection that was as unwelcome as it appeared to be unlikely.

'Was Ken here?' I asked.

'It's not what you think, Andy.' She crossed her arms. The dog circled back to her and stood by her side as if he sensed something was wrong.

'I don't know what I think, Sheila.'

'I had one of the girls over last night. Ken appeared at my door, all agitated. I dragged him out here. He had a cigarette or two. Spouted all kinds of crap and then left.'

I don't know where the connection came from, but it was there, undeniable.

'Was Ken having an affair with my wife?' I asked.

'If Ken was here last night, it's none of your concern.' Sheila looked at me. Defiant. 'And as far as him having an affair with Anna…'

'Why are you protecting him, Sheila?'

'How dare you,' she said, her face going pink. She turned away from me and walked back inside. I followed her and read the hurt in the stiff line of her shoulders and back.

'I'm sorry, Sheila,' I said. 'I don't mean to offend you.'

'I offered my ex-husband an ear. That was all. And as far as…'

'Did he kill Anna?'

'He's a troubled man,' she replied. 'But a killer?' She shook her head.

'That time I was round here with the woman from human resources, you were worried that was exactly what he was.'

I saw Sheila in memory. The fear in her voice as she recalled how Ken had treated her. And the certainty that she would no longer put up with it, and the fear that he would eventually kill her if she did.

But now, she was dissembling. I recognised the symptoms. I had them branded.

He'd been round last night. Reminded her of his humanity. His vulnerable side. He was no longer the scary man from a nightmare, he was someone she used to love and he had appealed to the embers of that lost affection. She'd relented a little. Allowed a little warmth to build.

It was what I had done with Anna. Over and over again.

'What do you know, Sheila?' I pressed and stepped closer. 'Was Anna having an affair with Ken?'

She looked away from me. I could see her throat move as she swallowed.

'He told me he didn't lay a finger on her.' Her gaze returned to mine. 'And I believe him.'

'Really?' I asked. 'Ken? Your ex-husband? The man who regularly kicked shit out of you?'

'Don't, Andy,' Sheila said and scratched at her right cheek. 'He was different last night. Quieter. Less…' she looked at me, her eyes imploring my belief in her words '… less like himself.'

'It wasn't Jim,' I said firmly. 'And this boyfriend's the only other person I can think of.'

'A few minutes ago you were complaining about the gossip. You're every bit as bad.'

'Oh come on…' I stopped myself from saying something hurtful. Sat down.

The radio played a jingle at the end of a track and as Sheila and I lapsed into an awkward silence a voice announced the latest news bulletin. I heard the announcer say something about the murder of local woman, Anna Boyd, and listened with rising disbelief to the rest of her words.

'… Ayr detectives have released the name of the man they have in custody as local man, and brother-in-law of the deceased, James Boyd.'

23

When I got back to Mum's she was clearly fighting to retain some semblance of control. She didn't want the boys to see exactly how worried she was.

'Did you hear the news?' Her voice was just above a whisper.

I nodded.

'What are we going to do?' she asked and stepped inside my reach, resting her head on my shoulder. She mumbled something. It sounded like she was saying her boy was not a murderer.

I stroked her head, not sure I had the strength and reassurance she was looking for. All I could think about on the way over was that the police had questioned us both, but arrested Jim. What had made the difference?

I thought about the deep scratches on his forearm.

I'd watched enough TV dramas to know that Jim's skin tissue would have been underneath Anna's nails. Was that what had sealed it for the police?

'We'll get him a lawyer, Mum. The best. And they'll see there's not enough evidence to convict him. He was outside the house? Big deal.'

I felt a hand tug at the right knee of my trousers.

'Dad. What's wrong with Ganny?'

I looked down at Ryan's face. His eyes were huge and bright with tears.

'She's upset about Mummy,' I answered, getting down into a crouch and as close to his eye level as I could. As I met his teary gaze, I wondered how I could ever tell him his much-loved uncle was in jail for the murder of his mother.

'Come on and watch TV, Ryan.'

I turned to see Pat by the door. His frame was rigid with the determination that he would do his part in our family drama. It was as if, even at his young age, he could sense the adults needed the space to deal with the big stuff and he should try and keep his brother distracted, regardless of his own feelings in the matter. 'Aang is about to come on.'

I sent him a silent note of thanks over his brother's head and cringed at the effort Pat was making on our behalf; worried at the eventual cost. This was not something a child his age should have to contend with.

'Okay,' Ryan said, his voice subdued, not yet ready to be swayed into forgetting how upset his gran had been.

'Oh, Aang the Avatar,' Mum said, somehow managing to inject energy into her voice. She clapped her hands. 'I love that cartoon.' She reached down and took Ryan's hand and marched into the living room. As she reached the door she turned and spoke.

'The boys are running out of clothes and stuff. You need to see if you can get into the house for their things.'

I nodded. 'But it's still probably a crime scene. Not sure they'll let me in.'

'Ask the question,' she replied. And gave me a look. It said: do something.

I walked into the hall and picked up the phone. It was avocado green, sitting on a doily, beside a potted red-flowering plant and a small photograph of the boys in a gilded frame. All of this like a display for visitors, on top of a half-oval table with slender legs.

And right there, in this microcosm was the story of my mother's existence. Her affection for craft and plants, her need to keep in touch with the outside world, and her family.

My regret at the worry and pain I'd brought into her carefully constructed life almost had me buckling at the knee.

I pulled my wallet out of my pocket. Selected a card and reading the number, dialled it.

'Karen McPherson, please?' I asked, praying that she would be at work on a Saturday morning.

I heard her voice moments later and almost sagged with relief. I explained about Jim, and that he needed her help. And that I needed to get back into the house for clothes and toys for the boys.

'Let me look into it and get back to you,' she said before hanging up.

I replaced the phone on its cradle and leaned against the wall. From there I allowed myself to slide down until I was in a seated position.

Anna was dead.

Jim had been arrested for her murder.

If this didn't have the sense of the surreal, I wasn't sure my mind could contain the breadth and weight of it all.

Get a grip, Boyd, I told myself.

I had no idea how long I'd been sitting there when the phone rang.

I jumped up and answered. It was Karen calling back.

'You can visit the house for the boys' stuff. Can you be there in an hour? The police will need to chaperone you as they're not yet finished processing the scene.'

I nodded. Then realised I needed to speak. 'Yes. Right,' I replied. 'What about Jim? Have you arranged to see him?'

'I have,' she said. 'And you need to prepare yourself for some bad news here, Andy.'

'I do?' My chest tightened. Bad news? Wasn't there enough of that going round already.

'Afraid so,' she replied. 'Your brother confessed, Andy. He told the police that he killed Anna.'

24

Detectives Holton and Bairden were waiting for us outside my house. My lawyer, Karen, was sitting beside me in my car. She had insisted that she accompany me to the house in case the cops tried to wrong-step me into saying something incriminating.

From habit I parked in my drive, and then worried about how this might be perceived by the detectives.

'My head's full of mince,' I said. 'I don't know how to behave here.'

When I saw the officers climb out of their car, solid and sober with purpose, I couldn't have been more grateful for Karen's presence. I turned to her in the passenger seat and sent her a smile of thanks.

'Shouldn't it just be some uniformed officers?' I asked

'They want to rattle you, Mr Boyd.'

'It's working.' I exhaled. Felt a sharp twist low in my abdomen. 'Jim confessed? What the hell's he playing at?'

'You know him better than I do, Mr Boyd. Could he do it?'

'I can't even...' I shook my head. Looked over at my house. Saw nothing but shadow and threat.

Karen clicked open her seatbelt and looked over at me.

'Ready for this?' she asked.

I nodded.

'We'll stick to the living room and the bedrooms, okay?'

'Why...'

'You won't want to go into the kitchen,' she said and I heard the warning in her voice.

'Right.'

Anna died there. And my mind filled with an image of her prostrate body, limbs pointing at the various compass points. I pushed the picture from my head, released my seatbelt, tried to quell the roil and surge of nerves in my gut, and climbed out of the car.

The detectives met us at the front door. They both looked at Karen with surprise.

'Nothing better to do on a Saturday?' asked Holton. His tone was going for jocular, but his eyes were dismissive. As if he was questioning why she would be with a low-life like me.

She ignored his question. 'My Boyd will need to get a suitcase out of the loft, and then gain access to both bedrooms.'

'Understood,' said Bairden as he looked at me. His gaze was calm and accepting of the situation, but underlying it I could sense a quiet simmer of anger.

I was desperate to ask if they had forced a confession out of Jim. What evidence did they have against him? More than anything I wanted to know how Jim was. If I could visit him and ask him what the hell had he done.

Instead I remained silent, uncertain how my questions might be viewed. Worried that my behaviour might indicate guilt or innocence, I studied the ground.

Then I gave myself a mental ticking off. An innocent man shouldn't need to question how he acts.

'When can I bring my boys home?' I asked, looking at the three officials in turn.

'It's still a crime scene, Mr Boyd,' Karen answered. 'It will be released to you as soon as the investigation allows.' Her smile was reassuring and I thanked whatever god had put her in my path. 'In the meantime, let's get your stuff and get you back to those wee boys of yours.'

I walked into the house, half expecting Anna to be standing in the hallway, hands on her hips. I made my way upstairs and to the loft. As I climbed the stairs I kept my focus ahead of me. I didn't, couldn't, allow my eyes to stray in case I saw something that I didn't want to see.

In my mind's eye I saw a large-blue suitcase in the far corner of the loft and when I climbed up, it was exactly where I thought it might be.

Down in the bedrooms, I packed several changes of clothes for the boys and for myself. As I threw items into the case, Karen and Detective Holton stood by the door. One a silent support, the other a scowl in a brown suit.

'Right. Got a DVD for Ryan,' I said to no one in particular. 'Just need to get Pat's dinosaur.' I scanned the room but it was nowhere to be seen.

I looked at the walls and there, pride of place above Ryan's bed, was a poster of Spongebob Squarepants. And memories of happier times. This time last year, complete with buckets and small nets on the end of a two-foot long bamboo pole we'd gone jelly-fishing. Pat explained it all to the grown-ups patiently. We go fishing for jellyfish, he said. Put them in the bucket, count them, guess how many might be on the beach and then release them back into the sea.

Anna had been terrified that one of us would be stung. And then grew disgusted, to the boys' delight, when I said that if anyone did, we all had to pee on them.

I noted the feeling of sadness and tried to rid my head of the memory. I had to focus on the here and now.

'Might it be in the living room?' asked Karen and from the seriousness of her tone I guessed that she was a mother and well knew how disastrous it might be if I arrived at my mother's without the requested toy.

'There's no toys in the living room,' said Holton. 'In fact, the whole house is spotless. Like a show home.' He looked at me, studying me for a reaction. 'Apart from where the body was…' he tailed off.

I looked around and considered his words. Right enough, the house was spotless. I tried to remember if it had been like that when I'd come round to see the boys that night. Came up short. All I could see was their sleep-tousled faces as I bundled them into the car.

Both boys' beds were both made. In memory, they were dressed in different sheets. Had Anna also changed their bedding? Ryan's had the faint impression of a body on the surface of his quilt as if someone had lain there briefly. I couldn't imagine one of the crime of scene officers would have done that. That left Anna.

Did she lie there after I took the boys away?

Did she clean after I took the boys away?

She did keep a clean house, but was relaxed with untidy. I often heard her say that a messy home was a happy one. Had she gone through the house, cleaned and put everything back in its place after I left? Why would she do that? I walked to the top of the stairs and looked around as if the place no longer belonged to me. The appearance of the rooms held the feel of ceremony.

'Any ideas about this dinosaur then?' asked Karen.

I chewed on that for a moment. 'The garden,' I replied. Both boys often took toys with them when they played out in the back green.

'You'll need to go round the outside of the house,' Holton interrupted. 'You can't use the back door.'

'Right,' I acknowledged and walked down the stairs.

In the hallway, Holton got Bairden up to speed and the four of us stepped out of the front door and round the side to the back garden.

There was a spit of rain in the air and I looked up at the gathering mass of cloud in the near distance to assess if it might dump its load while we were outside.

Detective Bairden was walking alongside me.

'I meet men like you all the time, Boyd. They've got no place for their anger so they take it out on the person they're supposed to love the most. It's fucking depressing.' The heat of his irritation rose in his neck and coloured his face.

'Get out of my face, Detective,' I replied and lengthened my stride.

Karen caught up with me, a question in her eyes.

'S'all right,' I answered and shoved my hands in my pockets to hide the tremble.

The four of us stood in a line on the patio, house at our backs, facing the back fence.

'Anybody see a dinosaur,' asked Holton, his tone light as the realisation of the strange nature of his question hit.

'No, but I can see a man getting away with murder,' answered Bairden.

'Detective, that is out of line.' Karen was robust in her response.

So, the police weren't buying Jim's admission of guilt, or they thought I might also be involved somehow.

Feeling a weakness in my thighs I walked over to Ryan's swing thinking I could scan the grass from that central point. I was also keen to show them that I didn't care what they thought. Karen walked alongside me as if to protect me from the thoughts and scrutiny of the detectives.

'Did Anna smoke?' asked Karen, as she bent at the waist to study something lying between the blades of grass.

'No,' I replied and followed her gaze.

'Do you?'

I shook my head.

'Jim?'

'Nope.'

'Detectives?' Karen looked at Holton and Bairden. 'To your knowledge have any of the team come out of the house for a cigarette?'

'They know better,' said Bairden as if he was offended at my lawyer having the temerity to even ask the question.

'In that case you should get an evidence bag and bring it over here.' She looked around herself. 'There's another,' she pointed and said. 'And another.'

'A bird could have dropped them,' said Bairden.

'Three? In almost the same spot?' Karen scoffed.

I followed her eyes and spotted them. Three white stubs. Each of them with that distinct shape of the self-made.

'Whoever it was must have been standing here for some time.' She looked back up at the house as if imagining the thoughts of the smoker.

'Means nothing,' said Bairden.

'We won't know what it means until we analyse any DNA found on them,' Karen replied. She gave both men a smile of challenge. 'But I shouldn't need to tell you gentlemen how to do your job.'

'Ken Hunter,' I heard myself say.

'What?' Holton looked at me.

'He was married to Sheila from my work. He beat her badly. I was round at hers this morning. She had a collection of cigarette stubs just like that in her back garden.'

'So what?' asked Bairden.

'He's got a history of violence. Don't you guys do the DNA thing? Match those cigarettes with these. That puts Hunter at this house. There's no telling what that guy is capable of.'

'Jesus Christ,' said Bairden. 'Save us from the TV crime addict.'

'Sounds like a desperate attempt to deflect our investigation,' said Holton. The detectives shared a look that showed they gave my theory no credence whatsoever.

'And weren't you getting a wee bit too cosy with this Sheila? What exactly is going on here, Mr Boyd?' asked Bairden, taking a step closer to me.

'Mr Boyd?' Karen held a hand out, pointing towards the path round the side of the house. 'We should go.' She raised her eyebrows.

Bairden walked by my side as we made our way round to the front door.

'We know your brother didn't act on his own, Boyd.'

My mind was full of the implications of the cigarette stubs, thinking about the ones in Sheila's back garden, so I didn't respond.

Disappointed, Bairden moved closer to me, almost nudging me with his shoulder, his lips a thin line of loathing. 'We think big brother says jump and the other asks, sure, which window?'

25

'Tell me about Ken Hunter,' Karen said when we got in the car.

'I've known him for years,' I replied. 'If we'd had a yearbook at school on those days, he would have been the one voted most likely to turn serial killer. He was the kid who'd pull the wings off wasps, drown kittens or…'

'I'm getting that you don't like the man, Andy, but if you want to direct the police away from Jim and you, you need to give us something more concrete.'

'But Jim confessed…'

'Something's fishy,' she said. 'Doesn't quite make sense. If they have his confession, why are they trying to bait you?'

I shrugged.

The rain that threatened while we were in the garden, stepped up its efforts. It drummed on the roof and washed against the car windows, turning the world outside our metal shell into a rinse of colour.

'You should drive off,' Karen said as she looked out of her window towards the two detectives, who had been studying us in the car.

'Let's wait a moment. See if they stay there and get soaked.'

She laughed. And the note her amusement sounded was a reminder that beyond this painful drama there was living, and life.

I started the engine and pulled away from the kerb. As I drove I filled Karen in on Ken and Sheila's marriage. Ken's attempt to woo Anna when she arrived in town and, with reluctance, I told her about the night I attacked him in Billy Bridges.

'Was Hunter charged for his attacks on Sheila?'

'Why would that matter?'

'He'd be in the system. Easier to compare his DNA. And there would be evidence of a habit of violence.'

I searched my memory. I could remember Sheila taking time off and coming back to work, but couldn't think of her talking about any repercussions.

'I saw the mess she was in afterwards. Surely he wouldn't have got away with it?'

Karen crossed her arms. 'You'd be surprised. We are getting better, but domestic violence cases are difficult to process. And at times it's because the victim withdraws their support for the case…'

'As I said, I saw the mess Sheila was in and how determined she was to turn her life around. I find it hard to believe that she wouldn't want to see him get his just desserts.'

'But you don't remember if he went jail or anything like that?'

'No.'

She made a face.

I fell silent as I considered the implications of this. I remembered sitting in Sheila's living room and seeing the look of determination on her face. She would not let this man ruin her life. So wouldn't that mean she would ensure he feel the full effect of the law?

Did he still have some sort of hold on her?

When I was in her garden earlier and we spotted the cigarette ends, I didn't get the impression she was scared of him. She was calm and relaxed when his name came up. Perhaps not completely relaxed: she did get defensive, protective even.

What the hell was going on with those two?

Or was I just overthinking things?

Back at my mother's house, I parked behind Karen's large, black Vauxhall. Handbrake applied, I turned to her.

'Thanks,' I said. 'I couldn't have done that without you.'

'Just doing my job, Andy.' She smiled her support.

'Could I have just another five minutes of your time, please?' I asked. 'Mum is out of her skin with worry.'

Karen looked at her watch. Looked over at the house.

'I've…' she began, but stopped as if she'd seen something.

I followed her gaze to see Mum walking with purpose down the path towards the car. Her arms were crossed tight against her midriff as if they might help hold everything together. Her face was pale, her brow sliced with furrows. She looked as if she had aged ten years in the last ten hours and guilt scored a line across my heart.

We got out of the car and I walked round to the boot for the suitcase and pulling it out, rested it on the pavement.

'Mrs MacPherson,' I heard Mum say. 'Do you have a minute before you head off?'

'How can I help?' Karen replied.

'I need to speak to my son.'

'You should be able to get access through the police,' Karen said, her head cocked to the side with a question.

'He refuses to talk to me.' Mum reached Karen's side and stood there, twisting her fingers the way she might wring out a damp washcloth.

'In that case there's not a lot I can do, Mrs Boyd.'

'He won't see you?' I asked.

Mum looked at me, her face full of anguish. 'Why wouldn't he want to speak to me?'

I could only shrug.

I turned to Karen. 'Any chance you could find out what's going on in his head?'

'I'll see what I can do.' With that, she walked to her car, stepped inside and drove off.

I watched her car for as long as I could. I didn't want to look in my mother's face and see her hurt and fear. Not only that, as Karen left I felt myself unravelling. I needed her calm presence to keep me centred. I was supposed to be the mainstay that grounded everyone around him. I was worried that I was instead becoming the rock on which everything floundered.

I felt Mum's hand land light on my forearm, as if she was frightened she might scare me off.

'Andy…'

I stepped back from her and from the realisation I had nothing in that moment to give

'Andy, I think I know why Jim did it.'

'What?' I looked at her as if seeing her for the first time. Her face was almost unrecognisable in her anguish.

'Can't you see? He's trying to protect you and the boys.'

'What on earth do you mean, mother? Protect us? From what?'

'Can't we do this inside? People are watching.' Her eyes darted from house to house, checking to see if this was indeed the case.

'Mum, tell me what you're on about.'

'If you … If you did it…'

'What?' I shouted.

'Then you'd be put away for years and the boys would lose their mother and their father. He doesn't want that to happen. He'd do anything for those kids.'

'You think I actually killed Anna? Jim thinks I killed Anna?' I was incredulous.

'You were under terrible stress, son. People do terrible, terrible things under those circumstances…'

I could see she was lost. Nothing made sense, even the words that were coming out of her own mouth. As she was saying them, I could see the thought in her mind. *I'm trying to explain murder?*

'Mum, let be me clear…' I bent over so that I was at eye level with her. 'I did not kill Anna. Okay? It wasn't me.' I straightened up. Looked around me as if something, anything, in the air around me would make sense.

Mum actually thought I was guilty?

'This is…' I ran my hand through my hair. There wasn't a word to describe how messed up this was. 'Can you give me some time, Mum? I can't…' I looked down at her. ' … I can't.' With a look that I prayed might impart how lost I was and how much I needed some space on my own, I got in my car and drove off.

One by one I ticked off in my head all the places that normally offered the stillness that eased my spirit. In the days and weeks after

Patricia died I had made for the wind and sand on Ayr beach as if the energy there would scour the wounds from my heart. Other places helped, like the River Doon and Craigie Woods.

Now, I parked at each of those places in turn, sat in the car and studied the people around me as if they held some key. As if they had what I ached for. Peace. Stillness. An answer. They wore it like certainty, whereas the only thing I was sure of was that my life was an unholy mess.

At the River Ayr, on the cobblestone paving at the foot of the Auld Brig I saw a familiar figure. She was barely five feet tall, dressed in a grey sweatpants and a red-and-white striped sweater. Her long grey hair was gathered at the nape of her neck and looked to have the texture of a brillo pad. She was bent at the waist as if there was a broken hinge there.

Pat called her the Swan Lady. She was an often-seen figure down here. She would borrow a shopping cart from one of the supermarkets and ask them to fill it with stale bread. Once she judged she had enough, she would push the cart through the town, taking the bread to feed the swans that lived under the bridge. Her progress through the streets was as stately as a mad queen, no doubt hampered by the fact that she couldn't straighten her back. There was an eccentricity about her that warmed me. What I would give to be able to switch off from everything and be guided by the notion that all I needed to do was to gather the loaves and feed the birds.

But my respite was fleeting.

Worries clustered around my head the way a scrum of gulls hovered over the feeding swans, waiting to dive with sharp beaks, bullies in their greed for crumbs.

Anna. Jim. Mum. Pat. Ryan.

All of them needed me and I'd let down every each of them in turn.

Jim had confessed because he thought I did it?

Just a couple of hundred yards away, up the hill and past the back door to the Carnegie Library, was the local police headquarters, where my brother sat in a cell, waiting for Monday morning and an appearance in front of the local Sheriff.

From there he would be taken to Barlinnie Prison, or the Bar-L as it was known, until the trial began.

I had to see him. I had to find out what the hell was going on in his head.

The duty officer at the police station was stiff in a starched white shirt. Sleeves rolled up to display ropy, muscular forearms. Her smile was perfunctory. It said, I've seen my share of arseholes today; don't you be another one.

I explained what I wanted.

She nodded towards the seating area behind me. Red bucket chairs flanked by six-foot tall plastic plants. 'Take a pew. I'll go and see what the score is.'

I did as she asked and sat beside a lad in a black tracksuit and matching baseball cap. He was as thin as the leg of a standard lamp and sharp in profile. Three points; nose, chin and adam's apple.

'Aye,' he mumbled. 'She was nice to *you*. Wouldn't gie me the time of day.'

'That was her being nice?' I asked and leaned forward, elbows on knees, hoping that would be the extent of our conversation.

The duty officer returned to her desk.

'They'll no be long,' she said to me across the reception area. Her eyes met mine for less than a second before she went back to working on whatever she was doing before I rudely interrupted her.

'See what I mean,' the boy said. 'It's like I'm no here.'

'Maybe, instead of moaning about it you should go up and see what's what?' My version of brotherly advice.

He blew out of the side of his mouth and crossed his arms. 'Aye, right. She's scarier than my ma.'

Having exhausted my willingness to interact with the boy I sat upright in my chair, crossed my arms, and my feet at the ankles.

Taking the message, he shifted his buttocks so that he was facing away from me.

Time passed.

A woman came in and approached the desk. The duty officer heard her out, went back to her desk and returned with a piece of paper. The woman took it and left.

Another three people came in and this process was repeated.

With a huff, I got to my feet and approached the desk.

'Mind if I ask how long it will be?' I said.

'It will be as long as it will be,' she replied.

'Like the string,' I said.

'Exactly.'

'And how long is the string?' I asked, feeling a stir of irritation.

'Sir,' she stood up, 'this is a working police station. We don't work on an appointment system. Nobody asked you to come down here. Take a seat and someone will be with you as soon as they can.' She cocked her head to the side in an, *am I understood* motion.

I sat down. And just as my buttocks reached the curved plastic of the seat a door opened to the side of the reception area. Out walked Holton and Bairden.

'Must be our lucky day,' said Holton. 'Were you missing us already?'

'I'd like to speak to my brother.'

'He's helping us with our enquiries,' said Bairden.

'Nonetheless, it would be good if I could talk to him.'

'Am I talking in Dutch?' Bairden looked to the side and his partner. Then back to me. 'It's not happening, Mr Boyd. Why don't you go back home to your mother's and look after those two wee boys?' He smiled. 'While you still can.'

I took a step towards him. Hands in fists hanging low by my sides. Anger was a black-blue surge in my mind. Sharp and urgent like a heated knife. I was storing so much fucking anger and it needed a way out.

Holton stepped in between us, placed his right hand on my chest.

'Mr Boyd, go home.' His voice was low, his tone professional. 'You being arrested for a breach of the peace isn't going to help anyone, is it?'

'But my brother…'

'Mr Boyd, go home. You're not helping anyone here.'

'But…'

'Home,' he stretched out his right arm and pointed at the door, as if he was on point duty at a road accident.

'Leave him,' said Bairden. 'I'd be delighted to lock him up.'

'Prick,' I said, more loudly than I intended to, and felt the hot, white surge of satisfaction.

Holton grabbed my wrist. I pushed him off me, lashing my arm round with more force than was needed.

In less than a blink, I was on the floor, on my stomach, my right arm twisted behind my back and someone's knee between my shoulder blades. I tried to struggle against being pinned, but could only move my feet. I kicked out. And again.

'Hey, I saw everything, mate,' the guy with the baseball cap shouted over. 'If you want compensation, I'm your man.'

'Shut up, Leckie,' said Holton. Then to me. 'I'm going to let you up now, Mr Boyd, but if you feel this…' he applied some pressure to the hold he had on my wrist and pain flared '… you'll see that if you don't calm down I can easily restrain you again.'

The words reached my brain through the fog of anger. I heaved at the air, willing oxygen into my lungs. I could only concede that he was right. I was in no position to fight here. Nor was I helping my cause.

'Do you understand me, Mr Boyd?' Holton asked.

'Yes,' I croaked. 'Yes.'

He helped me to my feet and as I stretched to my full height, I kept my attention away from Bairden, who, I was sure, was gloating.

'Guys,' shouted over the duty sergeant. 'A call you need to take.' I heard the urgency in her voice.

'In a minute,' said Bairden. 'We've got a situation here.'

'Now, Detective,' she said in a tone that brooked no argument.

Bairden mumbled, 'For fuckssake,' walked over to the desk, stretched over and picked the phone from her hand. He held it to his ear and listened. Kept on listening. Then he looked over at me, his expression a complete contrast to what I expected.

Now, he wasn't worried about me. He was worried for me.

26

We were in my car. Bairden was driving.

'You going to tell me what the fuck is going on?' I asked him as he waited to join the traffic and exit the police station's car park.

'Ryan's been taken.'

'What?'

That made no sense. Ryan gone? He was at home with my mum. He was watching a video with his brother. Maybe he'd even made it into the garden to play. Mum hated them being stuck in front of a TV for too long.

'Mr Boyd,' Bairden shouted. He must have recognised my distant stare. I was dissembling. After everything that had gone on this was too much for me to take in. 'Ryan has been taken. That was your mother on the phone. A man calling himself Ken Hunter knocked on the door. Pushed his way in and took Ryan.'

'No,' I said. 'Cartoons. He's watching cartoons.' I was making no sense. What Bairden was saying made no sense.

Bairden took his eyes from the road for a moment. Studied mine. 'Your mother is unhurt and Pat is fine. They're both shaken but otherwise fine.'

Ryan.

I pictured his smile in my mind. He can't be gone. He's…

'Mr Boyd,' Bairden shouted again. 'I need you to focus. Take a breath. Nice and slow.'

Ryan taken. He wants me to fucking breath?

That bastard Hunter. I should have killed the fucker.

Meaning struck me, like a claw hammer to the head.

Ryan taken? I wanted to be sick and shit at the same time.

'Faster,' I shouted. 'Can't you put your blue light on?' I sat forward as if my head being nearer the windscreen would increase the speed of the car. 'Tell me again. What happened?'

Bairden repeated what he had already told me.

Hunter couldn't have chosen his moment better. He must have been watching the house and when he was good and sure I wasn't in, he stole my son.

'I told you Hunter was involved in all of this. If you had believed me about the cigarettes in the back garden…'

'That was only just this morning, Andy.'

Oh, it's Andy now.

The traffic lights just ahead changed to amber and the car in front braked. In my anxiety I was certain there was time for both cars to get past before the lights had fully gone red.

'Oh c'mon,' I shouted. 'Move, you prick. Move.' I moved my hand to the car door and tried to judge the distance to Mum's house. Would I be quicker running?

'Shit. Shit. Shit.' I intoned, drumming my feet on the foot well. Ryan gone. My little Ryan in that murdering bastard's hands. 'I swear if he touches him…' I couldn't finish the sentence. My breath was coming in heaves. My vision and hearing had narrowed. Pain was a hot weight in the base of my spine. I rocked back and forward in the seat. Changed to repeating, 'Be safe, be safe, please be safe.'

'We'll get him, Andy. Be sure of that. We'll get him back for you.'

'My wee boy,' I said, fighting to get the words out against the crush in my chest. 'My…'

'We need you to focus, Andy,' Bairden said. 'Your mother and Pat need you to be strong for them…' At these words my throat clenched. I didn't have strength for myself. 'And we'll need your help in finding Ryan. How well do you know this man?'

'Not that well.'

I told him how he was the first person Anna met when she moved to Ayr. How he had beaten Sheila. 'You know about the cigarette doubts,' I finished. My breathing had returned close to normal and I realised his question had been a tactic to calm me down a little and return my focus.

Crack up later. Save your boy first.

He had the decency to look a little ashamed at that. He stared out of the window and then briefly returned his gaze to meet mine, as if making a decision. 'We knew it wasn't Jim, by the way.'

'You what?'

'His confession was all over the place.'

'What the…?'

Jim, what the hell were you playing at?

'You guys must be really close,' Bairden said. I could only nod. 'I mean, I love my brothers, but I wouldn't cop a murder for them.' He looked at me. 'What's the deal then?'

I exhaled. Fought to take this in and add it to the teetering pile of thoughts in my head. A column of calamity. 'Fucked if I know,' I eventually answered. 'He hasn't been himself of late. It's like he's depressed or something.'

'Your brother thought you did it, Andy.'

'Fucking idiot.' I sat back in my seat, crossed my arms and then reached up with my right hand and held my palm against my forehead, as if the heat from that might stop the stir of emotion. 'I'd never kill Anna. I couldn't harm a hair on her head.'

'Yeah, well. If you'd seen the number of battered wives I have…'

'Any battered husbands?' I asked.

'More than a few.'

'Do you get as hot under the collar about them?'

He shot me a look. Tried to work out where I was coming from and decided not to go there. 'Anyway. We realised quickly that he was off beam and thought we'd keep him in – helping us with our enquiries, to put pressure on you.'

I tried to read his tone.

'Is that you apologising?'

'It is what it is.'

We fell into silence. I resented his use of cliché. What the hell did it even mean?

My mother's house hove into view and I placed my hand over the seatbelt release so I could exit the car as quickly as possible.

I looked in the car mirror and saw that Detective Holton was behind my car. A marked police car was behind him.

As soon as Bairden brought the car to a halt, I was out and on the pavement. I ran to the front door and was met by my sobbing mother and son.

'I should go in first…' Bairden shouted at me. I sent him a silent, 'yeah right'.

Mum's face was a welter of anger and physical pain. She was furious that someone would do this to her family and completely unmindful of the swelling at the right side of her face.

I gathered Pat to me and his small body shook with the force of emotion. 'I'm sorry, Dad,' he said. 'I couldn't stop him.'

'Hey,' I replied. 'Don't think any of this is on you, son. Okay?' He was pressing his head into my hip, so I put my hand on his head and shifted it so that he had to look up at me. 'Okay?'

He nodded. I looked to my mum.

'You neither. This is not on you.' I held a hand out to her and lightly touched the side of her face. 'He hurt you.' Another mark on the post. I found a grim certainty. Clenched my teeth against it. I only hoped I found him before the police did, because there would be a reckoning.

'It's nothing,' Mum said. 'Just a bump.' She smiled. It was weak and jagged with disappointment that she hadn't managed to stop Hunter.

Bairden arrived at my back and said, 'We should all go inside.' And I realised we were still standing in the hallway.

In the living room, I sat on the sofa with Mum and Pat on either side. The room then filled with police officers, which I found simultaneously reassuring and frustrating. Who was out there looking for this guy?

Bairden walked over to the mantelpiece and picked up a photograph of the boys. He held it up and looked at Mum and me. 'Is this a recent photo?'

We both nodded.

'Do you mind if we take it?'

'Take what you need, officer,' Mum said.

He handed it to one of the uniformed officers, a young man who didn't look old enough to shave. The young man left without a word.

'He's going to take it to the CCTV Centre so we can get the team looking for him.' Bairden looked at his wristwatch. 'There's a shift change due in five minutes. The shift due on have all started early and the shift due to finish are going to stay on till we've found Ryan. All of them will be issued with a copy of the photograph, okay?' His eyebrows were almost at his hairline in his effort to demonstrate how earnest he was.

Mum moved closer to me and reached for my hand. She gripped it and said, 'We will find him, Andy. We will.'

I felt myself smile at her, desperate to agree with her notion of hope, but frightened to allow myself to go there.

'Mrs Boyd, if you could carefully repeat what you told the officer on the switchboard?' Holton asked. He took a seat on one of the armchairs. Bairden moved to stand by his side, feet spread as if he was ready to spring into action the moment Mum stopped speaking.

'The door went and I thought it was Jean next door. Every now and again she pops in for a cuppa, you know? Only it was that guy...' She stopped speaking. Held a hand to her mouth, before gathering her courage. 'He pushed past me, shouting Ryan's name.' She gasped at a breath. 'The wee soul was in the living room. He came out, wondering who was shouting his name. He grabbed him by the arm. I reached for the other one and we began to pull against each other.' She looked at me as if frightened at what she had to say next.

'Go on, Mum.'

'He pushed me away. I fell and...' she touched her head where she had been hurt '... and he said that he didn't want to hurt me. That he only came for what was rightfully his.' She paused as if collecting enough strength to continue. Her right hand was at her throat. Fear feathered in the dark of her eyes. 'He said if you tried to find them the boy would go the same way as his mother. He'd killed once already, it didn't matter if he did it again.'

'He said those exact words?' asked Bairden.

Mum nodded and the detectives exchanged a look.

'Rightfully his?' Bairden said. 'What did he mean?'

Mum was still shaking her head. 'I was screaming at him. Bloody nutter. Ryan's a Boyd, it shines out of him.' She looked round the room as if expecting everyone in it to back her up. 'He said it was practically the last thing Anna said to him before she died. Said she rubbed his nose in it.' She looked at me. 'The man you hate more than any other bringing up your son.'

27

Mum asked everyone if they wanted a tea or a coffee. It was less a request than a command. She needed to be doing something. And if she couldn't go out into the street and start looking she'd fall back onto routine.

Everyone gave her their order. She responded to each with a grim nod.

'Give you a help, Mum?' I asked.

'Sure, son.'

I got up, Pat came with me and the three of us walked into the kitchen.

'Why don't you go up to your room, Pat,' I said, fretting at the need in his face.

'The boy needs to be with his dad, Andy,' Mum said with a soft smile.

'Course you do, son.' I sat down on one of the kitchen chairs and pulled him onto my lap, regretting my impulse to remove him from my line of sight. Once in position, he rested his head on my shoulder as if trying to draw strength from me.

'Hey, buddy,' I said. 'Everything will be fine. Ryan will be back here before you know it.' Sent that prayer to whatever God was in situ.

Mum busied herself with the kettle and the cups, repeating the drinks orders like it might save her sanity. To the music of spoon on clay, I stroked the silk of Pat's hair and tried to make reassuring noises. Both of his mums dead and now his brother missing. How would his young mind translate all of this?

Hunter, you will pay for this, I promise you.

I heard the reassuring sound of water being poured into mugs and looked over at Mum. She stopped what she was doing when she sensed my focus on her.

'Sorry to ask this son, but is there any chance that Ryan is this man's son?'

'Mum,' I warned, looking pointedly at Pat.

'He's gone through a lot, Andy. This is no time to pile secrets on to this mess as well.'

'Ryan is my son. You just need to look at him,' I said. My assertion was weakened by the fact that Ryan looked nothing like me and was one hundred per cent his mother's son. 'Anyway, what does that lunatic want with a child?'

I saw Anna in front of Hunter, eyes blazing, words wounding, fists a blur. For her to use this against him there must have been an outside chance for it to have happened.

Folk had warned me Anna was having an affair.

A memory of her at the birthing suite when Ryan was born, asserting that the child was late while the nurses tried to say he was early. It had bypassed me at the time. What had been going on in her head then? Was there something about the dates that might actually put Ryan's parentage into question?

'And what have you ever done to him to make him hate you so much?' Mum asked, interrupting my thoughts.

I shrugged. 'He was just one of those kids that were on the periphery at school. Didn't join in. Maybe he saw me – good at sport and relaxed with girls – and his dislike started there?'

Then there was Anna. And I even became friends with his ex-wife, Sheila, after they split up. Perhaps, in his mind I got the women, the happy family life, and he was on his own with his version of the truth. Twisting my perceived good fortune into a reason to hate.

'You know, until the man explains himself – if he's able to – this is all just guesswork,' I said.

Bairden walked in. 'Sorry to interrupt.' He looked at the row of mugs and smiled. 'Just to let you know that Jim has been released.'

Mum put a hand on the worktop to steady herself and allowed a small smile. 'Good. What will happen to him?'

'It's up to the Procurator Fiscal.' Bairden made a face of apology. 'He might be charged with wasting police time. Or even perverting the course of justice.'

'Really?' Mum blanched.

'Worst-case scenario?' I asked.

'I'd rather not speculate,' he said. 'Let's wait until we get Ryan back and worry about it then.'

'I should go get him.' I eased Pat off my knee and got to my feet.

Bairden held a hand out. 'His flat is easy walking distance from the police station, aye?'

I nodded.

'Word we got was that he was going to go there and sit under the shower for a few hours.'

I managed a smile at that. Sounded like Jim. He was so fastidious, the thought of being in the same clothes for too long and in a jail cell would have him wanting to scour his skin.

The house phone rang. Mum jumped to her feet, a weak smile of anticipation on her face. 'That will be Jim.' She all but ran into the hall.

'Did Uncle Jim get out of prison then?' asked Pat and it seemed to be from a need to hear some good news on repeat.

'He did, son.' I patted his head and winked. 'Let me hear what Gran says, eh?' I walked to the door and looked at Mum, who had the receiver to her ear.

'Jim, son,' she said, her face pink with relief. 'But you're okay? You sure you're okay?' She listened for a moment, turned to me and nodded. 'He wants to speak to you.' She held the phone out to me.

I was by her side in three strides.

'Hey, bro. It's me.'

'I know it's you, ya chump. I heard about Ryan. Fuck. What's happening? We need to find this bastard and get him back.' His voice filled my ear and everything seemed to settle just a little. It had always been Jim and me against the world; whenever he was nearby I could face almost anything. It was just a shame I forgot that while I was with Anna.

'The police have got everyone on overtime and they've got the CCTV team on it as well.' As I said this I forced enthusiasm into my tone. For Bairden's benefit. Just the slightest encouragement from Jim and I'd be out there, ignoring the police advice to stay away and driving down every street in the town.

'Aye,' barked Jim. 'That's the police. What are we doing? I can't just stay here scratching my arse.'

'The police are here at the moment, Jim.' I warned. 'They're doing everything they can.'

'Course they are. That's great. But they're not family.'

I heard some static from a police radio in the living room and held the phone away from my head, the better to hear what was going on.

Bairden appeared at my side. 'A CCTV operator has seen a boy of Ryan's description in the High Street. He's with a solitary male. Slim. Early thirties.' Hunter. Has to be. 'They think he has gone into the Early Learning Centre.'

Ryan's favourite toyshop. How did Hunter know that?

'I have to go to him,' I said to Bairden.

'I understand,' he said. 'But please don't. Let the police do their job. We have a much better chance of a positive outcome if you stay out of the way, Andy.'

'But he's my son,' I pleaded. I had to do *something*.

'From what your mum reported, your presence is likely to inflame Hunter. Best to stay away. You have another son. Being with him is you doing something.'

'He's right, son,' said Mum as she put a hand on my shoulder. I nodded, but was thinking, to hell with this, I need to get out there. Then I remembered that Jim was still on the phone. I held it back up to my ear.

'Jim?' I said.

Nothing. He was gone.

28

In the kitchen, I leaned against the sink and looked out of the window. Mum had a neat back garden, the grass clipped, a clothes pole posted at each corner and bordered on each side with hedges, shrubs and small flowering plants.

I looked at the sky, at the clouds sliding past and the scraps of blue in between and thought that somewhere under that sky, not that far from here, my boy was walking with a man who had murder in his heart.

'Can I suggest you sit with Pat, Andy?' Bairden came up behind me. The rest of the police officers had left the house at the first sighting of Ryan. 'He needs to be distracted somehow.' Subtext: so do you.

'So you're our Family Liaison Officer?' I asked him.

He nodded.

'Cos you've got the skills,' I said, wanting to wound.

'Andy,' Mum said. 'That's enough. This is not a good situation for any one of us. Let the man do his job.'

I straightened my back and crossed my arms, unwilling to acknowledge that my attitude was suspect. To hell with Bairden. If his feelings were injured he should get himself down to the job centre.

My mind returned to Ryan. Those big, blue eyes of his were a demonstration of why Disney gave their cartoon animals that same feature. To most humans they were irresistible. Most humans.

I saw Ryan. Trusting. His small hand in Hunter's. Walking with the man, completely unaware of what was going on. Every adult he'd ever met had been a source of affection and fun. To Ryan, why would this guy be any different?

I felt emotion build. Knuckled a tear from my eye.

'Pat,' I said, forcing light into my tone. 'Fancy a kickabout in the garden? Maybe Detective Bairden would like to join in?' I looked at the careful shine on his black brogues and took some satisfaction that between us we might dull that a little. To his credit, Bairden was unfazed.

'Yeah,' he said. 'Great idea.'

We passed an utterly surreal thirty minutes in the garden, kicking the ball back and forward, each of us listless and distracted.

'The Early Learning Centre?' Bairden broke the silence.

'Yeah, what about it?' I asked.

'I don't have kids and I assumed, from the shop name, that it would be kind of a boring place for kids. You know, learning centre? Doesn't say come in: you'll have a blast.' He shrugged. 'How would Hunter know to take him there? The CCTV operator said that was the only shop they went in to.'

'Maybe they walked near it and Ryan pulled Hunter in?' I suggested.

His radio buzzed and voices issued from it. We all stopped moving.

'They're not here, Detective Bairden,' I heard a voice say.

Bairden held his hand to his radio and spoke. 'Any sign of them?'

'Negative.'

'Liaise with CCTV. See if they took up his tracks when he left the shop?' He signed off the call, our eyes met and he sent me a determined look. *We will get him.* He beckoned to Pat to give him the ball. 'If he's buying toys, that's a good sign, no?' he asked me.

'Sure. The psychopath is buying shit for my son.'

Bairden opened his mouth as if to explain what he meant, but changed his mind and closed it again.

We heard the house phone ring. Moments later Mum opened the kitchen window and called to me.

'It's for you, Andy. One of the guys from work.'

'What do they want?' I asked no one in particular. 'You guys keep working at your skills,' I winked at Pat and sent a smile of apology to Bairden. 'I better go and see what can't wait for Monday.'

When I walked into the hall Mum handed me the phone and whispered, 'It's Jim.' She then gave me a look of warning. 'I don't know what you two are up to, but if it gets any of my boys hurt I'll bloody kill you.'

I looked at her as I held the phone up to my ear. 'Nothing to worry about, Mum.'

'Yes?' I said into the phone.

'If you'd get yourself one of those mobile phones that would have made this a whole lot easier.'

'What's going on, Jim?'

'The young lassie that works in the Early Leaning Centre recognised me. Said that Ryan was quite chirpy when he was in…'

'You didn't—' I tried to interrupt.

'I didn't let on anything was wrong. Kidded on the wee fella was with a mate while I was buying him a present in another shop.'

'And?'

'The weirdo bought Ryan a fishing net. You know, one of those wee nets at the end of a long pole? And a red bucket.'

'Anything else?'

'A dinosaur,' Jim said with a *what else* tone.

'Right,' I said thinking out loud. Listened for noises from the back garden and was satisfied that Bairden and Pat were otherwise occupied. 'Where are you now?'

29

I gave Mum a peck on the cheek, a hug, and said, 'I'm going to get my son.'

I couldn't face her if she was showing any negativity, so I walked out of the front door without looking back. By the time I reached the end of the street Jim had arrived in his big, black car.

I got in and looked at him.

'Fucking idiot,' I said.

'Well-meaning fucking idiot,' he corrected me.

'Why would you even think … and why would you…?' The questions crowded my mind and I couldn't articulate what bothered me most about his 'confession'.

'Andy, let's do that later, eh? We have a wee boy to find.'

'Drive then,' I replied.

We drove in silence for a few minutes and the route brought us down Holmston Road, with the town cemetery on our left and the ranks of mature, broad-leafed trees that bordered the River Ayr on the right. I remembered happier times and walks down by the river. Skimming stones on a small beach just beyond the foot bridge with the red handrails.

'So Hunter's got it in for you, then,' he said. 'There's a surprise.'

'Mad fucker.' I paused. Ground my teeth. 'What the hell did I ever do to him?'

'You got the girl. You got the happy ever after.'

'Yeah,' I gave a snort. 'Look how that turned out.'

'He was always a bit jealous of you,' Jim said, his eyes on the road, but his mind clearly back in the past. 'I remember one time, you must have been in third year at school, playing against Belmont

Academy. You skinned Hunter. Made him look like he had wooden feet. His eyes? I've never seen anything quite like it.'

'So, he hates me cos I made an arse of him on the pitch?'

'He's a nut-job. Whenever do folk like that need a reason to do anything?'

'Wait till I get my hands on him…'

'I understand the impulse, brother, but if you get yourself locked up for ripping into him, how does that help the boys? No mum and then no dad?

'Down there,' I cocked my head to indicate the river. 'Do you think he'd take Ryan and his net down the river?'

'Worth a look.' Jim indicated and pulled in at the side of the road, parking under the tall wall of the cemetery.

We crossed the road and half walked, half ran across the bridge and then made our way down to our left and a small pebble beach. There was no one there except a bald guy and his yellow Labrador.

'Bob,' he shouted, threw a stick downstream and the dog was off after the missile like his life depended on it.

'Seen a man with a wee boy?' Jim asked.

'Sorry, mate. Haven't seen anyone,' he replied.

I looked around the beach. Noted empty cans of beer, the tinfoil of a disposable charcoal barbecue and an empty, clear-plastic pack that had once held burgers.

'Might have cleaned up after themselves,' the bald guy said when he saw where I was looking.

Nodding, I walked away. I was too disappointed to make conversation. Then called myself an idiot. What did I expect? To find Ryan that easily?

Back on the path, returning to the car, I asked Jim.

'Where would someone go with a kid, who had no idea about kids?'

Jim looked at his watch. 'It's nearly tea time. He'll be looking to feed the wee man.'

'Fast food, eh? He doesn't have a car,' I said, thinking out loud. 'That suggests Burger King on the High Street. Right next door to the Early Learning Centre'

'Shit,' said Jim. 'I didn't think to check in there.'

'Let's go,' I said, picking up my pace.

The burger bar was a bust. We walked the length of the place three times studying all the kids, almost got ourselves into a fight in the process when the father of what turned out to be a wee girl took exception to our presence.

The manager had to intervene to calm things down.

'We're looking for my son,' I said. 'He's two and he's with a tall, skinny bloke.'

A look of recognition on the manager's face. 'We had the police in earlier showing the photo of a wee lad.' Pause. 'That's your son?'

I could only nod, my ability to speak temporarily on hold as disappointment took over. 'Sorry, sir.' He made a face of pity and I wanted to punch it out of him. 'No one recognised the boy.'

Jim tugged at my arm. 'Let's go, Andy. 'He's not here.'

Outside, I leaned against the window.

Fuck.

Where were they?

I closed my eyes in prayer and felt the heat of the early evening sun on my face.

'It's turned out a nice day,' said Jim.

I looked at him.

'Where might a wee boy with a fishing net want to go on a lovely summer's evening like this?' he asked pointedly.

And we were off at a run to the car again.

At the beach, Jim parked up at the harbour end and we walked down to the water's edge. We turned and faced the wide curve of Ayr Bay. The tide was out so we set out across the wet, sticky sand.

'We should split up,' said Jim as he looked to his left and the low grey wall that ran along the beach. Groups of people were clustered along its length, families taking advantage of the break in the weather, no doubt trying to get their kids into nature and away from TVs. 'You walk along the water. I'll take the wall.'

''Kay,' I said and strode off, studying every child I saw.

'Look for a net,' Jim shouted after me. 'And a red bucket.'

As I walked and searched I was encircled by good cheer at the simple things in life. Sunshine, sand and salt water lapping at my feet. All around me children of various ages, smiling parents and dogs. Laughter and barking. Screeches of joy. The high call of gulls.

And it all reached my senses through the filter of my fear. My heart was a cold zone. The only thing that would reach it, my son safe and sound in my arms.

I saw a small boy at the water's edge. He was jumping each lazy wave and celebrating safe landing at the other side as if he was an Olympic winner. His parents celebrated with him and I wanted to shout at them: how can you be happy at this moment?

Three kids in a group were clustered around a jellyfish. The creature was about the size of a large pizza and they were daring each other to poke at it with sticks.

A black-and-white collie, his head low to the ground, sprinted past after a ball. Just beyond, a small boy on his own.

With a lurch, I recognised the blond tuft of hair and his wide-footed stance. I ran over, grabbed him, he turned, a cry coming out of his mouth.

'Sorry, son,' I managed to say, when I saw it isn't Ryan. The boy wailed, frightened. I heard a stampede behind me and two people I assumed to be his parents reached us. They both looked like they were in their late teens. The mother was red-faced with indignation and the father all beard and bristle.

'What the hell are you playing at, mate?' The father demanded.

'I'm so sorry, wee pal,' I said. The boy was in his mother's arms, head on her shoulder. 'So sorry.' I reached out to try and touch him, but the mother twisted him away from my reach.

'What's your deal, pal?' asked the father.

I looked at them, thinking that should be me. Protecting my son. I opened my mouth to explain. Closed it again. I didn't want their pity. Or their judgement. Face burning, I turned from them, mumbled another apology and strode away.

'I'm phoning the polis, you freak,' shouted the father.

I turned to him and held my hands out in a placatory motion. 'Please,' I said, 'I'm so sorry. I thought he was…' I turned away again. I didn't want them to understand. I didn't want them to do anything but leave me alone.

I kept walking. Kicked at the surf. Skirted a couple of giant jellyfish.

Ryan, where are you? I stood still and, hand up to my forehead, scanned the length of the shoreline. Nothing I could see gave me hope.

Over to my left Jim was walking on top of the wall. Good idea, I thought. That would give him scope to check beachside and those people who hadn't ventured onto the sand.

Beyond him I could see the four white towers of Ayr Pavilion. There was a kid's soft-play area there. Pirate Pete's. It would be worth checking if our beach search proved unsuccessful.

Jim had paused in his walk and was looking down at me at the water's edge as if wondering what I was doing. I waved him on and continued walking.

More jellyfish.

More dogs.

More kids.

No Ryan.

30

Keep moving, I told myself. Keep moving.

You'll find him.

A heavy lurch in my gut and a sourness in my mouth.

But what if…

I stumbled. Breath caught in my throat. I hunched over, hands just above my knees and forced air into my lungs. Don't go there, Andy. He's not been gone a day yet. You'll find him. Besides, Hunter was a bully and, like all bullies, it was a sense of power he was trying to assert over his victim. Ryan was a small child, therefore his 'power' was assured. There was nothing to assert.

It was flimsy reasoning, but for that moment it offered me some hope. And in that moment hope was all I had.

At this end of the beach, the curve of the water's edge brought me closer to the wall and I could see Jim walking on the pavement, a grim expression on his face. He stopped an elderly couple. Spoke. They each shook their heads. The woman reached out and touched his arm before they walked away.

A toddler and his sister walked in front of me, hand in hand. The sister gave the boy a stone and told him to make a big splash. He threw it, his arm coming across his body but the stone plinked into the sand just inches away from him.

'Way,' she cheered. 'That was good.'

'Again,' he chanted. 'Again.'

I put a spurt on. Their happiness was a wound I couldn't bear.

Just ahead of me was the Seafield end of the beach. There was a ramp from the road down to the water's edge, a flat-roofed shop and restaurant and beyond that a stretch of sand dunes.

We played here a lot as kids, the marram grass that topped the dunes the bane of my short-trousered legs. But as a teen it was the perfect spot to take a girl to engage in some heavy petting. You could set a towel down among the dunes and hide from the world together.

This end of the beach was quieter and therefore easier to navigate. As I passed the shop I could see just a few people ahead of me and none of them were the height of Ryan.

I wondered if I should stop here and turned to see what Jim was doing, but he was obscured by the height of the dunes and the lack of a shout from him suggested that he had kept on walking.

Minutes later I was approaching the small estuary where the River Doon flowed into the sea. There was nothing here but swans and gulls, so I turned to look for Jim. The dunes were much flatter at this point, so I could see him. He was on top of the wall, arms stretched wide in question. I shook my head and turned to walk back.

Hopeless, this was hopeless.

I kicked at the water.

Fucking hopeless.

Hands deep in my pockets, shoulders hunched, I made my way back along the beach.

A hundred yards away a man was crouched at the water's edge, trousers rolled up past his knees. Where did he come from? I looked to my right and the sand dunes. He must have been sitting up there, out of sight.

I walked closer. Something about him was familiar. And as I did so I could see that his bulk was hiding the shape of someone else. A small someone else.

A boy.

I tried to speak, but it came out in a squeak.

'Ryan?'

I picked up my pace. Cleared my throat.

'Ryan?'

Was it him? I held my expectation as I might hold my breath.

The man was being solicitous. His shoulders were moving in laughter. I could see him put his hand on the boy's back. Offering support. And the breeze brought me the sound of his answering laugh. High and unrestrained.

They were so caught up in their game, neither of them heard me approach. The boy stepped beyond the man in search of something in the water. My heart turned solid in my chest and I somehow managed to speak.

It was the small red bucket at his feet that did it.

'Ryan?' I said.

31

They both turned to face me at the same instant. Hunter's face lengthened in surprise. Ryan's burst into a smile.

'Daddy,' he sang. 'Daddy.'

Hunter rose out of his crouch and held Ryan back.

'Clever daddy found us,' Hunter said.

'Jelly fishing,' Ryan said and pointed at his bucket. 'Jelly fishing.' From where I was standing I could see that the bucket was almost full to the brim. The water was opaque with little bits of pink.

'What are you playing at?' I asked and with every cell in my body I wanted to crash through Hunter, pick up Ryan and carry him away to safety, but I reined myself in. I had to do this in a way that had least impact on my son.

Words first.

If that didn't work I was prepared to use whatever would.

'Anna played us both,' Ken said. 'She was a damaged woman, but at least …' he looked down at Ryan with a smile that surprised me in its warmth '… at least she brought me this wee charmer.'

'If you think you are walking off this beach with my son, your brain has taken up residence in Mars.'

'Thing is, big guy. He's not your son. He's mine.'

As he spoke the light in his eyes died and they took on a dark lustre that almost had me take a step back. A shadowed part of me recognised that darkness, refused to give it a name, reeled from its danger.

'And when, in this fairy tale of yours do you describe to the boy how you killed his mother?' I hissed.

'He'll understand one day.' He shrugged as if her murder was the matter of a simple disagreement. 'In a way, it was what she really wanted.'

'Gimme a break, mate…'

'You're not hearing me, *mate*. She *wanted* me to kill her. It was like she'd had enough. She'd tried for long enough to goad you into it, but she knew I didn't have the same weakness.'

'What the hell are you talking about, Hunter?'

'Daddy?' Ryan's face tightened as something in him noted the change in atmosphere.

'It's okay, son,' I said. 'We'll be going home to Gran's shortly.'

'What part of, *he's my son*, don't you understand?' Hunter took a step to the side, hiding Ryan behind his legs.

'She was lying to you, Ken. It's what she did. She worked out what would mess with your head and she'd lay it on you.'

'I was shagging her for years,' Hunter crowed. 'And you, Mr Pillar of Society knew nothing.' He grinned. Feral. 'Anna told me everything. We used to laugh when she'd describe how you just lay there and took it. The big rugby player couldn't hit back.' He sang the last sentence with an effeminate tone. 'Call yourself a man? You're pathetic. There's no way you have the balls to father a son like this. *That's* how I know he's mine.'

'I wouldn't hit a woman,' I said, my anger threatening to spill over. 'But I can as sure as fuck take a piece of you. So, step aside, let me take my boy home and we'll say no more about it.'

'This…' Hunter reached into a back pocket, brought out a knife and flicked it open '… says otherwise.' It was a small weapon, but I had no doubt it could cause a serious amount of damage.

'I'll shove that knife up your arse.'

'You'd like to try,' said Hunter, flashing his teeth. He pulled Ryan round so that he stood at the side furthest from me.

Ryan squealed in surprise, his eyes large with fear.

Hunter pointed the knife at Ryan. 'What do you think?' he asked in a reasonable tone, as if he was about to take him to the shop to buy an ice-cream. 'You let us leave the beach and no one gets hurt.'

'Yeah, cos that's good fathering right there,' I said. 'Aren't you a great example? Wasn't it enough that you killed his mother?'

'I'd rather kill him too than see you walk off with him.'

A cold calm came over me. 'Anything happens to that boy and I will rip your head from your shoulders.'

Hunter chuckled. Threw his head back and belly-laughed as if that was the funniest thing he'd ever heard.

'You're a pussy, Boyd. You've proved that a thousand times. Sure, you can swing a punch, but actually do any harm?' He snorted. Grew serious. Pulled Ryan in to his side with his left arm and with his right held the knife under his throat. 'One movement and it will all be over. The wee lamb won't even feel a thing.'

'Hurt him and I swear to God…' I took a step closer, my breath coming in gasps.

'Pussy, Boyd. You're a pussy.' He took a step to the side.

I could rush him, but there was a strong chance that Ryan would get hurt. I looked around me for a weapon. Nothing, apart from the bamboo pole and the bucket.

I thought about scooping up some sand and throwing it in his face. Discounted that. I scanned the beach around me.

Not even as much as a stick.

The red bucket.

'Okay, Hunter.' I took a step closer. 'If you're convinced Ryan's yours, why don't we take a test. A DNA test will sort it once and for all.'

He stepped to the right. Ryan briefly struggled against his grip, looked up at the man who had been kind to him so far. Confusion brought a trembling lip and then tears.

'I want my daddy,' he cried.

'You're upsetting him, Ken,' I said and moved closer again.

'There, there, wee buddy,' said Hunter. 'It will soon be over. Don't worry.'

I heard a shout from behind me and the rapid approach of several pairs of running feet.

'Put down the weapon,' I heard a male voice shout.

I turned. It was Detective Bairden with Jim and a pair of uniformed policemen. They were about twenty metres away.

'Yeah, that's going to happen,' Hunter laughed. Then shouted, 'All of you keep back or the boy gets it.' From his fixed and determined expression I knew he was serious. I had to do something before the police reached us. The space between Ryan's flesh and that knife was getting shorter and shorter.

While Hunter was distracted by the police, I lunged forward, picked up the bucket of jellyfish and threw it in his face.

He screamed. And in his drive to put his hands to his face, dropped the knife and released Ryan.

I dived for my son, pulled him into my arms, and scrambled out of Hunter's reach.

Ryan burrowed into my shoulder. He was sobbing, his little body thrumming with fear.

'What have you done to my face?' screamed Hunter and fell to his knees. 'Somebody wash it off me. Wash it off me.'

Detective Bairden reached me, patted Ryan on the back and smiled over at Hunter. 'That looks quite painful,' he said. 'Or is he just a big wean?'

Now that Ryan was safe and the bogeyman was reduced to a quivering wreck the atmosphere changed. Apart from Hunter and Ryan everyone else was relaxed. It was all I could do not to break into a shaking fit of laughter.

Jim reached my side and held his hands out for Ryan.

'If you fancy having a kick at his nuts, I don't think any of these officers will stop you,' he grinned, relief pinking his face.

'I think the burning feeling on his face will be sufficient for now,' I answered.

We all clustered round the squealing Hunter and watched him as, on his knees, he feverishly splashed himself with water.

'I need medical help,' he shouted. Stopped splashing to look at all of us in turn. 'Somebody help me.'

Jim pretended to reach for his zip. 'I heard that urine was a good treatment for jellyfish stings. Do you want it straight from the pipe, Hunter?'

32

My mother was a rock during the few days leading up to the funeral service. From her spirit and energy no one could tell that she was about to stand by her son's side as he buried his second wife. She did everything: got in touch with the funeral director, arranged the flowers, spoke with the priest.

Jim's confession and Ryan's abduction meant that my feelings of grief for Anna's death had been pushed to the far side of my thoughts, but now that everyone was safe, they forced themselves centre stage.

The boys clung to me like limpets that following week. I even had to leave the door open whenever I went to the toilet, such was there distress when they couldn't find me in the very moment they sought me.

Ryan asked for his mother several times over the next few days, then learned not to as each request was met with downcast faces. Bed time was the worst. Ryan always preferred his mother's touch just before he went to sleep.

On the day of the service I debated whether Ryan should go, but my mother argued that he should be allowed to say goodbye. I couldn't disagree with her. If he became distracted and noisy, then she would take him outside.

One should never discount a child's sensitivity. Ryan behaved beautifully. He held my right hand through the service, while Pat held the other. He looked at the faces long with grief around him and was hushed by the emotion evident in everyone's stance.

Death touches us all, particularly when it leeches life from one as young as Anna; particularly when it brings violence along by the hand. The church was full. People who worked with her, people who knew her only briefly, people who'd never set eyes upon her until they'd picked up a newspaper, they were all there to express their sadness.

The priest's eulogy was short and for this I was grateful. I couldn't have listened to someone speaking about Anna, filling in the holes of their knowledge of her with generalisations.

At the graveside people offered their hands in condolence. Each one I accepted with royal patience when I would have rather screamed at them: leave me alone. There's me, my boys and my grief. Leave us be. I wanted to look over Anna's short, sad life and pick at it like a fisherman would examine his nets. Perhaps in the picking there would be a mending and I could make some sense of it all.

More hands, more lips pressed against my cold cheek.

Leave me be.

I said nothing. I permitted a smile to curve the ends of my blood-less lips and continued to acknowledge the mourners. I could feel a tear like a salt pendant hanging in the corner of my eye, waiting for the moment when I would let it sail.

Two men stood away to the right, heads bowed. I didn't recognise them. The thought occurred to me that they might be from Anna's family. I sent them a message of hate; they were the start of all of this. People around the two men moved off and I could see that they were both wearing council uniforms.

They were simply waiting to shovel the earth over the coffin. This was just another day to them and I envied them their sense of distance.

Ryan and Pat were standing just off to my left with Mum and Jim. Cold had begun its journey through the veins in my feet, the muscle and tendon of my legs, the flesh in my groin, but I would not let it journey any closer to my heart. If life had robbed these boys of a mother each, I would not let it take their father. I believed then and I believe now that it is not what happens to you that determines your happiness, but how you react to what happens to you. I had a choice and right there and then, I chose joy.

It was difficult to find, but standing there on that graveside I found joy in Anna's existence. The night before she died I'd caught a glimpse under the hard carapace. I'd been granted a reminder of what the real Anna Boyd was like. The real Anna who had been buried under the thick shield of her defences. The Anna that the boys would celebrate with a happy and fulfilled existence.

I thought about what Hunter said as he held a knife to Ryan's neck. Anna had goaded him into killing her. Anna would certainly have known what Ken Hunter was capable of. He was one of the first people she met when she first came to the town. She had at one stage worked with his wife, Sheila. She was a master of manipulation. Had she hand-picked him for the role? Had she orchestrated the whole thing? She would have known that Hunter was insanely jealous. Did she deliberately provoke him? Until he grabbed a knife, granting her wish for release.

I had tucked away Hunter's accusation that he was Ryan's father. That was surely just part of Anna's efforts at manipulation. Kids are always born early, aren't they? Two weeks was nothing. No. Ryan was mine and I wouldn't allow any other possibility.

I considered her last act as a mother. The phone call. It was nobody, she'd said. Repeated it. But by offering the boys to me she knew they would be safe. Safe from any damage that Hunter could inflict on them. They would also be safe from the psychological damage of hearing her screams.

I shook my head as if trying to rid my head of these terrible imaginings. Was all of this just me looking for some sense in the chaos?

The funeral crowd was beginning to disperse. People returning to their homes, to heat themselves with the gratitude that it wasn't their wife, their partner or their child who had just been described as ashes and dust.

I spotted Sheila with a number of my bank colleagues. As she was getting into a car she turned to look for me. The distance faded and I could see the affection in her eyes as she caught sight of me. My heart flipped. There was something between us. Those beautiful eyes did not read only of sympathy, there was a world of caring there too.

I hoped she would have patience enough to wait for me; my boys would have my full attention until I was sure they could cope with their mother's loss.

Jim walked towards me, Ryan perched on his right arm, Pat walking at his side, holding on to his left hand.

'Right, Dad, let's go and get these boys something to eat.' In his own fashion he was reminding me that I had two very good reasons to live. It was completely unnecessary but I loved him for it.

We looked a strange sight in our sombre clothes, Jim, Mum, the boys and I, as we trooped into McDonalds. In this moment I craved the normality of it, the reminder that no matter how sharp my grief was now, it would fade. It also gave me the chance to see the boys smile, perhaps hear them laugh with the pleasure of receiving a new toy.

We ordered and I carried a tray of questionable calories over to a table. Everyone sat down and, as if this was any other day, they tucked into the burgers, chicken and fries. As the boys played a pantomime out on the table with their new plastic characters, the last words I heard Anna say sounded in my ear.

'Boys…'

They turned to me, the distraction having worked for the moment. Their eyes were bright, their attentions successfully shifted from the sadness around them. The bogeyman was locked up and would never bother them again.

'Did I tell you that your mother loved you both very much?'

Acknowledgements

My huge thanks to:

My very first readers of this book all those years ago: Stuart, Nan, Jackie, Sheila, Alison and Angela – see what you guys started!

Maggie Craig and Douglas Skelton for helping me all these years later to see that there was something worth pursuing with this story.

Sam, my sounding board.

All of my colleagues in the crime scene and fellow scribes. The shared moans and giggles are what keeps me sane (along with the coffee).

The unflagging Karen Sullivan for believing in this book and being able to see through that first draft to the real story beneath – and for helping me chip away at it until we found it.

And, above all, YOU – the bloggers, reviewers, booksellers, librarians and readers – without you guys this is just a block of paper and a bunch of squiggles.